W9-BZD-134

A *Texas* CHRISTMAS

Six Romances from the Historic
Lone Star State
Herald the Season of Love

A *Texas* CHRISTMAS

Cathy Marie Hake
Ramona Cecil, Lena Nelson Dooley,
Darlene Franklin, Pamela Griffin, Kathleen Y'Barbo

BARBOUR BOOKS
An Imprint of Barbour Publishing, Inc.

Here Cooks the Bride © 2005 by Cathy Marie Hake
A Christmas Chronicle © 2005 by Pamela Griffin
To Hear Angels Sing © 2010 by Ramona Cecil
The Face of Mary © 2010 by Darlene Franklin
Charlsey's Accountant © 2009 by Lena Nelson Dooley
Plain Trouble © 2009 by Kathleen Y'Barbo

Print ISBN 978-1-63409-033-9

eBook Editions:
Adobe Digital Edition (.epub) 978-1-63409-583-9
Kindle and MobiPocket Edition (.prc) 978-1-63409-584-6

All rights reserved. No part of this publication may be reproduced or transmitted for commercial purposes, except for brief quotations in printed reviews, without written permission of the publisher.

All scripture quotations are taken from the King James Version of the Bible.

This book is a work of fiction. Names, characters, places, and incidents are either products of the author's imagination or used fictitiously. Any similarity to actual people, organizations, and/or events is purely coincidental.

Cover Image: JenniferPhotographyImaging, GettyImages

Published by Barbour Books, an imprint of Barbour Publishing, Inc., P.O. Box 719, Uhrichsville, OH 44683, www.barbourbooks.com

Our mission is to publish and distribute inspirational products offering exceptional value and biblical encouragement to the masses.

Printed in the United States of America.

CONTENTS

Here Cooks the Bride

by Cathy Marie Hake

CHAPTER 1

September 1879

"Excuse me, sir."

Jeff halted mid-motion, his shovel full of coal. Black dust swirled around his thick boots as he glanced at the young lady. Oh, and she was definitely a *lady*. Judging from her so-very-proper Boston accent, the Daddy-has-money traveling suit with all the fuss and bother, and her wide hazel eyes, this gal wasn't just out of place; she was lost.

"Might I impose for a moment to inquire as to the location of your local diner?"

He dumped the coal into his wheelbarrow and stood to his full height. "Diner's closed. Best hop back aboard the train and try Meadsville."

The feather in her stylish hat swayed back and forth as she gave her head a small shake. "I fear I did not make myself known. I'm Lacey Mather, and I've come to help my great-aunt Millie at the diner."

"Millie's your great-aunt?" Jeff couldn't hide the surprise in his voice. On her better days, Millie looked as if she'd been caught in a whirlwind. Most of the time, she looked like she sorted bobcats for a living. No man in his right mind would imagine Millie as kin to this dainty blond beauty.

"Yes." Miss Mather folded her white-gloved hands at her

waist and gave him a charming smile. "I'm eager to reacquaint myself with her. Could you please direct me to her place?"

"Sure. Go on through the station here, and you'll see Main Street turning off to the west from Ranger Road. Millie's is the first place on the right side of Main."

Miss Proper-and-Pretty leaned forward ever so slightly. "Would west be to my right or left?"

Jeff tamped down a groan. Helpless. The woman wasn't just lost, she was utterly helpless. What kind of assistance did she think she could give Millie, clear out here in the wilds of Texas? He heaved a sigh. "Give me a minute. I can show you the way—long as you don't mind coal dust."

Laughter tinkled out of her—from behind her gloved hand, of course. "Sir, after riding a train for the past three days, I assure you, I could shake out my skirts and fill your wheelbarrow!"

The woman had a point. He nodded, then directed, "There's a bench over yonder. I'll just be a minute."

Chestnut-brown skirts whispered as she turned to walk away. The whisper might as well have been a shout, because the narrow-cut front of that fancy dress hadn't prepared him for this view. Row upon row of ruffles draped over a sassy bustle and spilled to the ground. Dainty, swaying steps led her away from the bench and toward a trunk, valise, and hatbox.

She really does plan to stay.

The realization made Jeff groan aloud. Bad enough that Millie couldn't cook a lick. Put both women in the kitchen, and most of Cut Corners would probably die of food poisoning. Resigned to continue to prepare his own meals, Jeff dumped more coal into his wheelbarrow and muttered, "Lord, I know I'm not supposed to question Your wisdom, but seems to me a homely old spinster who knew her way around a stove would be a much better choice for us here in Cut Corners."

The train whistle blew, adding an exclamation mark to his opinion.

"You've been too kind." Lacey clutched the cording from her hatbox and smiled at the stranger. He'd not yet introduced himself. These western men were a rough lot—rough but strong. He'd filled the biggest wheelbarrow she'd ever seen, then hefted her trunk across the handles as if it weighed no more than a pillow. Shoving the heavy burden through the rutted streets didn't even leave him breathless. He'd stayed in the street but next to the boardwalk so she'd not have to contend with the hazardous road any more than necessary.

"Open the door. I'll tote in your belongings."

Lacey rapped on the door to what appeared to be the residential portion of the diner.

"Open it," he ordered as he lumbered up. "Millie's probably knocked out from the laudanum Doc gave her."

"Oh. I see." Though it felt intrusive to barge in, Lacey understood the necessity. "Very well." The door creaked open to reveal a jumbled mess. Lacey yanked the door shut. "If you'd be so kind as to leave the trunk here, I'll drag it inside later."

"You couldn't drag this thing if it were empty. Get the door."

She shook her head. "I'm dreadfully sorry. Truly I am. I'm not trying to be difficult, and I appreciate your strength. It's just that. . .oh, dear. Well, Aunt Millie's hurt. She simply hasn't felt up to tending to matters."

Her trunk thumped loudly on the boardwalk. The man looked at her like she'd taken leave of her senses. "Suit yourself." He wrapped huge, blackened hands around the handles of his wheelbarrow and trundled back across Ranger Road to the smithy. Suddenly the width of his shoulders and his uncommon strength made perfect sense. Lacey tilted her head to read the sign. Jeffrey Wilson. Blacksmith.

"God, please bless Mr. Wilson."

"Which one?" a frail, raspy voice asked from behind her.

Lacey whirled around. From the wild wisps of her gray hair to the tattered hem of her dressing gown and the sling on her arm, the woman looked positively ghastly. "Aunt Millie?"

"In the flesh. Which Mr. Wilson?" She motioned with her good arm for Lacey to enter.

Lacey gripped her hatbox and valise as she stepped over the threshold. She'd never seen a place in such a sad state. Afraid she'd blurt out something hurtful, she grasped at the slim thread of conversation. "How many Mr. Wilsons do you have in this town?"

"Three. The old codger who used to be a ranger, the sheriff, and the blacksmith."

"I see. The blacksmith just escorted me from the train station." She set her valise and hatbox on a nearby table and patted the woman's good hand. "I'm here to help you now."

"Imagine that." Aunt Millie quirked a lopsided smile. "So why don't you tell me who you are?"

The question nearly felled Lacey. Then she recalled the blacksmith mentioning how the doctor gave Aunt Millie laudanum. No wonder the poor dear soul was a bit confused! "I'm Lacey, Tobias's daughter. I've come to help you since you hurt your arm."

The old woman squinted, then bobbed her head. The tortoiseshell comb holding up her wispy gray bun slid lower, and her topknot loosened into a precarious nest of tangles. "I remember you. Last I saw you, you were clinging to your mama's fancy ball gown and missing your front teeth. I see good, sound ones filled right in."

Having her teeth remarked upon as though she were a mare under consideration for purchase stunned Lacey. Then again, poor Aunt Millie dealt with gruff men all day long. No doubt, now that she had feminine companionship, the gentler side of her nature would shine. "How kind of you to remember Mama.

I only hold a few memories of her. Perhaps, after you rest, you could share some of your recollections." Lacey took her aunt's arm and led her toward an open doorway. Surely this must lead to the residential portion of the building.

"You hungry, girl?"

"I confess, I am. Perhaps you'd like me to prepare us lunch."

"Then we're headed the right direction." Aunt Millie shuffled ahead and blocked Lacey's view for a moment. When she stepped to the side, pride rang in her voice. "How do you like it?"

A fair-sized kitchen spread before Lacey. Well, she thought it was a kitchen. Pots, pans, kettles, and roasters lay stacked on the stove and counter and hung from the ceiling. Towers of plates listed perilously close to the edge of what she supposed was a sink. Glass canisters formed a jumble in the center of a table, and a cat lazed across the far side of that table, soaking up warmth from a sunbeam. Pretending to ignore the sad state of the room, Lacey pulled off her gloves. "It's plain to see you have a well-equipped establishment. I'll get to work. Is there anything in particular you'd fancy?"

"Jeff."

The hammer clanged down on the horseshoe one last time; then Jeff set the piece back into the fire. "Yeah?"

Two old men hovered by the rail in his smithy. No one stepped beyond that rail—he'd established that rule straight off, and never once had he regretted it. It kept folks from getting hit by the hammer, sparks, or worse. It also kept them from meddling with him when he worked.

Not that anyone ever managed to keep what the town collectively called "the meddling men" from sticking their noses into other folks' business. Four retired Texas Rangers had founded the town after they'd spent the bulk of their adult years directing and fixing issues and problems. Now, in a peaceful town, the old guys couldn't limit themselves to dallying with dominoes or grumbling over checkers. From their vantage point on the boardwalk, they were worse busybodies than a pack of gossipy widows.

And here two of them were. His uncle Ebenezer leaned forward and cleared his throat. "Pretty filly you were escortin' down the avenue this morning."

Big old Swede nodded his silver-blond head. "Ja. So, what is this? Did you send for a bride?"

"A bride?" Jeff burst out laughing. "Not a chance."

"It's past time you married up," Uncle Eb declared. "Your cousin's happy as a clam now that he married up with Peony."

Mentioning Peony and clams in the same breath seemed daft, but Jeff didn't bother to share his opinion. The less he said, the better off he'd be. Once someone took a mind to challenge the meddling men, the old men took it as a personal affront and reckoned they had to defend their honor by proving themselves right.

"So who is this pretty girl?" Swede asked.

"Millie's kin. Gustavson's mare threw a shoe. I need to get her shod before he comes back."

"Millie's kin, huh?" Swede crammed his thumbs into his belt and rocked to and fro. "Think she can cook any better than Millie?"

"Anyone can cook better than Millie," Eb said in a wry tone.

"No telling," Jeff said gloomily. "Could have inherited Millie's recipes."

All three men sighed. Jeff used his pinchers to pull the horseshoe from the fire and hooked it over the conical end of the anvil, then started pounding it into shape again.

"A man has to have a cast-iron stomach to survive Millie's food. I suppose I'd better keep payin' Lula at the boardin'-house for chow." Swede frowned. "Even my nephew cooks better than that."

Jeff purposefully clanged his hammer extra loud just to

drown out their conversation. After all, the two men were directly responsible for matching up his cousin Rafe with Peony, the dressmaker, last Christmas.

Ever since then, the bachelors in Cut Corners had been manipulated into any number of situations wherein the meddling men tried to match them up with anyone in a skirt.

"Of course he will, won't you, Jeff?" his uncle half shouted.

Jeff knew better than to agree when he hadn't heard what they'd said. He shoved the horseshoe back into the fire and picked up the awl so he could drive holes into the shoe and be done with it. "Don't know what you were jawing over."

Swede harrumphed. "No offense, you understand."

Jeff looked to his uncle for an explanation.

"We were discussing how you've sorta let yourself go. It's the heat and coal and all. . .but I'm sure now that we've called it to your attention, you'll spruce up a bit."

Even though he stood right beside the forge, Jeff's blood ran cold. "I'm not trying to impress anyone."

"Didn't say you had to." His uncle pretended to be interested in a sample brand burned into the wall. "But you'd do well to take your Saturday night bath—"

"And get your hair trimmed," Swede tacked on for good measure.

They were reaching for something to needle him about. Because of the grime from the smithy, Jeff bathed every day, whether he needed to or not. Why, he probably bought more soap from the mercantile than a family of eight. Instead of saying a thing, he snorted.

"You've been keepin' company too long with horses, son. Snortin' and tossin' your mane like a riled stallion."

"Jay Harris took his shears to me just last week."

"Humph." Swede managed to use that sound to great advantage. Jeff wondered how long it took him to cultivate just the right tone to make it dismissive and disparaging all at the same time. Probably did it for survival's sake, because he had that lilting tonal quality as part of his accent that made him seem more like an affable farmer than a gritty Texas Ranger.

Jeff grabbed nails and stuffed them into the pocket of his leather apron, then slung the horseshoe on the anvil and closed one eye as he measured and punched the holes with a steadiness borne of experience. Done with that, he plunged the shoe into the water bucket and relished the satisfying hiss it produced.

"You men'll have to excuse me." Jeff nodded curtly toward them and headed out the side door to the corral attached to his place.

"Forget about that mare and think about the pretty filly across the street!" his uncle called.

Jeff scowled. "Why don't you go tell Swede's nephew about her?"

The two old men exchanged a conspiratorial look and hotfooted out of the shop.

Jeff went over to the mare, stooped, and held her leg fast between his knees. In no time at all, she boasted a perfectly fitted shoe.

He straightened up, gave the mare a chunk of carrot, and chuckled. "I ought to feel guilty about sending them to Erik, but it's every man for himself."

"Excuse me, sir."

He tensed at the sound of that soft feminine voice. Silly Boston woman. Exact same words she used early this morning at the train. Was that her standard greeting? Jeff turned. "Yes?"

"Aunt Millie tells me you deliver coal to her. Could I trouble you to bring over more?"

"Sure."

The woman had changed into a simple calico dress, but it looked anything but plain on her. Judging from the damp tendrils corkscrewing around her flushed face, she'd been busy. She smiled—a friendly, sort of shy smile. "Thank you ever so much."

"I'll be by shortly." There. That served as a polite dismissal. It was the best he could manage. She might be pretty as a picture and smell sweeter than a rose garden, but Jeffrey Wilson wasn't looking for a wife, and with Uncle Eb plotting and scheming, the last thing Jeff wanted was to be seen near Millie's niece. He wanted her to go away. The sooner the better.

CHAPTER 2

"Wonderful! Thank you." Lacey stood to one side as Jeff brought in a full scuttle of coal.

"Don't mention it."

She inched back a bit farther and stood on tiptoe to swipe a smudge off the wall. "You've been so kind. Would you care to join us for supper?"

"No."

He answered so quickly, Lacey wondered what she'd said to offend him. She hid the soiled cleaning rag behind her back and offered, "Maybe another time."

He hitched his shoulder and headed out the door.

Lacey didn't dwell on his terrible manners. She had too much to accomplish, and troubling herself over his surly ways would be a waste of time. She'd dealt with fractious children and found it wisest to ignore such dark moods. Most often, they blew away like a bank of unwelcome thunderclouds. Not that he was at all like the little girls she'd worked with. Mr. Wilson belonged to that mysterious gender with whom she'd rarely interacted. Growing up in a young ladies' academy severely limited her ability to associate with men. To be sure, with his imposing physique, deep voice, and unmistakable strength, Mr. Wilson was the epitome of masculinity.

Still, it would have been nice for him to notice what she'd accomplished.

But he didn't see the place. *I shut the door so he wouldn't know how Aunt Millie let the place fall to rack and ruin. Well, no matter.* Lacey felt the satisfaction of a job well started. Certainly she couldn't consider it well done. Too much remained on her to-do list.

The list lay on the table—the clean, catless table—weighted down with two of the freshly scrubbed canisters. Every last dish, pot, and pan now rested neatly in a hutch, cabinet, or crate. She'd used sink after sink of water and half a cake of soap to wash them all. The windows and floor shone.

So did her nose.

Lacey giggled at herself for that vain thought. No one here in Cut Corners would give a fig for what she looked like or how she behaved. They'd simply be glad Aunt Millie had help and the diner offered decent meals. It would be fun to do this—sort of a holiday. All the other young ladies at the school got to go on trips and vacations, but she'd always remained on the premises. Father never managed to arrange his important business schedule in such a manner as to be home during the school term breaks. Well, this was her vacation. Once Aunt Millie healed, Lacey would pack her trunk and head back to Boston, where a more prestigious school had offered her a very flattering position.

In the meantime, plenty needed doing. Poor Aunt Millie was behind the times. She'd never read Beeton and didn't live according to the all-important maxim that ruled a woman's world. "A place for everything and everything in its place," Lacey quoted as she strove to decide how to make a place for the hundreds of unmatched knives, forks, and spoons she kept unearthing in odd nooks and crannies. So far, she'd resorted to dumping them into three buckets she'd set on a table in the diner.

The diner. She shuddered. The place was a veritable pigsty. No one had come to help clear the tables from the meal Aunt Millie had been serving the day she broke her arm. It had taken every scrap of Lacey's fortitude to collect and scrub those dishes. Bless Aunt Millie's heart, she'd slept through the day thanks to a dose of laudanum. Before the poor old woman woke, Lacey still had several things she wanted to accomplish. If she stayed on the schedule she'd set for herself, Lacey estimated she'd have the diner open for business the day after tomorrow.

—∞—

"Excuse me, sir. Could I trouble you to fill this?"

There she goes again. "Excuse me, sir." Her pretty little head must be full of manners and empty of brains. Jeff told himself he wasn't going to turn, but he did. Resplendent in a light purplish dress, Miss Mather handed a list to the grocer. Jeff couldn't decide whether the grocer smiled because of the woman's charm or because the long list would make for a profitable day. Either way, Miss Mather had just made herself a friend in Cut Corners.

"No trouble at all." Lionel Sager beamed at her. "I'll have it done in a trice. I heard tell we had a new lady in town. No one mentioned you were so lovely."

"You're too kind."

The way her thick lashes lowered might well be a practiced response, but Jeff couldn't deny that the fetching blush filling her cheeks was genuine. She acted as if men didn't shower her with compliments all the time. He grew angry with himself for paying any attention and spun back around. Soap. He'd come to get more soap.

A moment later, Miss Mather stood by his side. A wooden basket was looped over her arm, and she'd already put two cakes of lye soap inside. She stood on tiptoe to look farther back on the display. "Good morning, Mr. Wilson." She helped herself to two more bars of soap—fancy ones. Larkin's Sweet Home and Larkin's Oatmeal Toilet Soap.

"Morning." He grabbed an ordinary bar of Pears.

"It's a pleasure to see Cut Corners boasts such a well-stocked mercantile."

He nodded, then headed toward the counter. Gordon Brooks walked past him, leaving a choking cloud of Hoyt's cologne in his wake. The smirk on the saloon owner's face left nothing to the imagination, and Jeff spun back around. He didn't want his name paired up with Miss Lacey Mather's, but he couldn't leave a poor, defenseless lady to the schemes of a rogue.

"Gordon Brooks at your service." Brooks doffed his hat.

"Thank you," Lacey said as she added knitting needles to her baskct, "but the storekeeper has already offered his capable services."

Jeff watched in amusement as she breezed around a corner and busied herself with choosing a ball of string. Brooks followed. "I was merely introducing myself. Here in the untamed regions, a man learns to introduce himself to a lady. Otherwise, someone else will beat him to her since ladies are so few and far between."

"Sir!" Lacey pressed a hand to her throat and gave him a shocked look. "I saw several God-fearing women as I came down the boardwalk and must protest the slur you've made upon their good character."

"I did say there were a few," Brooks said in a placating tone. "I meant no offense. My intent was merely to make your acquaintance and ask you to supper."

"I'll have to refuse your invitation."

"Why?" Brooks looked flummoxed that his oily charm hadn't worked on her.

"Because I must."

Jeff didn't bother to smother his smile. She actually made that flimsy excuse sound like a reason. He'd thought the little lamb needed to be rescued from the wolf, but that wolf was starting to resemble a whipped puppy. Still, it wouldn't be wise for her to make an enemy of such a man. Jeff cleared his throat. "The lady is being discreet. Fact is, she and her aunt already asked me to supper."

"Yes, yes, we did." She gave Jeff a look of sheer gratitude.

Lionel Sager rounded the corner with a bag on his shoulder. "Miss? This is the last of my sugar. I'll wire for more on the next train, but if you don't mind, I'd like to split the bag so I can keep some stock."

"Please do." She edged farther away from Brooks. "I don't believe I have beans on my list. Do I?"

"Come take a look."

As she walked to the counter, Jeff growled at Brooks, "Leave her alone."

"You Wilsons are all cut from the same cloth—think you run the town." Brooks shook his head. "You got it all wrong. Money is power, and I'm the one in Cut Corners with more of it than most of you put together."

"To my way of thinking, the important things can't be bought."

"Maybe not." Brooks paused, then tacked on, "But that's because those are the things you win." He tugged a pack of poker cards from his vest pocket, then shoved them back down. "Anytime you want, there's room for you in a game."

Jeff grinned. "Sitting at a supper table's my style. Card tables don't hold any appeal."

Vivian Sager approached them. "Pardon me, but I need to get a tin of lard for Miss Mather's order. It's behind you, Mr. Brooks."

Gordon Brooks's suave facade slipped as he scrambled out of Vivian's way. Known for being clumsy, she managed to drop or bump things with disconcerting regularity. He straightened his coat and headed for the door. On his way out, Brooks began to whistle.

"'The Girl I Left Behind Me.'" Vivian identified the tune as she grabbed the bucket of lard. "He'd better not be whistling that about me."

"Allow me." Jeff grabbed the five-gallon tin from her before she crippled one of the two of them by dropping it. He took it to the counter and set it with a rapidly growing pile of groceries.

Lacey stood by the spice display and kept chucking tins into her basket. "Since you're here, Mr. Wilson, perhaps you could tell me if you prefer stewed tomatoes, butter beans, or succotash for supper."

Succotash. He loved succotash. Then again, no use spoiling one of his favorite things by having her massacre it. "Whatever's easiest."

"It's all the same to me."

I'll bet. Just like it is to Millie. How did I rope myself into eating over there tonight?

"I have asparagus," Lionel suggested. "End of the season. Won't be in again until next year."

Jeff shrugged. "I'll leave the menu up to Miss Mather." In all actuality, he hated asparagus. Never did seem quite right, gnawing on something that looked like a bloated, sickly pencil. Then again, he'd be needing bicarbonate after the meal anyway.

Miss Mather set her basket on the counter. The thing overflowed with a crazy collection of luxuries and nonsensical things. Soap, knitting needles, string, paprika, cloves, thyme, tooth powder, and two licorice ropes. "I think this is the last of it."

Vivian scratched off the last thing on the long list and squinted through her thick glasses. "If you think of anything else, you can run back. It's not like Boston where you'd have to take a buggy and need an escort."

"You must enjoy that freedom." Lacey's voice carried a tinge of longing. "It's so refreshing to be here."

"I'll put this on Millie's account." Lionel added the last few items and circled the total.

"Oh no." Miss Mather promptly pulled a small purse from the bottom of the basket and drew out a dozen or more ten-dollar greenbacks.

"Perhaps you'd like to go to the bank and deposit that," Lionel half choked.

"I've already been to the bank," she said blithely.

I had this woman pegged from the start. Daddy has money. That confirmation felt like the last nail in Jeff's coffin. No woman from a wealthy family learned to cook. He silently set a bottle of Peabody's Seltzer on the counter.

CHAPTER 3

"I declare, Aunt Millie, you'd think that man's been starving for a decade," Lacey said as she finished washing the supper dishes. Jeffrey Wilson had come over, asked a nice blessing over the food, then taken very modest portions. After the first few bites, he'd practically inhaled the remainder of the food on his plate and accepted seconds with gusto. . .then taken thirds.

Aunt Millie rested her elbow on the table and propped her head in her hand. "Barely said a word, but his mouth was full."

"So he's usually more talkative?"

"Not much." The cat jumped up into Aunt Millie's lap. "He's got a weakness for critters, though. Talks to horses, dogs, and cats. Isn't that right, Tiger?"

Tiger purred in response.

"Oh, that plate you're washing belongs to Peony Wilson. She brought over some meals for me. I'm surprised she hasn't bustled over to meet you."

Suds splashed everywhere as Lacey dunked the plate. "Don't tell me I asked her husband or brother here for supper and didn't invite her!"

"No, no. She's married to Rafe—the sheriff. He's Jeff's cousin. That's a mighty fancy apron you've got on."

Lacey didn't bother to glance down. She owned four aprons—all of them cut off the same pattern, each with a different floral pattern embroidered across the bodice. "All of the young ladies learn needlework at the academy. This is an everyday one. There's another that's my Sunday-best."

"You'd better plan on wearing mine. Stains'll never come out of that white cotton."

"Madame taught us how to handle each type of spill." Lacey smiled. "But I thank you for your generous offer. What time do you normally serve breakfast?"

"Half past six, I unlock the door. Folks wander in whenever they've a mind to. Wouldn't expect too many to come tomorrow. They won't know the diner's open for business again."

The next morning, Lacey cracked the very last egg she'd bought into the skillet. She'd planned for those eggs to last three days. They hadn't lasted three hours! Aunt Millie tromped into the kitchen and wedged two more plates into the crate beside the sink. "Erik Olson wants another order of flapjacks."

"Another!" Lacey flipped several on the griddle, then shuffled the spatula beneath the egg and slid it onto a plate that held a sizzling slab of ham and handed the plate to her aunt. "I'm out of eggs."

Aunt Millie headed toward the dining room and called over her shoulder, "Not to worry. Just whip up some more flapjacks."

"More flapjacks? But I don't have eggs!" Lacey chased after her. "We'll have to close till lunch."

The entire noisy dining room suddenly went silent. Lacey stood in the doorway and stared at the shocked faces of what looked like the entire population of Cut Corners. Four older gentlemen glowered at her. One thumped his coffee cup on the table. "Can't do that. It's criminal."

"Don't worry," Aunt Millie said. "I told her to just make more flapjacks."

"I don't have eggs to make more batter for—" Lacey shrieked, "The flapjacks!" as she whirled around and ran back to the stove.

Half of them were acceptable. The others— She scraped them off and winced.

"Finally got 'em cooked all the way through. I wasn't sayin' anything, but those others looked half-raw to me." Aunt Millie shoved out a plate and set the charred ones aside. "Crispy ones taste the best. 'Specially with apple butter on 'em."

"Bless you," Lacey said softly. Her great-aunt showed great consideration by speaking such kind words when those pancakes were only suitable for—

"Well?" a deep male voice asked. Lacey looked over and started to laugh. Half a dozen men crowded the doorway. She wasn't sure who had asked. "I believe Aunt Millie said Erik Olson ordered flapjacks. He has five coming to him. There are. . ." She took quick inventory and reported, "Seven more left."

"I'll pay a nickel apiece for 'em!"

"I'll pay a dime!"

"I'll wash the dishes," a woman said from the other entry, "if you share your recipe."

—∞—

Four old gents hunkered over the barrel and pretended to study the checkerboard. Ebenezer Wilson said, "Can't let this one get away."

"Only had breakfast," Stone Creedon muttered. "Don't know if she can cook anything else yet."

"Who cares? I'll settle for breakfast."

"We must come up with a plan." Chaps reached over and methodically jumped his checker. "King me."

Swede grumbled, "Ja, ja. I king you."

Eb lowered his voice. "Swede, your nephew liked her flap-jacks. If we tie her apron strings to a man here in town, that'll make sure she stays at the stove!"

"Erik saw her. Says she's pretty but she talks funny."

No one made mention of Swede's accent. Then again, no

one made a comment about Chaps's English accent, either. Stone let out a snarling sound. "He can get used to her accent if he likes her cooking."

"It would be wise to have other gentlemen express interest," Chaps mused. "Nothing makes a woman more attractive than the fact that other men want her."

"Who cares about other men wanting her? The fact that she knows her way around a kitchen is recommendation enough."

"It doesn't matter what we think," Eb Wilson said. "We gotta convince some young buck here in Cut Corners to pay her court."

"Your nephew's a good prospect." Chaps leaned back and smirked at the checkerboard. "He's the first man to see her, and he's already been a supper guest."

"Eb and me, we already tried to convince him." Swede's voice dragged with disappointment. "He isn't interested in her much."

Stone kicked the toe of his scuffed boot against the edge of the boardwalk to dislodge a dirt clod. "Who cares if he don't like her mush? She can cook plenty of other stuff."

Ignoring the fact that his old crony's deafness had him speaking nonsense, Swede announced, "I know what to do."

"What?" Chaps and Eb asked in unison.

"This." Swede leaned forward, took a checker, and hopped it across the entire board like a cricket on desert stones. Scooping up all of Chaps's pieces, he slapped his knee with the other hand and chortled. "You got the king, but I got the game."

"Crazy old coot," Stone muttered. "I thought he figured out something important."

Eb watched as Lacey sashayed down the boardwalk and into the mercantile. Every last bachelor either stared or followed after her. "Fellas, we might not have to do much a'tall. Seems Miss Lacey Mather might need our help to fight off the men instead of us draggin' 'em to her doorstep."

—ꟷ—

The doors to the diner didn't stop swinging. From the moment the folks in Cut Corners discovered Lacey Mather could cook, they'd beat a path to her door. Morning, noon, and night, she'd dash out with chalk in her hand, write up a menu in the fanciest script ever seen, and run back to her stove. Well—to Millie's stove. Only no one wanted it to be Millie's. They all loved Millie just fine, but her cooking could gag a skunk. Even now, folks could tell what Lacey prepared and what Millie made. Lacey's biscuits rose to fluffy perfection; Millie's would make fine sinkers if someone planned to go fishing. Lacey's batch of gravy could coax a full sentence of praise from grumpy old Stone Creedon; Millie's had lumps big enough to fool a man into thinking he got a dumpling.

Clang, clang, clang. Jeff worked on repairing Heath's plow. He'd sharpen it free of charge. Though it took a little extra time, he always wanted his customers to feel they got a good deal. Besides, he could sit outside the smithy by his large whetstone and watch the parade of swains going to eat at Millie's. The food tasted great, but word around town was the bachelors had more than just a full plate in mind. Many intended to court the pretty little gal. Lacey might think they were claiming their steak; Jeff knew they were staking their claim. There went Harold Myers, hair slicked back and a string tie, and it was just an ordinary Tuesday night. Bay rum wafted clear across the road as Ticks McGee headed into the diner.

Yup, no doubt about it. I've got a front-row seat for first-class entertainment.

"Hey, son." Uncle Ebenezer sauntered over. "Ain't it 'bout time you cooled off, cleaned up, and chowed down?"

"In a while."

"Best you not wait. Miss Mather might run outta grub again." Uncle Eb's head jutted forward as he imparted, "Happens 'least once a day."

Jeff jabbed his thumb back toward the forge. "Beans already on the fire."

"You're fixin' to eat your own cooking?" Eb shook his head. "Heat from that forge must be fryin' your brain."

"You taught me how to make 'em," Jeff replied. "They've been good enough all these years."

"Son, when you ain't got nuthin' but a mule to ride, you ride it. Only a fool keeps on a-riding that flea-bitten old beast when someone offers him a high-steppin' filly."

"You're assuming I aim to go somewhere. I'm happy to stay put."

—∾—

"I'm flattered, sir, but I simply cannot." Lacey refilled Ticks McGee's coffee mug and moved on down the table, topping off the mugs.

"Why not?" Mr. McGee demanded. "You'd never want for nothing. I'd treat you real good. My job at the telegraph even comes with the upstairs rooms for us."

Everyone in the diner awaited her answer. Lacey hadn't realized the men were being more than friendly until Ticks just proposed to her in front of everyone. She'd thought the gangly telegraph operator had been joking. He wasn't. *Men are fragile creatures—their pride is easily damaged.* Madame's words echoed in her mind. Lacey set down the big blue enamel coffeepot and gifted Ticks with a gentle smile. "You've honored me with your offer, sir. Truly, I'm flattered, but I cannot accept because I'm set to take a position at Le Petite Femme Academie once my aunt is better."

Angry roars and denials ripped through the diner.

"The matter is settled." She headed toward the kitchen for refuge.

"What was all that noise?" Aunt Millie asked as she sat at the table and made another bowl of coleslaw. "And where's the salt?"

Lacey scooted a cup toward her aunt. "Here. I measured this

out for you already." The fact that the cup held sugar instead of salt—well, Lacey had to do something. Aunt Millie seemed to have very. . .unique notions about her recipes. Rather than offend her aunt, Lacey simply started supplying bowls with already measured dry ingredients so her aunt could still be helpful. So far, the solution had worked wonderfully.

"How about adding a little kick to this with some chili powder?" Aunt Millie asked after adding the sugar and taking a taste.

Chili powder in coleslaw? Public marriage proposals from near strangers? Lacey shook her head in disbelief.

"No?" Aunt Millie looked disappointed.

"Raisins. They'll complement the pork roast, don't you think?" Lacey swiped the chili powder from the spice rack and slipped it into her apron pocket. No use leaving temptation on hand. "You've made a wonderful suggestion, though. We could make chili and corn bread for lunch tomorrow."

Mollified, Aunt Millie dumped raisins into the coleslaw. "Best you get plenty of peppers from Sager's. These men are Texans. They like their chili hot."

Aunt Millie's idea of hot would no doubt have every last man in Cut Corners on his knees, praying for redemption. With that concern in mind, Lacey hovered over the stove the next day. Jeff Wilson lumbered in with more coal. As he filled the box and added more coal to the stove for her, he sniffed. "What is that?"

"Chili." She smiled at him and tapped the edge of the enormous pot on her left. "This one is regular. The other is hot."

"Hmm." He washed off at the pump, dried his hands, and swiped a spoon. After taking a taste of the hot pot, he gave her a patient look. "Miss Mather, back in Boston you fix beans with brown sugar and molasses. That's all well and good, but you're in Texas."

"Why, of course I am."

"Texas chili doesn't use beans—but just this once, we'll overlook that."

Another peculiar thing about Texas. At least he was nice about telling me. And the chili tastes perfectly fine the way it is.

"The real problem is, that stuff's milder than kissin' your sister." Jeff grabbed a bottle of hot sauce and upended it over the pot. "Millie, head on over to the mercantile. Grab up half a dozen more bottles, a mess of peppers, and grab me a ginger ale while you're at it."

"Sure thing!" Aunt Millie shot Lacey an I-told-you-so look and rushed out the door.

Horrified at how he blithely spoiled a perfectly decent pot of chili, Lacey spluttered. Just the fumes from the Tabasco had her gasping for air.

"Now that she's gone," Jeff said, continuing to give the bottle emphatic shakes to empty it, "I'm going to talk turkey. Your aunt's a fine woman, but she's a miserable cook. I heard tell you plan to leave once she gets better. Take pity on us all and teach her your recipes, will you?"

Staring at the pot in utter dismay, Lacey said, "You seem to share her chili recipe."

"Simple rule: In Texas, you make the chili so it blows off the top of your head when you take a taste." He grinned. "Then you triple the hot stuff." He gawked at the spice rack. "Where's the chili powder?"

Lacey pulled it from her apron pocket. "I had to hide it from Aunt Millie so she wouldn't put it in the coleslaw last night."

His features looked pained. "So that's what she does to it." He dumped an eye-popping amount into the first pot, then as much into the second, and finally set down the tin. "At least she won't be able to do it again until you buy more."

"You emptied the chili powder and Tabasco into it!"

"Yup." He stirred the pot.

Aunt Millie returned so fast, Lacey suspected she'd already

sent word to the mercantile to have everything ready. Lacey couldn't even cut more peppers. Her eyes, nose, and fingers already stung. Jeff grabbed a knife, hacked the peppers into an unsightly mess, and dumped them into the chili as Aunt Millie merrily shook hot sauce into the second pot.

Lacey put another pan of corn bread into the oven and wondered how she'd ever explain to the hungry patrons that the main dish had been spoiled.

Jeff tilted his head toward the icebox. "Now get yourself some milk."

"Would you care for a glass?"

"Don't need it." He waited until she had a glassful. "Now taste this."

Lacey didn't want to sample it. Then again, she didn't want to be rude. At least he didn't have a lot on the spoon. She opened her mouth.

CHAPTER 4

"Oh. Ohh." Lacey's hand went up to her mouth. The strangled sound coming out of her made Jeff drop the spoon and grab the milk from her.

"Here. Drink." He lifted the glass and tried to peel her hand from her mouth. Her big hazel eyes filled with tears that overflowed and spilled down her cheeks.

"It'll help. Drink!"

Both of her hands clamped around his. The poor woman could scarcely breathe, but she took a sip and fought to swallow.

"Drink it all. Fast." Jeff hadn't ever seen such a pitiful sight. Proper little Lacey Mather broke out into a full-on sweat, and her face rivaled a tomato for color. Tears poured down her face, and she kept making a sound of pure anguish.

"Wa—" She tried to scramble away. "Wa. Ur."

"Oh no. No water!" Millie stood in front of the pump by the sink.

"More milk." Jeff sloshed milk into the glass and shoved it back at Lacey. "Milk cools the fire." She couldn't decide what to do or where to go, so he yanked out a chair and shoved her into it. As she drank the milk, Millie flapped a dish towel to cool her off.

"I gave her a taste out of the milder pot," he said to Millie.

Lacey said something—it sounded sort of like "murder," but

he wasn't sure. Maybe it was "mother."

"Millie, let's have her lie down." Jeff half lifted Lacey from the chair. She clutched the milk bottle for dear life. "Yeah, princess. You bring that along."

With Millie as chaperone, it would be decent enough for him to escort Lacey back to the bedchamber, only Lacey didn't cooperate. They'd scarcely gotten into the parlor when she pulled away and sank onto the horsehair settee and gulped more milk—directly from the bottle.

"She can't breathe," Millie said as she shoved at his shoulder. "You go on back and stir the pot."

Jeff took his cue and left. Women and their stays. Once Millie loosened Lacey, then she ought to improve. Or so he hoped. He stirred the pots, tasted each, and couldn't fathom why she'd reacted at all. They were still blander than rattlesnake. Well, Lacey wouldn't try another taste, so he might as well go ahead and finish seasoning the pots so they'd be ready for the lunch crowd. She'd done fine with the garlic and onion, but the woman didn't have a hint on how much zing and heat to add. Satisfied he'd salvaged lunch, Jeff decided he'd better try to rescue the fair maiden.

"How's she doing, Millie?"

"Hot," Lacey croaked.

Jeff tore open the icebox and chipped out a chunk of ice. His bandanna wasn't exactly clean, but it would have to do. He wrapped the ice in it and ventured back into the parlor. Ever since she'd arrived, the woman always looked like a page straight out of that *Godey's Lady's Book* his aunt used to pore over. Not any longer. Hair askew, clothing loosened, and apron off, Lacey looked like she'd been dragged through a knothole backward. The sight of her melted his heart.

"Ice." He slid it across her forehead. "Millie, I'll just put the pots on the table and let folks serve themselves today. Why don't you put the corn bread out?"

Lacey grabbed his wrist. "No. Dumb. Keyhole."

"Princess, I'm not going to dump it out. It won't kill anybody." The accusation in her eyes had him squirming. "Just drink a little more milk. Trust me."

Her pretty round jaw dropped open in shock, then clamped shut. Jeff figured it was a good thing she couldn't talk much right now.

—∞—

Lacey stood in church and held the hymnal, but she didn't sing. Couldn't sing. Ever since yesterday's chili debacle, her tongue and throat belonged to a dragon. A whole day now. An entire day of not being able to speak much, taste at all, or sing a note. And the men! Every last bachelor in town—except Jeffrey Wilson—wouldn't leave her alone. They'd tasted that pot of bubbling brimstone, declared it the best they'd ever eaten, and vowed they'd never let her leave Cut Corners. Unable to deny any responsibility for that vile dish, she'd become a celebrity.

Jeff Wilson—that rascal—didn't let on. No, he didn't. Neither did Aunt Millie.

Both of them ought to visit the altar and confess their dirty deeds.

Only staying mad didn't make sense. Truly this group was a lot of fun. They managed to find the good in just about anything. The fact that they'd eaten every last bit of that dreadful chili proved her point! They helped one another out. Peony Wilson had come to the diner the first morning it was open and helped wash all of the dishes. Vivian Sager dropped by each morning to see if Lacey needed anything from the mercantile. The old gents who whiled away their days on the boardwalk playing games all kept watch on the children as they darted across the road on their way to and from school. Jeff brought over coal and sharpened her knives. Aunt Millie, for having a painful arm, still kept a cheerful attitude and did her best to help.

When the last chord on the piano died out, Lacey sat down

between Aunt Millie and Peony on the bench. Rafe had gotten called to go check something and worried about his wife, so he'd brought her by to "help" get Aunt Millie ready for church. One glance told Lacey why he'd fretted so. Peony alternated between blanching and taking on a peculiar green tint. No wonder Rafe started showing up for breakfast at the diner! Her new friend deserved to reveal the wonderful news when she took a mind to—and not a moment earlier. That being the case, Lacey opened her silk fan and managed to waft it more toward Peony as the parson approached the pulpit.

"We are all part of the family of God," Parson Clune said. "Working together for the betterment of one another and to promote the kingdom of God."

Aunt Millie reached over with her good hand to give Lacey's leg a loving pat. Ever since Mama had passed on and Father had sent her to the academy, Lacey hadn't been part of a family. She didn't have anybody. Well—back in Boston, she didn't. Here, she had Aunt Millie. If it hadn't been for Father's housekeeper sending the telegraph message on to Lacey, she wouldn't have known her great-aunt still lived.

"Instead of considering it a duty to help our brothers and sisters, it is a privilege and honor to serve them in the name of Christ. Christ displayed an attitude of humility by washing the disciples' feet. You can't get any more down-to-earth than that."

Folks in the congregation caught the pun and chuckled.

Parson Clune smiled and continued, "We want to be like the Savior. That means caring for each other in the everyday, mundane, little matters. . . ."

As the sermon continued, Rafe arrived. He scooted onto the bench next to his wife and slid his arm behind her. She immediately leaned into him and relaxed.

"A lady sits upright at all times. Back straight. No slumping. Only a lazy woman rests against the back of her chair. . . ." Madame's lessons darted through Lacey's mind, and for the

first time they all seemed petty and nonsensical. Rafe cherished his wife, and she wasn't feeling her best. To support her back while she sat on this hard old bench was—well, it was an act of everyday love. It was like in the fairy tales. A happily-ever-after kind of love. *And they're going to have a family.*

After the service, Lacey couldn't get that image out of her mind. Something tugged at her—a longing she couldn't escape. How wonderful it would be to have someone to love and to be loved by! Oh, if she wanted to, she could accept the very next marriage proposal and become a wife within a week. Men asked for her hand with stunning regularity. *But none of them love me, and I don't love them. I can't live day in and day out when there's no love beneath the roof.*

A small voice inside taunted, *You already have—all your life at the academy.*

Lacey shoved that thought aside. It was untrue. The younger girls flocked to her, and she adored them. And she admired Madame. If anything, the sermon opened her eyes. She could love in Christ's name and by His example in dozens of tiny ways each day. But that plan didn't take away the odd feeling that she was missing out on finding her own happily-ever-after.

CHAPTER 5

Hoo–oo–ey!" Jeff finished filling the coal bin, took out his bandanna, and flapped it in the air. "Now that you can fire up the stove, I'll open the door and air out this place."

Millie winked. "Long as I've been here—and I'm one of the founding folks of Cut Corners—Ticks McGee never put on any airs for me."

"Put on airs!" Jeff hooted. He opened the door and fanned it back and forth to dispel the overwhelming scent the telegrapher had left in his wake. "The man did a backstroke through bay rum to deliver that telegram."

"Oh, stop that." Lacey continued to peel potatoes, but laughter tinged her voice.

"I don't dare." Jeff kept fanning the room. "If this place isn't aired out by supper, folks'll all think you got a polecat under the planks."

"Not with all the flowers," Millie said in a droll voice as she stood on tiptoe over at the spice rack. "I'm flat running out of jars for 'em."

"They look pretty on the tables," Lacey said as she set aside a potato, got up, and smoothly took the tin of spice from her aunt. "I'd like to save these cloves for the ham, Aunt Millie. I hope you don't mind."

Millie frowned. "Then what're you going to put on the roast beef?"

"I was thinking maybe we ought to do something together. Madame taught us to mix spices and jar them so we'd have ready-made seasonings specifically for chicken, pork, fish, or beef. It saves a lot of time. After I leave, it'll simplify things for you."

"Great idea!" Jeff beamed at her. "Tell you what: I was fixin' to go to the mercantile to get a few things. I'll bring back some of those nifty Ball-Mason jars. What spices do you need?"

"I'll make a list. We can write the recipes down, too." Lacey smiled at her aunt. "And you can be sure to give me your cowboy cookie recipe and that sweet cornmeal mush. The girls at the academy will love it."

Jeff grinned at her. Lacey Mather exhibited more tact than anyone he'd ever known. She hadn't even spoken a cross word when Jay Harris and one of the Baxter boys both brought in goldenrod and had everyone in the diner sneezing all day. Men kept bringing her posies, and she'd have her aunt stick them in jars on the dining tables—along with everyone else's. That way, according to Lacey, everyone could enjoy the beauty of Texas. Far as all those men were concerned, Lacey was the Beauty of Texas. But Beauty never once showed the least bit of interest in any of the men.

Millie and Peony did a fair job of sitting on either side of Lacey at worship services; otherwise, a passel of lovesick cowboys all practically trampled the poor woman in hopes of having the honor of sitting by her side. Ticks McGee actually knocked over a bench in church in his rush to be near her.

That wasn't all. She'd befriended the women in town, and even old sourpuss Lula Chamberlain sang her praises. Youngsters were crazy about her, too. Why, she'd taken to baking cookies only the children were offered if they'd finished their meals. Folks in town speculated on how good they must be, and the kids practically licked their plates clean to earn one—but Lacey didn't let the adults have them. She declared it as a rule.

Only she'd set one on the ledge by the coal box for Jeff each time he made a delivery. A special one—extra big. Continuing to fan the door, he bit into the cookie. "Mmm."

"I've been meaning to speak with you about increasing the delivery of coal to every other day."

Jeff took another bite and waggled his brows. Mouth full of incredible taste, he suggested, "How about every day?"

Her gaze went from the remains of the cookie to his eyes, then back. "I wouldn't want to cast aspersions on your character or motives. Shall I presume the offer stems from the fact that winter is almost upon us?"

"Miss Mather." Jeff tucked the last portion of the cookie in his mouth, chewed and swallowed it with relish, then grinned. "I wouldn't take offense if you assumed my offer had anything to do with a tasty fringe benefit. No man in his right mind would pass up an opportunity to eat your cooking. As for winter—well, the weather's getting snappy."

She opened the cookie jar and held it out to him. "I've been thinking about that. Perhaps it's time to place an order with Sanger's so the diner isn't without necessities. When do we expect the first snowfall?"

"Snow?" Millie let out a cackle and grabbed a cookie.

Jeff helped himself. "More often than not, it doesn't snow here until late, if at all."

A stricken expression crossed Lacey's pretty face. "You don't have snow for Christmas?"

"A few times we have." It hadn't ever mattered to him, but clearly the thought rocked Miss Mather to the core.

Millie dusted a cookie crumb from her lips. "A bigger mess you've never seen. Folks tracked slush and mud in here and never gave me a moment's rest. All they wanted was coffee, soup, and pie. Can't make much of a profit on that."

"With all the rain we've been getting, I thought—" Lacey let out a small self-conscious laugh. "I suppose it doesn't matter. You're both happy without the snow, and I'll be back in Boston up to my boots in snow for Christmas."

Suddenly the cookie tasted like sawdust. Jeff looked at Lacey and couldn't imagine her leaving. "You don't have to go."

Her eyes widened and glistened with sincerity. "But of course I shall. I've given my word."

—∞—

"Frankly, I don't like the looks of this." Dr. Winston supported Aunt Millie's arm and carefully moved it. "It's healing more slowly than I'd hoped."

"Don't tell me you're going to splint me up again. I won't have it."

Lacey took corn bread from the oven and popped in pans of chocolate cake. "What do you recommend, Doctor?"

"Not another splint." Aunt Millie's repressive tone matched her taut face.

"If we keep it heavily bandaged and in a sling, that ought to provide enough protection. You cannot use the arm yet for anything. Even lifting the lightest object might well snap the bone again."

"I don't need to be mollycoddled. Using the arm will strengthen it."

Doc folded his arms across his chest. "Millie, you're old, you're stubborn, and you're wrong."

"Two out of those three aren't flaws," she shot back.

"But that still means the doctor needs to bind up your arm," Lacey said.

"Not till after I eat a chunk of that corn bread. Doc, have a seat."

Lacey smiled at the physician. He'd about hit his limit in dealing with her aunt. "Please do sit down. Would you rather have vegetable barley soup or potato cheese?"

"Have the potato cheese. She wouldn't listen to me and add cinnamon or nutmeg to the vegetable barley." Aunt Millie shot Lacey a disgruntled look. "Everyone knows you add nutmeg and cinnamon to things with grains in them."

The doctor choked, coughed, then rasped, "I'd like the vegetable, please. And Miss Mather, you cannot possibly leave yet. At this point, your aunt still needs your assistance."

"I suspected as much. I'll send a telegram today." The thought of staying in Cut Corners awhile longer filled her with happiness.

The happiness lasted all through serving lunch, clear until she approached the telegraph office. Facing Ticks McGee after she'd turned down his marriage proposal qualified as more than a little awkward. In the time she'd been in Texas, there hadn't been a single day during which she hadn't received a gentleman's offer to take her out for a walk. . .and more than a few had actually embellished the invitation clear into a proposal that she walk down the aisle to him! Once she'd informed the populace that she'd be returning to Boston, Lacey presumed the nonsense would stop. On the contrary, it only got worse.

That scamp Jeff Wilson seemed to find the whole thing hilarious. Indeed, Lacey supposed it was. She tried to keep a sense of perspective. These men were lonely. And hungry. Madame said a man who had a full plate and a quiet woman who listened to him was a happy man. These men were seeking happiness. She oughtn't fault them for following their nature. Lacey just wished their nature would lead them to some other woman.

"Well, well! Miss Mather, what can I do for you?" Ticks perked up.

"Good afternoon, Mr. McGee. I'd like to send a telegram." She'd already composed it back at the diner, so she took the paper from her reticule and handed it across the counter.

"This is quite a lengthy one." He pulled the pencil from

behind his ear and dabbed the lead on his tongue. "We could shave it down and save you a bundle."

Lacey suppressed a shudder at the fact that his hair oil slicked the pencil. "I appreciate the offer, sir, but that isn't necessary."

His brows scrunched into a deep V. "It costs a nickel per three words, Miss Mather."

"Yes, I know." She smiled. "I counted it at a hundred fifty-nine words. According to my arithmetic, it should total two dollars and sixty-five cents."

He tapped his pencil against her paper. "It goes against my grain to take advantage of a lady. I'm sure I can help you out. You can't squander your money like that."

"My finances are not your concern, sir. The matter is important, and I'd appreciate you taking the utmost care in transmitting the letter precisely as I composed it." She set the exact cost of the telegram on the counter.

Muttering to himself, Ticks went over to the telegraph key. He settled into the oak chair, poised his finger over the apparatus, then squinted at the missive. His head shot up. "You're staying?"

"Only for a while longer."

"Why don't you have a seat? You can wait for a reply."

The last thing she wanted to do was spend more time in the stuffy office with a man far too eager to drag her to the altar. "Forgive me for asking you to deliver any reply to the diner. I have a few errands to run."

Exiting the office, she headed for Sanger's Mercantile. Perhaps if she and Vivian looked at what was in stock, they could concoct a softer, more comfortable bandage and sling for Aunt Millie.

Dear Aunt Millie. Lacey fretted over what to do about her relative. The old woman had plenty of spirit and a heart as big as the sky, but there didn't seem to be any reason behind some of her actions. *I'm sure it's the laudanum that makes her forgetful,* Lacey told herself. Then again, Chaps Smythe called her an "odd duck." The appellation did fit—after all, who else would think a roast beef ought to be topped with sugar? Well, regardless, Lacey loved her great-aunt. She wasn't in the least bit upset about extending her stay. What would Jeffrey Wilson say about it, though?

—∞—

"Are you okay?" Jeff hovered in the doorway.

"Depends on who you're asking." Millie gave him a jaded look as she shuffled across the floor. "I say I'm fine. Doc still wants me trussed up like a coast-to-coast parcel."

He hadn't come to check on Millie's arm, but Jeff nodded. "You do what he wants. We need you completely healed."

"Yes, we do." Lacey stood by the sink dabbing peroxide onto a wad of cotton.

Jeff crossed over toward her and grabbed hold of her hand. Studying her slender fingers, he asked, "Did you cut yourself?" He'd heard she'd bought peroxide at the mercantile, and he'd hotfooted it over here to be sure she was all right. He'd heard other news about Lacey, too, that he wanted to confirm.

"No. I got some drippings on myself when I put the roast in the oven. Peroxide removes bloodstains." She slid her hand loose and continued to fiddle with the front of her too-fancy-for-the-wilds-of-Texas apron. What call did a woman have wearing anything that pristine and frilly when she stood in front of a stove?

"All those facts are a waste, what with you living at that school." Millie dumped sugar into her coffee and shook the spoon at Lacey. "Those girls won't use that knowledge a lick. They'll marry rich men and have maids and cooks to do the work for 'em."

He saw hurt darken Lacey's eyes. Clearly she felt she'd found what God intended her to do with her life. Having others disparage it upset her. Though he agreed with Millie's assessment, Jeff couldn't bring himself to say so aloud. Instead, he teased lightly, "According to Ticks, the girls will have to make do without you for some time yet."

Lacey nodded. "I'll be staying until just before Christmas. That'll give Aunt Millie plenty of time to heal."

"I think I'll buy another fireplace poker from you, Jeff." Millie winced as she placed her arm on the table. "I'll use it to prod Ticks out of here. The man's making a pest of himself."

"Your niece has been good for business, Millie."

"Amazing what a pretty face'll do." Millie nodded. "Brings 'em all in, and they don't seem to mind that the food's seasoned all wrong. The girl cooks like an easterner."

"I've been able to thank God with a clear conscience for every last meal she's cooked."

Millie gave him a worldly-wise look. "Ecclesiastes 2:24: 'There is nothing better for a man, than that he should eat and drink, and that he should make his soul enjoy good in his labour. This also I saw, that it was from the hand of God.' That's you, Jeff Wilson. You're happy just to have a full belly and a hot forge."

"Contentment is a fine quality," Lacey said quietly. "Jeff works hard, and his heart belongs to God. In my estimation, that's more than admirable." She turned back to trying to remove the blot on her apron.

Jeff appreciated her compliment. Lacey wasn't one to pass out flattery. He patted the edge of her apron. "Well, you need to take a little credit for that contentment. I'm doing all of my eating here these days."

"You're always most welcome," Lacey said.

Most welcome. Was that just polite banter, or did she mean I'm more welcome than anyone else?

—∞—

Peony took a sip of tea and gave Lacey a grateful smile. "It's helping. Thank you."

"Lemon's supposed to help, too. Here. I made lemon spritz cookies for you." Lacey urged her friend to nibble. For the past week and a half, she'd been bringing little meals and treats to tempt Peony. Rafe took all his meals at the diner, and from the lines creasing his face, Lacey knew he was beside himself with worry.

"Dr. Winston says my tummy will settle down in another few weeks."

"Of course it will." Lacey smiled brightly. "In the meantime, since you don't have to worry about cooking, we need to plan your wardrobe for the *accouchement*."

Peony smiled. "Your propriety is so charming. How wonderful to grow up with such refinement."

Lacey urged her to nibble on a second cookie. "I'd scarcely call a school full of chattering girls refined. We were trained in all matters of conduct, but there weren't many opportunities to actually put the lessons into practice."

"I grew up with women, too—but not ones of respectability."

Reaching out, Lacey covered Peony's hand with hers. "Do you think such a thing matters to me? We have no say about the circumstances we're born into. It's what we do with ourselves that matters."

"I felt it only right to confess it. There are those who cannot—"

"Pardon me for interrupting you, Peony, but I cannot abide those with narrow minds and even narrower hearts. From the moment you stepped foot into the diner and offered to help wash up the breakfast dishes, you showed your true heart. God sent you to me as a friend, and I'm thankful. So now that we've settled that, why don't we design a dress for you to wear through Christmas? I'm sure with your clever sewing we could take deep seams to let out as your delicate condition progresses."

"I did order a length of beautiful green paisley."

Once she'd made sure Peony had finished the tea, cookies,

and cheese, Lacey headed back to the diner. Aunt Millie was supposed to be placing an order over at Sanger's, and they'd already prepared the chicken pasties. Lacey would start popping them into the oven and have them ready just in time for the lunch crowd. She turned the corner and saw smoke billowing out of the diner window.

CHAPTER 6

"Well!" Millie plopped down in the chair and fanned herself with a damp, charred dishcloth.

Jeff stamped on another ember and poured one last bucket of water down the wall. The entire window frame looked like a chunk of charcoal, the panes were cracked, and what had once been curtains now made a sad pile of ashes on the floor.

"Aunt Millie!" Lacey barreled into the room.

"Over here. No use fussing."

"Are you well? Did either of you get burned?" Lacey's voice quavered as she made her way to her aunt.

"Wasn't nothing much. No real harm done." Millie shrugged. " 'Cept a couple of the pastries for lunch are singed."

"No one cares about that, Millie. We're just glad you didn't get hurt." Jeff set down the water bucket.

Lacey watched him solemnly. Her hazel eyes reflected a mix of horror and gratitude. One glance at the place told just how close this had come to being a disaster. "Thank you." She stumbled toward the other door and opened it wide. Smoke drafted on the breeze from the first door to the second.

"Smoke follows beauty." Jeff didn't intend to speak aloud. Once he realized he'd done so, he crooked her a grin. "I don't think there's much damage here. Nothing a little sanding, a few replacement boards, and glass won't solve."

"Erik Olson can handle that." Millie leaned back in her chair.

"I'll see him about it after lunch." Lacey stepped through the water puddles on the floor and opened the oven door.

"Careful!" Jeff cinched his arm about her waist and lifted her up and back. He'd barely managed in time. Gray water with gritty bits of soot and coal spilled from the appliance and splattered on the floor.

"Oh my."

Oh my. Jeff wanted to echo Lacey's words—but for an entirely different reason. He'd just grabbed an armful of woman, and he hadn't anticipated the effect. He didn't want to put her down. The sweet scent of her perfume engulfed him.

"The oven's stone-cold."

"Yep." He didn't tell her it took eight buckets of water before the dumb thing stopped steaming—all of course, after the half dozen he'd used on the wall and window. At the moment, he doubted she would accept that information with much poise.

Patting his arm, Lacey said, "You did a wonderful thing, Mr. Wilson. Heroic. There's no doubt you rescued my aunt and the diner."

From the way she twisted, he knew she wanted to be put down. Jeff took a few long strides and grudgingly set her on the dry patch of planks on the far side of the table. "I just happened along."

"Thank the Lord!" Lacey cast a glance at the shelves of towel-covered sheets. "You've already done so much. I do hate to impose, but would you mind awfully if I used your forge?"

"My forge?"

Twenty minutes later, Jeff stood beside Lacey at his forge. The crazy woman was dressed in her calico dress and a frilly white apron; she held a potholder in one slender hand and a long pair of tongs in the other. She'd dug out the biggest pot in the diner, given it to him, and now had lard melted and bubbling in it. "I'd far rather bake these. It's much more healthful," she said as she snagged the chicken pasties from the pot and replaced them with more.

"Smells great."

"Hey, there." Uncle Eb stood over at the rail. He shot Jeff a wily grin. "What's happening here?"

"Your nephew is saving the day." Lacey flashed Uncle Eb a smile. "He put out a fire at the diner, and he's letting me fix lunch here."

"What say, folks just drop by here to pick up their lunch? Looks like they can carry them meat pies."

"I don't know. . . ." Lacey looked up at Jeff. "What do you think?"

"After all the rain, it's a fair day. Ground's dry. We can stick out a bucket of apples and call it a picnic lunch."

"A picnic!" Her face lit up. "Oh, I love picnics. I know just what to do."

By the time lunch was scheduled, Jeff stood back and shook his head at the event. At Lacey's urging, he'd set out a pair of sawhorses and stretched a few solid planks across them. She'd covered them with a red-checkered tablecloth from the diner. A big vat of potato salad, a dish of pickle spears, slices of buttered bread, and a bucket of apples sat along it. Six more tablecloths lay on the ground, weighted by rocks and each holding one of the jars of flowers from the diner. She stepped back and sighed. "If only we had some music!"

"You could sing."

She turned the exact color red as the checkers in the tablecloth. "I'd scare away the diners. I confess, I cannot sing at all."

"No?" Her admission caught him off guard. "I thought those fancy girl schools turned you out with all sorts of musical accomplishments."

"They're supposed to. I failed abysmally. The music master despaired of teaching me to sing. I'm utterly and completely tone deaf. Even worse, I developed the revolting habit of getting hiccups whenever I attempted the flute." Her smile turned charmingly winsome. "It produces the oddest sounds."

"But you played the piano last week at church."

"Only because the pastor implored me to since no one else was more capable. I'm afraid the piano master pronounced my playing 'somewhere between painful and passable.' "

He scowled. "Was everyone there that cruel? I thought they pampered you at those places."

"Honesty is the best policy. How could I work on my shortcomings if no one pointed out the flaws? I do, however, hope to mention my impressions with a bit more tact when I'm overseeing the girls at my next post."

Her next post. She said it so blithely. What did she think she was doing, leaving a dotty aunt and a town full of people who cared for her, just to go back to an institution where truth wasn't tempered with compassion? Jeff wanted to roar. He wanted to rattle some sense into her. No way was he going to let her go.

CHAPTER 7

Erik Olson pounded in one last nail, then stood back to survey the repairs. "Ja. The window, bigger is nice."

"You outdid yourself," Aunt Millie declared. "I think the man deserves a cookie, don't you, Lacey?"

Lacey nodded. She didn't dare actually open her mouth to reply for fear that she'd start to giggle. The Swedish carpenter had been casting longing looks at the cookie jar from the moment he came over to assess the damage. To his credit, even when he'd been alone in the kitchen, he'd never sneaked a single crumb. His sense of honor touched Lacey. Then again, it didn't exactly surprise her. Erik was Jeff's friend—and as she'd been taught, a man could be judged by the company he kept.

"My niece made you a whole dozen of your own, Erik. You go ahead and enjoy 'em—every last one." Aunt Millie scooted a plate across the table.

Erik grinned and pulled out a chair. "Then I will eat them here. My uncle and the other old men—they will gobble up the plate if I go outside."

"Milk or coffee?" Lacey offered.

"Both." The carpenter gave her a boyish grin. "Milk for to dunk the cookies. Coffee to remind me I am no longer a boy, even though I enjoy the treat you keep for the children."

Lacey set the beverages before him, then turned back to the oven. She opened the door and pulled out the roaster just long enough to dump in the carrots and potatoes.

"Mmm, mmm, mmm. Something smells great."

She didn't even turn around. "Is there anything you don't like, Jeff?"

"Cranberries." His boots rang across the planks, and coal shuffled into the bin.

"Asparagus. He does not like that, either." Erik grinned. "He calls it 'ugly pencils.' "

Lacey wheeled around. "And I served you asparagus the first time you ate here!"

"Your asparagus is good. Millie, I still think you need to teach her chili doesn't take beans."

The older woman sighed theatrically. "You can lead a horse to water. . . ."

"Aunt Millie! Are you comparing me to a horse?"

"Don't get all het up and scandalized." Aunt Millie's face puckered. "Horses are fine creatures. Loyal. Hardworking."

Jeff shot a look at the new window ledge. "Good work, Erik."

"Thank you."

Lacey took the hint. She grabbed the cookie jar and held it out to him. He looked down at his sooty hands. "Here." Fishing out a pair of cookies, she slipped them into his hands.

"Much obliged." Jeff cast a look at Erik, who was plowing through the plate of cookies like a starving man. "If the old rangers catch wind of you eating those all by yourself, your days are numbered."

"You do not tell them. I will not tell them you eat a cookie each time you come to deliver coal." Erik bit off another chunk. "This is a good bargain. You come out better."

Jeff pounded his friend on the shoulder and belted out a chuckle.

The male camaraderie astonished Lacey. She'd never had

an opportunity to watch men interact. The whole time Erik worked, Jeff had tracked in and out, lent a hand, and silently left. Neither of them ever said a word about the assistance. Rafe Wilson was the same way. He and Jeff were cousins, and they often seemed to carry on entire conversations over the dining table without saying more than a cryptic one- or two-word phrase apiece, grunt, nod, and grin.

Those masculine grins—Jeff's in particular—were oddly gratifying sights. Men, for being such odd, rough creatures, never looked very approachable. But when Jeff's mouth kicked up and his eyes sparkled with laughter, an odd sense of contentment washed over Lacey. Longing to keep him smiling, she said, "I've been thinking about Thanksgiving."

"Diner's closed Thanksgiving and Christmas. I made that mistake the first year. Worked myself silly, and all because everyone else was too lazy. Since then, I have a free pot roast luncheon for all the bachelors on Christmas Eve Day. That's as good as it's gonna get." Aunt Millie rapped the knuckles of her left hand on the table. "Let each of 'em cook their own turkey or goose."

"My goose is cooked, all right," Jeff muttered. He scowled. "Come on, Millie. It's stupid for me to make a whole turkey just for myself."

"You got an uncle and a cousin and his wife. Your family'll take you in."

Lacey inhaled sharply. "Oh, but Peony can't cook. It's too hard for her."

"Good." Jeff's smile looked downright smug. "Then we'll all show up. You name the time."

"Ja, name the time." Erik bobbed his head.

"If you come, Swede will tag along," Aunt Millie groused.

"Of course they will," Lacey chirped. Excitement welled up inside. She'd always had to endure lonely holiday meals with the cook at the academy. This would be her first time to have a true holiday feast. "And so will Stone Creedon and Chaps

Smythe. They sit and play dominoes and checkers with Swede and Ebenezer Wilson every day. I can't abide the thought that they'd feel left out."

"Child, you're talking yourself into a heap of work." Aunt Millie shook her head. "With my arm like it is, I'm barely helping out as is. You try cooking a whole fancy feast, and—"

"We'll all pitch in," Jeff said.

Flashing him a grateful smile, Lacey said, "So it's settled."

—w—

Jeff whistled under his breath. "Wow."

Lacey beamed. "Isn't this fun?"

"You outdid yourself." He stared at the dining room. She'd pushed two tables together to form a big square. A snowy tablecloth covered it, and she'd folded napkins on the plates to form fancy fan-shaped designs. Apples, nuts, and ribbons cascaded out of a pair of cornucopias as a centerpiece.

"I'll have to ask you to light the candles just before we begin. I can't reach them."

"Sure." He'd come over early to help out—or as Millie put it, "rein her in." Lacey got some crazy notion that this was supposed to be a seven-course meal. For the past week, he and Millie kept cutting down Lacey's grand plan and nixed over half of the menu items.

It started when Lacey asked his preference between oyster bisque and some other fishy-sounding soup. "To be honest, I've got my mouth set for turkey."

"Naturally, we'll have turkey. I'm talking about the soup course, though."

Millie had chimed in. "Why waste time making that? They won't care. Give the men what they want."

"Very well." Lacey sighed, then brightened. "Then let's discuss appetizers. I was thinking how lovely it would be to have an assortment of—"

"Turkey, child. The men want turkey."

"And stuffing," Jeff had tacked on. "I couldn't care less about a bunch of little morsels. I'm saving all my room for the good stuff."

Good stuff. He hadn't known just what that meant to Lacey, but now he was finding out. "Did you sleep at all last night?"

"A little." She bustled toward the kitchen and over to the stove, where she lifted the lid on a pot and gave the contents a quick stir. "Aunt Millie, if you'd put the baskets of rolls on the table, I'd appreciate it. Jeff, would you please move this pot of potatoes onto the table so I can use the burner for something else?"

Hefting the pot, he asked, "Want me to drain the water?"

"Not just yet. It'll keep them hot until I mash them." She set a coffeepot on to percolate, then opened the oven. The nearly overpowering aroma of turkey burst into the room, but Lacey reached beside the huge pan and pulled out another dish. She opened the lid, drizzled butter atop yams, and sprinkled brown sugar over it all.

Jeff's stomach rumbled. "I'm not going to be able to wait another half hour to eat."

"Yes, you will." She waggled her spoon at him. "I have this all scheduled, and no one is going to destroy my plan."

"Oh, give the man a cookie," Millie laughed as she came back in.

"It'll spoil his appetite."

"I'm not a child."

Lacey paused and looked up at him. Her lips parted, then closed. Though she'd already been rosy from the heat of the stove, her color heightened. "No one could mistake you for a child. Forgive me."

"It'll cost you a cookie." He winked. "You can buy me off cheaply."

"Spoken like a true friend," Millie said as she pulled butter from the icebox.

"Friends and family—that's what today's all about." Tears sheened Lacey's eyes, turning them into glistening pools of gold.

"Being thankful to the Lord with those we love."

A knock sounded at the door. She smoothed her skirts and went to answer it. Millie watched her go, then murmured, "I didn't figure it out till last night. Did you know that gal hasn't had a family Thanksgiving since her mama passed on? She was only six. Ever since then, she's been stuck at that snooty school. It's why she's so dead set to make today perfect."

"Then let's make her dreams come true."

—∞—

The turkey skidded off the platter and onto the table. Ebenezer Wilson growled, stabbed the bird with the carving fork and knife, and wrestled it back onto the platter, then proceeded to hack the beautiful golden brown bird into unidentifiable chunks.

"You made succotash!" Jeff shot Lacey a huge smile as he lifted the lid off the dish. "My favorite!"

"I'm glad." *Well, at least that went well.*

"What's this in the dressing?" Stone Creedon stabbed at something with his fork.

"Oysters," Lacey said as a sinking feeling swamped her. Didn't Texans use oysters in their stuffing?

"I say!" Chaps Smythe reached over, speared the oyster straight off Stone's plate, and gulped it down. "Excellent! I haven't had oyster stuffing in years." He then proved his liking for the dish by scooping almost a third of the bowl onto his plate.

Rafe kept trying to coax Peony to have a little taste of each item as the dishes were passed around the table. Lacey secretly thought it a marvel her friend wasn't abjectly ill just from the sight of her husband's heaping plate with gravy dripping off the edge. Lacey tried to distract herself by helping serve Aunt Millie.

Finally, everything had been around the table, and Lacey relaxed. She promised herself she was going to enjoy today. Picking up her knife and fork, she managed a smile. Everything wasn't exactly picture-perfect, but everyone seemed content.

Bang, bang, bang.

CHAPTER 8

Lacey jumped at the sound, turned, and tamped down a groan. Ticks McGee and Jay Harris both peered through the window.

"I'll take care of this." Jeff rose and headed toward the door. He opened it and said in a firm tone, "The diner's closed today."

"It can't be," Jay Harris said.

"Oh, I smell turkey." Ticks sounded somewhere between heaven and torture.

Memories of lonely holiday meals washed over Lacey. She rushed over to the door as tears filled her eyes. "Please join us. I should have thought to invite you. I'm so sorry."

"You don't have to do this," Jeff said in a low tone. His large body still blocked the door.

Lacey looked up at him. "I want to. Everyone deserves to belong and be wanted."

"Okay." He brushed her tears away. "You men wipe your feet."

Rafe came over. "And go wash off that bay rum, McGee. My wife can't take it."

Hours later, everyone wandered off. Lacey was up to her elbows in water, and Jeff dried the dishes. "We ran out of stuffing," she said.

"So what?" Aunt Millie awkwardly poured the last bit of

cranberry jelly from a bowl into a Ball-Mason jar. "If you wanna squawk, then talk about what Eb did to the bird."

"No harm done," Jeff said blandly. "It still tasted great."

"I should have made another pie."

"There was plenty until we got company," Aunt Millie said in a wry tone.

Heavy-hearted, Lacey nodded. "I should have planned better. I should have invited them and made more." She glanced at Jeff. "I'm sorry you didn't get any pie."

"I had my dessert before supper—remember the cookies?"

"You're a gallant man, Jeffrey Wilson."

His big hands stopped drying a platter. Eyes steady as could be, he studied her and said, "You're every inch a fine lady, Lacey Mather—but more than that, you're a good woman. This Thanksgiving was unforgettable."

"Thank you. I've never received a sweeter compliment. I wanted to do something special so we could all look back fondly. Years from now, I know I'll always treasure this day that I spent with you."

"There can be more of them, you know." He reached over and brushed a bubble from her sleeve.

Her hands sank to the bottom of the sink, and her heart went right along with them. "No. I'll go back to Boston soon." Forcing a smile, she tacked on, "Where I'll even have a white Christmas."

—~—

"Stubborn woman." Jeff brought the hammer down again to punctuate his opinion. What was wrong with Lacey? Couldn't she see her life was here in Cut Corners?

"We came to talk sense into you," Uncle Eb said from beyond the rail.

Jeff glowered at him and the other three meddling men. "What now?"

"You can't let Lacey Mather go back East," Chaps declared.

"It's simply unacceptable."

"You're thinking with your belly," Jeff said. It irritated him that these men only cared about Lacey because she could cook. Didn't they see past that? Couldn't they understand that she deserved to be loved and have a family surrounding her?

"Plenty of young bucks around Cut Corners. Every last one of 'em thinks she's a fine catch," Stone Creedon said.

"Better make a quick move," Swede advised.

"I think we've said enough," Uncle Eb declared. He nudged Chaps. "Let's get back to the game. I'm going to whup you like a rented mule."

"Pride goeth before destruction, and an haughty spirit before a fall." Chaps inspected him for a moment through his monocle—an action intended to lend impact to his words. The old ranger then straightened his shoulders and marched out with the others close on his tail.

Uncle Eb stuck his head back into the smithy. "Son, don't let pride keep you from love. She might well be a great cook, but the truth is, since she's come, you're a different man. Puts me of a mind on how I was once I met my wife. When God gives you that blessing, you have to accept it."

After he left, Jeff shoved the iron back into the fire. *Lord, I feel like that bar—You're going to have to heat me, bend me, and hammer me into the man Lacey needs. You're going to have to bend her spirit, too, because she's so dead set on taking a different path.*

—∞—

Dear Mrs. Delphine,

I deeply regret to inform you that my great-aunt's health is still unstable. Her physician recommends that I remain with her until the New Year. Please forgive me for any inconveniences my absence causes you and the plans you've made for the holiday season.

Sincerely,
Lacey Marie Mather

Ticks read the telegraph and cleared his throat. "I'd be honored to have you sit with me for the Christmas Day service."

"Your offer is most kind, Mr. McGee, but I don't believe that would be wise." Lacey tried to speak gently. He was a nice man—but not the one for her. "When a reply comes, please give it to my aunt. I'll be out running errands."

"Sewing with Peony again?"

Lacey gasped. How did he know where she went and what she did? The very notion that he kept track of her made chills run down her spine. "Good day, Mr. McGee." She set payment for the telegram on the counter and left with what Madame termed "purposeful decorum."

Bless her, Peony had offered to have them sew back in Aunt Millie's parlor. After the fiery debacle the last time, Lacey knew nothing but relief that her friend understood the necessity of keeping close watch over the situation. Lacey stepped foot into Peony's place and asked, "What shall I carry?"

"Rafe already took it over. He refuses to let me lift a thing." She cast a look across the street. "Lionel Sager hired me to make a dress for Vivian for Christmas. Just wait until you see—it's a blue, button-down wool."

What a wonderful surprise! I can't keep anything from Aunt Millie. She's more curious than any cat, so you know what I did?"

"No, what?"

"I sent away to Boston for Christmas gifts!"

"How clever of you!" They stepped out onto the boardwalk.

"She's a clever gal, all right," Swede declared as he hunkered over the checkerboard. "I'm thinking I ought to challenge her to a game."

Stone snorted. "You just want someone new to beat."

Peony dipped her head and kissed Ebenezer Wilson on his weathered cheek. "I'm going to Millie's to sew, Father. If anyone comes to the shop, you can tell them where I am."

"Okay, darlin'." The old man smiled at his daughter-in-law,

then patted her hand. "Don't work too hard."

"I won't let her." Lacey held Peony's arm and led her down the boardwalk. The genuine affection between Peony and Eb never failed to touch her deeply. She couldn't recall a single time when her own father had given her the merest scrap of attention. "The Lord has blessed you so much," she said to her friend.

"Hasn't He?" Peony beamed. She glanced around and lowered her voice. "I confess to being selfish, though. I've been praying, Lacey. I've asked God to keep you here so I'll have a friend when my time comes."

Lacey's step faltered. "Now, Peony—"

"I put it in God's hands. Neither of us is going to snatch it back." She continued to sashay along the gritty boardwalk. "I do declare, I believe that you, Vivian, and I are the only ones who sweep in front of our establishments."

"You're trying to change the subject."

"And you'll humor me because you're such a dear." Peony's laughter tinkled on the crisp air.

"Ladies!" Ticks McGee looked like a crane as he lifted his knees high to pick his way across the rutted road. He waved a piece of paper. "Telegram!" Face flushed, he stood before them and straightened his shoulders. "'Dear Miss Mather—'"

"I'm able to read the telegram, Mr. McGee."

Ticks ignored Lacey and read, " 'I shall hold your aunt in my prayers. Please extend my wishes for complete recovery. Your loving care surely blesses her. I've arranged for someone to stay with those who are unable to go home for Christmas. Looking forward to seeing you in January. Sincerely, Amanda Delphine.' Isn't that the finest news? You'll be staying here in Cut Corners!"

"Only through Christmas, Mr. McGee." Lacey held out her hand.

Instead of giving her the telegram, he shook her hand!

Thunderstruck by his forward behavior, Lacey stood frozen to the planks beneath her feet.

"Miss Mather isn't a water pump, Ticks." Jeff sauntered over and slapped Ticks on the back in a friendly way.

"She's staying through Christmas!"

Jeff looked straight into Lacey's eyes. "That," he rumbled in a thrillingly deep tone, "is the best news of the year."

—w—

"What is that racket?" Jeff rolled out of bed and yanked on his jeans. Shrugging into his shirt, he headed toward the door. The instant he realized what and where the commotion came from, he jogged toward Millie's.

"Shoo fly, don't bother me," one of the cowhands from the Gustavson spread sang.

"Stop that caterwauling," Jeff snapped.

"Shoo fly, don't bother me." The cowboy took his hat from where he'd been holding it so earnestly over his heart and flapped it toward Jeff.

"Leave the man alone. He's shher–en–ading hishh lady love," one of the other cowboys slurred drunkenly.

Lacey Mather deserved far better than a penniless saddle tramp and his sotted sidekicks. Irritated, Jeff barked, "Hush. It's the middle of the night!"

"It's called a moonlight ser–a–nade. It's romantic." The cowboy glowered at him.

"That shhong didn't work. Try a differ'n one," one of his pals urged. "What 'bout 'The Bear Went Over the Mountain'?"

"I'm partial to 'Turkey in the Schtraw,'" another hiccupped.

" 'Old Dan Tucker' or 'Little Brown Jug,'" a third suggested.

"Those ain't romantic," the suitor snapped.

"And 'Shoo Fly' was?" Jeff couldn't believe this ridiculous scene. "It's the middle of the night. Leave the poor girl alone."

"You just want the girl for yourself."

The accusation hung in the crisp air. Jeff widened his stance, stared at the men, and asked in a very still tone, "What if I do?"

CHAPTER 9

"What if I do?" Jeff's words seeped into the room, and Lacey muffled her gasp. Awakening to the so-called serenade had been surprise enough for the night. An embarrassing surprise. Lacey hadn't opened the curtains or the door because she didn't want to encourage such nonsense. Aunt Millie slept through the whole thing, but Lacey didn't delude herself into believing that meant the rest of Cut Corners would do likewise. By tomorrow, she'd have to face all of the diners' smirks and teasing comments.

But now, Jeff put himself on the line. Of all the bachelors in this crazy town, only he hadn't pestered her. Oh, he'd definitely had his share of observations regarding her would-be suitors. Never once did he stoop to being cruel or unkind about those men, and he made it clear he found her worthy of such attention, however bumbling it might be. But he respected her ambition to go back to Boston and become a teacher. He alone hadn't asked her to change to suit his pleasure.

Such chivalry, she thought. *He's putting himself between those men and me. And honorable! He didn't tell a lie. They asked him, but he only responded back with a hypothetical question.*

Lacey leaned against the wall and drew her robe about herself more tightly. *It's all so confusing. I don't understand these men. I ought to be happy to go back to Boston, back to the company of genteel women whom I understand and young girls in need of guidance.*

I ought to, but I'm not sure I am.

—⁓—

"Come back in half an hour." Millie slammed the door in Jeff's face.

He stood out in the rain with a huge scuttle of coal. The last thing he wanted to do was traipse across the street again, then interrupt his morning's work to redeliver this fuel. Irritated, he booted the door open and groused, "I'm a busy man."

Feminine chatter suddenly stilled, save one high-pitched squeal.

Jeff stopped dead in his tracks.

Peony stood on crate, and Lacey knelt on the floor, pinning the hem of her dress. They'd stuffed a pillow or something under the skirt to allow for Peony's increasing size due to her delicate condition.

Peony let out a choked sob.

Lacey jumped to her feet and stood at an angle to block Jeff's view. "Why, Jeff. Yes, you are a busy man. No use in holding you back." Her voice stayed quite calm. All of those years of training served her well. "If you'll please fill the stove, I'd appreciate it. Oh, and I've been making gingerbread. It's not iced yet, but you're welcome to cut yourself a piece."

"Don't mind if I do." Given that reprieve, he hotfooted it into the kitchen. It always struck him as silly for everyone to pretend to ignore the fact that the Lord was blessing a woman with a child. Nonetheless, Peony tried so hard to observe every societal dictate. Given her background, Jeff understood why it was so important to her. Lacey—well, she'd salvaged a bad situation with her smooth thinking.

Making it a point to be noisy so they'd be able to track his whereabouts, Jeff dumped the coal, clattered around to cut a huge chunk of the gingerbread, and shouted, "Thanks, Lacey." He strode through the diner and half slammed the door to reassure them he wasn't about to scandalize them with his presence again.

"What you got there?" Stone Creedon squinted at him.

"Gingerbread."

The old ranger spraddled closer and tore off a huge portion of the fragrant treat. "Guess it'll have to do. I was hopin' you'd bring out cookies."

"You know how Lacey is about those."

"She does?"

Jeff gave Stone a quizzical look. Given an opportunity, the old guy usually talked enough to explain his odd mishearings. Confronting him with them or asking him to use his ear horn only got him riled.

"Mayhap she oughtta git her some new shoes then. Or socks. Good cotton ones—not them silk kind."

"Jeff." Rafe sauntered up. He cocked his brow and grabbed for what little gingerbread remained. "We need to talk."

"Sure do. Jeff, tell Rafe all about it. He can talk sense into Peony, and then she can make Lacey see reason."

"What's happening with Lacey?"

Stone brushed crumbs from his droopy mustache. "She's got bad toes." He perked up. "Tell you what. Me and the others, we'll come serve lunch and supper today. Thataway, Lacey can soak her feet."

"Great idea," Rafe said. He and Jeff watched as Stone headed toward his cronies. "Are you going to fetch Doc Winston?"

"I don't think there's any need. Stone just jumbled up what I said. So what do we need to talk about?"

"Word around town is you have Gustavson's cowboys sore at you. I saw the tail end of what happened last night, and I know you too well. If you were just trying to get rid of them, they'll be back and pester her half to death. If you're serious, then you need to make it clear to everyone that the little lady is yours."

Jeff leaned against the diner's wall. "Rafe, convincing them isn't going to be the hard part."

—∞—

"Have you seen the sign-up list for the bachelors' dinner?" Peony asked Vivian as they decorated the church.

"No. Why?"

"Because I didn't know there were that many bachelors in Cut Corners. Gordon Brooks even signed up, so the Tankard will be closed!" Lacey tacked up a swag of pine. "I'll need to order more beef."

"Just tell me how much," Vivian murmured as she shoved her slipping spectacles higher on her nose. "I'll make sure we have it in the mercantile for you."

"That's not what I was talking about." Peony let out an exasperated sound. "Millie put out the list, and the page was almost full before lunch ended. Jeff wasn't at lunch, so when he caught wind of that list, he went and put his name at the very top in huge, bold letters."

Vivian clasped her hands over her heart. "Lacey, I'm sure the man has a tendresse for you."

If only he did. Lacey shook her head. "No, no. He's just being a very good friend. He's trying to shoo away all of those men so I don't have to deal with any more awkward proposals."

"I've never gotten a single proposal," Vivian said quietly as she lifted her hem and carefully got onto a stepladder.

"Neither had I until I came here," Lacey said crisply. "And I wouldn't consider any of the offers I've received as being serious. Those men want a cook. If I ever marry, it'll be because the man loves me, not because he loves my suppers."

Erik Olson entered the sanctuary. "But your cookies—they could win any man's heart." His light blue eyes danced with a teasing light. "I will settle, though, to have you as my sister in Christ."

"That's sweet, Erik," Peony said. "What do you have?"

"I heard you ladies were decorating the church, so I made

this. It's the Advent wreath. Vivian, you have the right colors of the candles at the store, ja?"

"I'm sure we do." Vivian scrambled down the stepladder and over to him. "Wouldn't that look positively splendid in front of the pulpit?"

Erik smiled and turned to Lacey. "I am supposed to ask you a question. The bachelors' dinner—Ebenezer wishes to know if widowers are also invited."

"He never went before," Vivian said.

"Lacey was not doing the cooking then." Erik chuckled. "Please do not take this wrong, but Millie's cooking—it is bad. We all love her, so we took turns eating at the diner to make her feel good."

"She is lovable, isn't she?" Lacey looked at all of them. "So are you. What you all have here in Cut Corners is so special—you all care for one another."

"You could stay, you know," Peony said.

"Ja, you should stay." Erik nodded.

"Maybe she wants more adventure in her life," Vivian said. "Ticks told me a woman is a telephone operator in Boston now."

"Boston is altogether different from Cut Corners." Lacey dipped her head and pretended to concentrate on binding the pine boughs to form the next swag. The school in Boston had her pledge, but Cut Corners had her heart. *Lord Jesus, what am I to do? Please show me Your will.*

—w—

Jeff couldn't stand it anymore. He'd barely endured the bachelors' pot roast luncheon. Lacey turned the whole thing into a veritable feast. Oh, she'd gone way overboard—and though she'd had Mary Jo Heath, Vivian Sager, and even the young Widow Phelps there to help her serve, the men barely spared those single women a glance.

Every last one of those men fancied himself in love with Lacey. Jeff knew better. He alone suffered that particular malady.

Lacey and the girls were picking up the dessert plates, but none of the men took the hint to leave.

Jeff wasn't about to depart until every last man had vacated the premises.

Lacey finally halted at the door to the kitchen and clasped her hands just below her bosom. The pose came naturally—it wasn't meant to be coy, but it drove Jeff daft. When she stood like that, it called his attention to her tiny waist.

"Gentlemen, you're all invited to return this evening at seven. The whole community is welcome for a Christmas dessert reception."

The men all rumbled their delight.

Jeff stood up. "The lady's being polite, men. Now scat so she can get things ready." The guests trundled out, but Jeff's hackles rose when he spied Harold Myers slipping Lacey a note. Then and there, Jeff knew what he had to do.

CHAPTER 10

"Place looks awful fancy." Aunt Millie's grousing tone didn't sting one bit because of the wide smile she wore.

"So do we," Lacey said. "Your new dress is marvelous!"

Aunt Millie ran her left hand down the skirts of the blue delft print. "Never had someone give me a store-bought dress. It's like putting a wreath of flowers on a mule."

"Nonsense!" Lacey pulled her Sunday-best apron over her new Christmas gown. For tonight, she'd attached a collar with little green sprigs embroidered along the edge and added a wide green sash. The festive look matched her mood. "I hope we have enough food."

"As much as the men ate today at lunch, they shouldn't be able to wedge another bite in sideways for three days," Aunt Millie said. She sighed. "I may as well confess, I don't blame 'em. I guess we've all grown accustomed to your eastern recipes. My pot roast never tasted like that."

"Her recipes aren't all she brought with her from Boston," Jeff said as he let himself in. He held the door wide open. "Take a look."

Lacey tilted her head to look around him. "Snow!"

"Yup." He grinned. "Merry Christmas."

"Oh, snow!" She dashed past him and out into the gently falling flakes and turned her face upward. "Thank You, Jesus!

Now it really feels like Christmas!"

"Here." Jeff wrapped something around her.

Lacey glanced down at the soft white merino wool shawl and gasped. "This is beautiful, Jeff."

"Merry Christmas. I figured if we didn't get snow, you'd still have something white falling onto your hair and shoulders."

"That's the most thoughtful thing anyone has ever done for me."

"Lacey. . ." Jeff turned her toward himself.

"Hoo–oo–ey! It's snowing!" Stone Creedon shouted as he and the other old rangers ambled up. "Hope you got lotsa hot coffee on the stove, missy."

"I do. Please, come in." Lacey wished Jeff hadn't been interrupted. He'd looked very intent. Then, too, she'd wanted to tell him her news. Would it make him half as happy as it made her?

"I'm gonna drink a pot all of my own," Stone continued to ramble.

Lacey cast Jeff an apologetic look. She needed to assume her duties as a hostess.

He heaved a sigh. "Go on."

All of Cut Corners turned out for the Christmas Eve dessert reception. Lacey wove in and out of the crowd, chatting with her friends and neighbors while setting out more pies, tarts, cakes, and cookies.

Happiness bubbled in her like the coffee perking on the stove. She'd asked God for direction, and He'd been faithful. The letter from Amanda Delphine today released her from her commitment to the Ladies Academie. From now on, she'd have a home—here, with Aunt Millie.

Jeff followed her into the kitchen. "Want me to take that cake there on into the other room?"

"Oh no." She smiled. "Tomorrow is Rafe's birthday. I made that cake so we could celebrate."

"Come here." Jeff dragged her from the kitchen to the parlor.

"But everyone—"

"Everyone can wait." He cupped her face in his rough hands. "Lacey, I've tried my best to respect your wishes. I know you want to go back to that fancy school, but I can't let you go. I want you to stay here. With me. Lacey, I'm not good with words. What I'm trying to say is, I love you. I want you to marry me."

"*This is all so sudden.*" Madame drilled all of her young ladies to stall for a moment with that phrase so they could gather their thoughts. Lacey laughed. She didn't want to pause. "Oh, Jeffrey. How can you say you're not good with words? Those are the best words I've ever heard. Nothing would make me happier than to stay in Cut Corners and be your wife."

His eyes lit with joy.

"I received a letter from Mrs. Delphine today. She said the other woman is working out well, and if I didn't mind, she'd like to allow her to keep the position. I'm free to stay here, with you."

"And I'm not going to let you go." He pressed a swift kiss on her cheek, then grabbed her wrist and dragged her back into the diner. "I have an announcement! Lacey's going to marry me!"

Everyone cheered.

Old Ebenezer Wilson slapped him on the back. "No time like the present. What do you say, Parson Clune?"

"It's a fine time to be married."

Everyone hastened across to the church. Peony quickly untied Lacey's apron and removed the green-trimmed collar. Vivian pulled a length of elegant white lace from her pocket. "Here. And I have a bouquet, too."

"You do?" Lacey stared at her in amazement.

"Of course I do. Jeff came to the mercantile today to buy your ring. I thought you'd probably get married after church tomorrow, but I brought everything over to the sanctuary tonight before your party."

The sanctuary was nearly freezing, but the crispness in the air made the pine boughs more fragrant. "It's too cold to sit in the pews," Parson Clune decided. "Everyone stand around the edges in a big circle."

In a matter of minutes, everyone held a bayberry candle. By that glow, Uncle Eb escorted Lacey to the altar.

Solemn vows, a kiss, and then Jeff swept Lacey into his arms. "This is the merriest Christmas since Christ came!"

"And there's a wedding cake back at the diner," Aunt Millie declared. "It's Rafe's gift to the bride and groom."

Jeff carried Lacey outside and halted as snowflakes danced about them. She snuggled close. "I love you."

"Now that's an even bigger miracle than snow for Christmas."

"Hundreds of years ago, God touched our souls with the gift of His Son. Tonight He touched our hearts again with His gift of love for one another. I'm in your arms, Jeffrey. I'm home."

"Welcome home." He dipped his head and sealed his greeting with a kiss.

Brown Sugar Cookies

2 cups light brown sugar
1 cup melted butter
3 eggs
¼ cup milk
1 tbsp. vanilla
1 tsp. baking soda
5–5½ cups flour

Mix ingredients in order given. Add just enough flour to make dough firm enough to roll. Cut into shapes as desired. Decorate with raisins or brown sugar, bake at 350° for 8–10 minutes or until edges are lightly browned.

Cathy Marie Hake is a Southern California native. She met her two loves at church: Jesus and her husband, Christopher. An RN, she loved working in oncology as well as teaching Lamaze. Health issues forced her to retire, but God opened new possibilities with writing. Since their children have moved out and are married, Cathy and Chris dote on dogs they rescue from a local shelter. A sentimental pack rat, Cathy enjoys scrapbooking and collecting antiques. "I'm easily distracted during prayer, so I devote certain tasks and chores to specific requests or persons so I can keep faithful in my prayer life." Since her first book in 2000, she's been on multiple best-seller and readers' favorite lists.

A Christmas Chronicle

by Pamela Griffin

DEDICATION

A big, Texas-sized thank you to all my crit partners and writer friends who helped on this project. And to Jon Jones, Linda Rondeau, and Calvin Wood, a special thanks for info regarding the square dance and calls.

As always, I dedicate this book to my patient, sweet Lord, who taught me what it really means to please Him, yet accepted me just as I was.

For do I now persuade men, or God?
or do I seek to please men?
for if I yet pleased men,
I should not be the servant of Christ.
GALATIANS 1:10 KJV

PROLOGUE

Cut Corners, Texas
1881

Stone Creedon eyed the checkerboard with unsuppressed glee. Victory over Swede would finally be his. "I got ya now, you old goat. Take a long, hard look at Cut Corners' new champion." He cackled out a laugh.

Swede only harrumphed a couple of times. Watching from nearby, Mayor Chaps Smythe brought his monocle to his eye to peer more closely at the board, while Eb Wilson shook his head slowly in amazement. Trim and tall, he was the only one of the four who hadn't changed all that much since their younger days as Texas Rangers.

"Mark Olson, you get that overgrown puppy out of the store this instant! You know my brother doesn't allow animals inside." Vivian Sager's words to the boy were so high-pitched, even Stone could hear them, and he winced when her shoes clomped his way. "Why, he's tracked muddy paw prints all over my clean floor!"

Quick as greased lightning, Vivian swished past, her elbow knocking into Stone's head and her ungainly skirts knocking board and checkers off the barrel and onto the oak planks. Swede roared with mirth and slapped his knee. Stone seethed words not fit to be aired under his breath, as the board—and his sure victory—clattered to the floor while the wooden disks rolled and landed with ricocheting spins and plops even a partially deaf man could hear.

"Oh, Mr. Creedon, Mr. Olson, I'm so sorry." Vivian raised long fingers to both cheeks, which were flushed beneath her round spectacles. "Did I hurt your bad ear, Mr. Creedon? Are you alright?"

"Stop your fussin' gal, I'm fine."

"I certainly didn't mean to. . .well, I hope you know I never would have. . ." Appearing to be plumb out of words, she colored as red as a ripe tomato, picked up her skirts, and hastened to the back storage room as if a fire had been set beneath her heels.

Stone blew out a disgusted breath and bent to help Swede and the others pick up the checkers. "You know," he said, "I think it's time we get her hitched."

Swede straightened in surprise. "Who? Vivian?"

"See any other woman round here?"

"That's a pretty tall order, don't you think?" Eb asked.

Stone scratched his whiskered jaw. "I reckon us four could do it. We got the other three hitched, didn't we? And who woulda thought Erik would stop bein' so mule-headed and finally marry up with Anna?"

"Ja, but Vivian?" Swede dumped the checkers on the board he'd replaced atop the barrel.

"Swede's right," Eb put in. "Rob Baxter was the only man to show interest in Vivian, you'll recall. Interest he lost directly after that little accident when she waited on him. Doc says he'll most likely never walk right again."

"All the more reason why we need to get her married up," Stone stressed, "so she can stay home like most womenfolk and raise young'uns. It's time she was put in her place. Her brother'll probably thank us for gettin' her out from underfoot."

"Hmm, I am not so sure." Swede studied Stone with narrowed eyes.

"I say," Chaps inserted in his very British way, "have you someone in mind, Stone?"

"Matter of fact, I do. When that last mail delivery batch came through, a letter from my nephew Travis was in it—he's one of them chroniclers that gallivant throughout the West, totin' a camera. Takes pictures for some fancy magazine back East."

Swede nodded. "I heard of them, these chroniclers."

"Well, he wrote that he'll be ridin' through Cut Corners nigh unto three weeks."

Grinning at the idea that now filled his head, Stone settled back in his chair and eyed his three matchmaking partners. Their present work was a far cry from the old glory days of bringing law and order to the Wild West, but attempting to bring order to these youngsters' lives by trying to find them lifelong companions was just about as important, he reckoned. Besides, once the couples were hitched, they tended to stop interfering in his affairs. Ever since that dunk in a frozen river years ago, when he'd rescued a lad from being swept away by the current and had consequently caught a high fever, losing most all his hearing in his right ear, the women had been fussing over him like he was a little boy in britches. Especially that old gossip, the widow Chamberlain, though he figured nothing could be done about pairing her up with anyone.

"Yep." He laced his hands across his thick paunch. "I reckon Travis'll do just fine."

CHAPTER 1

Almost one month later

Travis McCoy settled his shoulder blades comfortably against the wooden chair and rubbed his stomach. "I declare, Mrs. Chamberlain, that was by far one of the best meals I've had in weeks. Make that months. One doesn't get fare like this while traveling the plains. Hardtack and beans are my usual diet."

As if waiting for such approval, Lula Chamberlain, the fiftyish owner of the boardinghouse, hovered beside the table where Travis and his uncle Clive "Stone" Creedon were eating. She beamed a gap-toothed smile at Travis then looked at Stone. He didn't say a word.

"Thank you for speaking your mind, Mr. McCoy. My pecan pie is some of the finest in all of Cut Corners, as my dear deceased husband Roderick Chamberlain III used to claim, may he rest in peace. Now that young Lacey Wilson who runs the diner? I heard tell she uses white sugar in her pies, though she's tight-lipped when it comes to revealin' her recipes to anyone but family, so I can't be certain. But that fancy white sugar is something which I just don't abide. You can't get the right texture and flavor when you use white sugar for the filling, but will she listen? Not a whit. It's like trying to talk sense into a flea."

His uncle raised his cup. "I'll take more tea."

"Not tea," she said more loudly. "Flea."

"You got fleas?" he shot back.

"Oh, never mind." Exasperated, she swung her hands into the air. "Whyever don't you use that ear trumpet of yours?" She scooped tea leaves into Stone's cup and poured steaming water over them.

"Cain't stand the thing." His gray mustache twitched as he gave a sniff. "Fool thing don't work right, nohow."

She blew out a breath, causing the straggle of silvering hair that had escaped her bun to fly upward. Again, she turned her gaze toward Travis and smiled. "You do have such an interesting occupation, Mr. McCoy, in using your cameras to take photographs of the landscape and such. I have a brother who's also lived quite the adventurous life. He was a Pony Express rider, but then he took himself an Indian wife, and now he lives like a savage, wild on the prairie. . . ." She tsk-tsked, gossiping on as she'd done nonstop since Travis had arrived in Cut Corners hours ago.

"Well, my occupation does fill a need," Travis replied when he could get a word in edgewise. Yet his thoughts were anything but modest. He loved his work and knew he was good at what he did, striving to be the best. His was a lonely job, but lack of companionship was a sacrifice he was willing to make. Truth be told, if the good Lord didn't want him to continue in his pursuit of chronicling the West, it would probably take a knock upside his noggin for him to get the picture.

"You'll be staying in town for the harvest dance next week, won't you?" Mrs. Chamberlain loudly inquired. "I imagine a number of young ladies from these parts will have quite a hankering to meet you. Ranchers' families come from miles around for the occasion."

Stone abruptly cleared his throat, stood, and stared at him. "How about we step outside for some air?"

"Alright." Travis pulled his napkin from his collar, sensing his uncle wanted to talk.

"What about your tea?" Mrs. Chamberlain asked.

"It'll keep." Stone shuffled outside onto the porch, and Travis followed.

Due to the sharp wind that blew from the north, Travis was glad he still wore his coat. He would have preferred the warmth of the cozy parlor he'd glimpsed upon his arrival but kept his thoughts to himself. Glancing to his left, he caught sight of two young boys approaching his wagon. They poked at the tarpaulin covering the back, as if hoping to get a peek at what lay underneath.

"You there," he called. "Get away from that wagon!" His livelihood was inside, and suddenly he questioned the safety of leaving his conveyance there. Maybe he should camp in the rear of the wagon, crowded though it was, rather than partake of the luxury of a room at the boardinghouse.

"Don't worry about them two," his uncle said with a dry chuckle as they watched the lads skitter down Main Street and head toward Ranger Road, the only two streets the town possessed. The wind blew orange red dust in a swirl around the boys' legs. "They're curious as young chickens in a new barnyard, but they know better than to fiddle with the equipment in your What-izzit Wagon."

At that, Travis grinned. When he'd first stopped in front of the boardinghouse, people drifted across the street from the mercantile, clustering around as he pulled back the tarp to show his uncle the wagon's contents. Someone asked the inevitable question, "What-izzit?"

Travis had joked that Matthew Brady, the famous Civil War photographer he so admired, had soldiers who posed that very question upon seeing his array of boxlike cameras and other equipment. And so Mr. Brady's wagon had been dubbed "what-izzit" from that point on. Now Travis's wagon bore the honor of that same title.

"Remember that young gal you met at the mercantile?" his uncle asked casually, tucking the fingers of his gnarled hands in his suspenders.

Travis drew his brows together. "I can't say as I recall any girl."

"Well then, you must be losin' your eyesight, since it was a woman who waited on you when you bought them groomin' tools of yours."

Travis wiped a hand across his smooth jaw, feeling civilized again. It was a relief to have gotten rid of the scratchy beard, though he'd kept the mustache. He'd learned that the town had a barber, but Travis preferred to groom his own face. Something about allowing a stranger to put a blade to his throat didn't sit well with him. "You mean the woman who knocked over the stand of shaving brushes when she collected one for me?"

"Yep, that's the one."

While he stared at the weathered board walls of the mercantile directly across the street, Travis tried to form a mental picture. An image of a woman almost as tall as he, gangly, and skinny as a post came to mind. Spectacles. A thick cloud of dark hair. He shrugged, setting his sights on the wooded bluffs beyond the store. The setting sun filled the sky with a blaze of orange, and purple shadows buried deep into the hills. He longed to find the perfect spot, set up his camera, and get started.

"Well, I'd consider it a favor if you'd ask her to the harvest dance."

"What?" Stone's words knocked Travis from his mental photograph. "You can't be serious."

"Sure am. She's decent folk, goes to church. Helps her brother run the mercantile."

"That's all well and good, but I'm not looking for a companion. Besides, I'm not even sure I'll be here next week to attend any dance."

"Well, that's another thing," Stone said quickly. "I talked to

Chaps—the town's mayor—before your arrival, and we'd like to requisition your services to take us a photograph of everyone in this here town. It'd be nice to frame and keep for posterity's sake." He sounded as if he were parroting the Englishman, whom Travis had met that afternoon. "We figure sometime in mid-November would be best."

"Why so late? Why not now?"

"Well. . ." Stone shuffled his feet, his gaze going to the glimpse of railroad tracks near the church. "Fact is, there's a few citizens who got business outta town and won't be back till then. Chaps wants them in the shot. They're important to the town, you see."

Why did Travis get the feeling his uncle was making this up as he went along?

"Mrs. Chamberlain said you're welcome to stay here at the boardinghouse as long as you like. Her fees are purty reasonable." Stone cleared his throat. "Anyhow, Chaps asked me to talk the matter over with you, bein' as you're my nephew and all. I'll make sure you get a handsome price for your troubles."

Travis pondered the idea. "I suppose I could put off leaving till then."

"Good. Then there'll be no problem about the dance. If I was you, I'd ask Miss Sager soon—tonight even. A lady likes to have enough time to get herself a purty dress and all them doodads."

"Whoa there, back up a minute." Travis lifted his hands out to his sides. "I never said I was going to any town dance. And how would you know what a lady likes? You've never been married."

"Spending time at the mercantile every day, a man hears women chattering about all sorts o' things he has no business knowin'." Stone scratched his gray-whiskered jaw. "It's just a dance. I ain't askin' you to court her or nothin'."

Travis thought a moment. "One thing isn't exactly clear to

me. Why would this be a favor to you?"

"I told her brother I'd ask. Lionel's a right nice young man—plays a mean game of checkers—and his sister's a sweet little gal. So I'd go if I was you. Cain't hurt nothin'."

Narrowing his eyes, Travis surveyed his uncle. He stood a good foot shorter and stouter, his straight hair unkempt, his clothes clean but well-worn. Travis had a feeling that Mrs. Chamberlain was responsible for any cleanliness concerning the man's garments. An idea came to Travis, one that made him fight back a smile. Triumphant, he played what he was sure was his trump card.

"Alright, tell you what, Uncle. I'll go to your town's shindig and ask—what was her name again?"

"Vivian. Vivian Sager."

"I'll ask Miss Sager to accompany me—but on one condition."

The zeal ebbed out of Stone's eyes. "What condition?"

"That you do exactly the same. You ask to escort Mrs. Chamberlain to the harvest dance."

"What? That old gossip?" Stone scoffed and shook his head. "Nothin' doin'."

Travis allowed the smile to spread across his mouth. He was glad he remembered what his mother had said about her brother Clive being a confirmed bachelor. The ex-Texas Ranger claimed in a former letter to his sister that he wanted "nothing to do with womenfolk cluttering up his personal lifestyle." The nickname of "Stone" fit him well. With the kind of existence Travis led as a nomad photographer on the plains, he was destined for a life of bachelorhood like his uncle.

His gaze going to the hills, Stone grumbled loudly to himself, pulling down hard on his suspenders until Travis thought they might be in danger of popping undone. The wind picked up as twilight descended. Travis was just about to seek the warmth of the front parlor, and a second slab of pie, when Stone turned.

"Alright, Nephew, you got yourself a deal. I'll ask that woman to be her escort—and you'd better do the same and ask Miss Sager first thing after sunup tomorrow."

At a sudden loss for words, Travis only stared, caught in his own trap.

—ʍ—

Vivian swept the spilled sugar into her cupped hand, disposing of the grains into a nearby bucket set on the floor expressly for refuse, then once more carefully went about measuring the sugar Anna Olson wanted. The two fair-haired children, Mark and Molly, longingly eyed the candy jars along the counter. Lacey Wilson slowly paced, smoothing the back of her baby daughter, whose rosy cheek lay upon her shoulder. Peony Wilson, the sheriff's wife, waddled into the shop, her extended stomach evidence that her second child would soon be born, only a month after Anna's was due. Peony's little girl, Lynn, smiled widely when she caught sight of the Olson children and toddled their way, her dark ringlets bouncing.

"Good morning, Anna, Vivian." Peony nodded toward each woman, then caught sight of Lacey near the pickle barrel. "Oh, there's the little one! Why, hello there, Mercy Mae." She headed that direction and began cooing baby talk.

Vivian went about her work, preparing Anna's order, her ears attuned to the three women visiting and chattering away, happily content in their roles as wives and mothers.

She had never fit in with those women. They'd never treated her rudely, though they rarely sought her company. But maybe that was partially her fault. Being around them made Vivian all the more aware that she would never have what they did. They were all beauties with engaging personalities; she was plain with the social skills of a turtle—and just as awkward. In the past three years, all three of those women had found love during the Christmas season, each of them receiving proposals during that month of goodwill and cheer. A few of the local yokels joked that Cut Corners at Christmastime always brought Cupid in for a spell. Of course, the four ex-Texas Rangers, who'd been dubbed the Meddlin' Men, had had a lot to do with pairing off those couples.

Vivian doubted that either Cupid or the four matchmakers could help her find a husband. Not that she would ask any of those aged gentlemen for assistance. No, sir. She didn't get along well with people; they always seemed to be watching her, as if waiting for her to trip over her huge feet. Besides, she wanted more to life than just getting married and raising babies, though she did love children. She wanted adventure, as well. Doubtless, she would be denied both.

Sighing, with her face poised toward the front of the store, Vivian stilled as she recalled those fantastic stories from the dime novels she kept hidden beneath her bed. She wouldn't wish any of their maladies upon herself, of course, but those stories were always full of excitement—spinning yarns of gamblers on steamboats, sharp detectives donning disguises and solving impossible mysteries, cowboys chased by war-painted Indians—and many contained braver-than-life heroes rescuing fair damsels in distress.

The door to the mercantile swung open, and Vivian watched as a tall, handsome stranger strode inside, his mink dark eyes focused on her. She blinked, lowering the scoop from where she'd held it in midair.

"Good morning, sir," she managed, her voice crackling hoarse. She cleared her throat and shook from her mind images of heroes. "How can I be of service to you today?"

"I understand there's a dance in town next week."

Vivian raised her brows, not fully comprehending. "Yes?"

"My uncle mentioned it last night, and. . ." He shuffled his feet, looking discomfited. He smoothed his palms along his trouser legs. "I was wondering. . . ."

The three women ceased talking with one another, their

curious gazes darting back and forth from Vivian to the stranger. He glanced their way then blurted, "Give me a penny's worth of those."

"You want lemon drops?" Vivian asked, uncertain.

"Uh, yeah."

A lengthy silence followed as she collected the sugar candy from the jar.

"Well, I suppose it's high time I return to the diner," Lacey said slowly, as if she'd rather not go. "I don't know what possessed me to come here this time of morning. Aunt Millie must be wondering where I am. Lovely to see you ladies. Vivian, I'll return this afternoon after the lunch crowd thins and tend to my shopping then."

She breezed through the door, baby over her shoulder. Anna and Peony glanced at the silent man then at each other. Peony grabbed her little girl's hand as both women made their excuses. "Come along, Molly and Mark," Anna said.

"Can't we have a piece of candy, too?" the boy asked.

"Not today. But remember, if you do as you're told and clean your plate at the diner, Miss Lacey will give you each a cookie."

Mark and Molly shot for the door. "We'll be good, Auntie Anna!" Molly cried. "Bye, Miss Vivian!"

"Good-bye." Smiling, Vivian glanced at the children as they and the women left the store. She recalled how after she'd sprained her ankle last year and was laid up on a cot that Lionel had placed in the storage room—since she couldn't maneuver the stairs—the children had often come to visit her while Anna worked in the mercantile. Mark had played with her crutches, pretending to be a wounded cowboy, while Molly perched on Vivian's cot and kept her informed about the music box they were helping their Uncle Erik make for Anna. She hadn't invited the children's company, but when they were gone, she'd found she missed it.

Vivian wrapped the candy in parcel paper and handed it to

the stranger. He gave her a penny, which she put in the till, and then she replaced the glass lid on the jar.

"Miss Sager." He cleared his throat. "W–would you accompany me to the dance next week?"

It was a good thing Vivian had replaced the lid, because she would have dropped it if she hadn't. She felt as if she'd turned hard as rock candy, unable to move.

"Pardon?" She must have misunderstood.

The paper parcel rustled in his grasp. "The dance. The harvest one. Would you accompany me to it?" This time the offer came out hurried, clipped, almost as though he would rather she decline.

Incredulity warred with indignation. "Sir, I don't even know your name. If this is your idea of a prank, I consider it to be in poor taste. Now, if you require no further assistance, I have other business to attend to."

Surprise made his features slacken. "But we have met— well, not formally. You sold me the shaving brush yesterday and a clean shirt. My uncle is Stone Creedon."

"You're Mr. McCoy?" Incredulity made her eyes widen as she spouted the awed words. She adjusted her glasses, pushing them higher.

The shaving kit, not to mention a haircut and good cleansing, had done wonders for this man. The scruffy beard had concealed the strong lines of his well-shaped jaw and firm chin. Without that brown curly fuzz covering his cheeks, his cheekbones were more defined, and his dark eyes stood out even more, especially with the way his shiny, thick hair curled at the temples. A closely trimmed mustache slanted down both sides of his thin upper lip and curled a bit at the corners of his fuller bottom one. Suddenly she felt somewhat light-headed and clutched the countertop between them with her fingertips in an unobtrusive manner. "And you wish to take me to the dance."

"Yes. That is, if you haven't any other plans."

"I. . ." Her brain suddenly quit, as if a mental candle had been snuffed out. She couldn't string two words together.

Lionel picked that moment to amble in from the storage room. "Well, howdy, Mr. McCoy. I couldn't help but overhear your offer, as I was in the back doin' book work. And as Vivian's guardian, I just want to say that I heartily approve of you taking my sister to the harvest dance." Almost as tall as Mr. McCoy, he shook Travis's hand. Both men smiled at one another.

"Well, alright then. What time should I come by and pick her up?"

"Seven o'clock is fine."

"I'll be here." Without even so much as a farewell nod to Vivian, Travis left the store.

Vivian's rock candy blood simmered to boiling sugar as she frowned at her brother and crossed her arms over her chest. "Honestly, Lionel. I can't believe you would just grant permission like that without seeking my opinion on the matter."

He raised thick skeptical brows. "You would have refused him?"

"No. Perhaps. I don't know. I simply would have preferred the pleasure to make my own choice since it wholly concerns me."

"Really?" Her brother's level look made her uncomfortable, underlining what she already knew.

Vivian twisted around and busied herself tidying shelves with a feather duster. As one of the clumsiest old maids in Cut Corners, her marriage prospects were slim pickings. Only one man had ever proposed, and it hadn't been out of burgeoning love but rather the desire for a woman to cook for him and his brother and run his home. After Rob Baxter's clumsy proposal while she waited on him as he bought hunting supplies, shock had made her drop the cask of gunpowder on his foot, breaking his toe. Since that day, he'd hobbled clear of her.

Vivian had passed the old maid marker years ago and was fast approaching her twenty-fifth birthday. She had resigned herself to the fact that she would always live under her brother's roof. Mr. McCoy's invitation had shocked her speechless, especially since she hardly knew the man. One meeting, exchanging items for cash, could hardly be construed as an introduction.

Yet it was evidently enough for her brother, who'd started courting the widow Matilda Phelps this past summer. Perhaps neither of them wanted two women running Lionel's household, since Vivian was sure a proposal to Matilda was forthcoming; and out of desperation, Lionel was trying to match her up with the first available stranger who moseyed into the store.

Also knowing that Stone Creedon was Mr. McCoy's uncle, Vivian felt positive that the Meddlin' Men were up to their tricks again. Why else would the newcomer ask her—a stranger—to the dance, unless egged on by his uncle? She should be upset, but that emotion was absent for some reason.

Remembering Travis's good looks and his exciting, adventurous profession, Vivian decided that one arranged evening with the man—even without her consent—could be managed.

Vivian turned to face her brother. "Very well. I'll go."

She wished she could take her duster and erase that knowing grin right off his face.

CHAPTER 2

Sorry," Vivian muttered as she lagged behind Travis.

While the ring of men and women joined hands and traveled in a wide circle south, Vivian worked to get her feet to go the right way on the elevated oak-board dance floor built just for the occasion.

"Possum on a post, rooster on a rail, swing your honey round, and everybody sail!" the caller yelled in a singsong voice from his place near the lively fiddle players.

"Oof!" Seth Baxter exclaimed from behind when Vivian barreled into him.

"Pardon," she murmured as Travis brought her round again.

The rest of the caller's instruction she should be able to manage fairly well, as long as Travis didn't go too fast.

Travis was going too fast.

Vivian cringed as she almost ran down the couple in front of her while everyone returned to their starting positions. It was a wonder she didn't have them all catapulting off the foot-high stage Erik Olson had built. The caller shouted another direction, placing her among the three women of her square to form a ring. They joined hands and traveled in a circle north a few times; then she returned to Travis to be swung around in the opposite direction. Travis and the other three men formed their own circle, each putting a hand out to form a wheel and going round and round, south.

Dizzily, she watched them, clapping and trying to keep time to the music, as everyone else did, though her clapping seemed off by a mile. The call came for Travis to return to her side.

"All jump up and when you come down, swing your honey, go round and round."

They gave a little hop—then Travis linked elbows with her, swinging her around again and again. Vivian lost all balance and fell into him, her big foot clomping down squarely on his.

He winced.

"Sorry." She gave him a sheepish smile.

Four more calls followed, including an allemande—the men going one way, the women the other in the same circle, interweaving and clasping hands as they did. Then came a promenade, with Vivian paired off with Travis, and again stumbling in her large boots—and the square dance was thankfully over. They bowed to each other, then to those at their sides.

The fiddles picked up another lively tune. At Travis's rapid-fire suggestion that they sit this one out, Vivian heartily agreed.

Although the night air was chilly, she was perspiring. Travis offered to retrieve some refreshment, and she thanked him. She wished for a fan to cool herself such as some of the women had, but she never carried such trifles. Plucking at the damp pouf of curls stuck to her forehead, she vainly tried to fluff them back into shape, then slid her hands to the back of her upswept hair to make sure none of it had come unfastened.

As long as Travis was gone—two songs worth—Vivian wondered if he was ever coming back or if he'd fled the dance. She wouldn't blame him if he had.

After a moment, she spotted him talking with his uncle in a golden circle of torchlight. The two seemed to be in disagreement. She wondered what topic of conversation would have both men frowning at one another and talking so fast.

Vivian's gaze wandered back to the dancing. Her lips tipped

upward in a smile when she caught sight of Mark and Molly off to the side of the stage, spying on the adults and giggling behind their hands. Mark bowed to Molly, and she curtseyed. Then the children linked elbows and attempted their own dance in the calf-high grass, awkwardly skipping round and round till Molly's white blond braids were bouncing. On them, "awkward" looked adorable.

Travis finally returned and handed Vivian a mug of cool cider. The tart taste of apples teased her tongue and refreshed her. Travis sat stiffly beside her on the boardwalk, his focus nailed to the dancers.

Vivian cleared her throat. "I do apologize for that fiasco out there, but dancing was a pastime my brother never thought important enough to teach me."

That seemed to snag his attention a bit. He gave a nod, angling a glance in her direction. "I suppose I'm as much to blame. I'm out of practice. You mentioned your brother. Are your parents still living?" As he spoke, his gaze drifted back to the dancers, and to one young couple in particular. Red-haired, blue-eyed Mary Jo Heath, her laughing smile wide, kicked up her skirts as she expertly danced with Ned Turner.

"They died of cholera when I was a child," Vivian said a little more loudly. "Lionel raised me."

He gave a half nod in reply.

At least he didn't watch her with eagle eyes, as many of the townsfolk frequently did, seeming to anticipate her next graceless move. Vivian sipped her cider before trying again. "I have a question that's been puzzling me, Mr. McCoy. Lionel told me about your What-izzit Wagon and all the cameras you keep inside. But why keep so many? Why not just one?"

That fully sparked his attention. "The size of the negative I wish to make has a huge bearing upon the camera size. For a wide panorama, I need a bigger camera. And of course, a smaller camera captures miniature photographs. Head shots, for instance."

"Then you take photographs of people, too? I wondered, since your uncle formerly mentioned that you captured scenic views of the West."

"Yes, I've captured images of cowboys on a cattle drive, workers on a railroad in progress, and a wagon train party I tagged along with for a few hundred miles. I even obtained permission to photograph residents on an Indian reservation on the other side of the Red River." His dark eyes fairly blazed with excitement.

"Oh? And did you happen to see Mrs. Chamberlain's erstwhile brother there?" As soon as the flippant words left her mouth, she regretted them. "I do apologize; I shouldn't have spoken so. I simply don't understand why she's so bothered about him taking an Indian for a wife. The woman converted to the faith, after all. Oh, dear, now I sound like a gossip. Forgive me. Perhaps I should drown my tongue in this cider." She took a sip, embarrassed. Honestly. She wasn't accustomed to making social conversation, and she feared she was failing at this as miserably as she did at dancing.

He chuckled, a light in his eyes as he studied her. "I can't say that I've had the pleasure of meeting the couple. But many of the tribe I met—the Tonkawas—were friendly and amiable about having their photograph taken. Only a few of the elderly held themselves in reserve and refused. Of course, I respected their wishes." He fully twisted his body in her direction so that he faced her. "I have wonderful images of the experience that I held back from those photographs I sent to the magazine. I'm forming my own private picture collection of life in the West."

"Really? How interesting. I'd love to see them."

"Would you?" His gaze grew thoughtful.

"Yes, I think your profession is so exciting, and I just love adventure." She almost admitted to being a dime novel enthusiast but, since some frowned upon a lady partaking of such a reading pastime, decided not to. "Please tell me more." Turning toward him, she perched on the edge of the boardwalk so that their knees were only inches apart.

The rest of the evening flew by. Vivian found herself caught up in his tales—some humorous, some dangerous, all of them riveting—and it wasn't until the fiddlers stopped playing that she looked around the area to see that only a few people remained. She watched as men began to douse the torches that had provided light.

"I wonder how late it must be," she murmured the thought aloud.

"Forgive me, I didn't mean to go on so."

"Oh, pshaw. Perish the thought, Mr. McCoy. I heartily enjoyed hearing your reminiscences. It would be exciting to witness exactly how a photograph is taken. I can piece together the information in my head through what you've told me, of course, but experience is by far the most worthwhile teacher." Oh, dear. Now it sounded as if she were finagling an invitation to join him. "I mean. . ." What did she mean?

He smiled. "I think that can be arranged."

Thoroughly flustered by her ill-mannered gaffe, she quickly stood and smoothed her blue calico skirts. "No, please. I wouldn't dream of imposing. Forgive my tongue for wagging the wrong direction a second time."

He, too, stood. "It would be no imposition, Miss Sager. I would welcome your company."

Vivian eyed him, uncertain. He sounded as if he truly meant it. Studying his earnest expression in the nearby torchlight, she could almost believe that he did.

"This Wednesday, I plan to journey to a spot near the Red River, one I glimpsed from afar during my travels here. I would appreciate having someone to talk with, as the lengthy process of photographing inanimate objects does tend to get lonesome at times. If the possible lack of chaperones distresses you, I can persuade my uncle to ride along with us and take Mrs.

Chamberlain, too." He grinned as if at a private joke, and two crescent dimples appeared in his tanned cheeks.

"Well. . .I. . ."

"Please. Say you'll come." His gaze was almost tender, and she felt drawn in by his expressive brown eyes. "Who can tell? You might enjoy the prospect of photography so well that you'll be inclined to seek a profession as one of the first women photographers in the West."

If she did decide to go, her interest in the art of chronicling wouldn't be the sole reason for changing her mind. Taken aback by that errant thought, she took a slight step sideways—and promptly connected with the edge of the boardwalk. His hand shot out to grab her upper arm, preventing her from a fall and further disgrace.

Warmth radiated through her sleeve where he touched her, but it couldn't rival the heat that sailed even to her ears. "I—" She took a quick step back, loosing herself from his hold. "Perhaps I might. That is, I will. But for now I—I should go."

With that, she lifted her skirts, managed to turn without breaking a leg, and set off at a fast pace to the familiar shelter of her brother's blessedly empty mercantile a few buildings away.

—ℳ—

Travis finished setting up the boxlike camera, the size of a small, potbelly cookstove. It sat on its three-legged stand facing the mighty Red River, the barrier between Texas and Indian Territory. When he'd left Cut Corners, the day was clear, but now only a ray of sun shone through a mass of cottony white clouds that swept by, picking out orange and red streaks in the river and purple in the bluffs surrounding it. It was a shame that cameras weren't able to photograph color.

"This spot is lovely, in its own rugged way," Vivian breathed from nearby. "With all those small sandbanks in the middle of the rushing water. And that stretch of gray grass growing over the one over there—appearing almost as if it were a huge scraggly eyebrow. And those wooded bluffs flush up against the water. I've never been this far out along the river. I find it quite peaceful."

"Don't be fooled, Miss Sager. Looks can be deceptive. Both men and cattle have drowned while crossing this river's depths."

"Yes, I've heard of its dangers." Her voice quieted, as if she were lost on another thought trail. "As brilliant a blue as the sky is today, it's a crying shame that the image you take will only show up in black and white."

Astonished that she'd voiced a thought similar to the one he'd had earlier, Travis lifted his gaze from making sure the camera was secure on its tripod. "One day in the future I'm confident such an achievement will be realized."

"Really?" Reflective, she looked back out over the landscape. "I wonder if it'll happen in our lifetime."

His decision to invite Vivian Sager had given him as much surprise as it appeared to have given her on the night of the dance, but it wasn't often he found someone genuinely interested in his work. After the initial curiosity, most people got a glazed look in their eyes when Travis went into a detailed discourse concerning his profession, but Vivian's face had never lost its expression of eager interest. The thought again crossed his mind that he might very well be inspiring the first woman photographer of the West, and he chuckled. Somehow, as clumsy as she was, he couldn't picture Miss Sager in such a role.

He watched her walk toward the front of the wagon where Lula and Stone still sat—Lula as chattery as a pert mockingbird while his uncle sat off to the side, mute as a cheerless crow. Vivian promptly stumbled over something in the dirt and barely caught herself before falling. Shaking his head, Travis returned to his task.

His uncle hadn't been one bit happy that Travis had volunteered him and Mrs. Chamberlain to be chaperones—not that he was courting Vivian. Far from it. But he did want to protect her reputation. At the dance, Travis had insisted his uncle was being downright rude not to venture even one reel with the lively widow, and now he seemed further to be proving himself as a miserable companion—not that Lula seemed to take notice or care. Travis smiled and reckoned she could keep the conversation going for both of them. He wondered if she and Peony Wilson were related. That dear lady had nearly talked his ear off when her sheriff husband, Rafe, had introduced her to Travis at the dance.

Sensing someone behind him, he looked over his shoulder. Vivian smiled. "What are you doing now?"

"I've prepared the plate and put it in its holder." Travis again focused on his work. "Now I'll place it within the camera."

"Is there anything I can do for you?"

"No." He quickly straightened and turned partway, almost as if he would stop her if she tried to come forward. The image of her bumping into him and the precious glass he now carried lying in shards on the rocks entered his mind. "This equipment is highly delicate."

Her expression clouded. "Oh. I only meant to ask if you'd like me to bring you the canteen or if you'd like anything to eat. I wasn't offering to help with your equipment."

He forced himself to relax. Of course she wasn't. Seeing the eager light had been doused from her features, he felt like a cad. "You're welcome to watch," he offered, in an effort to be kind. If she stayed her distance, he could foresee no catastrophes arising.

"I'd like that." She advanced.

"Well, I didn't mean—"

But it was too late; she had come to a stop a little behind him, at his elbow. He tried to focus on his work, withdrawing the glass slide, inserting the plate holder, raising the slide, and after a count of six covering the lens—but the lingering scent of rose water proved to be a constant reminder of her presence.

"Would you mind explaining what you're doing?" she asked.

He welcomed the distraction as he forced the slide down with gentle firmness and withdrew the plate holder. "I've just taken the photograph and am now preparing to enter my dark tent to complete the process." He wasn't expecting her to follow him, but after almost snapping off her head earlier, he didn't have the heart to tell her to wait outside. He did, however, tell her not to come too close since he was working with acid.

In the dusky glow of the dark tent lined with orange calico and reeking of the medicinal smell of ether and other chemicals, Travis quickly set to work before the collodion could dry. He poured a solution of pyrogallic acid over the glass. Within seconds, an image appeared, rapidly increasing in brilliance.

"Oh, my," Vivian gasped in wonder, stepping closer. "It's the river—and there are the sandbanks and bluffs—and in such vivid detail, too!"

Travis smiled, though he spotted a blur in the corner near the bluffs, depicting a failed attempt. Perhaps a prairie animal had raced across the grasses while he'd closed the shutter. Nevertheless, he rinsed the developed plate well with clean water, then poured potassium cyanide over it, afterward again washing it in water. He would keep it for his collection.

"Light that candle over there, would you?" After giving the low command, he wondered at the intelligence of his words. Would she drop the lit match and set the tent on fire?

Vivian managed to strike the match against the large matchbox and light the candle without mishap. Travis thanked her and rapidly moved the plate over the flame, continuing this maneuver until it was dry. While the plate was still warm, he varnished it.

"This is all so amazing," she said. "I don't see how it can be done, to transfer such a detailed image to glass, but there it is." She was quiet a moment. "It is a messy process, though, isn't it?"

"Actually, I'm using the wet-collodion process, which is almost obsolete. In recent years, pretreated, gelatin-coated plates have pioneered a much faster dry process, dispensing with the need of a dark tent like this to develop the photograph immediately. Unfortunately, a crate of treated plates I ordered never arrived at my destination spot last spring, so I must resort to old methods until I can purchase them."

"How awful. We have no such items at the mercantile, but we do have a catalog, and I can see about ordering them if you'd like."

"That won't be necessary." He smiled to show his gratitude. "I'll be leaving for Dallas within several weeks, and I'll procure the plates there."

"Of course." She tipped her head as though pondering a dilemma. "Odd, though."

"What?"

"It seems as painstaking as this process appears—and since you said there are other plates that are so much better—that you would wait until you got those plates and not put yourself through such tasking methods."

Incredulous, he said. "And give up chronicling?"

"Only for several weeks until the new plates arrive."

He busied himself closing bottles. "Not even for that short time will I consider quitting. I strive for excellence, Miss Sager. To have my work recognized. To be the best at any given craft or job, one must work hard at it every day."

"Yoo-hoo," Mrs. Chamberlain called from outside the tent. "What are you two doing in there?"

"It's alright, Mrs. Chamberlain," Vivian hastily called back. "Mr. McCoy is just showing me the process of developing a photograph."

The tent parted, and the plump woman took a step inside, wrinkling her nose. "Oh, it is odorsome, isn't it?"

"One of the drawbacks of the trade," Travis said lightly. "I would like to attempt another photograph, if you have the time. This one is marred and not fit for publication." He showed Vivian the blur.

"We're here by your generous invitation, Mr. McCoy," Vivian said quickly. "I have no need to get back any time soon since Lionel said he would watch the store. Actually, I could stay here all day. Despite my earlier comment, I consider this quite exciting and have enjoyed viewing how it's done."

Mrs. Chamberlain frowned at her exuberance. "Yes, well, Mr. Creedon has expressed his desire for supper."

"Please," Travis said. "Go ahead without me. I'll eat after awhile. I know we spent some time reaching this destination and then hunting and picking out what I felt was the perfect spot, and I imagine you both must be starved."

"If it's alright with you," Vivian said, "I'd prefer to watch the process from the beginning. I'm not all that hungry yet, and I wouldn't feel right eating without you."

"Very well." Mrs. Chamberlain exited the tent.

Again Travis gently warned Vivian to keep her distance as he poured the viscous collodion over a new plate, then immersed it in a bath of silver nitrate. At her request, he described every step along the way and why he was doing it. He'd never had such an interested pupil.

Once he slipped the wet plate, now a creamy yellow, into its holder, he exited the tent to make another attempt at a perfect photograph, something the *Atlantic Monthly* would consider worthy to publish. He so desired to be as accomplished a photographer as the famous Matthew Brady, Alexander Gardner, and T. H. O'Sullivan. But as he'd told Vivian, to be the best at any craft took countless hours of tedious work and a constant striving for perfection. Except for Sundays, he worked every day.

Vivian walked beside him, asking questions and recounting all he'd told her, as if to double-check facts. He was amazed to discover she had such a keen mind, quick as a steel trap, and one that recorded details so well.

As they neared the camera on its tripod, Vivian suddenly stumbled on some loose rocks. "Oh!"

Without thinking, Travis dropped the slide and grabbed her before she could fall headlong down the cliff and into the rushing muddy water. Her arm flew around his waist in an effort to prevent her fall. He stared down into her flushed face, inches from his.

"Oh, Mr. McCoy, I'm ever so sorry! I certainly never intended. . . I never meant. . ." Her face went rosier. "It's these horrid boots. Well, that's not the entire truth—I'm also hopelessly clumsy. Please forgive me."

Travis didn't respond. He'd grown lost in her eyes. . . eyes so big, so blue. Framed with long lashes that curled at the tips. Never had he noticed how lovely they were. At the harvest dance, the lighting had been dim, even with the torchlight all around. And in the store, the area had also been poorly lit, with a counter separating them. But now her eyes stared up at him, only inches away. So big. . .so bright. . .the color of a crystal-clear lake shimmering amid the mountains farther West.

"Mr. McCoy?" With her forefinger, she pushed the dislodged spectacles back up the bridge of her nose.

He released her. "Boots?" His voice sounded as if it had a frog in it, and he cleared his throat.

She averted her gaze to her skirts and smoothed them. "Yes, well, never mind. I apologize for ruining your glass plate, especially when you had to go through such painstaking methods to get it ready. Of course, I'll have it replaced."

"No, never mind. It's not necessary." Travis hunkered down to retrieve the cracked glass. He needed the action to try to clear his head, to think, to separate himself from the vision of twin blue lakes. "I'll just go and prepare another. I have hundreds."

This time she didn't follow him to the tent.

The second attempt to take a photograph didn't go much

better, though he did produce a presentable piece of work. Throughout the entire process, she didn't speak a word to distract him, but Travis couldn't keep his mind—or gaze—from wandering to the tall, rail-thin woman who stared out over the Red River, her attention rapt.

CHAPTER 3

Vivian could scarcely believe that Travis had agreed to accompany her to a picnic after the church meeting. As was often the case on warm days, families gathered with neighbors to sit beneath the oaks that stretched along the creek behind the church.

After the mishap, when her tumble caused him to crack his glass plate, Vivian felt sure Travis would want nothing more to do with her, but she later felt the necessity to be polite and return the favor of an outing by inviting him on a picnic. While she tucked a checkered cloth around the fried chicken in her basket, she silently mocked her own thoughts. Be polite? Want to return the favor? If she were honest with herself, she would admit that she was thoroughly smitten with Mr. Travis McCoy. Visions of a fourth Christmas wedding daily filled her thoughts since she'd met the man two weeks ago, visions she repeatedly told herself were far-fetched and ridiculous. Something only she would think up, in all probability spurred by the idealistic dime novels she read.

She stilled her motions with the cloth and lifted her gaze. If only. . .

The noise of her brother's boots thudding across the planks snatched her from impossible daydreams. Embarrassed to be caught woolgathering again, she hastily patted down the cloth, though it was already secure.

Lionel sniffed the air appreciatively. "Something sure smells good in here."

"It's for the picnic with Mr. McCoy," she explained, "and his uncle and Mrs. Chamberlain."

"I figured that. If I weren't accompanying Matilda, I'd join you." He poked at the cloth as if to get a look at what was beneath it. Vivian playfully slapped his hand away. "I'm sure Matilda Phelps's food will be just as delightful."

"Yeah, I reckon. She's just about as good a cook as you are." He swallowed hard, his Adam's apple bobbing up and down. "Fact is, I might be asking her to marry up with me. Today even, if I can work up the nerve."

"Oh?" Vivian studied him in surprise. She'd known all along her brother had been planning to propose to Widow Phelps, of course; she just hadn't realized it would be this soon.

"And unless I'm missing my guess, I won't be the only one marryin' up in the near future. You and Mr. McCoy certainly have been keeping time together."

Heat rushed to Vivian's face. "He merely invited me to view his work and see how it's done since I showed such an interest at the dance. And I repaid the favor by asking him to a picnic. I would hardly call that 'keeping time together.'"

Lionel's bucktoothed smile grew wide.

She hadn't fooled him one bit.

"Oh, just take this, will you?" She thrust the picnic basket at him. "We'll be late for the church meeting if we stand here lollygagging any longer."

"Yes, ma'am." The grin remained on his face.

As Vivian and her brother commenced their short walk to the church on the corner, Lula and Stone left the boardinghouse, also wearing their Sunday going-to-meeting clothes. Travis appeared behind them, and Vivian took in a deep breath. His black sack suit fit nicely to his slim form. Above his pin-striped, buttoned vest, he wore a dark tie wrapped around his stiff winged collar, making him appear the embodiment of charm. She'd never seen him look so handsome.

He didn't join her but instead kept company with his uncle. Vivian harbored her disappointment and turned to catch up with her brother, who walked a few feet ahead. Catching sight of her, Travis tipped his tall crowned bowler hat. Giddiness sailed through her, and she offered a shy smile before pulling her wool shawl more securely about her and hastening to Lionel's side. As they approached the church, she noticed Rafe Wilson stood in a huddle with his father, Eb; his cousin, Jeff; and Erik Olson. Both Lionel and Travis moved toward them, and the other men raised their voices in greeting. The younger men's wives had formed their own ring and motioned for Vivian to join them.

"What a lovely dress," Peony said. "Is it new?"

In confusion, Vivian stared down at the button-down, blue frock with its frilled bustle plumped out in the back, the same dress she'd owned for almost two years. "No, it's what I wear every Sunday. The dress Lionel asked you to make me."

"Oh, yes, of course," Peony agreed. "I recognize it now. It's just that you look so different today. Your face is absolutely glowing."

"It certainly is," Anna added with a grin. "And I like what you've done with your hair, too. Having those tendrils hang down near your temples suits you."

Vivian wasn't sure how to reply. She offered an uncertain, embarrassed smile and continued inside, selecting the same pew she and her brother always took. One with a beautiful carving of Jesus raising Jairus's daughter from the dead. Erik Olson, the town's gifted carpenter, had crafted each pew from oak, each with a different biblical carving on the end that faced the center aisle. The gift of engravings he'd given to the church.

To Vivian's shock, Travis and his uncle filed into the pew

directly behind hers, even though Stone Creedon always sat on the other side.

She didn't miss her brother's knowing grin as he slid in beside her but refused to acknowledge it. Instead, she tried to cover her clunky boots with her skirt hem as best she could, not wanting Travis to catch a glimpse of the ugly things. To think, the day he'd saved her from her fall into the river, she'd almost made yet another social gaffe and blurted that her feet were so large women's boots didn't fit her. She wore serviceable men's boots instead. The mercantile didn't have a size that fit well, so she'd chosen them overly large instead of painfully tight. Now she wished she'd given in to vanity and ordered a custom-made pair. Soft kid boots with button tops like Mary Jo wore. With rounded toes and not old-fashioned square ones. . .

My, where was her mind trailing now? Why should she be thinking of boots, of all things, when her focus should be on worship?

"All please stand," Pastor Clune said from the front.

Along with the rest of the congregation, Vivian did so. She concentrated on singing the worship hymns and listened to the message that followed—a message that gave her pause and caused her to examine her heart.

Travis sat with his long legs sprawled out and his back against an oak's trunk, watching as Vivian spread out food over a blanket. She had seemed quiet after the service, and he wondered what was bothering her.

All around, townspeople gathered in spots over the grass, some seeking shade under the trees, others taking advantage of the bright spots—that is, when the weak sun peeked from beyond its covering of thick white clouds. Neighbor talked with neighbor as the womenfolk prepared the food for their individual families and the children played tag. Beyond the trees, a creek shimmered, and a few dragonflies darted over the water, late summer guests now that autumn was here. With the thick copse acting as a wind barrier, the day wasn't too cold for a gathering.

"This is a nice place," Travis said. He closed his eyes in contentment.

"Yes, it is. Many of us gather here after services when the days aren't too cold and the weather's nice." Vivian worked to unscrew the band around a glass top from a jar of pickled beets. "Of course, there probably won't be many more days like this. It gets pretty cold in Cut Corners." She pressed her lips together as she twisted and pulled. Suddenly, with a loud *pop* the lid came off—and beet juice spattered onto her skirt.

"Oh, dear." Quickly she set the jar down and worked to mop up the stain with a napkin.

Travis sympathized. "I should have offered to open that."

"It's not your fault. Likely I would've spilled something else if it hadn't been that." As if it heard her, the jar of beets toppled from its precarious stance on the uneven ground and fell, splashing red juice onto the blanket.

"Mercy!" She set the jar upright. "I hate being so clumsy. It's no wonder people don't want to be around me." Her face went as red as the beets, and she lifted her gaze to his. "Please, forget I said that. I really don't know what I'm saying." She took a deep breath and smiled, though it seemed a tad shaky. "Would you care for some potato salad with your chicken, Mr. McCoy?"

"Please." He grew thoughtful as he watched her scoop large servings of potatoes onto the plate beside three golden brown chicken pieces. Her hands trembled as she offered him his dinner, and he quickly grabbed it before his trouser legs were christened with the yellow lumpy concoction.

Travis looked around the area for his uncle and Mrs. Chamberlain but didn't spot them. He offered to say the blessing, and Vivian agreed. Afterward, he went into a deep study, thinking about how to broach the topic he wanted to discuss.

"Miss Sager, if you'll permit me saying so, I believe you're much too hard on yourself."

Her expression seemed guarded. "Oh?"

"Take, for example, the minister's message earlier on how we're not to give great heed as to what others think about us but instead how we should only strive to please God." He took a bite of chicken. "This is delicious, by the way."

"Thank you." She forked a modest amount of green beans into her mouth. "Please, continue."

Travis thought a moment. "Relating to this morning's message, allow me to demonstrate further. Sometimes, as humans with flaws, we tend to see those flaws as if they were enhanced, like the detailed image that appears once a negative has been immersed in silver nitrate. But that's all we see, and we're certain that's all others see in us."

She furrowed her brows and pushed her spectacles higher on her nose with one finger. "I'm not certain I understand."

"The image of the river you viewed the other day was just that—an image. You concentrated on a small fraction of everything that river and those bluffs actually are. A small frame of a larger picture. Nor could you see what was hidden within the river. Or beyond its bluffs. Those who've never been west and view that photograph will see the image, not the whole panorama. They'll think of that river in no other way—though at least they'll have the ability to view a portion of its magnificence, even if it is in monochromatic grays and ivory."

He smiled sheepishly. "But I digress. Sometimes we as humans tend to do the same regarding our flaws. They're the only image we see—gray and white—and we take no notice of the complete colorful beauty of all that lies beyond. We worry so much about what people think of us, we see nothing but those flaws we feel are separating us from a pleasant union with others and concentrate on them alone. As a result, though we often try to hide what we view as our shortcomings, they come to the forefront each time."

She sat back, regarding him with wonder. "I perceive, sir, that you're a professor in disguise."

He laughed. "Hardly that. I've had the hard hand of experience as my teacher."

"Hard?"

Travis thought back to his childhood and was silent.

—w—

Vivian shouldn't have asked the question. His pleasant expression faded, and a grim one took its place, clouding his eyes. She wondered if she'd offended him. Before she could apologize, he cleared his throat.

"I had a horrible stuttering problem in my youth, something my father could not and would not tolerate."

Vivian was amazed. He spoke so confidently, even eloquently, at times.

Travis settled back against the tree trunk, his forearm propped atop an upraised knee, a chicken leg dangling from his hand. "The one image I saw of myself in those days was of a boy with huge, flapping lips. I had nightmares of that very thing. It wasn't until my grandfather took an interest in me that I thought of myself as anything but a stutterer. When I was around those I wanted to please most—those people I wanted to think well of me—I invariably found my tongue tripping against the roof of my mouth and wound up making a fool of myself."

Thinking of her clumsiness, Vivian could relate to his embarrassment.

"My grandfather was teaching me about cameras one day in his studio—he was a daguerreotypist, which is how I got the interest in photography—and he could tell I was upset. I told him about some boys who'd poked fun at me and how I hated myself because I stuttered. I was only thirteen," he explained with a boyish grin, one that brought out the crescent moons in his cheeks. "Anyway, he said, 'Travis, there's a lot more to you than just your mouth. So stop putting all your efforts into trying to please others, who are just as flawed, and trying to make them like you, when you should be striving to please your Maker instead.' " Travis chuckled. "Grandfather once thought of becoming a preacher."

"So what happened?" Vivian asked.

"I got to thinking about what he had said and did just that. I spent more time listening during church services instead of playing with the things I carried in my pockets, and I began to talk with God while I was fishing at the creek. The next time someone made fun of me, I thought about how everyone was flawed in one way or another, and the taunts didn't hurt as much as they used to. I stopped seeing only the image of myself as a boy with big flapping lips and began to see traits I approved of. I'd already shown a propensity toward photography, and my grandfather told me I would make a good photographer someday. I spent countless hours in his studio, assisting him and watching him make miniatures of his customers. One afternoon, I realized I'd spoken for five minutes to a stranger—a situation that normally would have made me nervous—and I hadn't stuttered once. So I suppose you could say that I got over my problem by no longer caring what negative things others thought of me but by instead focusing on the full panorama—the view of how God pictured me."

His words gave her a lot to think about, ideas to ponder later when she was alone in her room. The more she grew to know Travis McCoy, the more impressed she became with the man.

"How is it that you never married?" She hadn't realized she'd murmured the thought aloud until she saw surprise cross his face. "If you don't mind my asking," she quickly uttered. "It's just that you're so much different than your uncle and don't seem the bachelor type at all."

Oh, dear. That sounded worse.

He took a large bite of chicken and washed it down with a swig of ginger ale before answering. "Some see my profession as a flaw. I live the life of a nomad, traveling and living out of my wagon much of the time. I never stay in one place long enough to set down roots. My dream is to become one of the best chroniclers in the business."

"And?" Vivian shrugged, not satisfied with his answer.

"What sane woman would embrace such a life?" His words were incredulous.

"I would." She spoke without thinking. "I mean—" She scrambled for words to save herself. "I'm certain there's a number of women who would consider it a privilege and an adventure, besides. Um, yes, well, I think it's time to go. It looks like rain." Hurriedly she began gathering the items to replace in the basket.

"Miss Sager." Travis's words were solemn. He laid his hand over her wrist as she tucked the cloth around the food. The warmth of his touch made her feel a little light-headed.

After taking a few seconds to compose herself, she looked up into his sober eyes.

"I never intend to marry. For some, it's the natural way of things, I suppose. But I fear I'm more like my Uncle Clive—Stone, as you know him. His true love married another, and he made the decision to remain a bachelor. For me, my love is photography."

"Of course." She smiled, hoping to portray indifference, though inside her heart felt weighted with iron. "You must travel the course planned for your life, Mr. McCoy, as we all must. I was merely curious as to why you came to such a decision. You've satisfied my curiosity quite well." She looked toward the creek, and he dropped his hand from hers as if just realizing he still grasped it. "I wonder where your uncle and Mrs. Chamberlain have gotten to. I thought they'd planned to eat with us."

His attention remained fixed on her. "There's one thing I do miss in all my travels, and that's companionship. Perhaps it's presumptuous of me to ask this, in light of our recent conversation, and I'll understand if you refuse, but I should very much like for us to share a friendship while I'm in Cut Corners. I'm comfortable talking with you, and given the fact that I don't partake of social conversation to a great degree, and when I do, I don't do it well, that's saying a lot."

Vivian was surprised. "Why should you think I'd refuse your friendship? And that you must seek my permission?"

He hesitated, as if he might not speak. "In my few days here, I've learned a lot about the town. I've come to realize that my uncle is one of four men who like to meddle in others' affairs and they've all played the roles of matchmakers, as you doubtless know already. An odd state of affairs, if you ask me, since three of the men are old bachelors. But I think you should also know, they've been playing the same game with us, manipulating us, like they do their checkers and dominoes—and I heartily apologize for my uncle's interference. I hope it didn't cause you undue distress."

She hardly knew how to reply. On the one hand, she was embarrassed that he should correctly surmise her interest in him; on the other, she was grateful for the manner in which he framed his apology so as not to cause her further humiliation. At least he hadn't come right out and said, "I have no interest in courting you, Miss Sager."

But a rejection was still a rejection, and Vivian felt deflated. Her gaze searched the area, anything to keep from looking at him. The wind had picked up, scattering those leaves that had fallen, and gray clouds made a slow sweep over the sky. "There's your uncle now," she said, catching sight of the old man and Mrs. Chamberlain walking together toward them, both deep in conversation.

Travis turned his head to look, and his mouth dropped open in surprise.

"I do apologize for missing your picnic, Vivian," Lula said as they approached. "But Clive and I had a few things to talk over.

Since the weather looks as if it's taking a turn for the worse, I feel we should head on home. I have a mincemeat pie, among other foodstuffs, so you have no need to concern yourself about us. We'll get along just fine."

Clive? Since when did Lula address Stone by his given name?

"Time's a wastin', woman," he said, seeming jumpy. " 'Stead of jawin' about the goods, let's put 'em to use afore they spoil."

"Oh, hush up, old man," she said in mock exasperation. "You'll get plenty. The good Lord knows that I baked enough to feed King David's army."

"You think I'm bein' smarmy?" He pouted like a little boy. "Never. I ain't no apple polisher."

Mrs. Chamberlain rolled her eyes to the storm clouds. "Whyever won't he use that ear horn of his?" she asked, addressing the heavens.

Once the two had left, Vivian hurried to pack the basket. "We should be going, as well. Thank you for a lovely afternoon, Mr. McCoy."

"Please tell me I haven't h–hurt you with my slipshod apology," Travis said. "Perhaps I m–m–misconstrued the matter."

Hearing him stutter, Vivian looked at him in surprise. His eyes had closed. After a long moment elapsed, he opened them, shrugged, and his lips tugged into a faint smile. "Sometimes, when I'm upset, the s–stuttering returns. Once I calm, it disappears."

Hearing his boyish-sounding admission, she felt closer to him than ever before. If she couldn't have his love, she would take the next best thing.

"I should dearly prize a friendship with you while you're in town, Mr. McCoy."

"Travis. . .please."

"Alright, then. Travis." Her face warmed as she repeated his name. "And you must call me Vivian." She hoped she wasn't breaking all codes of etiquette by asking such a thing.

"Vivian it is." His smile was wide, bringing the crescent moons out in his cheeks, while his rich brown eyes positively danced.

Vivian held back a sigh. What peculiar twist on life's path had brought her to the point of truth she now faced? She was falling hopelessly in love with a happily unattached chronicler.

CHAPTER 4

Mark Olson, you get over here right this minute." The exasperated voice of Anna Olson came to Travis's ears as he set up the camera for the town photograph. Anna shrieked. "Oh, my! Whatever did you get in to this time?"

Travis looked up from pushing the plate holder into the camera. The young boy had mud from the bottom of his trousers to the waist of his untucked shirt. "See what I found!" he exclaimed in delight.

He thrust a dripping frog her way, obviously expecting an enthusiastic response. Anna screeched, as did Mark's sister, Molly, who backed away.

"Now, now," Erik soothed, calming his wife. "Mark, put the frog away. Tuck in your shirt and just stand behind Molly. That way your trousers will not show. We have already taken too much of Mr. McCoy's time."

"Aw, it's just a frog. It ain't hurtin' nobody." But the boy placed the amphibian within his shirt and obediently took his place in the second row of the group of forty-two townspeople, counting babies, lined into three rows.

Travis kept his focus on the camera until he was sure he could look up without breaking into laughter. Idiosyncrasies aside, he was becoming fond of this small town and toyed with the idea of extending his stay several more weeks, as his uncle had urged him to do, until the New Year. Other than his parents, Uncle Clive was his only living relation, and business in Dallas could surely wait.

"Everyone hold as still as a tree," Travis said. Rapidly he managed the camera, going through the steps necessary to take the photograph. He pulled out the plate holder. "Finished. You have permission to breathe again."

The sound of relieved laughter and jovial voices raised in conversation followed Travis while he rushed into his nearby dark tent. As he poured the pyrogallic acid over the plate and the image grew more vivid, he noticed a blotch and peered more closely. He chuckled.

What appeared to be a frog peered out from the collar of Mark Olson's white shirt.

The tent flap opened, and a stream of unwelcome sunlight illumined him, covering the plate as an intruder entered and walked his way. "No!" Travis commanded, upset, sure the negative was now damaged. "Leave this tent at once!"

He glimpsed Vivian's astonished face as she whirled around to go—and caught her foot on the center stake. The tent gave a protesting *whooof* as it pillowed down atop their heads.

Vivian stood as still as a stunned squirrel, unable to see anything but orange cloth before her eyes. Humiliation warred with remorse. These past two weeks she'd done well to avoid accidents or stumbles while in Travis's company. Having heeded his words concerning his personal experiences, she'd grown more at ease around him and less inclined to embarrassing acts of clumsiness. But now this—her worst blunder yet!

The canvas shifted as Travis pulled on it, and she heard the crunch of his boots coming closer. She wished she could dig a hole, sink into the ground, and cover herself from what was sure to be his accusing stare—but too soon, the weighty canvas lifted from her head, the tent resumed its upright position, and she looked up into Travis's face.

Her spectacles had been knocked off, but he was close enough that she could make his features out clearly. He didn't appear angry, just bemused.

"I do apologize," she said, her words no more than a breath. How many times had she used that phrase in reference to him?

She felt a tear slide over her bottom lashes and, embarrassed, lifted her hand to whisk it away. Before she could bring her hand all the way up, two of his fingertips slowly brushed the wetness from her cheek. She held an astonished breath.

"I shouldn't have yelled," he said quietly, his words oddly distant. "I startled you."

"No, I. . ." She couldn't think when he was staring at her in such a manner. "I should have been more careful and watched where I was going."

He didn't respond, only continued to study her eyes, her face, her mouth. His hand moved so that his palm lightly cradled her cheek. He stared at her a moment longer before his head lowered a fraction toward hers.

Vivian inhaled a soft breath, certain he would kiss her. Tilting her face upward ever so slightly, she let her eyes flutter closed. But the kiss never came, and the warmth of his hand left her jaw.

Confused, she opened her eyes again. He had straightened and appeared disconcerted, now unable to meet her gaze. He bent down, retrieving her spectacles. "They don't appear broken."

"Thank you." She took them from him and slipped them back over her ears.

He turned away. "If you wouldn't mind informing the others that a second photograph will need to be made, I'd appreciate it." He righted an overturned bottle on his table. She was relieved to note that the lid was still intact and nothing had spilt. "Once I prepare for another shot, the sun will be too low in the sky for a worthy image. Please inform everyone that we'll try again tomorrow."

"Of course." She clasped her hands at her waist. "I just want to say—"

"Please." He awarded her a glance. "No further apology is necessary. I was as much at fault as you." He presented his back to her as he worked at securing the center stake that was once again holding up the tent.

Vivian stared at him a moment longer then moved to go. Suddenly remembering the reason she'd come into his dark tent in the first place, she stopped and pivoted. "Actually, I came to tell you the most amazing news," she said before he could order her to leave again. "News I thought you might like to know. Lula just announced to everyone that your uncle proposed."

"What?" Travis jerked upright, his hand still around the stake.

The tent pillowed down atop their heads once more.

Seconds of silence elapsed—then Vivian giggled. The giggles turned into unstoppable laughter, and as Travis unearthed them a second time, Vivian was grateful to see him smile.

CHAPTER 5

Feeling melancholy, Travis sucked on what was left of his lemon drop while he stood outside the boardinghouse and stared at the mercantile across the street. The sheriff's wife, Peony Wilson, bustled through the door, holding her little girl's hand. Behind him, another door opened.

"Thought I'd find you out here," his uncle muttered as he came to stand beside him. "You ought to go on over there and talk to that gal, the way you been starin' over there and moonin' all mornin'."

Turning his full attention on his uncle, Travis cocked an eyebrow. "Are you referring to me? I'm not the one getting hitched."

Even Stone's ears turned red. "Yeah, well, maybe you should think on it some."

"And what about you? Are you really going through with it?"

His uncle shrugged. "Don't see why not. Widow Chamberlain's been after me to marry up with her since I moved into the boardinghouse. She's got a right carin' heart beneath all that chitter-chatter, and she kin throw fixin's into a kettle and come out with somethin' to please any man's belly. Like no other woman I know, exceptin' maybe Lacey Wilson. And Miss Sager."

Travis ignored the not-so-veiled reference to Vivian and waited, sensing there was more.

"Fact is," Stone said, scratching his whiskered jaw, "she ain't so hard on the ears once she stops blabberin' about other folk and their problems. Sometimes it helps bein' partial deaf." He cackled at that.

Travis shook his head at his uncle's remark but couldn't help the smile that spread across his face. One thing he'd learned—the gossip had died down in Cut Corners since Lula joined his uncle Stone as a chaperone. After their first two disastrous meetings, his uncle had actually seemed to enjoy the widow's company. "Well, then, I can honestly say I'm glad you found yourself a good woman, even this late in your years, Uncle. But that kind of life isn't for me."

His uncle snorted. "And just why not?"

"Because I've got other plans, plans that don't include a wife."

"Balderdash. I reckon every young buck thinks like that at some point in his life. I told you about Erik Olson, didn't I? And Rafe Wilson?"

Travis was getting mightily tired of hearing about the town's "mule-headed young men" and how they'd finally "wised up" and proposed to their gals at Christmastime.

He crunched down on his lemon drop and swallowed it. "My mind's made up, Uncle. You're not going to change it."

Before Stone could argue, a shout came from across the street.

"Hey, Stone," Eb called. "We're just shufflin' the dominoes. Get on over here."

Travis motioned with his arm toward the mercantile, where the other three meddlers now sat in chairs on the boardwalk, with a square board on a barrel between them. "Your cronies are waiting for you, Uncle. And for the record, it would be best for everyone concerned, especially Miss Sager, if you four dispense with hatching any further plans of trying to 'pair us up and get us hitched,' as I overheard Swede say last night. My course in life is set, and there's no room for a wife. Good morning, Uncle."

Travis settled his hat on his head and headed north down the boardwalk.

"Where you headin'?" his uncle called after him.

"While I'm still here, I plan to visit Lacey's Diner, after having heard so much praise about the food there," Travis answered without turning around. "I'll be leaving Cut Corners earlier than planned—this coming Monday. I've decided I want to reach Dallas soon, after all."

"What?" his uncle called in shock. "What about your plan to stay through Christmas, like you said last week?"

But Travis kept on walking. He'd just made the decision and reckoned it was the wisest course to take. Having seen the determined gleam in his uncle's eyes, he was positive the old-timer wouldn't give up, nor would his friends; and Travis wanted to spare Vivian any further embarrassment. It was best for all concerned that he cut his visit short and leave town before the four old coots could cause more damage.

Vivian looked over her shoulder to make certain no one was in the store before giving in to the desire to turn the cheap wood-pulp pages of the latest novel that had arrived. Another shocking detective yarn with a strong, virile hero named Old Sleuth—whose favorite disguise was that of an aged man—involved a spine-tingling mystery regarding the trail of a missing woman. . . .

"Miss Sager, did you hear what I said?"

Startled, Vivian threw the thin book up in the air. It landed on the floor with a rustle, front side up, showing the black-and-white illustration of a terrified woman in a frozen scream.

Mrs. Chamberlain's brows sailed to her bonnet.

"I—I was just straightening the shelves." Vivian grabbed the duster she'd left near the cash till.

"Ahem. Yes." Lula stooped to retrieve the dime novel and laid it on the counter. "I have no earthly idea why your brother would sell such trash in this store. Pure drivel. I really should have a word with him. . . ."

Vivian hoped her face wasn't as red as it felt, betraying her guilt. Mrs. Chamberlain was one of a few ladies in town who thought such novels unfit for decent Christian folk. Yet to Vivian, they offered a glimpse of excitement in her otherwise dreary existence. She saw nothing really evil about them.

"Well, back to why I came. I'd like for you to come to my wedding." Lula adopted a flustered look, batting her eyelashes as a young girl might. "Since Mr. McCoy is leaving day after tomorrow, Clive decided we might as well not tarry. We're saying our vows tomorrow morning in front of Parson Clune—just a quiet gathering, nothing fancy. I do hope you can be there. As you know, I haven't any family nearby; and since if it wasn't for you and those outings we took, Clive may have never gotten the idea into his head to marry me, I want you there to share in my happiness."

Vivian only stared, while shock wrapped around her mind like cotton wool, and she grappled with what Mrs. Chamberlain told her. Travis had changed his plans again and was leaving early—two weeks before Christmas. He was leaving Cut Corners in two days.

"Vivian?"

She blinked and swallowed hard. "Yes, of course. I'd consider it an honor to attend your wedding. I look forward to it."

Once Lula left the store, Vivian allowed her shoulders to droop. Why hadn't Travis mentioned he was leaving when she'd spotted him eating a meal in Lacey's Diner yesterday? He hadn't said a word to her about going. Just nodded in acknowledgment and invited her to sit with him. Of course, she'd declined, thinking others might look upon them sharing an unplanned meal together as much too forward on her part. But, oh, how she'd wanted to stay!

Now he would never know how much she loved him. Not

that she ever planned on telling him so.

Sighing, she replaced the novel on the shelf. Even Old Sleuth and his daring escapades couldn't rouse a spark of interest right now. Despite what Travis had said about remaining unattached at the picnic weeks ago, Vivian had hoped against hope for a Christmas proposal to top Cut Corners' tally of three.

The day progressed as slow as molasses on a cold morning. When the hour finally came to close up, Vivian did so gladly. After supper, she meandered to her room and turned up the smoky glow of her kerosene lamp, but the stack of dime novels waiting for her beneath her bed didn't appeal. Regardless, she pulled them out, more out of habit than from any desire to read one. For a long moment, she stared at the illustration of a woman posed in a frightened stance with the hero's hand protectively at her back as they both stared in horror at something the reader couldn't see. In a rare fit of frustration, Vivian kicked the stack over, losing her balance. She fell to a sitting position on her patchwork quilt. Tears clouded her vision as she stared at the mess on the bedside rug.

"Oh, Father in heaven. Why? Why can't I find happiness like Lacey and Anna and Peony—and even old Mrs. Chamberlain? Am I doomed to a life of caring for my brother only? But soon I won't have even that." Removing her foggy spectacles, she swiped the tears from her cheeks with her fingertips. She wouldn't cry again.

"Why is it that men run when they see me coming? Not all the women of Cut Corners are ravishing beauties—such as the ones in those novels—yet most all have found husbands. I still have every one of my teeth, and they're straight, too, unlike Mrs. Chamberlain's." Remorse niggled at her conscience for making such an unworthy comparison. "I just don't understand it. Why is it that no man finds me the least bit dear to claim as his wife?"

No—not *no* man. *The* man. The only man she desired for a

husband. Travis. Mentally she whispered his name, as if by doing so she might treasure it all the more.

With Travis, she'd found companionship, something she'd never had in great quantity with anyone else in town. They'd shared similar dreams and laughed together. He had helped her to see herself as God saw her, and as a result she didn't feel the necessity to try to satisfy everyone else—a thankless task since no one was ever wholly pleased with the way she was or the way she did things. He'd taken her on mental journeys with him out farther west—regaling her with scenic wonders of striking red sandstone cliffs in their odd formations, hot desert sands, and magnificent, towering, snowcapped mountains.

Now he was going back to them and other places like them and leaving her behind.

Well, she would no longer make a fool of herself over the man nor cause him further distress. She would allow him to slip out of town as quietly as he'd come in.

Clicking her tongue against her teeth in self-reproval concerning her former fit of weakness, she replaced the novels and scooted them back into position under the brass rail of her bed. The books were pleasurable reading, but lately they failed to quench an ache that had been growing inside her. She readied herself for the night then reached for God's Holy Word and opened it to where she'd left off during her last quiet hour with her Savior. Too long ago.

As she read His words of instruction and promise from the book of Hebrews, they convicted her but also acted like balm to her troubled soul. One verse stood out: "Let your conversation be without covetousness; and be content with such things as ye have: for he hath said, I will never leave thee, nor forsake thee."

Recognizing her earlier murmurings as a thin veil for coveting what her neighbors had, Vivian repented. "Lord," she whispered, head bowed, "help me to be content with what I already have, with who I am, and with what You've blessed me with. We observed Thanksgiving a few weeks ago, but I see now that I've hardly been grateful. I take comfort in Your promise that You'll never leave me and will always be there for me. I love You, my sweet Jesus."

As she hugged her Bible to her chest, tears again pricked her eyes at the gentle words that responded deep within her heart.

"I love you, dear daughter. And I have only your best in mind."

CHAPTER 6

All through the ceremony at the front of the empty church, Vivian avoided Travis's gaze. He supposed he couldn't really blame her for treating him like an oncoming plague of locusts—he'd never known her to avoid him so—but still it smarted after the easy friendship they'd shared.

Couldn't she understand that his dream of being the best chronicler in the West was the most important thing in his life? It was imperative that he reach Dallas—and soon—to get on with his photography business. He needed those treated glass plates. At least that's what he told himself spurred his desire to leave earlier than planned. That and his wish not to see her get hurt more than she already must be.

Despairing of ever catching her eye, Travis returned his attention to the beaming couple and those clustering around them now that the service was over. Lacey's great-aunt Millie, her hair flying in all directions even beneath the beribboned bonnet, took Lula's hands in hers as if they were schoolgirls and kissed her on both cheeks.

The other Meddlin' Men clustered around his uncle, offering their congratulations and best wishes. Swede slapped Stone's back with an open palm. Mayor Chaps Smythe, with lingering British correctness, stood tall and shook Stone's hand. "Bully for you, old boy!" He cited words about a good life and prosperity in his precise English accent, while Eb Wilson, with suspicious moisture in his eye, winked at Travis and loudly joked, saying now that Stone had been firmly lassoed to the matrimony wagon, they had tackled their most stubborn pair yet. Then he wished Stone a marriage as happy as his own had been.

"Don't know about bein' stubborn," Stone said in his quiet, gruff way. "But I reckon mulishness runs in the family. 'Cause I know someone even more set in his ways than me."

Travis had no doubt his uncle was talking about him, since he stared straight at him as he spoke. Before he could defend himself, Lula cleared her throat.

"Now, now. Let's not get into a discourse on who's the most stubborn of the bunch. Each of you old goats has your fair share of that trait, if you want the truth." Lula said the words lightly, casting a smiling glance Travis's way, as if she were his ally. "I made three lovely pies yesterday—one of them pecan. For a wedding present, your dear daughter-in-law gave me her recipe, Eb—the same pie she serves at the diner—and you're all welcome to come over to the boardinghouse and sample a slice or two and let me know what you think. Parson Clune, you and your wife and children must come, too."

Everyone agreed. As the hubbub once more increased, Travis watched Vivian slip quietly away from the circle and head down the middle aisle. He waited a moment then hurried to catch up with her. As his boots hit the boardwalk outside, he caught sight of her tall figure stepping off the same boardwalk and onto the muddy strip of land before the other walkway began. The clouds had grayed and looked as if they'd drop more rain sooner than later. Travis hoped the weather would stay clear for his departure.

"Aren't you coming over to the boardinghouse?" he called after her. She halted and hurriedly lifted a hand to her face, then dropped it to her side and turned. He moved to join her. "Mrs.

Chamberlain will be mighty disappointed if you don't sample her pecan pie."

Her blue eyes shimmered behind the glasses. "I'd like to." She gave a weak smile. "But I promised Lionel I'd get back as soon as possible after the ceremony to mind the store."

"Oh." Travis was disappointed.

"I'm happy for your uncle and Mrs. Chamberlain. . .er, Mrs. Creedon," she went on to say. "As you likely know, Stone Creedon is the last person anyone ever thought would marry, and I'm truly happy for both of them. Please extend my apologies for missing out on the festivity, and wish them well for me." Her voice caught. "I really must go now. Good-bye, Travis."

He wanted to stop her, to talk to her awhile longer, but what could he say? Truth was, nothing he could say would change things; so instead he helplessly stood in the middle of the road and watched her hurried trek toward the mercantile.

Inside, he felt lower than a worm.

Vivian wiped the counter with a vigor that should have taken away the oak grain. She heard Lionel's boots scuff on the planks behind her.

"Travis McCoy is leaving town this mornin'," he said.

"So I hear." Under the window glass's black-painted words DRY GOODS, she could clearly see the commotion surrounding Travis's wagon in front of the boarding-house. Despite the light rain that sprinkled the ground, a number of people had ventured out to tell him good-bye. Vivian knew from overhearing talk in the store that many of the townsfolk admired him. Small wonder.

A long pause ensued. "Well, I reckon it's the right neighborly thing to do to wish him well and bid him godspeed. Don't you?"

"I reckon it is." She scrubbed harder when her cloth encountered a patch of stubborn dirt.

Lionel snorted and headed for the door, mumbling something under his breath. Once he was gone, Vivian lessened her brisk scrubbing, straightened, and massaged her aching shoulder. It wasn't that she intended to scorn Travis or that she didn't want to tell him good-bye; it would just hurt too much. Rend her heart to pieces and bring home to her the realization that her dreams of a Christmas proposal were now firmly buried in the ashes of all her other unfulfilled hopes. Yes, she wanted him to realize his ambitions and nightly prayed that every last one of his dreams would be realized—even if, for that to happen, she must sacrifice her own desires.

But she would not say good-bye.

Trading the cloth for a broom, she began a brisk sweep of the mercantile.

A tinkling above the door announced Lionel's return. "I'm glad you hung those bells over the door last week," she said, her back to him. "It's nice to know when a customer enters the store."

"I'm not a customer, but I like those bells, too."

She froze then whirled to face Travis. His expression was grave, and she dropped her gaze to the top button of his long frock coat, unable to meet his eyes.

"On second thought, I am a customer." He hesitated. "Give me a penny's worth of lemon drops."

She raised her eyes to look at him. "You want lemon drops," she repeated, doubting it.

"Sure do. And a penny's worth of those, too." He pointed to a jar of horehound drops.

Her actions forced and erratic, Vivian moved behind the counter to gather his purchases. She handed both small paper parcels into his hand and waited, but he didn't offer any change. Finally, she looked up. Raindrops dripped from his hat brim. She lowered her gaze to his face, and the sadness in his brown eyes made her heart catch.

"I couldn't leave without saying good-bye," he admitted.

She nodded once. "Then I'll be wishing you well." Vivian shifted her feet. "That'll be two cents, please."

He dug the coins from his pouch and laid them in her palm. Her nerve endings tingled at his touch, and she pulled her hand quickly from his.

"I'd like to write you, if I may," he said after a moment.

She averted her gaze to the counter. To what purpose would it serve, except only as a continual reminder of all she'd lost? "I'd rather you didn't."

"Why?"

"Now that you're leaving, I just think it'd be best if each of us goes our own way and forgets about one another."

When he didn't move, didn't speak, she again inched her gaze upward. She couldn't place the look in his eyes. But his mouth was drawn tight enough that the crescents in his cheeks appeared.

"Then I guess there's nothing more to say." His words came clipped. "Except for good-bye, Miss Sager." He nodded once then strode out of the door and out of her life. For good.

Soon she heard his wagon's harness and the creaks of the huge spoked wheels as he drove hurriedly away. Inside, she crumpled and wanted to give in to the moisture that heated her eyes. Instead, she brushed at her lashes and resumed her efforts to give the floorboards a thorough whisking with the broom. Regardless, the tears continued to fall.

The bells tinkled as the door opened. Hurriedly, she wiped her face with the back of one hand before facing her customer. "Oh. Hello, Molly. Mark. What can I do for you today?"

The two children eyed her as if uncertain. "We come to get some stick candy," Mark said. "Uncle Erik said we could."

"Of course." Vivian briskly moved to the counter and laid aside her broom. Knowing their favorites, she pulled the snow-white peppermint sticks from a jar.

"Were you crying?" Molly asked, her pale blue eyes anxious.

She let go of her brother's hand to relinquish her two pennies.

The last thing Vivian needed was for those two to tell everyone they'd caught her in tears. She tried to smile. "What makes you think that?" She handed the children their treats.

" 'Cause your cheeks are all wet and your glasses are foggy."

Vivian busied herself with putting their pennies in the till.

Molly looked down at her stick candy a moment then cupped her hand over Mark's ear and whispered something to him. He looked at his sweet and nodded. Both children snapped off the tops of their candies and handed the sticky chunks to Vivian.

"Uncle Lars says sugar candy always make a body feel better," Molly explained. Her smile was wide as she grabbedMark's hand, and together they ran, giggling, out the door.

Touched, Vivian looked after them then at the stubs of candy in her hand. Not for the first time, she wished she could have children as dear as those two. Obviously it was never meant to be. She must accept the plan God had for her, whatever plan that was, and stop hoping for impossibilities.

CHAPTER 7

Vivian and Lionel shared a light supper late on Christmas Eve, a full two weeks after Travis's departure. Earlier in the day, Lionel had taken part in the elaborate bachelors' pot roast luncheon that Lacey's great-aunt had started as an annual celebration—his last year to partake of it, since he was marrying Widow Phelps in the spring. Later, Lacey opened up the diner to the entire town, her third year to do so, and doled out scrumptious desserts free of charge.

Determined not to let Travis's absence ruin her Christmas, Vivian had walked over to the diner to join in the fun and had even managed to smile and sample some mincemeat pie and delicious fudge. All of the women—especially Anna, Lacey, and Peony—had been so kind, and the memory of their gentle words and sympathetic smiles caused tears to cloud Vivian's eyes even now. From their hesitant way of speaking, Vivian realized they, too, had thought Travis might propose.

She simply must get her mind off that man.

Forking a last bite of potato pudding into her mouth, she shot up from her seat to set the butter in the sideboard and collect the dishes to wash them.

"I declare, Vivian." Lionel leaned back in his chair, eyeing her. "These past two weeks you've been as fidgety as a jackrabbit with an itch. Sit down a spell and drink your coffee while it's hot."

Keeping her hands in motion helped her to stop thinking on things she had no business thinking about. But there was one matter she needed to discuss with her brother. Might as well be now. Smoothing her hands down her apron, she reclaimed her seat.

"Actually, we do need to talk, Lionel. You'll be marrying up with Matilda come spring." She cleared her throat. "And I noticed an ad for employment in the last mail-order catalog we received. They're looking for a bookkeeper in Kansas City. I've sent a letter applying for the position. I feel it's time I move on."

"What?" Lionel's cup hit the saucer with a bang, startling Vivian into lifting her gaze. His brows were bunched together. "Never. I won't hear of it."

This wasn't the answer she expected. "Why not?"

"Don't you like it here?" His tone became uncertain.

"It's not that, but soon Matilda will be living here, too, and it's time I made other arrangements."

"Vivian." He reached across the table to lay his hand over hers in an uncharacteristic show of affection. "You're always welcome in my home. I talked with Matilda, and she agrees. After all, you're all the family I've got left."

Tears pricked Vivian's eyes at his warm response. All this time she'd thought his was a grudging hospitality and that he wanted her out from underfoot. She shook her head, still unsure. "But didn't you help Stone Creedon and the others in trying to pair me off with Travis McCoy? I saw you talking to the old men the day he arrived."

Lionel's face reddened, and he cleared his throat, pulling his hand back. "Well, yes, I did. But only with your benefit in mind. Before Ma died, she made me promise to look after you, and as your big brother, that's what I thought I was doing. Looking after you by helping to find you a husband. I'm sorry it turned out so badly. I never would've figured. . . ."

"Yes, well, never mind that." Vivian shifted in her seat,

her attention going to her coffee. She took a sip. "Thank you for talking to me about all this, Lionel. I've always thought of myself as an imposition."

"Never." The word came out fast and sure.

She smiled. "Then I can leave Cut Corners all the more content, knowing I'll have a home to return to if things don't work out."

He seemed troubled. "You're still planning on going?"

She nodded. "I'm tired of reading about other people's adventures. I want some of my own."

"Those stories all tend to lean on the melodramatic side, Vivian. Nothing like real life—or real people."

Shocked, she set her cup down fast, spilling her coffee. "You know?"

"About your liking for dime novels? Sure. I never had a mind to read, not like you. Seems you've had your nose stuck in a book since you were in pigtails. Course then it was the classics you were drawn to."

Vivian cleared her throat. "How'd you find out?"

"I do inventory each week, remember, and it seemed too much a coincidence that whenever a new crate arrived, one of them novels would always disappear off the shelf that day, regardless if we had one of the few customers with a liking for them visit the store or not."

So her secret was out. A wave of shame lapped through her, though of course she'd put coins in the till for them and hadn't taken them outright. "How long have you known?"

"Since Old Sleuth made his debut, I reckon. Aw, don't look so humbled, Vivian. There's a lot worse things in life, and I'm not sure I cotton to what some of them persnickety old women say about them books being evil. Far-fetched, definitely. But evil?" He shook his head. "Their gossiping tongues always a-yappin' and spreading poison about others is more evil, to my way of thinking. As long as you don't get fooled into believing them stories are what life's truly about, I don't see how they can do any harm."

"I know they're not real. I'm not that naive. But I always wanted a smidgen of adventure, Lionel. Ever since Pa used to tell of his skirmishes with the Apaches when he first traveled west, and his encounter with those wolves that time, and meeting up with those crooked fur traders, and—"

Her brother laughed and stretched out his long legs, his back pressing flush against the chair. The wood creaked, protesting the added weight. "No quiet hearth at home for you, huh? Yep, I remember them bedtime stories of Pa's. Liked to have scared me witless, but, oh, how we clamored for more, didn't we?"

They continued to reminisce a while longer in harmonious union before Lionel rose from his chair and stretched.

"I'm going to call it a night. I suggest you do the same. The church bell will bc ringing before we know it, gathering everyone for Christmas services."

"I just want to do some straightening first."

"Don't stay up too long." He stooped to hug her, and surprised, she hugged him back, then watched as he headed to his sleeping quarters.

An hour passed. Then two. Vivian couldn't have slept had she tried.

Once the dishes were washed and put away and the kitchen was fully straightened, she headed downstairs and transferred her whirlwind cleaning to the store. She was glad for the soft kid boots with the fashionable heels that she'd finally broken down and ordered from the most recent mail catalog. All she'd needed to do was send in her measurement by drawing an outline of her foot on parcel paper, and weeks later she'd become the proud owner of a pair of *ladies'* boots that actually fit. What a difference it made in the way she walked and even carried herself! Oh, she was still clumsy at times, but her stumbles had greatly decreased with the advent of her new boots.

With the shelves straightened, dusted, and put in order, she grabbed the broom. Minutes later, she looked up from her whirlwind whisking to see a sight that made her mouth drop open. Broom in hand, she hurried to the door and swung it open, certain her eyes must be playing tricks on her.

A fine dusting of snow fell from a soft, powder-gray sky. She stood, amazed, and lifted her face to let the cold flakes kiss her cheeks. Snow—in Cut Corners, of all places.

Only once before could she remember them receiving snow at Christmastime—the year Lacey Wilson got married—and some winters they didn't get snow at all. Surely, this was a night for miracles. Even the sky seemed hushed, stilled, as if to remind her of the awe-inspiring miracle that had taken place almost two thousand years ago on a night much like this one.

"Oh, Lord, You are wondrous, and Your ways are wondrous to behold."

The whisper had barely left her lips when she heard the vague sound of a creaking harness and the rapid clopping of horses' hooves coming from a distance. She turned her gaze toward the railroad tracks to look. Possibly Doc was out to deliver a baby. Anna's was due any day.

A wagon came rumbling and clattering around the bend of Ranger Road. And for the second time that night, Vivian stood speechless.

—w—

"Whoa!" Travis pulled on the reins as he drove up in front of the mercantile, and his focus went to the woman silhouetted against the light coming from the store. Vivian stared at him as if he were an angel come to announce the birth of the Savior. Nothing so dramatic, but he did have an important announcement, and he was bound and determined to get his words out before his lips froze to his teeth. He prayed he wouldn't stutter. He was more nervous than a plump goose on Christmas Day.

"Vivian," he called out, low enough so as not to wake the

entire town. "I've been a fool. It took me a whole week in Dallas to recognize the truth—that what I really want in life I left behind in Cut Corners. I came as soon as I could get away."

Still clutching a broom, she took a step forward until she stood at the edge of the boardwalk. The light from the overhead clouds illumined her face. "Travis?"

"Yeah, it's me." He pulled up the brake lever and wrapped the reins around it. Swallowing hard, he stepped down from the wagon. After the curt way he'd behaved when he last told her good-bye in the store, he wouldn't blame her if she turned her broom on him and shooed him out of town. But he must answer to the strong desire that was even now playing a song within his heart at the very reality of seeing her again. He'd driven all day and night; he wouldn't play the coward now that the moment had finally arrived.

He pulled off his hat, bringing it to his chest, and dropped to one knee on the ground just beginning to collect patches of snow. Icy water soaked his trouser leg, and he shivered at the contact.

"Vivian Sager, I've been a downright fool, and I wouldn't blame you if you never wanted to see me again. But I'm going to say my piece, come what may. I love you." With those words out in the open, the rest came easy. "There's no way I could ever live my life and forget you like you said I should. I've come back because my life has been empty and dull without you by my side. So I'm asking—begging—would you do me the honor of marrying a dim-witted nomad like me and share in my life of chronicling the West?"

Her broom dropped to the planks with a clatter. "You want to marry me?"

"Yes. With all my heart." His knee in danger of turning to a hunk of ice, he stood unsteadily. "Will you be my wife?"

"Will I!"

"Yes?" He took an uncertain step forward.

"Yes!"

She ran off the boardwalk toward him. Throwing his hat to the wind, he planted his hands at her waist and hoisted her high in the air. She clutched the tops of his shoulders as he swung her around, and both of them laughed. All at once, his shoe slipped on an icy patch, and he lost all balance. Before he knew what hit them, they tumbled into an undignified heap on the frozen ground.

"Are you alright?" he was quick to ask.

She rubbed her hip, but she was smiling. "How can I be anything but glad when you've just fulfilled my every dream?" Her eyes sparkled, and she removed her dislodged spectacles, now speckled with snow.

Suddenly she laughed aloud. His heart full of joy, Travis joined her.

"Vivian, you're beautiful."

"Beautiful?" This time her laugh sounded choked. "Me?"

"Yes, you. You have the loveliest blue eyes, the sweetest smile, the most tender heart."

Drawing close to her, he cradled her satin jaw in his palms and saw the response of love in her eyes before they fluttered shut. The touch of her warm lips against his cold ones was all he thought it would be—and more.

"You two ever gonna get up off that ground and stop your carryin' on so we decent folk can get some shut-eye around here?" Stone yelled from a top window of the boardinghouse. The point of his striped nightcap lay slung over one eye.

"Uncle," Travis called, unable to wipe the smile from his face. "Wish me well—I'm getting married!"

"Buried, you say? You look healthy enough."

"He said 'married,'" Lula loudly proclaimed from behind him.

"Well, glad to hear you finally wised up," Stone said. "But unless you're plannin' on marryin' her tonight, could we get some sleep now?"

Lula stuck her head with its frilled nightcap out the window. "Oh, don't mind him. Come on up, Travis, and I'll ready a room for you quick as a wink. First I received that letter from my brother today, saying as how he and his dear Indian wife and family will be visiting in the spring, and now this. It's all so exciting." Her bubbly voice trailed away.

"A night for miracles," Vivian added, her voice soft.

"Amen to that." Travis stood to his feet and, taking hold of her hands, helped Vivian up from the ground. They stared at one another a moment longer, until he slowly drew her close for a parting kiss. Travis could hardly wait for morning to roll around when he'd see her again. He wondered if dawn was too early to come courting.

EPILOGUE

I now pronounce you husband and wife." Pastor Clune's voice boomed throughout the church decked in all manner of greenery. He grinned. "You may kiss your bride."

Vivian felt lighter than air as Travis gave her a tender kiss that curled her toes. Her heart leaped an excited little beat at the loving look of promise in his eyes before they both turned their attention to family and friends, who stood nearby with wide smiles, and accepted their well wishes. The Meddlin' Men clapped one another on the back and shook hands as if congratulating each other. Vivian knew it was the Lord who'd brought Travis back into her life, but she wouldn't begrudge the four old men their fun.

"I'll surely miss you, little sister," Lionel said as he hugged Vivian.

She embraced him just as hard, realizing that in a few short hours she would be leaving him, their first time ever to be separated. "I'd stay longer, but Travis has to return to Dallas—he has clients waiting there. Then, as soon as the weather clears, we're traveling farther west, on to New Mexico and Arizona and even up through Colorado. But when the time comes to settle, years on down the road, we plan to return to Cut Corners and make our home here."

"I know. He told me. I guess you're getting that adventure

you always dreamed of."

"Yes." She drew back, taking hold of his hands. "Oh, Lionel. Please be happy for me. I do love him so."

"That's the one thing that makes it bearable losing you. That, and knowing he'll take good care of you. And God'll take care of you both." He squeezed her hands before letting her go.

The next few hours passed in a blur of activity that left Vivian breathless. First came a party at the boardinghouse, with a huge dinner followed by dessert—and both Lula and Lacey plying everyone with their scrumptious cakes, pies, and cookies. A host of well-wishers flocked around the bridal couple. All too soon, it was time to pack up and say good-bye.

Dressed in her new smart traveling clothes of deepest blue, Vivian hugged each of those members of Cut Corners who'd become so dear to her. In past weeks, she'd gained the courage to open up to the three women she so admired and form friendships with them. Now she felt as if they were the sisters she'd never had. First came Anna, who'd delivered a healthy son named Michael four minutes before midnight on Christmas Day. Vivian kissed the top of Michael's downy head poking through the swaddling blanket then bussed Anna's cheek.

"I'll never forget you, Vivian. You must write to us and let us know how you're doing."

"I will."

"Do you hafta go?" Mark asked from beside Anna.

Vivian smiled. "Yes, but it's a good thing. It's not a bad one."

"Will you hafta ride on the train like we did?" Molly chirped up.

"No. We'll be traveling in Travis's wagon."

Mark's pale blue eyes grew wide. "The What-izzit Wagon? With the cam-ruhs?"

"Yes."

Molly and Mark looked at one another then back at Vivian.

"But if you go," Mark said, "who'll give us candy?"

Vivian laughed. "I guess my brother'll have to take over that job."

"That's enough, children," Anna chided softly. "Miss Vivian and Mr. Travis have to leave now, before it gets too dark and there's not enough daylight to see."

Molly suddenly moved forward, her small arms going around Vivian's blue skirts. "Good-bye, Miss Vivian. I wish you didn't hafta go."

"Me either," Mark added.

Emotion clogging her throat at the unexpected sweet gesture and words, Vivian stooped down to hug both Mark and Molly close. "I'll miss you children. Be good. Stay out of trouble."

Next came Lacey, who, with tears in her eyes, offered Vivian a basket piled high with delicious-smelling food from her diner. "I tucked a dozen of my best ginger cookies in there, too," she whispered before pulling away.

And finally, Peony, large with child, waddled up to embrace Vivian. "You're a special woman, Vivian. Don't let anyone ever tell you otherwise. I'm sure you'll make your husband proud as you chronicle the West together."

They kissed cheeks, and Vivian laid a gentle hand atop little Lynn's curly head. Unable to speak for the tears, she pivoted sharply and offered a hasty good-bye hug to each of the sometimes irascible but always loveable old-timers she would fondly remember as the Meddlin' Men—Stone, Chaps, Eb, and Swede. Lula and Lionel she hugged last, before she moved away.

Travis helped her step up into the wagon. Once seated, she looked out over the cherished people she'd known a good part of her life. Their sometimes-quirky, sometimes-crazy mannerisms and character traits, she would never forget.

Travis clicked his tongue as an order for the horses to proceed.

"Good-bye!" The townspeople called and waved.

Holding her hat, she turned in her seat and waved back,

watching as they continued to walk forward and wave. She watched until they were little more than the size of grasshoppers on the prairie.

"Regrets?" Travis asked suddenly, voice somber.

Vivian turned her attention to her new husband. "None. I'll miss them, yes, but I wouldn't choose being with them one more day if it meant I'd have to be without you."

He smiled and reached across the space between them to grab hold of her hand. Bringing her glove to his mouth, he kissed her fingers. "Look in the sack by your feet."

Puzzled, Vivian reached for the burlap bag and pulled the string. Withdrawing a framed object, she gasped. Fresh tears clouded her eyes. In her hands, she held a photograph of all the townspeople of Cut Corners. She smiled at their sober faces, though she noticed a few cheery ones, too. And she laughed aloud when she saw what appeared to be the frog that caused such a ruckus peeking out of Mark Olson's shirt.

Was any woman ever so blessed to have such a thoughtful husband as her Travis?

"I made that picture from the negative I assumed was ruined when the dark tent fell on our heads," he explained when she didn't speak. "I was able to save it, and I thought you'd like to have it. We can make that photograph the start of a family memory book. An album. And we'll add photographs of our children once they start coming, should God bless us so."

At his mention of the little ones they might one day have, her heart soared even as she felt a blush rise to her face. As cold as the day was, the sudden surge of warmth inside felt good. Sliding closer to him, she wrapped her gloved hand through the crook of his arm. "Have I told you yet today how much I love you, Mr. McCoy?" she said, feeling like a young schoolgirl out riding with her beau.

Grinning, he turned his head to plant a swift kiss on her cheek. "A man never gets tired of hearing it, Mrs. McCoy."

She giggled. "Well, I do love you. And I'm sure that today—the start of 1882—is destined to be the best year yet, due to the wonderful way in which it began—with me becoming your wife, and you my husband. I doubt any woman in the whole wide wonderful West could be happier than I am right at this moment."

Travis stopped the wagon. Mystified, Vivian turned to look at him, but before she could ask what was wrong, he drew her into his arms and gave her a lingering, heart-escalating kiss.

"I love you, Vivian," he whispered, pressing his cold cheek to hers. "I was a fool not to realize it sooner."

She held him close, certain no dime novel could ever compare to the wonderful adventure she was about to share with this dear man.

Grandma Vera's Creamy Pecan Pie

(Guaranteed to be as good as Lula's and Lacey's)

1 cup light corn syrup
1 cup sugar
3 lightly beaten eggs
2 tablespoons melted margarine or butter
1 teaspoon vanilla
1½ cups pecans
9" frozen deep-dish pie crust

Preheat oven to 350°. Stir corn syrup, sugar, eggs, margarine (or butter), and vanilla in large bowl until blended well. Stir in pecans. Pour into frozen crust. Bake 50-55 minutes—pecans should be light to medium golden brown and have "cracked" look to them. Cool and cut. Top with dollop of whipped cream, if desired. Enjoy!

Pamela Griffin lives in Texas with her family. She fully gave her life to Christ in 1988 after a rebellious young adulthood and owes the fact that she's still alive today to an all-loving and forgiving God and to a mother who steadfastly prayed and had faith that God could bring her wayward daughter "home." Pamela's main goal in writing Christian romance is to help and encourage those who do know the Lord and to plant a seed of hope in those who don't.

To Hear Angels Sing

by Ramona Cecil

DEDICATION

To my beloved Texans, both transplanted and Texas born;
Jennifer, Galen, Matthew, Gabriella, and Emily.

CHAPTER 1

Suddenly there was with the angel a multitude of the heavenly host praising God, and saying, Glory to God in the highest, and on earth peace, good will toward men.
Luke 2:13–14

Pinewood, Texas, October 1883

Seth Krueger sat up straighter at the train whistle's shrill blast. From his seat on the bench in front of the Pinewood train station, he narrowed his eyes toward the bend in the tracks.

"I have better things to do than to fetch some schoolmarm," he grumbled beneath his breath.

The next moment, the train chugged into view, its earsplitting whistle filling the air. With a loud *hiss* of rolling steam, the locomotive came to a stop.

Breathing a sigh of resignation, he stood to get a better view of the disembarking passengers. A stream of people flowed down the lowered iron steps. Every female appeared to be either attached to other passengers or hurrying to embrace loved ones waiting on the platform.

Seth yanked off his hat and ran his fingers through his hair. He scanned the milling crowd in an attempt to identify and cut out of the herd the woman Violet Barton had sent him to fetch.

A green velvet hat atop a tumble of bright, copper-colored curls caught his eye. The woman reminded him of the porcelain doll he'd seen in the general store's front window. Dressed in a traveling dress and cape that matched her hat, she struggled to maneuver a trunk half her size down the steps. She seemed alone and glanced around as if lost.

Though the woman didn't fit Seth's notion of a spinster schoolteacher, he ambled toward her. At the bottom step, a heavyset man puffed past her, bumping against the girl so hard she almost toppled. Seth watched her chin quiver and hastened his steps.

Once on the platform, she lifted her face. The most beautiful, big green eyes he'd ever seen met his, and Seth's heart bucked.

He reached up to drag his hat from his head, then realized he had it in his hand. "Miss O'Keefe?" he finally managed, unable to wrest his gaze from her glistening eyes.

"Y–yes," she hesitated, taking a half step backward.

"I'm Seth—Seth Krueger. Mrs. B.—that is, Mrs. Barton, Mrs. Violet Barton—sent me to fetch you." Seth called himself every kind of imbecile for tangling his words like a six-year-old with a lariat.

"But where are Sally and Van Taylor? I thought they would. . ."

Lord, don't let her cry.

Half shocked at the prayer spilling from his desperate heart, Seth cleared his throat. "Reckon you'll have to take that up with Mrs. B. Just supposed to fetch you, that's all." He grasped the leather handles of her trunk and forced himself to look away from her lovely features that were threatening to crumple.

"Sally told me what a wonderful woman Mrs. Barton is, sponsoring our ministry."

Seth's heart lifted with the timbre of the girl's voice, and he smiled. "Yes. Yes, she is."

She rewarded his reply with a smile that melted his heart like butter beneath the Texas sun.

Lifting her to the wagon seat took no more effort than lifting a newborn calf. In the easy motion, an intoxicating scent of lavender caressed his nostrils. His hands ached with regret as they relinquished her tiny waist.

"Is the orphanage far?" The false cheerfulness in her voice could not mask the fear that rendered it breathless.

Seth's heart constricted and he gentled his answer. "No, not far, but we'll be goin' to the Circle B."

"But Sally said we would all be staying at the orphanage—"

"Hope you won't mind, but I need to stop at the general store and pick up a couple bales of barbed wire." What he really needed was to steer her away from asking any more questions—especially now that his mind had plain stopped working.

Don't be an addlepated fool. All right, so she's a right pretty girl. Not like you ain't never seen a pretty girl before.

After riding a short distance, Seth pulled hard on the reins and brought the wagon to a halt in front of the general store.

"What—what is that?" The girl dug a snowy white handkerchief from her black beaded reticule and pressed the cloth over her nose and mouth.

He followed her gaze to the wagon that had pulled up next to them. "Hides. Deer and elk, mostly. Probably some alligator hides from the swamps in the piney woods, and maybe even a buffalo hide or two. Reckon they are a mite ripe."

Although unpleasant, the smell was just one of many distasteful odors Seth had learned to tolerate. But the delicate creature beside him appeared overcome by the stench.

Even worse, One-Eyed Jake, the buffalo skinner, leered at her with his good eye as he climbed down from his wagon.

"Reckon maybe it would be best if you came in with me," Seth mumbled.

She answered with an emphatic nod and pressed the handkerchief harder against her face.

He guided her inside the dark, dusty building.

The moment they stepped inside, Jake entered behind them. In what appeared to be an intentional move, the skinner brushed against the pretty newcomer.

Miss O'Keefe shrank from the foul-smelling man and moved closer to Seth. Her nearness sent a pleasant warmth flooding through him and set his heart pounding like an Indian war drum.

"I suggest you watch where you're goin', Jake." Seth kept his voice low but glared a threat at the man, whose lecherous gaze slid down the young woman's form.

"Beggin' yer pardon, miss. Didn't mean no harm." Jake displayed a yellow-toothed grin and lifted a greasy black felt hat from his sweaty, balding pate.

Jake pushed past them, and Miss O'Keefe's hat shook as if she were shuddering. Perhaps bringing the woman into the store had not been the best idea.

Remorse struck Seth like a punch in the gut. He wished Jake Tuley was the worst the schoolmarm would face today.

—w—

Bridget's bottom felt bruised as they bounced along on the wagon that wound through mile after mile of tall grass and groves of pine trees.

Lord, help me. What have I done?

Her heart shook with trepidation. Only weeks ago, the calling had seemed so clear. She should follow her friends Van and Sally Taylor and take the gospel to the Indian orphanage Violet Barton and the Women's Missionary Union established near Pinewood, Texas. But now she doubted the wisdom of leaving her safe, familiar teaching job in Chicago.

Her unsteady fingers found the gold cross pendant hanging at her throat. She caressed it, wishing her mother could send strength and reassurance to her from heaven.

Despite the warm Texas sun, she shivered. Surely, the horrible-smelling, filthy man with the eye patch would visit her in nightmares. Only now, out here in the open country, did she feel safe enough to mention the subject.

"Are there many like him?" She tilted her head toward the man beside her who guided the team of horses through yet another grove of pines.

"Many like who?" Seth Krueger glanced across his right shoulder at her.

"Men like that—that man in the store." Fear gripped her again. She tried to hide it by uselessly brushing at the pine needles the stiff breeze kept depositing in her lap.

"One-Eyed Jake?" Somehow she found the man's smile comforting. "Naw, Jake's pretty much one of a kind. He's an old buffalo hunter from up around the Red River and Wichita Falls. Him and others hunted out the buffalo to deprive the savages of 'em. But with most all the buffalo gone now, and the savages corralled up at Fort Sill, Jake came down here to harvest sundry hides from the piney woods." He gave her a sidelong grin. "Jake brings the hides to Pinewood to ship out on the railroad."

The man's disparaging term for the Indians raised Bridget's righteous ire. "Savages? Is that what you think of the Indians? They are God's children, too, made in His image as surely as you and I." He gave a sarcastic snort and she bristled. Stiffening, she glared at him. "I feel privileged that God has led me on this mission to bring some of the young ones to Christ."

"Well, I couldn't tell you what God looks like, but I'm right certain it ain't no murderin', red-skinned heathen," he drawled with a chuckle. "If you ask me, this whole scheme of Mrs. B.'s is folly. Tryin' to save the redskins' souls." He snorted again. "Way I see it, you can't save somethin' that don't exist."

While Bridget tried to think of a scathing retort, the man nodded.

"Well, here we are—the Circle B." His announcement drove all other thoughts from Bridget's mind.

Two tall poles flanked the gently curving road with a swinging sign suspended between them. Into the sign was burned a capital *B* nestled in the center of a circle.

Bridget could see why Seth Krueger's voice swelled with pride. A short distance away, an imposing two-story log house crowned a knoll wreathed by stately pines.

They came to a stop in front of the house, and apprehension gripped Bridget's stomach like a cold fist. The man climbed down from the wagon, then came around and helped her to the ground. Her legs wobbled up the porch steps, and she thanked the Lord for the man's strong arm supporting her. She would feel better as soon as she saw Sally and Van again. Her heart pounded with happy anticipation of their warm reunion.

Inside, he led her along a narrow entranceway that opened on the right to a large, bright space. The room, dominated by a gigantic fireplace made from smooth gray stones, exuded an atmosphere of rustic elegance.

A middle-aged woman dressed in black rose from a maroon velvet chair near the fireplace. She wore her salt-and-pepper hair parted down the middle of her head and pulled severely back in a bun. A sad smile graced her kind face.

"My dear Miss O'Keefe." She walked toward Bridget with one hand outstretched. With her other hand, she dabbed a lace handkerchief at her tear-filled blue eyes.

A sense of foreboding filled Bridget. "Where are the Taylors? Where are Sally and Van?"

"My dear girl. I'm so sorry." The woman's warm fingers curled gently around Bridget's trembling hand. "They are gone. The Lord has taken them."

CHAPTER 2

The large log room beyond Violet Barton's distraught face swirled around Bridget. What the woman had just told Bridget was impossible.

It has to be impossible.

As Bridget's legs buckled beneath her, Seth Krueger reached an arm around her waist, preventing her from collapsing to the knotty pine floor. He helped her to the horsehair sofa.

"Oh, I was afraid of this." The woman fretted, anxiously rubbing Bridget's hands. "Seth, go to the kitchen and tell Sadie you need to fetch a glass of cool water for Miss O'Keefe."

Seth seemed reluctant to leave but finally released his firm grip on Bridget's waist.

Bridget was vaguely aware of Violet Barton rubbing her hand and whispering unintelligible laments.

The next moment, she felt the warm strength of Seth's arm supporting her shoulders and helping her to sit up. He held a glass of water to her lips. When the cool liquid hit her shock-constricted throat, she coughed.

"Slow," he whispered, "real slow now."

His warm breath fanned her cheek. She gazed into his pale blue eyes. In her excitement and apprehension, she hadn't noticed until now what an exceptionally handsome man he was. He looked to be only a few years older than she. Blond hair, bleached nearly white by the hot Texas sun, framed his tanned, boyish face. He carried the scent of leather and a faint whiff of smells that reminded her of the Chicago stockyards. Altogether, not unpleasant aromas.

"You don't know how sorry I am that you had to learn this way." Violet Barton's voice sagged with regret. "When it happened, we'd already received your telegraph saying you'd left Chicago."

"How?" Bridget managed to rasp.

"Last Saturday they were on their way to Pinewood for supplies. We think something spooked their horses. We don't really know." Violet shook her head as if still struggling with her own disbelief. "Seth and my husband, Andrew, found the wagon at the bottom of a gulch with the couple beneath it." She stifled a strangled sob and dabbed at her eyes again with the handkerchief.

"Do you think they suffered?" Bridget couldn't bear the thought. She'd grown close to the young, enthusiastic missionary couple who had attended her church in Chicago.

Seth shook his head. "I'm sure it was quick." His kind blue gaze met hers squarely and she believed him. The thought soothed her.

The next moment the broader realization struck, and panic seized her. She now faced an altered future. Would she live at the orphanage and try to do alone the jobs the three of them had planned?

"You will be staying here at the ranch of course," Violet Barton said, as if reading her mind. She turned to Seth Krueger. "Seth, please take Miss O'Keefe's portmanteau up to the yellow room."

"Yes, ma'am."

Bridget's mind raced blindly through a fog of uncertainty, grief, and confusion. What would become of her now? Someone else had her teaching job in Chicago. There was no going back.

—∞—

"Violet told me what you did. . .for Van and Sally. Thank you." Bridget glanced at Seth as they bounced along on the buckboard. Though Violet had urged her to rest for a few days before visiting the orphanage, Bridget was determined to make the three-mile trek the next morning.

Seth fidgeted and cleared his throat. "I'm sorry. Reckon I shoulda told you what happened when you got here. I—"

"No. You were right to wait. I'm glad I was at the Circle B with you and Violet when I learned." Gratitude filled Bridget's heart as tears filled her eyes. "Violet told me how you stayed with them—Van and Sally—until Andrew could get help." She brushed a tear from her cheek. "She said you sat with them for over two hours, keeping away. . .animals." Her voice snagged on the last word.

Seth's Adam's apple moved with a swallow. "It was the decent thing to do. Anybody would have—"

"I don't think so. I think it took someone very special to do that." In light of what Violet had told her, Bridget's opinion of Seth Krueger had risen greatly since their first meeting in Pinewood yesterday afternoon. His disparaging words about the Indians notwithstanding, she was beginning to understand why the Bartons held their ranch foreman in such high regard.

He gave her a sad smile that sent her heart tumbling. "I wish I could have done more." He shrugged. "If me and Mr. B. had come along a few minutes earlier. . ."

She touched his arm. "You did all you could. More than most. And the lovely crosses you made to mark their gravesite—you didn't have to do that."

His face turned red, and he cleared his throat again, his gaze sliding to the toes of his dusty boots, perched against the wagon's angled footboard. There was something very sweet and touching about his embarrassment at her praise.

Looking up, he bobbed his head. "House is up yonder."

Bridget followed his gaze, and a broken-down farmhouse soon came into view.

As Seth pulled the buckboard to a stop, Bridget's spirit wilted. Weathered gray boards covered the two-story building. An eave creaked as it swung precariously in the breeze. If the house had ever had a coat of paint, the relentless Texas sun and wind had long since worn it away.

"Hasn't anyone even tried to fix it up?" she asked.

"Violet said the Taylors planned to before. . ." Allowing the unfinished thought to dangle, he wound the reins around the wagon brake and jumped to the ground.

He helped Bridget down then climbed back onto the wagon.

"You're not coming in with me?" Surprised and hurt, she looked up at Seth, who looked everywhere but at her face.

He dragged off his stained gray hat and studied the sweat-band lining its bowl for a moment before slapping the hat back on his head. "Naw. I'd rather stay out here. Maybe catch forty winks." The muscles worked in his jaw.

Bridget's stomach twisted in a nervous knot. Irritation buzzed inside her like the flies tormenting the pair of horses hitched to the wagon. Even a cowboy unschooled in social graces should know enough to not leave a woman alone.

She grasped the dark leather reins sagging against the nearest horse's rump. "You promised to escort me. You can't just leave me alone in an unfamiliar place."

He blushed but still didn't meet her eyes. "Old Ming Li won't hurt ya," he said gruffly. He jerked his head toward the ramshackle house. "I've got no business in there."

From his derisive comments yesterday, Bridget took Seth to mean he'd rather not go near Indians.

"Have a nice nap!" She couldn't keep the sharp edge from her voice. How was it that a man who'd otherwise shown himself to be kind and caring could, at the same time, hold orphan children in disdain simply because they were Indians?

Heaving a sigh, Bridget headed for the house. Seth Krueger was an enigma.

She felt ridiculous shoving open the rusty-hinged gate. A couple of feet away, a great gap in the broken-down picket fence offered easy entrance to the yard strewn with pine needles. Her pounding heart drowned out the sound of her knuckles rapping against the weathered wood of the door.

The door opened to reveal a Chinese woman who smiled and bowed. The knot in Bridget's stomach loosened a bit.

"I am Bridget O'Keefe, the new teacher."

"Ah, yes, Missy Teacher. Come in, come in. I Ming Li." Ming Li's upper torso bobbed her invitation as she backed into the foyer.

The smell of stewed chicken and indiscernible spices welcomed Bridget into the house.

"Missus Violet say you come. Missus Sally, too, and Mr. Van. So sorry. So sorry." The smile vanished as she shook her head.

"Thank you." Bridget could not help staring. She guessed Ming Li's age to be about forty. Strands of gray threaded through the shiny black braid down her back. Instead of a dress, she wore a charcoal gray tunic with voluminous sleeves over baggy pantaloons. Remarkably tiny feet were covered with white cotton socks and tucked into flat black slippers.

According to Violet, the widowed Ming Li's husband had been one of the Chinese immigrants who'd helped to build the railroad.

"I call children." The woman's smile returned, pushing rosy cheeks up to slits twinkling with dark eyes.

"Come! Come now!" Ming Li clapped her hands sharply twice. The sound echoed around the sparsely furnished room. Nothing happened. "Come, come, I say!"

Gradually, little copper faces emerged from side rooms. Bridget lifted her gaze to the old creaking stairway where four more peered down through rickety spindles.

When they had all gathered around Ming Li like chicks around a mother hen, Bridget counted eight. Most were not yet in their teens. A boy, perhaps twelve or thirteen years of age, looked to be the oldest; a girl about seven years of age, the youngest.

"Missy Bridget, new teacher."

The children remained silent and somber-faced at Ming Li's introduction.

Bridget smiled. "I will be coming here soon to teach you English, arithmetic, and all about Jesus. Lots of wonderful stories from the Bible." Her announcement was met with stony stares, and the knot in Bridget's belly tightened. Though the children were undoubtedly grieving the loss of Sally and Van, Bridget hadn't expected them to be so reticent.

A girl who looked to be about ten emerged from behind Ming Li. Her pleasant copper face registered no fear, only curiosity. "They are afraid you will go to heaven like Mrs. Sally and Mr. Van."

Bridget's heart crumbled. She should have thought. These poor children had known so much loss. First their parents, then Sally and Van. She could see why they were reluctant to welcome anyone else into their lives.

Bridget looked into the girl's intelligent dark eyes. "Someday I will go to heaven, but God willing, not for many, many years. So tell me, what is your name?"

"Singing Bird, but my aunt called me *Liebes Mädchen*. She was my second mother when my mother and father died. Then the soldiers came and killed her and my grandfather and all the other grown people of our tribe."

Choking back tears, Bridget gave the girl a hug, overcome by the thought of how much grief this little one had experienced. She asked each child his or her name, then said her farewells, promising to return soon.

A few minutes later, Bridget was still blinking back tears as she and Seth bumped along the dusty road. "Do you know how the children were orphaned?" Perhaps if Seth knew their story, he might be more sympathetic.

He gave an indifferent shrug. "Some kind of a skirmish when the soldiers were roundin' up renegade bands of Comanche back in seventy-seven."

His matter-of-fact tone infuriated Bridget. "Those children's parents were murdered in front of them."

Seth turned steely blue eyes to hers, and the muscles worked in his jaw.

"Miss O'Keefe, Indians were not the only ones killed that day."

"I know. Sally told me there was a gun battle between the soldiers and the Indians." Bridget tempered her voice. Nothing would be accomplished by quarreling with the Bartons' foreman. "I just meant it must have been horrendous for them—the children, I mean."

"You ask me, they should be up at Fort Sill with the rest of the savages. But Mrs. B., well, she got wind of it and was dead set against that."

"Thank the Lord!"

At her pronouncement, a wry grin lifted Seth's lips. When her heart fluttered—a now familiar response to the handsome ranch foreman's smile—Bridget couldn't decide if she was angrier with herself or with Seth.

"Not sure what the Lord had to do with it. What got it done was Mr. B. ridin' ramrod on the Chisholm years back with the Fort Sill commander."

"They've been in that drafty house for six years?" On this one point, Bridget had to agree with Seth. Accommodations at the fort might have been better.

"No. Until last year, they lived in a little house in Pinewood with Ming Li. When the house was torn down to make way for a railroad spur, Mrs. B. moved 'em to that abandoned farmhouse on Barton land." He gave her a lopsided grin and Bridget's heart turned another somersault. "That's when Mrs. B. and her bunch of church women started lookin' for someone like you and the Taylors to teach 'em."

"You mean the Women's Missionary Union."

"If you say so." He snorted. "As if keepin' 'em wasn't enough, now they're determined to educate 'em."

His grin evaporated, replaced by a puzzled look that wrinkled his brow. Alert, he squinted at a cloud of dust in the road ahead.

Bridget followed his gaze and fear slithered down her spine. Out of the rolling dust emerged a mule-drawn wagon, its dirty canvas top billowing against the pale blue sky like a storm cloud.

After the frightening encounter at the general store, Bridget had hoped to avoid the foul animal skinner. So as the wagon rumbled nearer, relief surged through her. The driver was not the repulsive One-Eyed Jake.

Indeed, as the other wagon came up even with theirs, she saw that two pewter gray eyes shone from the man's bewhiskered, grandfatherly face.

He smiled. "Could you kind folks direct me to Mr. Andrew Barton's ranch, the Circle B?"

The pleasant scents of fresh-cut wood, tung oil, and varnish wafting from the wagon's interior tickled Bridget's nose.

"That's where we're headed." Seth rose a few inches off his seat and reached a hand out to the old gentleman. "I'm Seth Krueger, Circle B foreman." He shot a glancing smile at Bridget. "And this is Miss Bridget O'Keefe, a friend of Mrs. Barton's."

"Gabe Noell. Happy to make your acquaintance." The man tipped his worn brown hat toward Bridget, then clasped Seth's hand. His bare forearm beneath rolled-up sleeves looked remarkably firm and strong for a man of his apparent years.

He eyed Seth and Bridget with what felt like a soul-penetrating gaze that warmed Bridget's face. Did he think them sweethearts? The thought compelled her to clear up any such misconception.

"I'm the new teacher at the Indian orphanage sponsored by the Women's Missionary Union," she blurted. "I've just met my students for the first time, and Mr. Krueger is escorting me back to the ranch."

"Ah." Gabe's bushy dark brows bristled up and he lifted his hat higher this time, giving her a good peek at his salt-and-pepper hair. "A most admirable occupation in the service of our Lord, miss." Merry wrinkles creased the corners of his eyes with his widening smile. "As for myself, my trade is that of carpenter, wood-carver, and some say purveyor of sawdust sermons." His gaze bounced between Bridget and Seth. "I met Mr. Barton in the Pinewood General Store the other day. Said he'd like me to come by, that he had a couple woodworking projects for me."

Seth tensed beside Bridget, and though his smile remained, it looked forced. "You're welcome to follow us to the ranch, Mr. Noell. It's only a couple miles northeast of here."

As they jostled toward the ranch with the wood-carver behind them, sadness gripped Bridget. Seth had acted congenial to the stranger until Gabe Noell spoke of his faith. The wood-carver had just confirmed Bridget's niggling suspicion that Seth remained outside Christ's fold—and was quite content to stay there.

CHAPTER 3

"Teach me to ride."

At Bridget O'Keefe's bright voice, Seth pushed away from the corral fence he was leaning against and swung around to face her. His heart gave its usual leap when he gazed at the diminutive teacher. The morning sun danced over her russet curls, turning them to burnished copper.

"Is that an order?" He couldn't stop the grin tugging at his lips.

"No, it's a request."

"Sounded like an order to me." He forced his eyes back to the wild mustang colts bucking and prancing in the corral. If the rush of warmth he felt spreading over his face showed, he'd rather she didn't see it.

"If I could ride, you wouldn't have to take me to the orphanage every day."

Confident he had his features under control, Seth turned to her again. "It ain't safe for you to ride out there alone."

The obstinate lift of her chin indicated what she thought of his concern. "We've been traveling that road for a week now, and the only remarkable animal I've seen was that armor-plated little creature that scurried across the road in front of the wagon yesterday." Her green eyes flashed over her cute turned-up nose, which was sprinkled with golden freckles.

If Seth had ever seen anything more beautiful than Bridget O'Keefe, he couldn't remember when. "Oh yes, the ferocious armadillo," he managed in an almost normal-sounding voice. Try as he might, he could not rein his galloping heart to a walk. He had no interest in looking for reasons to spend less time with her.

His gaze moseyed over her, drinking in her beauty. Her blouse, the color of a green apple, matched her eyes perfectly. Her sturdy-booted stance, along with her outfit—a brown riding skirt and a vest that hugged her curves—told him she wasn't likely to take no for an answer.

"There's plenty of dangers you couldn't begin to imagine. An inexperienced rider has no business out there alone."

"I could ride one of those." She nodded toward the mustang colts. "They are not very big."

Seth chuckled. "And I just might sprout wings and fly! They're mustangs—wild horses. They haven't been saddle-broke yet."

"Well, if you won't teach me, I'm sure Tad will." Giving a huff, she turned and stomped toward the Barton's nephew, who was heading for the corral with a saddle slung over his shoulder. "You'll teach me to ride, won't you, Tad?"

"Now, there's a chore a man wouldn't mind." Tad grinned. Lifting his hat, he pushed dark curls from his forehead with the back of his hand. His bright blue eyes traveled lazily over Bridget.

She flashed her pretty smile at Tad Riedel, and an uncomfortable feeling twisted in Seth's gut. He strode toward the pair, his fists clenched. "No, he won't." He narrowed his eyes at the young cowboy barely out of his teens and as undisciplined as the mustangs in the corral. Seth couldn't abide the thought of Tad lifting Bridget on and off a horse. He had no intention of allowing them to ride out of the paddock together.

"You've got work here to do." Seth glared at the boy, intent on making his meaning plain. "Start lead-breaking that black mustang."

"Right, boss." A heavy sigh followed Tad's reply. "Miss." With a sad smile and a lingering look, Tad lifted his hat toward Bridget before complying with Seth's order.

Bridget spun toward Seth, eyes flashing and fists planted stubbornly on her hips. "If you won't let Tad teach me, then I'll just find someone else!"

"Whoa, there. Don't get yer Irish up. I never said I wouldn't teach you." Grinning, Seth laid his hand on her shoulder. He had to admire the spunk of this slip of a girl who had come halfway across the continent to teach orphan Comanche. "I just said you couldn't ride the mustangs. I'll find one you *can* ride."

He saddled a lady-broke mare and helped Bridget mount it. During the next hour as they rode over the land, Seth's admiration for Bridget grew. Her fear soon turned to confidence, and he never found it necessary to repeat an instruction.

Brains, courage, and beauty, all in one comely little package.

Bridget O'Keefe was more than a man had a right to dream of. Certainly more than *he* had a right to.

She clicked her tongue and kicked the mare to a quicker pace. At her smile, Seth's heart bolted like a colt at a rifle shot.

"How am I doing?" A happy laugh warbled through her voice.

"Like you were born to ride," he said, unable to budge his gaze from her face as their horses cantered along side by side. A gust of wind blew a bright curl across her forehead. Giggling, she caught it with the crook of a finger. The heart-stopping beauty of the picture took Seth's breath away.

They crested a hill and Seth reined his horse to a stop. Bridget's horse stopped beside his.

Her eyes widening with wonder, Bridget panned the acres of fescue and johnson grass below them edged by vast pine forests and dotted with several hundred head of cattle. "How far does

Circle B land go?"

"Further than the eye can see, includin' five hundred acres of pine forest beyond this pasture." He enjoyed watching her childlike astonishment as she took in the spreading vista. "The Bartons own two thousand acres. About a quarter of that in grazin' land and the rest in loggin' forests and land they share-crop off for corn and cotton farmin'. One day I plan to have a place as big—maybe bigger."

Seth realized with a jolt that he had never shared that dream with anyone. Yet something about this girl caused him to want to open his heart and display his dreams like treasures before her.

"That's what you were buying at the store the day I arrived." She pointed toward a string of barbed wire sagging on the ground between two posts.

At the sight, Seth's anger flared. Dismounting in a leap, he strode to the fence and kicked at the downed wire in disgust.

"What is it?" Before he could caution her not to, Bridget dismounted.

"Poachers." He ground the word through his clenched jaw. "They look for places like this away from the loggin' sites to get access into the woods for game." He cocked his head toward the longhorns grazing in the distance. "Trouble is, it usually don't bother 'em to do some rustlin' on the way in and out. Even a few Caddo Injuns in the next county have been complainin' about poachers."

He walked the fence line, checking for more damage, keenly aware of Bridget's presence behind him. A few yards later, he found another length of cut wire and blew out a long breath in frustration.

"Why do you hate them so?"

Turning, Seth smiled at her. She'd obviously misread his dismay at the vandalism.

"The poachers? They make my job a long sight harder, and

Mr. B. ain't gonna like hearin' what I found. But I can't say I downright hate 'em."

"No. Why do you hate the Indians?"

Her question stopped Seth in his tracks. He swallowed hard, resting his hand on the top of a fence post. This sweet, spunky girl he admired—no, more than admired—had just dragged him back to a place he didn't care to revisit.

He allowed his eyes to meet hers and found no hint of reproach, only kind curiosity and a longing for understanding.

"It was a long time ago." He shoved the words through his tightening throat.

"What happened?" The caring touch of her hand on his arm warmed him as if the sun had split the canopy of gray clouds overhead.

"When I was twelve years old, my pa got the notion to sell our land in Pennsylvania and move the family to Texas." Seth marveled at how the story he hadn't recounted for years began to spill out at Bridget's gentle nudging. "So he bought land up by the Red River and started a dairy farm. Right smack in Comanche territory. My folks thought if they were kind to the Indians, the Indians would be kind to them. That's what they believed. They learned different."

The memory of his parents' trusting innocence soured Seth's tone. "I'd gone to the barn to start the mornin' milkin' when I heard the Comanches' whoops. I looked through a knothole in the barn door and saw my pa tryin' to reason with a war party." The picture flashed again before Seth's eyes, and he gripped the fence post until his hand hurt.

"What happened then?" Her kind voice prodded him on.

"I watched one of the painted devils split Pa's head open with a war axe." Seth ignored Bridget's gasp. "They took my mother and my sister."

"What did you do?"

"What *could* I do? I was twelve." Seth regretted the anger

in his voice. He didn't want Bridget to think it was directed at her. Tempering his tone, he continued. "I buried my pa, then walked to the next county. An old couple, the Pritcherts, knew my family and took me in. After they died I started ridin' cattle on the Chisholm. That's where I met Mr. B. He took me under his wing. Him and Violet have been like parents to me ever since."

"I'm sorry, Seth." At her sweet compassion, he swallowed hard.

A jagged flash of lightning ripped across dark thunderclouds along the southern horizon. The cattle in the pasture below set to bawling.

Seth turned his face toward the approaching storm. "Better head back, I reckon." A thunderclap swallowed his words. The wind had picked up, snatching at his hat and blowing the copper curls framing Bridget's face.

He turned toward the horses, glad for a reason to change the subject and leave the painful memories behind.

"Seth, I know how difficult it is to be left alone as a child." She seemed unwilling to let it go. "I was orphaned myself at the age of eleven. My parents died of typhoid fever. I guess being orphans is something we have in common."

Turned up to his, her smiling face looked like delicate pink and white porcelain.

He stood mute, surprised by her revelation and mesmerized by her beauty.

The silence exploded with a deafening *crack* followed by bone-jarring thunder, jerking Seth from his trance. The next instant, a vague sensation of tremors worked its way up through the soles of his boots. At a distant rumbling sound, he turned and looked southward.

Barely visible amid a cloud of dust, a brown and white wall of cattle raced straight toward him and Bridget. The animals' long horns stretched out like curved sabers in front of them.

Seth glanced several yards north to where their grazing horses had wandered, now with their heads up, alert. Fear twisted a knot in his stomach.

"What is it?" Though obviously unaware of the approaching danger, Bridget's face reflected the alarm in his.

"Stampede!"

CHAPTER 4

Bridget stood paralyzed at the sight of the bawling wave of cattle bearing down on them.

"Hurry!" Seth gripped her hand and they raced toward the horses. Before she could catch her breath, he flung her up onto his horse sidesaddle. He mounted behind her and kicked the horse into a gallop toward the sprawling safety of a lone oak tree. Perched between the saddle's pommel and Seth, Bridget twisted and pressed her face against his chest. "God, protect us. Please protect us both." Trembling, she murmured her prayer against the coarse wool of his shirtfront.

They sidled up against a gigantic oak tree. Seth clung to the reins with one hand, while his other arm held Bridget tight against him. "Shh, steady now, steady." The soothing words, no doubt meant to calm the snorting and shifting horse beneath them, comforted Bridget's terror-filled heart.

The cattle herd thundered around them. Bridget coughed from the dust and ground her face harder into Seth's chest. His strong arms, wrapped securely around her, offered a sense of security amid the tumult. When the din faded and the earth became quiet again, she lifted her face.

He leaned back so he could see her face but kept his arms clamped around her. "Are you all right?" Beneath pale brows drawn together, his blue eyes were filled with concern.

Bridget realized that she had never been so "all right" in her whole life. "Y–yes. I think so." She knew she could not entirely attribute her hammering heart and breathlessness to fright.

The tension in Seth's arm muscles relaxed a bit. In the long moment of their shared gaze, a silent understanding passed between them.

It happened slowly, as in a dream. His arms tightened around her again, and his eyes closed an instant before she closed her own. When his lips touched hers, the gathering storm, the distant sound of bawling cattle, the whole world around them vanished. Only the two of them existed. Held in his secure embrace, she felt weightless beneath his kiss while his lips caressed hers with a tender urgency.

His lips relinquished hers, and he cleared his throat as if embarrassed. "I'm sorry. I shouldn't have done that."

Bridget opened her eyes and blinked, regretting that the tender moment had passed. She had never known such exquisite joy. It spread through her whole body. Every nerve ending from her scalp to her toes tingled as if she'd taken a direct hit from the lightning bolts slashing across the slate gray sky. "Don't be," she managed in a breathless whisper. "I'm not." She'd never spoken truer words. Of the many emotions surging through her, sorrow was not among them.

For a long while they rode in silence. Bridget's heart thundered within her like the stampede that had just passed them. What was she feeling? What did it mean? Guilt filled her, squelching her joy. *He's not a Christian. How could you? How could you feel like this about him?*

A chill wind gusted, nipping at her face. She couldn't resist leaning against the warmth of Seth's chest.

"Are you cold?" He leaned closer as if to shield her from the wind.

"A little." She snuggled against him. "Why do you think they did it?" They were wending their way through a tranquil sea of cattle. The stupid beasts that only a few minutes earlier had been charging in panic now grazed leisurely.

"Stampede?" His chest moved with the chuckle that rumbled up from deep in his throat. The sound sent a ridiculous thrill through her. "The thunder and lightning, I reckon. I should have thought—"

"My horse!" Remembering her abandoned steed, Bridget stiffened in the saddle. She didn't like to think she'd cost the Circle B a horse.

"She knows her way home."

This time she gave in to the rich sound of his throaty laugh and relaxed once more against him.

Sure enough, a few minutes later when they rode into the barn, they found the mare in a stall munching happily on hay.

"See, I told you she'd be here." Seth dismounted and reached up to help Bridget down.

Joy swept through her as his strong hands held her in a secure grip. *You can't. You mustn't allow. . .* If only he was a Christian. If only he was a believer.

A thought struck her with a jolt like the lightning that had caused the stampede. She could witness to him. She could bring him to Christ. Perhaps God did mean for Seth Krueger to be part of Bridget's mission work here.

"I could. . ." He cleared his throat again, a habit Bridget had begun to notice about Seth whenever he seemed uncomfortable or embarrassed. He looked at the straw-covered dirt floor. His sweet shyness touched her heart as softly as the music of the rain now drumming on the barn roof. "I could ride out with you to the orphan house. . .until you get used to riding." He met her gaze now, hope shining from his eyes.

"I think that would be a wonderful idea." Her words tumbled out in an eager rush. She wasn't nearly as enthused about making the trip without him as she had earlier thought.

He blew out a long breath as if he'd been holding it.

Bridget knew she must crack open the door to the subject of faith if there was ever to be hope of a relationship between them. If he could not accept Christ, she must nip in the bud this blissful feeling in her chest before it bloomed. Her heart ached with the thought. Yet she must not falter.

She laid her hand gently on his arm and mustered her courage with a deep breath that frayed at the edges when she let it out.

"Seth, I know you're not an especially God-fearing man. I hope you don't blame God for what happened to your parents and sister. You shouldn't. And you shouldn't hold it against the Indian children." He drew back, but she forged on. "It wouldn't be fair. Just as it wouldn't be fair for me to hold a grudge against the Polish immigrants who infected my parents with typhoid when my folks helped them move into our tenement." She grasped his hands, which had turned rigid. "Don't you see? These Indian children are orphans, too, just like us. They need to be taught about God's love—about Christ's commandments that we love our neighbor as ourselves."

He stiffened and pulled away from her, his face reddening. A thunderclap sounded in the distance, as if it were generated by his stormy countenance.

The shift in his demeanor frightened Bridget. Feeling the blood drain from her face, she shrank from his growing anger.

"God? You speak to me of God? God turned His back on my family when they needed His help!" Muscles worked in his taut jaw, and he shook with the fury she'd unleashed. "Yes, I blame God! And maybe I don't want to stop blaming Him, or the Indians." His glare sizzled into her like a branding iron. "And maybe, Miss O'Keefe, thou art just better than me!"

Bridget's heart shredded. Unwilling to let him see the angry tears filling her eyes, she turned and ran from the barn, through the driving rain to the ranch house.

A half hour later she still lay face down on her bed, sobbing.

The howling wind assailed the windowpane with loud splats of rain, interspersed with the crackle of lightning and the deep rumble of thunder.

Bridget gave free rein to her emotions, glad for the noise of the storm drowning out the sound of her anguish. Why had she allowed herself to care for Seth Krueger? She wadded the Texas star quilt in her fists, as angry at her own weakness as with Seth's stubborn rejection of God and his bias against the Indians.

His words—said in a sarcastic tone, which had skated dangerously close to blasphemy—rang in her ears. He had actually accused her of having a "holier than thou" attitude.

Sniffing, she pushed up to a sitting position and swiped at her wet cheeks with the back of her hand. Seth Krueger was a stiff-necked clod, and she was acting like a silly girl. She would simply squelch her feelings for the man. He wasn't the reason she came here. She came here to teach and minister to the Indian children.

As if mocking her resolve, the memory of Seth's kiss returned, enveloping her in sweet despair. Her heart throbbed with a deep ache. Falling out of love might not be so easily accomplished after all.

CHAPTER 5

A cool breeze greeted Bridget as she stepped onto the porch that ran across the front of the Bartons' home. With Violet and her cook, Sadie Russell, working on preparations for tomorrow's big meal, the kitchen seemed overcrowded. Besides, the day was far too pleasant to work inside when she could just as easily peel apples in the fresh air.

She set her basket of Jonathan apples on the porch boards. Settling into one of the two rocking chairs, she nestled the empty crockery bowl, complete with paring knife, in her lap. In front of her, the midmorning sunshine poured like molten butter over the bare ground between the house and barn, then reached the porch, splashing across her feet.

The chair creaked softly as Bridget bent and plucked an apple from the basket. She tried to remember a late November day this warm in Chicago but couldn't think of one. She should have utilized these rocking chairs out here on the porch sooner. This would be a perfect place to sew, plan her lessons, or read her Bible.

She knew why she hadn't.

Seth.

The porch was in plain view of the barn and the bunkhouse—Seth's domain. They hadn't spoken since their argument last week following her horseback riding lesson. His judgmental words still stung like a lash across her heart, and she was not eager for their next meeting. She'd consciously altered her movements to lessen the chance their paths might cross, and she suspected he was doing the same.

This morning Violet had mentioned that Seth had left early for the piney woods to hunt for their Thanksgiving turkey, so Bridget had felt she could avail herself of the porch without risking an awkward meeting with him. Trouble was, keeping him out of sight hadn't kept him out of her mind. . .or her heart.

Sighing, she sliced the knife's blade into the scarlet-striped skin of the apple, releasing the fruit's fresh, crisp fragrance.

"From the long look on your face, you'd think tomorrow was a day of mourning instead of a day of thanksgiving."

At Gabe Noell's voice, Bridget stopped working the knife around the apple and glanced up. She hadn't seen much of the old wood-carver since his arrival at the Circle B. According to Violet, Andrew had hired him to add decorative pieces around the porch eaves, but so far she'd seen no evidence of his work.

"Sorry, Miss—O'Keefe, is it? I didn't mean to startle you." His gray eyes twinkled as he dragged his battered brown hat off his head.

"You didn't. Well, maybe a little," she said with a laugh. "I must confess I was lost in a muse." The old fellow's kindly demeanor put Bridget at ease. His presence felt almost comforting.

"Ah, muses." He gazed down at her with a grandfatherly smile. "As the apostle Paul tells us in his letter to the Philippians, 'Whatsoever things are lovely, whatsoever things are of good report; if there be any virtue, and if there be any praise, think on these things.'"

Bridget smiled up at him. "That is one of my favorite Bible passages." She wasn't at all sure, though, that her previous thoughts fell within the parameters of the apostle's admonitions.

The crinkles beside his eyes deepened. "Don't let me bother you. I just came to take some measurements." He pulled a folded carpenter's ruler from the pocket of his baggy pants. Unfolding a length of the ruler, he went to work, holding it up to the porch eaves. Then he took a stubby pencil and scrap of brown paper from his shirt pocket and scribbled something.

For the next several minutes, he and Bridget worked on their separate tasks in silence.

"Mmm. I have to say, those apples sure smell wonderful." Gabe ambled toward her from the far end of the porch.

Bridget cut in two the apple she'd just pared and held a half out to him. "Please, have some, Mr. Noell. I have more apples here than I will need for two pies."

He dipped his head in a bow. "Thank you, ma'am. I'm much obliged." He accepted the piece of fruit. "If you don't mind. . ." He nodded at the empty rocking chair beside her.

"Not at all, Mr. Noell, please sit." There was something intriguingly incongruous about this old gent, who dressed like a beggar yet possessed the manners and speech of an educated gentleman.

"But I much prefer Gabe to Mr. Noell." He lowered himself to the chair with a soft sigh.

"I will call you Gabe if you call me Bridget."

"Deal." He reached his gnarled hand across the chairs' arms, and when she clasped it, Bridget was surprised at the firmness of his grasp.

Settling back in the rocking chair, he took a bite of the apple. "Mmm. I like when the tartness gets me right here." Grinning, he tapped his cheek.

"Then I will be careful not to put too much sugar in the pies for Thanksgiving supper tomorrow."

"Ah, yes, Thanksgiving supper." He gazed beyond the porch with a distant look in his eyes as if remembering something pleasant.

Bridget couldn't help wondering why this obviously educated man had chosen such an itinerant life. Before she could ask, he swung his smiling face back to hers. "I reckon every day is an opportunity for me to thank my Lord."

"Amen, Mr.—Gabe," Bridget amended with a chuckle.

"But I do appreciate the Bartons' kind invitation to tomorrow evening's meal and must admit I'm looking forward to it. Trail fare gets a little monotonous," he said around a bite of apple, "and Mr. Krueger tells me Mrs. Barton sets a. . .how did he put it?. . .'rip-snortin' spread' on Thanksgiving." He rocked the chair back with his laugh.

At the mention of Seth, sadness gripped Bridget and she frowned. If only Seth possessed the faith of this old woodcarver.

Gabe stopped munching his apple and trained a scrutinizing gaze on her. "Did I say something to upset you?"

Avoiding his piercing look, Bridget focused her attention on peeling the apple in her hand. "I–I'm afraid Mr. Krueger and I are not on the best of terms."

"And why is that?" Bridget never knew her grandfathers, but Gabe's gentle tone sounded exactly as she imagined a grandfather's would.

She shrugged, suddenly feeling like an eight-year-old. Despite his kind coaxing, Bridget wasn't prepared to share her feelings about Seth with Gabe. "There are just some things we don't see eye to eye on, like. . .faith." Sorrow weighted her voice. "Let's just say I doubt Seth will be saying any prayers of thanksgiving at supper tomorrow."

Gabe nimbly plucked a dark seed from beside the apple's core. He held it up to the slice of sunlight that had encroached farther onto the porch. "I've often thought it a great miracle that something so small, if planted and tended, can grow into a tree that bears its own fruit." His voice held wonder as he gazed at the seed.

He dropped the seed in the breast pocket of his faded blue chambray shirt and looked at Bridget. "The Lord tells us that the seed of His Word, if tended with love and watered with prayer, can grow to bear wonderful fruit. Remember that, Miss Bridget O'Keefe. And never forget that with Christ, all things are possible."

He rose slowly with a soft groan, tipped his hat, and ambled down the porch steps and toward the barn.

Watching him disappear behind the barn, Bridget had no doubt Gabe's comments had to do with Seth. . .and her. It was almost as if the old man had read her mind. She realized she'd become the latest recipient of one of the wood-carver's sawdust sermons. She sighed. Though she liked to think her faith was strong, changing Seth's hard heart would require a mighty miracle.

"Miss O'Keefe, I. . ."

At Seth's voice, Bridget jerked around.

He stood in front of the porch gripping the bound feet of two dead turkeys, their featherless gray heads and red wattles dangling past his knees.

Heat flared in her cheeks, and she was sure he must hear her heart pounding.

"I—" He cleared his throat, and his gaze didn't quite meet hers. "I'm sorry for what I said to you last week. You know, in the barn."

Hope rose in Bridget's chest. Maybe, like Gabe had said, the seeds she'd sown in Seth's heart about God had actually taken root. She prayed that was true. Unless he changed his attitude toward God, they could never be more than acquaintances.

"Of course I accept your apology, Mr. Krueger. If you are truly sorry—"

"I just said so, didn't I?" Irritation flashed in his blue eyes, but it disappeared quickly. "I just want you to know that it wasn't you I was angry with." The sharp edge left his voice, replaced by a tone of contrition.

Bridget's hope withered. "So who *were* you angry with, Mr. Krueger?" She forced her hands to go back to peeling the apple she was holding.

He shrugged. "Nobody, I reckon. Just angry about how things are. I don't know."

Bridget swallowed down a knot of tears. "You mean God, don't you?"

He blew out a long breath. "I didn't come here to talk about God. Listen, I meant no offense to you, that's all." His hard tone smote Bridget's heart, but she had to try again.

She leaned forward over the crock of peeled apples. "I understand your anger, Seth. I was angry at God for a while, too, after my parents died—"

For an instant, his blue eyes turned icy. "I said I don't want to talk about God." He huffed a breath. "I declare, tryin' to say I'm sorry to you is harder'n tyin' down a bobcat with a piece of string!"

How could she get through to him if he wouldn't even listen? Was his heart the hard soil unable to accept the seeds of God's Word Jesus spoke of in the parable? Bridget knew that wasn't true. She'd seen his heart. It was soft and sweet. Beneath his pain, Seth Krueger was a good, kind, and caring man. To someone who had not learned of God's love from childhood as Bridget had, she could see how God might seem a malevolent power, a source of people's pain.

Seth shifted, his feathery burdens swaying. "So no hard feelings?"

"No hard feelings." She gave him a bright smile, and the tense lines on his face relaxed. "Looks like we'll have plenty of turkey." She eyed the two birds he was holding.

Grinning, he glanced down at the turkeys. "I figured we'd need two to feed ten people."

"Eleven people." Bridget slid the knife around another apple, divesting the fruit of its peel in one continuous spiral. "One of my pupils—Singing Bird—will be joining us."

Seth's grin faded and his tanned face went from chalk white to blood red. His Adam's apple moved with a hard swallow.

"Then I won't be there."

CHAPTER 6

Heat marched up Seth's neck as he entered the Bartons' dining room. He was late.

Mrs. B. had outdone herself. The long table spread with a fancy white cloth sparkled with Violet's finest china, crystal, and silverware. The two turkeys Seth had shot were baked to golden perfection and now lay steaming on silver platters.

He'd almost followed through with his threat to Bridget and stayed in the bunkhouse. But the thought of disappointing Violet and the surety of a tongue-lashing from Andrew had brought him to the dining room dressed in a starched white shirt, broadcloth coat and trousers, and a string tie.

Taking the empty chair beside Tad, he murmured an apology to Violet and Andrew for his tardiness and offered cursory nods and greetings to the two logging bosses, their wives, and the old wood-carver, Noell.

—◦◦◦—

His gaze lit on Bridget, seated directly across the table from him, and his heart bucked hard against his chest. Dressed in a shiny palomino-colored frock, she looked like an angel. Her bright curls piled atop her head sparkled in the candle's glow like a burnished copper halo.

Clearing his tightening throat, he gave her an unsmiling nod but refused to focus on the Indian child beside her. "Miss

O'Keefe," he managed in a voice that didn't sound like his.

"Mr. Krueger." She gave him a wobbly smile. "I don't think you've met Singing Bird." She looked down at the girl and back up to him, as if daring him to acknowledge the child.

For one sweet moment yesterday, he'd recaptured the harmony between himself and Bridget—until she'd mentioned this little Comanche. He forced a glance to the doe-eyed girl and bobbed a quick, begrudging nod in her direction. "Miss."

Paying scant attention to Andrew's long prayer of thanks, Seth instead used the opportunity to torture himself by feasting his eyes on Bridget and drinking in her beauty. He had no interest in thanking a God who seemed to enjoy giving just so He could snatch away the gift.

After the prayer, Seth ate in silence, tasting little of the meal as conversations buzzed around him. Making a concerted effort to avoid looking directly at Bridget, he found his gaze drifting to the Comanche child. Apart from an occasional shy glance at those around the table, she, too, ate quietly, despite attempts by Bridget, Violet, and Gabe Noell to coax her into conversation. Her head down, she fidgeted in a too-big blue frock that bunched at the front and shoulders.

Sympathy stabbed at Seth's chest, surprising him. *The kid's probably scared half to death.*

"Well, Seth, have you found any more?" Andrew's voice barged into Seth's reverie.

He snapped his head around to face Andrew Barton, who sat at the end of the table, wiping gravy from his graying handlebar mustache.

"Sir?"

"Cut fences, man. Haven't you been listening? Ben Shelton here says his loggers found evidence last week of more poaching—field-dressed deer and bear on Barton land. I was just wonderin' if you'd found any more cut fences."

"No, sir. Just those two lengths along the east string of the south pasture." Thoughts of the cut fence brought back other memories of that afternoon—memories of holding Bridget in his arms, the sweet taste of her kiss. . . .

Bridget's voice drew Seth's attention to her, leaving Andrew to resume his conversation with the loggers.

Bridget's soft pink lips—Seth knew how soft, he knew how sweet—were smiling at Tad, who was explaining the finer points of breaking mustangs. Her green eyes glistening, she listened in rapt attention to the boy's exaggerated exploits. Once, Tad even had the audacity to wink at her, earning him a kick in the ankle from Seth.

By the time Mrs. B. and Sadie cleared away the supper dishes, Seth had had more than his fill of the Bartons' nephew flirting with Bridget. Afraid he might do something he'd regret, Seth made his excuses and fled the house before dessert was served.

Out on the porch, he hooked an arm around a support post and gazed into the star-flecked indigo sky.

"Fine, Tad's welcome to her."

The only answer to his growled words was the cadence of a distant barred owl's call.

He inhaled a lungful of cool night air tinged with the scent of pine and slowly blew it out again. Other words flew into his mind, words from another life, another time. Words far truer to how his heart really felt. " 'Thou art all fair, my love—' "

" 'There is no spot in thee.' Song of Solomon, chapter four, verse seven."

Gabe Noell's quiet voice jerked Seth around. Since their first meeting, Seth had tried to avoid the old wood-carver. He didn't want any sermons. Not from Bridget and definitely not from some old tramp.

"Didn't mean to startle you, son." Gabe stepped closer, his footfalls nearly soundless on the porch boards. Folding his arms over his white dress shirt—which appeared to be one of Mr.

B.'s—he gazed into the deepening dusk. "It's easy to imagine Solomon writing those words on a night much like this one."

Seth had no interest in getting roped into answering any questions about why he'd quoted words from the Bible—something he didn't even understand himself—so he stretched and yawned. He gave the man a tepid smile. "Well, sir, reckon I'd best say good evenin' and get myself to the bunkhouse. Got a full day of work tomorrow."

"I was hoping you could help me with something." Gabe followed Seth off the porch. "It won't take long."

Seth wished he were immune to the old gent's disappointed tone. "Sure."

They walked together to the old tack shed behind the bunkhouse. Until Gabe arrived, the building hadn't been used for years. Seth had to admit he was curious to see what the woodcarver had been up to.

Gabe pulled a key from his pants pocket and unlocked the padlock securing the door. Inside, the smells of freshly cut pine and varnish greeted Seth. The old man took a kerosene lantern from a nail beside the door and lit it, casting a yellow glow over the space.

Lantern in hand, Gabe walked to a long, canvas-covered object near one wall.

He set the lantern on the floor and pulled back the canvas, revealing what looked like rectangular open box. "Mr. Barton commissioned me to make a breakfront cupboard as a Christmas present for Mrs. Barton. He wants it to be a surprise, so I'd be obliged if you kept this under your hat."

At least now Seth understood the secrecy, but what he saw didn't look like anything he or Andrew couldn't have put together. He shrugged. "Sure." The sooner he accommodated the old coot, the sooner he could climb into his bunk and start contemplating the hardest, nastiest chores to assign to Tad tomorrow.

Gabe lifted the lantern so its light shone directly on the box, and Seth moved closer for a better look. His eyes widened. An intricately carved design of flowers, leaves, and bunches of grapes decorated the top of the cupboard. Seth had never seen better woodworking.

"You do good work, Mr. Noell." Wonder filled Seth's voice as he slowly drew his fingers over the extraordinary carving.

Gabe smiled. " 'Whatsoever thy hand findeth to do, do it with thy might.' Ecclesiastes chapter nine, verse ten."

"I know." The admission escaped Seth's mouth before he could stop it.

Gabe cocked his head at Seth, and one eyebrow shot up. "You surprise me, Mr. Krueger. I'd gotten the idea you were not a man of faith, yet a little while ago I heard you quoting scripture, and you just admitted you're familiar with the verse I quoted from Ecclesiastes."

"I was raised Christian. My pa was Quaker and my ma Lutheran."

"But you're no longer a man of faith?"

"No." Seth barked the word, hoping to discourage any further talk of religion. His tone turned icy. "What can I help you with?"

Gabe nodded at the window on the other wall. "I need to move this under the window so I can get better daylight on my work. That is, if your thigh is not out of joint."

Irritation scampered up Seth's spine. "My leg's just fine, so let's move this thing." He picked up one end of the cupboard while Gabe picked up the other, and together they moved the piece with relative ease to a spot under the window.

Though he wanted to ignore it, curiosity about the man's comment got the better of Seth. "So what made you think I had a bum leg?"

Gabe straightened with a soft groan. "Don't you recall the story of how Jacob wrestled with an angel and the angel put his thigh out of joint?"

"Yes, I remember." When he was a child, it had been one of Seth's favorite Bible stories, but he couldn't see what it had to do with him now. "But I ain't been wrestlin' with anybody—'specially angels."

"I'm not so sure about that." Gabe picked up a small piece of wood from the floor and settled himself on the head of an empty barrel. A part of Seth wanted to turn and leave the old man to his babblings, but something kept him rooted where he stood.

Gabe took a little folding knife from his pocket and began whittling the wood. "Jacob wrestled with the angel to get God's blessing, but I believe more often, people wrestle with angels to get away from God's blessings. Why, much of the world even rejects God's greatest gift, Christ."

"Like I said, I ain't been wrestlin' with any angels, and anything God's given me with one hand, He's took back with two."

Gabe gave a little shrug and blew shavings from the piece of wood he was whittling. "Sometimes we don't recognize blessings. Or angels." He narrowed a piercing gaze at Seth. "Never wrestle with God when He wants to give you a blessing."

Seth turned to leave. He'd heard enough about angels and blessings and God. He took two steps toward the door before Gabe's next words stopped him.

"I'm just curious. Have you told Miss O'Keefe you were raised Christian?"

Seth stomped back to Gabe. The old man had gone past aggravating to meddling. His fists clenched, he glared down at the wood-carver. "And why do you think I should tell *her*?"

Gabe rose and pressed the piece of whittled wood into Seth's hand, then chuckled and clapped him on the shoulder. "Because you are in love with her, son."

CHAPTER 7

Bridget lifted her face to the cool wind nipping at her cheeks and tugged at her riding hat. She wouldn't have imagined she could love horseback riding so much.

After that first lesson with Seth, Violet had taken over as Bridget's riding instructor, accompanying her on her daily treks to the orphanage. But this morning Violet was attending a meeting of the Women's Missionary Union in Pinewood and had deemed Bridget accomplished enough to make the trip without her. Violet had assured her, though, that Gabe Noell would be doing some carpentry work on the orphanage today and would accompany Bridget back to the Circle B.

Clad in her brown wool riding skirt, Bridget hugged her knees against the mare's sides. Rocking with the gentle motion, she moved as one with the cantering horse. She thought of her first riding lesson, when Seth said she rode like she was born for it.

Seth.

Her heart throbbed with the familiar ache. No matter how hard she tried, she couldn't erase him from her heart.

Remembering his terse attitude toward Singing Bird at Thanksgiving, aggravation shimmied up her spine like a gust of the cool December wind. Why couldn't Seth see that by continuing to hate the Indians, he only hurt himself?

The sound of a wagon rumbling behind her broke into Bridget's musings. She smiled. Gabe must have decided to come out early to the orphanage. Did the wood-carver think he was her guardian angel?

As she reined in Rosie and waited for Gabe to catch up, Bridget grinned. Gabriel *was* the name of an angel.

When the wagon came up even with her, she turned toward it, ready to tease the kindly old fellow about taking his name too seriously. But instead of finding Gabe's congenial smile, her gaze met the decayed-tooth grin of the one-eyed buffalo hunter. Her smile vanished as icy fingers of fear gripped her chest.

"Mornin', miss." He lifted his battered black hat. "'Member you from the gen'ral store some weeks back, but don't b'lieve we was ever introduced properlike." He raised and lowered his hat again. "I be Jake Tuley. And who might you be?"

Her stomach roiling, Bridget turned her head to the fresh breeze, pretending to get better control of Rosie. The awful smell of the man's unwashed body, fanned by the lifting of his hat, was almost unbearable.

"Bridget O'Keefe. I teach at the Indian orphanage." She immediately regretted the honest answer, fearing he would follow her. Forcing a weak smile, she tried to look everywhere but at his disgusting face.

"The old McCallum place?"

Bridget never answered. Her mind raced, trying to decide if she should kick the mare into a run toward the orphanage, still only a speck in the distance. But before she could make a move, he reached out a grimy hand and grasped Rosie's bridle.

"Whaddaya say we mosey over to that pine grove yonder and get to know each other better?" His mouth twisted in a salacious smirk.

Panic rose in Bridget's chest. She gripped the reins tighter. "Mr. and Mrs. Barton would not appreciate you—"

"Right shame what happened to that Yankee couple." His

one bleary gray-green eye turned dead cold. "Hate to see somethin' like that happen to Barton and his missus. Or that tow-headed foreman of theirs."

—∞—

"Shouldn't you be workin' on Violet's cupboard?" Seth shot a sidelong glace at Gabe Noell, who was sitting beside him on the buckboard. Resentment rose in Seth's chest. Once again he'd been roped into doing something he didn't want to do, and worse, with the meddling old wood-carving preacher. True, in the two weeks since Thanksgiving, the old man had said nothing more to him about angels, God, or even Bridget. Still, Seth was less than happy when Andrew asked him to help Gabe with some work on the orphan house.

Gabe gave him a bright smile that did nothing to improve Seth's mood. "It's coming right along. Should be done well before Christmas Eve." He winked. "I told Mr. Barton I needed another project to keep Mrs. Barton from getting suspicious."

Seth only grunted and focused on the weathered farmhouse in the distance, partially hidden by a stand of tall pines. The sooner they got there and got the work done, the sooner they could leave the place.

"Mrs. Barton tells me the staircase railing needs several posts replaced, including the bottom newel." Gabe seemed determined to keep up some kind of conversation.

"Wouldn't know. Never been inside."

"And why is that?"

"Never had any business in there." Seth flicked the reins against the horses' rumps, urging them to a quicker pace.

Out of the corner of Seth's eye, he saw Noell dig into his pants pocket, and he groaned inwardly. He hoped the old man wasn't fixing to carve him another wooden angel like the one he had handed him Thanksgiving evening. A dozen times or more, Seth had thought to pitch the thing into the fire but hadn't been able to bring himself to do it. Even that simple little piece showed the old wood-carver's exceptional talent.

When Seth reined the team to a stop in front of the house, he saw that Gabe held not a knife, but a nail.

"Do you know what this is?" The old man gazed at the object he held between his thumb and forefinger as if he saw something beyond a sliver of pointed iron.

"A nail. Looks to be a horseshoe nail." Seth sighed. He was wearying of the old man's games.

"A broken horseshoe nail," Gabe said. "It came loose from the horseshoe it was holding and caused my brother's horse to stumble. My brother broke his neck. He died the instant he hit the ground."

"I'm sorry. . . ." Amid a rush of sympathy, Seth touched the old fellow's shoulder. He wondered why the man would share such a personal sadness.

"Would you like to know why I kept it?"

"S'pose you kept it to remember your brother."

Gabe shook his head, still gazing at the nail. "No. I kept it to remember the horse."

Seth stared at the old man. Maybe he *was* touched in the head.

A sad smile crept across Gabe's bewhiskered face. "You see, the day we buried my brother, I shot that horse. I was eighteen and grieving. I thought the only way to ease my pain was to make somebody pay for my loss. I've learned better since."

Seth understood what Gabe had felt. He couldn't count the times he'd itched to make a Comanche—any Comanche—pay for taking his family from him.

Gabe rolled the two-inch spike between his thumb and finger. "This nail reminds me that only forgiveness takes away the hurt." He fixed Seth with a knowing gaze. "Nails much like this one, only bigger, pierced our Lord's hands and feet, yet He asked the Father to forgive us, then died to buy us that forgiveness."

Realization of what the wily old coot was up to dawned on Seth. Irritation crawled up the back of his neck. If Gabe Noell thought his horseshoe nail story would make Seth abide the sight of a bunch of Comanche orphans, the crazy old man had another think coming!

Seth shot Gabe a slicing glare and jumped to the ground. "If you want to work in there, go right ahead." He cocked his head toward the house. "I'll stay out here and dig holes for the new fence posts we brought."

The sound of pounding horse's hooves yanked his and Gabe's attention eastward. Seth's eyes popped to see Bridget, atop Violet's old mare, Rosie, galloping at a breakneck clip right toward them.

Fear curled in Seth's belly. If the horse should stumble at that speed. . . It didn't bear thinking. With Gabe's story fresh in his mind, his pulse quickened and sweat broke out on his forehead. But before he could call out for Bridget to rein in her mount, she reached the front fence and did just that.

Seth rushed to her with Gabe at his heels. "Are you all right? Did somethin' spook the horse?" His heart thumping against his chest, Seth reached up to help her down from the mare's heaving sides.

Raw fear shone from Bridget's wide eyes. Her rusty curls tumbled about her face, and her cheeks flamed as crimson as a swamp hibiscus flower. Shaking, she slipped into Seth's arms, and it took all his willpower to not pull her trembling body close against him.

Her breaths came in gasps. "I—I guess I just got her running too fast."

Anger suddenly swamped Seth's fear. Grasping her shoulders, he glared at her. "I thought you were smarter than that, Miss O'Keefe. You could have broke your silly little neck! Don't you ever do anything like that again, you hear?"

She jerked away from his grasp, and her pretty face puckered up in an angry scowl. "I appreciate your concern, Mr. Krueger. But I'm not one of your cowhands and will do as I please!" Turning, she walked to the house, her back stiff as a branding iron.

Gabe clapped Seth on the shoulder. "You should go after her and apologize, son. I know she scared the liver out of you, but it's been my experience that women don't respond well to orders." He grinned. "Proverbs chapter twenty, verse three says, 'It is an honour for a man to cease from strife.'"

" 'But every fool will be meddling.'" Training a glare on the old man, Seth finished the verse, wondering how he remembered that.

To Seth's surprise—and aggravation—Gabe laughed. Smiling, he glanced skyward, then back to Seth. "God does work in mysterious ways, my boy. He does indeed." He went into the house still chuckling and shaking his head.

"Crazy old coot."

Seth strode to the back of the wagon and lifted out the post-hole digger. He stomped to the fence line and shoved the twin spades into the moist earth, a tangle of emotions balling up in his gut. "Angels and nails. None of it makes a lick of sense." He gave the handles of the auger a mighty twist. He shouldn't have agreed to come out here when there were at least a dozen other chores he'd rather be doing back at the Circle B. So why did he?

One word: *Bridget.* She'd burrowed deep under his skin and into his heart.

He glanced back at the dingy gray building behind him. Next thing he knew he'd be slapping a paintbrush across that sorry house. And in the bargain, he had to listen to old Noell preach about God's love when right behind him was a passel of Comanche kids, reminding him how God had turned His back on Seth's family.

Seth dug into his coat pocket and pulled out the little wooden figure of an angel Gabe had handed him Thanksgiving evening. The wings were etched to suggest feathers, and he could even see the folds in the robe. The angel's upturned smile seemed to mock him.

With a flick of his wrist, Seth tossed the thing in the dirt at the base of the post oak tree near the corner of the house. If only he could toss away his feelings for Bridget as easily.

CHAPTER 8

Tad, stop it!" Bridget giggled as Tad dropped a wreath of popcorn on her head. "It belongs on the tree, not me." She raked the fluffy kernels from her hair and tried her best to look perturbed.

A roaring fire popped and crackled in the enormous fireplace, washing the Bartons' parlor in a warm, cheery glow. The scents of pine and popcorn filled the room. Yet Bridget's heart ached, missing the one person who would make the tree decorating festivities complete.

Earlier, when Seth had helped Andrew and Tad carry the ten-foot-tall pine into the Bartons' parlor, he'd avoided Bridget's gaze. They hadn't spoken since last week when he'd scolded her for riding Rosie too fast.

Bridget's heart raced at the memory of Seth's arms around her, holding her safe, chasing away the terror that had gripped her. She'd sensed that if it hadn't been for the presence of Gabe Noell, Seth might have kissed her.

Somehow she'd mustered the courage to kick Rosie into a gallop and escape Jake Tuley. But the man's veiled threat had prevented her from sharing with Seth and Gabe what had transpired. She had no doubt Seth would have gone after Tuley. It sickened her to think the buffalo skinner might have somehow caused Van's and Sally's deaths. She couldn't chance putting

Seth in danger. Feigning anger at Seth's rebuke had given her an excuse to hurry into the house so he wouldn't guess there was more to her fright than Rosie galloping too fast.

"Popcorn angel, that's what I'll call you. You're no bigger'n a kernel of popped corn." Tad laughed and ducked around the Christmas tree's fragrant branches, evading Bridget's swipe at his arm.

Violet Barton stood in the middle of the parlor, shaking her head. "You two are as bad as a couple of children. We'll never get this tree trimmed if you don't stop the silliness." She chuckled. "Now, you both behave while I go look for the tree skirt."

"He started it," Bridget called after Violet, who headed up the stairs chuckling.

"I started it?" Tad pointed at his chest. "Who threw the first piece of popcorn?"

Bridget enjoyed the childish banter with Tad. It reminded her of her growing-up days at the orphanage. Like an overgrown puppy, Tad lived to play, never seeming to take anything seriously.

Without warning, he scooped Bridget up in his arms, and she let out a shriek. "Maybe we should just put you on top of the tree, popcorn angel."

"Tad!"

Seth's stern voice silenced their laughter, and Tad lowered Bridget's feet back to the pine floor.

The muscles of Seth's jaw worked as he trained steely blue eyes on Tad. "Did you replace those broken boards in the south end of the paddock like I asked?"

Heat suffused Bridget's face. She wondered how long he'd been standing in the doorway. Then, indignant anger leaped inside her at his frown. Just because he'd declined Violet's invitation to help decorate the tree didn't give him the right to ruin their fun.

"Not yet, boss." Tad reached down to fetch a shiny red glass ball from an excelsior-filled wooden box. "I'll get to it just as soon as we finish the tree," he said, his voice devoid of concern.

"Reckon I'll have to fix the fence myself while you play Christmas," Seth mumbled as he headed for the doorway.

Tad affixed the ornament to a branch and glanced over his shoulder at Seth. "Hey, boss, before you leave, would you bring me that box from the far end of the fireplace?"

"Get it thyself."

Bridget watched Seth stomp from the room, her jaw dropping at his use of the word "thy."

"Wonder what's put a burr under his saddle?" Tad murmured, seemingly unbothered by Seth's cross reply. He chuckled. "He sure must be mad, though, if he's revertin' to his Quaker talk."

"Quaker?" Stunned, Bridget stared at Tad. Seth Krueger a Quaker? Suddenly she remembered how he'd used the word "thou" in the barn. She'd thought his comment was an attempt to mock her faith.

At the sound of footsteps, she looked up. Violet descended the stairs with a small red, green, and white quilt in her arms.

"Seth is a Quaker?" Bridget asked and watched Violet's smile disappear.

"His pa was. I'm thinking he said his ma was Lutheran. In any event, theirs was a very religious family from what I understand." Violet crossed the room and knelt to spread the material around the base of the pine. "He seems to have turned his back on it all. Blames God for what happened to his family. Lord knows, I've prayed for him and tried to steer him back toward God's grace, but. . ."

Violet stood and raised her hands in a helpless gesture. "Andrew said Mr. Noell was surprised, too, when Seth mentioned his Christian upbringing." She gave Bridget a conspiratorial smile. "I suspect that may be why Andrew is finding little jobs to keep the wood-carver here even though he finished the lovely gingerbread work around the porch weeks ago. I think Andrew is hopeful that Mr. Noell can help in our efforts to nudge Seth back into Christ's fold."

For a moment Bridget's heart sang. Seth had been raised in a Christian home, so he knew of God's love and Christ's salvation. He just needed to be convinced that God still loved him. But why hadn't he told her he was raised in the faith? Everyone else seemed to know, even Gabe Noell.

The intentional omission sent Bridget's heart oscillating between hurt and anger. Seth cared for her. She had no doubt about that. He'd shared the story of his family's tragedy with her, so why had he kept from her something as important as his Christian upbringing—something that could draw them closer?

"Here." Bridget thrust a string of popcorn into Tad's hand. "I'll be back in a bit."

Her legs pumping with purpose, she ran out of the house, down the porch steps, and toward the south side of the paddock.

"Seth!" His name exploded from her lips.

Seth turned from pounding a nail into a new fence board. "You here to scold me for hollerin' at your beau?" His voice sounded as chilly as the December wind whipping at her skirt.

"Tad is not my beau."

"No? You two looked pretty cozy to me." He dug into his jeans pocket and pulled out two nails, sticking the flat end of one in his mouth.

"Why didn't you tell me you're a Christian?"

"Because I'm not anymore." He turned and stabbed a nail into the board, then drove it flush with two solid blows of his hammer.

"You were raised to believe that Jesus is your Savior. How can you turn your back on that?" Bridget couldn't tell if she shook more from cold or anger.

Seth's torso heaved with a deep sigh. He turned to face her. "Look, I'm not sure what I believe anymore. Except that the

God I prayed to for the first twelve years of my life allowed the Comanches to take my family from me."

"Seth, this world is not perfect. It's full of sin. Sin causes our troubles and griefs. In the book of Job the scriptures tell us, 'Man that is born of a woman is of few days and full of trouble.' No one is guaranteed a certain number of years on this earth." Bridget could not hold back the tears of frustration stinging her eyes. "Your family, my parents, and Van and Sally Taylor all went home early to God. But they were all Christians and will be celebrating Christmas together in heaven." She swiped at a tear, her fingers trembling across her cheek. "I want that for you, too, one day."

"Why? Why do you even care?" he asked around the nail dangling from his lips.

"Because that's what Christ has commissioned all Christians to do. 'Go ye into all the world, and preach the gospel to every creature,'" she quoted.

"Is that the only reason?" He took the nail from his mouth and pounded it into the board.

"You know it isn't." Shivering, she hugged her arms, rubbing the chill from them.

He turned his attention to the new fence board, pulling at it as if to check its sturdiness. "Stick with Tad. He's a church-goin' boy."

"I like Tad, but I don't feel that way about him." Surely Seth knew how she felt. Surely in that moment when their lips met he'd felt it, too. . . .

He gave her a critical glance. "You should go back into the house. It's too cool for you to be out here without a wrap."

So, that was it. He'd closed the subject. Anger dried her tears and raised her chin. "Why do you care?"

He dropped the hammer with a thud. Two quick strides brought him to her side. "You know why." His voice turned husky, and his smoldering gaze bored into hers.

Bridget gasped as he wrapped her in a canvas-coated embrace, pulling her to him. Hot tears slid down her face.

I mustn't allow this. I mustn't!

He pressed his mouth on hers. His kiss deepened, then gentled to a tender caress that curled Bridget's toes. Her body weakened along with her resolve, and she melted against him, her lips returning the sweet pressure of his.

"I love thee, Bridget O'Keefe," he confessed in a breathless whisper. "I loved thee the moment I first saw thee. And every day, I love thee more." He let her go, and his shoulders slumped as if the strength had drained out of him.

"You still use the words of your father's faith you learned in your childhood. Christ is knocking at your heart, Seth. Just open the door for Him. He still loves you and He never left you."

Glancing from the ranch house to the paddock, she waved her arm in a large circle. "He's given you a home and people who love you, and He can give you peace about what happened to your family. The peace that passes all understanding."

Seth did not answer. He simply turned his back to her, walked to the paddock, and with a savage blow pounded another nail into the fence.

Her heart crumbling, Bridget plodded back to the house. She'd tried to plant the good seed like Gabe Noell said but tomorrow she'd move out to the orphanage. She couldn't bear to see the man she loved day after day, knowing that unless he came back to Christ, they could never be together.

CHAPTER 9

"Missy Teacher, man from ranch here!" Ming Li gave two sharp smacks of her hands. The sound echoed like shots around the cramped space inside the orphanage's front door and, Seth assumed, all the way up the stairway where the woman had directed her summons.

Ming Li shuffled away, and left alone, Seth tried to rein in his heart. It bucked like a wild mustang with a belly full of locoweed in anticipation of Bridget's appearance. He must be a fool or a glutton for punishment to put himself through this torture. But when he learned that Bridget had moved to the orphanage, it was as if she'd ripped open his heart and scraped it clean. After what had happened between them yesterday, he couldn't leave things as they were. He grudgingly admitted that Gabe Noell was right—Seth had to try to fix things. At least maybe he and Bridget could part friends. So when Mr. B. asked him to cut a Christmas tree for the orphan kids, Seth had seen a chance to make things right with Bridget.

A sound at the top of the stairs drew his eyes upward, and the air left his lungs as if he'd been kicked in the gut by a mule. Even in her plain dark wool frock, Bridget's beauty took his breath away. His gaze slid from her lovely features to her unadorned left hand slipping down the banister.

Seth's heart constricted. *She should have my ring on her finger.*

She should be my wife. This ain't right. This ain't fair.

God stood between them.

He marked it as but one more cruelty God had visited on his life.

As she neared, the longing inside him tightened his throat. He cleared it, then glanced at the worn floorboards before meeting her questioning gaze.

"Seth." Her voice sounded breathless.

"Andrew said you wanted a tree cut."

"Y–yes." Beyond her obvious surprise, Seth could not interpret the several other emotions flitting across her face. She turned her back just as he thought he glimpsed tears in her eyes.

"I'll gather the children. They will want to help choose the Christmas tree." Her stiff, formal tone smacked painfully against Seth's bruised heart.

Hat in hand, he followed her to a large room awash in sunshine that streamed through three long, narrow windows. Torn and water-stained green paper covered the walls. The scuffed floorboards were bare except for several tattered rag rugs scattered over the floor's center. There, eight children of varying ages sat cross-legged around a blackboard supported by two easels.

Seth found eight pairs of curious dark eyes trained on him. He felt no anger or unease, just a surprising pang of sympathy.

Bridget walked to the chalkboard. "Children, this is Mr. Krueger. He has come to cut our Christmas tree. So get your wraps, and line up at the kitchen door behind Yellow Feather."

They all obeyed quietly. But the one called Singing Bird, who'd sat across from him at Thanksgiving supper, continued to gaze at him over her shoulder as she followed the others into the next room.

Bridget turned back to Seth. "You didn't have to do this, you know. Andrew could have had one of the loggers cut the tree."

"I don't mind. I've cut Christmas trees since I was a boy." It was a cowardly response, but evading her meaning seemed easier at the moment.

"You know what I mean." Her green eyes studied his, and Seth cleared his drying throat.

"Reckon I do." He fiddled with his hat. "I couldn't leave it like it was. I couldn't leave *us* like we were. . . ."

She clasped her hand over his, sending his heart bucking again. Her eyes glistened and a sad smile curved her lips. "I'm glad you came." Then she cocked her head and gave him a puzzled look. "I thought Quakers didn't have Christmas trees, or even celebrate Christ's birth."

Seth met her bewildered look with a grin. "My pa, bein' a Quaker, was dead set against it. But Ma was raised German Lutheran and was determined to keep her Christmas traditions. Ma, my sister, Elisabeth, and I always decorated a little tree on a corner table while Pa found somethin' he needed to do in the barn." Seth chuckled at the memory. "We got to have our Christmas tree, and Pa just pretended it wasn't there."

For one sweet moment they shared a smile, a fond gaze. If only it could last forever. But the next moment she turned. "Get your axe, and we'll meet you in the backyard."

Seth nodded and headed for the front door with a much lighter heart than when he arrived.

At the wagon, he flipped back the canvas tarp and lifted out the axe. A lump formed in his throat. How odd that something as simple as cutting down a tree could peel away the years, taking him back to a place he'd thought lost to him forever.

He hefted the axe, feeling the soft, worn wood of the handle in his grip and the cold iron axe head against the top of his clenched hand. From the time he was old enough to swing an axe, he'd cut his mother's little Christmas tree. He swallowed hard. How he would love to see his mother's face again, smiling approval at a *Weihnachtsbaum* he cut.

"You're the man from the fancy dinner."

Batting moisture from his eyes, Seth jerked around to find Singing Bird beside him.

"Shouldn't you be with the other kids?" The child had obviously lost some of the shyness she displayed at Thanksgiving.

"Teacher said I could come and tell you we found a good tree to cut." She slipped her hand into his, and Seth's arm stiffened at the unexpected touch then relaxed as her warm little fingers curled around his.

As they made their way around the side of the house through knee-high johnson grass, Seth found himself slowing his steps to match Singing Bird's shorter strides.

She tipped a smile up at him. "Teacher said we could make an angel from wet paper to put on top of the tree."

"Not a star?" Seth grinned down at the girl. He no longer saw her as a Comanche, or even an Indian. She was just a child. A child who probably longed for a father.

Singing Bird shook her head. "I like angels. Mr. Noell said we each have a special angel that watches over us. Do you have an angel, Mr. Krueger?"

Seth thought of the wooden angel Gabe had given him, the angel he'd thrown away. A pang of guilt struck.

"Not anymore."

Singing Bird frowned. Then seeing Bridget and the other children gathered near Sandy Creek, she let go of Seth's hand and, lifting her calico skirt away from her feet, sprinted toward them.

"I thought Christmas would get here before you two did." Fun sparkled in Bridget's green eyes. She glanced at a little red pine growing along the creek bank. "We've decided that this one is just perfect."

Seth had Bridget keep the children a safe distance away and commenced to fell the evergreen. A few sharp blows severed the little tree from its stump, and Seth enlisted the help of the largest boy—the one Bridget had called Yellow Feather—to help carry the tree back to the house.

Suddenly a scream pierced the winter afternoon, followed by a loud splash.

CHAPTER 10

Bridget gazed incredulously at the girl flailing in the swollen stream. "Singing Bird!" The child's name tore from her throat on a shriek. She instructed the other children who'd gathered near the bank—some hollering and some crying—to remain calm and stay back. She didn't need any more children in the flooded creek.

Though Bridget had never learned to swim and the swift, muddy water looked daunting, the sight of Singing Bird's tenuous grasp on a protruding dead tree limb eclipsed Bridget's fears for her own safety. She turned to start down the bank, but Seth grasped her arm, stopping her.

"Stay here. I'll get her. You get in that creek, and I'll just have to drag you both out." He pulled off his boots and stockings, as well as his wool shirt, and pitched them onto the bank. A chilly wind gusted, raising gooseflesh on his pale back.

"Be careful." Bridget's anxiety mounted as his bare feet slipped down the muddy bank and into the rushing water. Now two people she cared about were in peril.

He glanced back at her over his shoulder. "No different than pullin' a calf out of a creek, and I've done that a hundred times." The alarm in his eyes belied the false indifference of his tone.

Singing Bird's frightened whimpers squeezed Bridget's heart.

"Hang on, Singing Bird. I'm coming. Just hang on tight." Seth's calm, soothing voice—the same voice he'd used with his horse during the stampede—quieted the girl's heart-wringing pleas. Seth glanced over his shoulder at Bridget. "There's a rope in my wagon. Send the boy. He'll run faster."

Keeping her gaze fixed on Seth and Singing Bird, Bridget sent Yellow Feather for the rope and two other children to the house for blankets.

The brackish water swirled around Seth and Singing Bird as he inched closer to the panicked child. Twice, the girl's head dipped beneath the rushing stream.

Bridget gasped and sent up a desperate prayer. She couldn't imagine how the slight girl, whose fingers must be numb with cold, managed to retain her grip on the slippery branch.

Dear Lord, keep them both safe. And please, hurry Yellow Feather with the rope!

An instant after the prayer formed in her mind, she heard the tall grass whisper behind her. Yellow Feather handed her the coil of rope, and she moved as close to the rushing stream as she dared.

To Bridget's chagrin, Seth moved farther downstream instead of heading directly to Singing Bird. Suddenly the racing water tore the girl's fingers from the tree limb and sucked her beneath its unforgiving torrent.

Bridget gasped, then groaned in dismay. If he'd gone right to Singing Bird, he might have saved her.

The next moment, Singing Bird's head bobbed up. Seth reached out and snatched her from the water as the swift-flowing stream carried her past him. Now his actions became clear to Bridget.

The chilly wind stung Bridget's cheeks, turning her penitent tears to cold rivulets. *Forgive my uncharitable thoughts, Lord.*

Bridget tossed the rope to Seth. With one arm, he clutched Singing Bird to his chest, and with the other, he grabbed the rope.

Bridget ordered the children to line up behind her. Together they pulled on the rope while walking backward, towing Seth and Singing Bird through the rushing water and up the slippery gray brown mud of the creek bank.

Once on solid land, Seth kept walking while Bridget struggled to wrap him and the half-drowned girl in one of the wool blankets.

Seth glanced down at the drenched girl shivering in his arms and his stride quickened. "We've got to get her in the house and out of these wet clothes as soon as possible."

Back at the house, Ming Li took over. With a series of staccato orders in broken English, she sent the children to their specific tasks. Leaving a kettle whistling shrilly on the stove, she wrapped the blanket closer around Singing Bird. Then, spewing a string of Mandarin, she whisked the child away toward the girls' bedrooms.

"You should change, too." Bridget looked at the water dripping from Seth's soggy pants onto the kitchen floor.

"Reckon it'll have to wait." He cleared his throat as a ruddy hue crept over his face. Turning his back to Bridget, he hurriedly shrugged on his wool shirt that one of the children had retrieved from the creek bank.

"No, it won't." Bridget used her sternest teacher's voice. "Travel three miles with wet pants in forty-degree weather? You'll catch your death!" A grin pulled up the corner of his mouth, and her heart constricted. *Why does he have to be so handsome?*

"Don't see as I've got a choice." He picked up his boots and socks someone had set near the kitchen door.

"Yes, you do." Bridget straightened her back and struggled to maintain a no-nonsense tone. "Van Taylor was about your size. His clothes are still in their bedroom upstairs."

Frowning, Seth fidgeted. "It don't seem right somehow. I—I don't know as I ought to. . . ."

"Nonsense. Van was a very caring person, full of Christian charity. He would want you to." Bridget fought back the tears threatening to fill her eyes. *Lord, he is such a good, decent man, and I love him so much! Please, in Jesus' name, touch his heart and turn him back to You.*

She watched him start up the stairs, his bare feet padding on the worn treads.

"Seth." Swallowing down a hard knot of tears, she managed a small smile. "Van also would have thanked you for saving Singing Bird, and so do I."

Pausing on the staircase, Seth answered with a sweet smile that ripped at Bridget's heart.

"First door to the left," she murmured before tears drove her to the kitchen.

Bridget pressed her hand hard against her mouth to muffle a sob. Clutching the washstand, she shook in silent agony as the tears that would not be denied flooded down her face.

CHAPTER 11

Bridget bent over Singing Bird's bed and pressed the back of her hand against the child's hot forehead. At first, the girl had displayed no ill effects from her dunking. But now, two days after the accident, she woke with a sore throat and fever.

"Singing Bird must drink this." With her quick, shuffling steps, Ming Li scooted to the bedside with another cup of aromatic tea.

Frustration rose inside Bridget. Singing Bird needed *real* medicine. Not useless teas made from dried flowers, leaves, and herbs. The vision of an old woman from her tenement placing onions cut in half beneath her parents' sickbed floated before Bridget's eyes.

"Drink, drink." Ming Li slipped her arm behind Singing Bird's back, helping her to sit up. She pressed the rim of the cup against the girl's lips, plying her with the pungent liquid.

A fit of coughing shook Singing Bird's little body until she gasped for breath. Bridget could bear it no longer. Springing up from the chair, she started for the bedroom door. "I'm going to get her some *real* medicine." Pinewood had no doctor, but the general store should have some kind of fever tonic—if the store was open on Christmas Eve, and if the storekeeper agreed to put the medicine on the Bartons' tab.

Ming Li scowled. "This real medicine. This medicine fix!"

Ignoring Ming Li's objections, Bridget headed out of the room. With Singing Bird's life in peril, she couldn't worry about insulting the housemother.

Outside, she squinted at the sun, a yellow smudge hanging low in the pewter sky. It was already late afternoon. *Please, Lord, I need a Christmas miracle.*

Less than a quarter of an hour later, Bridget pulled on the reins, bringing Rosie to a stop in front of the general store. She'd managed to get the bridle on the horse but had decided against trying to lift the heavy saddle. Instead she'd simply thrown the saddle blanket over Rosie's back, climbed to the stall gate, and mounted the placid mare.

As she slid from the horse's back, Bridget sent up a prayer of thanks for her staid, dependable steed, then looked up and down the street, discouraged. She saw no one. Only a couple of other horses stood tethered to hitching posts along Main Street.

Half expecting to find the door to the general store locked, she was surprised when it opened with a jingle. She tentatively stepped a foot inside the dark, dusty store. She hadn't been in the place since her first day in Pinewood with Seth. The scents of leather, wood smoke, and tobacco dominated the dim space.

"Sorry, I'm jist fixin' to lock up." A young man emerged from the back room carrying a broom. Seeing her, he swiped at the lock of greasy brown hair dangling across his left eye.

Bridget made her way toward the counter, maneuvering between the potbellied stove and the pickle barrel. "I need medicine—fever powder. Please, I won't be long." She scanned the shelves behind the boy's head. Her heart lifted. There between the bootblack and a bottle of horse liniment sat several brown paper packets marked DR. JAMES'S FEVER POWDER.

The young man hesitated, scratching at his head with grimy

fingernails. "I don't know, my uncle Hiram done tallied up for the day. I'm jist supposed to sweep up and lock up."

Tears of frustration stung Bridget's eyes. "Please, someone is very ill. Can't you just add it on?"

The boy's eyes narrowed. "Hey, ain't you that schoolmarm from the Circle B?"

"Yes." Bridget had no interest in engaging the boy in conversation.

"Somebody sick at the ranch?"

"No, the orphanage."

"You mean them Injun brats at the old McCallum place?"

Bridget dug her fingers into the folds of her wool skirt and fought to keep her voice steady as anger rippled through her. Picking a fight with this ignorant boy would not get Singing Bird her medicine. "Yes. One of the children there is sick. Very sick."

He resumed swiping the broom across the floor, his voice hardening. "Like I said, we're done doin' business for the day."

"Please, have you no charity? It's Christmas!" Bridget hated the tears streaming down her face. She hated, too, having to beg this stupid boy for something no more than four feet in front of her.

He had the grace to look ashamed before he plucked a packet of the medicine from the shelf and plopped it on the counter. "That'll be one dollar."

Bridget expelled a relieved sigh and reached for the packet. "Just put it on the Bartons' tab."

"Can't do that." He snatched the packet away. "Uncle Hiram said I could only do that for the Bartons or Seth Krueger."

Fury pulsed through Bridget. She wanted to go behind the counter, rip the life-saving medicine from his grimy fingers, and run. Her hand went to her throat and she gripped her mother's cross necklace. Suddenly she could hear her mother's voice in her head, whispering God's will.

"You don't carry your faith in the Lord around your neck, Bridget. You carry it in your heart. Let the necklace go and save the child."

Somehow her trembling fingers managed to unhook the clasp, and she held the necklace out toward him. "Here, this is worth more than a dollar."

His eyes widened. "Reckon it is."

Grasping the packet of fever powder, Bridget fled the store. She stuffed the precious medicine into the pocket of her skirt and tried to push from her mind the vision of the boy's dirty fist closing around her mother's necklace.

Outside the store, she mounted Rosie from the top of a horse trough and kicked the mare into a gallop. The blood red sun rode low on the horizon. Bridget's wool shawl did little to fend off the icy wind. She pressed her face closer to Rosie's mane for warmth.

Suddenly she felt a jerk on the reins, and Rosie stopped so abruptly Bridget almost tumbled off.

"If it ain't Miss Bridget O'Keefe. We're finally gonna get to have that little talk." The sound of Jake Tuley's voice sent terror shooting through Bridget.

He brought his horse close. The stink of whiskey stung her nostrils. "You'll be a right purdy Chris'mas present to unwrap."

"Please, Mr. Tuley, I have to get— Ahh!"

He snatched her from Rosie's back and threw her to the damp grass.

Dear Lord, help me! Please help me!

Sobbing, Bridget pounded her fists against him. She kicked at his shins to no avail. He responded with bawdy laughter. Despair washed over her. She gagged and fought nausea, pushing with all her might against the suffocating weight and stench of his body.

Suddenly the offensive weight lifted off her. Bridget sat up, gratefully inhaling gulps of air as a miracle unfolded before her in the lengthening shadows.

The crack of Seth's fist against Jake's jaw reverberated in the heavy evening air.

"Seth." She breathed his name like a benediction.

Seth jerked Jake Tuley to his feet. "Now, get your filthy hide outta here!" He gave the man a hard shove toward his horse as Jake rubbed his assaulted jaw. "If I ever catch you on Barton land again or near Miss O'Keefe, I'll beat you within an inch of your sorry life!"

Bridget sat trembling as the hoofbeats of Tuley's horse faded in the distance.

Seth helped her to her feet and held her shaking body. "Shh, it's all right now, my love. Thou art safe."

Wrapped in the sweet sanctuary of Seth's arms, Bridget wept against his chest.

At length, he gently pushed away and looked into her face. "Did—did he hurt you?"

She shook her head. "No, I'm just a little bruised, that's all."

"What are you doin' out here, anyway?"

Bridget told him of Singing Bird's illness and her desperate ride to the store. She reached into her pocket for the fever powder but found it empty. "It's gone!"

"What's gone?"

"The fever powder. Singing Bird's medicine!" Frantic, Bridget beat at the tall grass with her hands, her eyes straining in the advancing darkness.

Seth gripped her shoulder. "You'll never find it in the dark. Shoot, even in the daylight you could look through this grass for days and never find it."

Bridget shrugged off his hand while tears flooded her eyes, further hampering her search. "I *have* to find it! God will help me find it!" She dropped to her knees, groping through the dewy grass. "Lord, *please* help me find it."

"Come away now." Though she batted at his hands, he gently gripped her shoulders, pulling her to her feet.

Exhausted, Bridget finally surrendered to Seth's warm embrace.

He retrieved her wool shawl from the grass and wrapped it around her shoulders. "Let's go back. Maybe the girl is better." He helped her onto his horse, tied Rosie's reins to his horse's bridle, and mounted behind Bridget.

Drained of strength, Bridget lay limp against Seth's strong chest. As they rode toward the purple, rose, and gold sunset smeared across the western sky, she prayed that Ming Li's teas had finally worked to reduce Singing Bird's fever.

But when they reached Singing Bird's bedside, they found she hadn't improved.

Singing Bird rolled her head on the pillow and faced Bridget, her eyes bright with fever. "Teacher. I dreamed you went away and didn't come back."

Bridget bent over Singing Bird and brushed a lock of hair from her searing face. "I'll stay right here beside you, Liebes Mädchen, I promise."

"What did you call her?"

Bridget turned at the odd tone in Seth's voice.

He stood in the doorway, his chambray blue eyes large in his ashen face.

"Liebes Mädchen," Bridget repeated, wondering at his strange demeanor. "It's the name she said her aunt had called her. I suppose it's Comanche—"

"No, it's German." Seth's voice sounded tight. "It means 'dear girl.' It's what my mother used to call my sister."

He stepped near the bed. "Singing Bird, was your aunt a white woman?"

Singing Bird nodded, and Seth's Adam's apple bobbed.

"What was her name?" He clenched his fists around his hat, crushing it.

"Elisabeth Sky-Eyes," Singing Bird said in a raspy voice.

Seth's eyes glistened in the lantern light.

Bridget touched his arm. "Your sister?"

He nodded. "Must have been."

Ming Li bustled into the midst of the quiet revelation, carrying a large cup of pungent tea. "Singing Bird need more tea. Tea fix."

Seth plopped his hat on his head. "I'm going to the general store for more medicine."

Bridget stood at his surprising declaration. "But they're closed now, and it's Christmas Eve."

"Hiram will open for me." He bent and kissed Singing Bird's forehead, then turned and brushed a quick kiss across Bridget's lips and disappeared through the bedroom door.

—ʍ—

Bridget jerked awake at the sound of quick boot steps echoing through the house, unsure how long she'd slept. The next moment, Seth appeared in the doorway, carrying a drawstring canvas bag.

"How is she?" Worry lines etched his forehead.

Bridget bent forward and touched Singing Bird's face. Her fingertips met cool skin and relief washed through her. "Her fever has broken. She's out of danger, praise God."

Seth blew out a long breath and set the bag down beside Bridget's chair.

Singing Bird stirred and opened her eyes. "Mr. Krueger. You are back."

Seth knelt beside the bed and drew the backs of his curled fingers across the girl's cheek. "Yes, Liebes Mädchen, I'm back. And thee must call me Uncle Seth, because I'm your aunt's brother. Are you feeling better?"

Singing Bird swallowed and touched her throat. "My throat doesn't hurt so much now."

Seth reached for the canvas bag. "I'm glad, because I brought you a present." He opened the bag and pulled out a red-and-white-striped candy stick. "This was your aunt's favorite Christmas treat when she was a girl." He grinned at Singing Bird and Bridget. "And I bought enough for the other children, too."

Singing Bird's eyes grew big and bright. Bridget's misted as she sent up a grateful prayer, marveling at the change in Seth's heart.

Singing Bird's expression turned serious. "I have a present for you, too, Mr. . . .Uncle Seth." She drew her hand from beneath the covers and held out a little wooden doll to Seth. It had wings and a carved robe that hung in folds. Beneath its smiling face was an impression of little hands steepled in prayer. "You said you didn't have an angel, so you can have this one I found."

For a long moment, Seth remained still, as if paralyzed. He finally took the doll and cleared his throat. "Thank you, Liebes Mädchen." His voice snagged on the endearment. "But I think I was wrong. I think God has given me two angels." He turned a tender look toward Bridget, and she swallowed down a sob.

Seth rose and slipped the angel doll into his pocket, then bent and kissed Singing Bird's forehead. "Thank you for the angel, little one. Now you must rest and get better. Tomorrow is Christmas, and Mr. and Mrs. Barton are coming to visit." He shot a quick grin over his shoulder to Bridget. "And Santa Claus might come, too."

Bridget smiled, knowing Gabe Noell had agreed to don the red wool Santa suit stitched by the Women's Missionary Union. She tucked the quilt under Singing Bird's chin, turned down the lamp, and followed Seth out of the room.

He slipped his arm around her waist as they walked to the front door. "Step out on the porch with me for a while, would thee?"

Still trying to assimilate all that had transpired this evening, she nodded mutely and fetched her shawl from the peg by the door.

The still, cold night met them outside where a full moon bathed the porch in a soft, pale glow. Bridget hugged the shawl around her while Seth leaned a shoulder against a porch post and looked up at the multitude of stars blinking down at them. "You know," he said at length, "my mother used to say if you're really quiet on Christmas Eve, you can hear the angels sing." He turned and drew Bridget to his side. "Because of you, I can hear them again."

"You're not angry at God anymore?"

"No." He reached in his pocket and pulled out the angel doll.

Bridget shook her head. "It's lovely. I wonder where she found it."

"Under the oak tree at the corner of the house, where I threw it."

Stunned, Bridget gaped at him. "But where did you get—"

"It was given to me by a very wise man, who told me to never wrestle with God when He wants to give me a blessing. So I won't." He knelt and took Bridget's hands in his. "I love thee, Bridget O'Keefe," he said, lifting pleading eyes to hers. "Will thee be my wife?"

A flood of joy cascaded down Bridget's cheeks. "Yes." Sobbing, she repeated her answer until he stood and silenced her with his kisses.

"I do have one request," he said at length. "I'd like us to adopt Singing Bird."

Bridget's happiness bubbled out in a giggle. "I'd like that, too."

"I almost forgot." He reached in his shirt pocket and pulled out something shiny. "I bought this back from Hiram."

Bridget gasped. "My necklace! Oh, Seth, thank you." She took the gold chain with trembling fingers and hugged her future husband's neck.

Her heart full to bursting, Bridget clung to her beloved,

thanking God for blessings more numerous than stars in the Texas sky, not the least of which was an old wood-carver and his sawdust sermons. She had no doubt that God had used Gabe Noell to bring about this moment. Bridget was sure that for many years to come, Gabe's little wooden angel would remind both Seth and her of God's love and grace. Together, every Christmas Eve, they'd think of the old wood-carver while they listened for the angels' song.

Ramona K. Cecil is a wife, mother, grandmother, freelance poet, and award-winning inspirational romance writer. Now empty nesters, she and her husband make their home in Indiana. A member of American Christian Fiction Writers and American Christian Fiction Writers Indiana Chapter, her work has won awards in a number of inspirational writing contests. Over eighty of her inspirational verses have been published on a wide array of items for the Christian gift market. She enjoys a speaking ministry, sharing her journey to publication while encouraging aspiring writers. When not writing, her hobbies include reading, gardening, and visiting places of historical interest.

The Face of Mary

by Darlene Franklin

DEDICATION

Seven months ago I moved to a new city and began the difficult process of starting over again. I dedicate *The Face of Mary* to the members of Draper Park Christian Church, who have been the hands and feet of our Lord to me in my hour of need.

PROLOGUE

Breading, Texas, 1880

Polly Jessup eyed the present she had wrapped for Jean Carpenter. Her friend fingered the pink ribbon, looking at Polly with a question in her eyes, but didn't say anything.

Yes, it's my hair ribbon. But I wanted something prettier than string. Polly reached up and patted her hair, dressed without adornment. Not that it ever looked nice these days without Mama to help her fix it.

Jean untied the bow and set it to one side before unwrapping the present. When she saw the plain cardboard cover, she wrinkled her nose until she opened the book. "Why, you've copied all the verses we learned in Sunday school this year." She turned a few pages. "And all of Psalm 119, with illustrations." Her fingers traced the letters, and she oohed and aahed over the minuscule drawings Polly had added.

"So you like it?"

"I love it!" Jean read the first verse softly. " 'For God so loved the world. . . .' "

"You said you wanted to win the new Bible they're offering for a prize at the scripture memory contest, and anybody who can quote all of Psalm 119 is sure to win."

"Only because you've decided not to enter." Jean flung her

arms around Polly and hugged her. "You know so much more of the Bible than I do." Jean started to slip the ribbon into the book but stopped. "You should keep this."

Polly's pride wanted to refuse, but she loved that ribbon. It evoked so many memories of her mother dressing her up. "Thanks." To cover her embarrassment, she hurried on. "After I won the adult contest last year, it didn't seem fair to keep competing. I'm practicing with Dolores, hoping she'll place. You and Abe Mott can battle it out for first prize." Polly grinned when Jean turned red at the mention of the young man's name.

"Did I hear something about Abe Mott?" a deep voice boomed behind them.

Polly jumped in her seat. When had Jean's brother, Joey, come into the room? Heat rushed into her cheeks, and she was sure her face turned the same dark shade as her friend's.

Joey took the book from Jean and opened it at random. " 'Let thy mercies come also unto me, O Lord, even thy salvation, according to thy word.' Psalm 119. You even copied the letter *Vau*. I couldn't have done it better myself."

Polly squirmed. Joey had the best penmanship in the school. Everybody knew that, and he could draw anything he wanted.

He smiled at the Liberty Bell she had painted in the margins, tracing the crack with his long index finger. " 'And I will walk at liberty: for I seek thy precepts.' I wrote an essay about that verse once."

"I remember." Jean giggled. "Isn't it beautiful? Polly wants me to memorize the whole psalm for the Bible verse competition this year."

"Now that she's retired from the memory contest, she wants you to win, huh?" Joey handed the book back to Jean and focused his brilliant blue eyes on Polly. "You've always amazed me with your love for God's Word. Any girl who loves the law of the Lord like the psalmist did is a woman after my lawyer's heart. If you don't have a beau when I come home from college, I think

I'll marry you myself." He smiled at the girls and left the room.

Speechless, Polly stared after him. Did Jean's handsome brother just say he might marry her someday?

His words engraved themselves on her heart.

CHAPTER 1

November 1884

Polly dallied longer than usual in the bedroom she shared with her two younger sisters. She wanted to look her best today. Not only was Jean Carpenter celebrating her engagement to Abraham Mott, but Jean's brother Joey had returned home after four years away.

Polly pulled her dark hair away from her face, but it continued to fall into a center part. Should she wear it up? No, at seventeen she was too young to dress her locks in the style of an old married matron, even if she did feel that way some days. Taking care of four younger brothers and sisters did that to a girl. She teased her fringe across her forehead, hoping it might curl.

Joey Carpenter. *"I think I'll marry you myself."* Her heart beat faster at the memory. How many times had she repeated his words when she learned a new verse from the Bible or studied something new? Even though she had retired from competition, she continued to hide God's Word in her heart. She hungered for it almost as much as she hungered for food, and prayed to walk according to God's law.

Did Joey even remember what he had said to her all those years ago? Would he mention it when he saw her today? She blushed. He had probably forgotten long ago.

"Hurry, Polly." Little Hazel dashed into the room. "Dolores is burning the beans."

Polly swallowed a sigh. Sometimes she wondered if the family would starve if she wasn't there to cook for them. Even when Dolores followed a recipe, things didn't turn out the same. Jean said cooking was a gift, like singing or painting. But Polly didn't think so. Mama hadn't had time to teach the younger girls before she died, that was all.

Polly doubted her cooking ability would impress Joey, however. After all, he'd become a lawyer. He probably hadn't spared her a thought in four years, let alone whether or not she could cook.

But oh, how she hoped he had.

Joseph Carpenter considered the top hat on the shelf of his closet and decided against it. Such finery might have been *de rigueur* among his set in law school, but his Breading friends would laugh him out of town. He fingered the narrow brim, imagining Alice Johnson's reaction to his big-city fashions. She might appreciate it—another reason why he enjoyed her company. With her style and class, she had a sense of life outside the small-town where he had grown up. Her father, owner of the town's only bank and its richest citizen, had made sure of that. A connection with Breading's leading family wouldn't hurt a man starting out his career.

But he wouldn't worry about that now, although he hoped Alice would enjoy the party. Today was about meeting old friends and celebrating Jean's happiness. As long as their parents focused on marrying off his sister, they wouldn't bother him about finding a suitable wife.

A knock sounded at his door.

"Who is it?" he called.

"Me." Jean opened the door with the word. "Are you ready yet? People are more eager to see you than me."

"I doubt that." He looked his sister up and down. She was dressed in a sage-colored dress with beige lace at the throat. When had she grown up? Of course he had seen her only twice in the past four years: once when the family gathered for his grandfather's funeral, and the second time when he graduated from school this past spring. He had spent the last few months closing his grandfather's affairs and making the difficult decision to return to Breading. "It's your special day." He smiled at her. With her upswept hair, she looked like a fine young lady, not the little sister he used to tease mercilessly. "I'm just the backdrop to your happiness."

"You know the people of Breading. They love an excuse to party. My engagement to Abraham isn't really news. People have been predicting this day since he broke my chalk on purpose back when we were in first grade."

"Including me, I know. But it doesn't matter. They won't see anyone else once you walk into the room." She radiated joy. Abe Mott was a lucky man. How had his sister found the man of her dreams at such a young age while the woman God had chosen for Joseph continued to elude him? His thoughts drifted to Alice Johnson again, and he wondered if she might be the one.

"We're praying our love will be as eternal as the Word of God. 'For ever, O Lord, thy word is settled in heaven.'" Grinning, Jean opened a well-worn book that looked vaguely familiar to a page where the text appeared beneath an artist's rendition of an evening sky. "I've used this little book so much that Mama says I should carry it down the aisle instead of the Bible I won."

The sight of the book triggered a memory in Joseph's brain. A dark-haired girl with bright brown eyes, smart as a whip, who could out-quote anybody when it came to scripture. "Polly Jessup gave that to you." He snapped his fingers. "For your thirteenth birthday."

"And then she helped me memorize every verse. She's the reason I won that year." The grin left Jean's face. "Polly hasn't had an easy time of it since her mother died. Promise me you'll say hello to her today."

"Of course. I'm looking forward to seeing all my old friends."

Jean's mouth opened but she didn't speak right away. "Good. Come down as soon as you're ready." She hugged him and disappeared out the door.

What was Jean about to say? Joseph mused. Give him time, he'd figure it out. After all, he *was* a lawyer.

He headed down the stairs.

"Polly Jessup."

Polly repressed a shudder. Of course Alice Johnson had come; everyone in Breading was invited. But her derisive tone made Polly's name sound like she was a misbehaving schoolgirl sent to the corner, even though Polly had excelled at her lessons while Alice had struggled. At the teacher's request, Polly had tutored the banker's daughter so she could pass English. The effort hadn't earned her so much as a thank you.

Polly reminded herself to be pleasant to Alice. After all, the Bible said she showed her love for God by how she loved others. Forcing a smile on her face, she turned around. As she expected, Alice was dressed in a style straight from the latest issue of *Godey's* magazine. The ecru silk and lace that adorned her claret-colored dress and outlined the bodice was not only expensive, it wasn't available locally. She might have had her father order the material all the way from New York.

"Look who's just arrived." Alice spoke to someone behind her.

Eyes as piercing blue as a summer sky, hair the color of hay in the fall. . .all six feet of him. Joey. *Her* Joey. With Alice.

"Joseph, you were asking after the Jessup girls earlier." Alice batted her eyelashes at Joey as boldly as any flirt. "As you can see, they're here." She twined a gloved hand around Joey's arm.

"Polly." Joey eased away from Alice and grasped Polly's hand. "Let me look at you." He looked her up and down, as if committing every detail to memory in case he needed to testify about her in court, and a slow smile spread across his face. "You and Jean grew up while I was gone. Come this way. I know my sister is eager to see you."

He offered Polly his free arm and walked with the two women to the corner of the room where Jean held court. At the sight of Polly, she stood. "Oh, good, you're here. Now we can get started. Mama? Papa?" She nodded at her parents.

Jacob Carpenter, an older, craggier version of Joey, clapped his hands for everyone's attention and motioned for quiet. "Mrs. Carpenter and I have invited you here today to celebrate with us. It gives us great pleasure to announce the engagement of our dear daughter, Jean Louise, to Abraham Mott. They're planning a spring wedding. Mrs. Carpenter insists they cannot do it any sooner."

Applause sprinkled with chuckles greeted the announcement. While Abe's father expressed his delight at the upcoming nuptials, Polly looked around for her father. Noise sometimes bothered him. She scanned the crowd and saw him in the corner. Her little sister was tugging at his arm and pointing at the table, where a specially decorated cake waited.

Maybe Hazel didn't realize she should wait for a piece of the cake. Polly decided she'd better check it out and excused herself from the people around her. Before she reached them, Pa nodded and headed for the table. A sinking feeling formed in Polly's chest, and she pushed through the edge of the crowd.

Mr. Mott was finishing his speech. ". . . you may all enjoy the cake that Mrs. Carpenter has made for the splendid occasion."

Every head turned in time to see Pa placing a corner piece with plenty of icing on a china plate and handing it to Hazel.

A high, piercing laugh floated across the crowd. *Alice.*

A look of panic replaced the pleasure on Pa's face, and he dropped the plate, the china shattering into dozens of pieces.

CHAPTER 2

One glance at her father's face erased any anger Polly felt. He reminded her of a cat that was unsure why people didn't appreciate the mouse he dragged into the house.

"Let's go find a seat, Pa." She led him toward the kitchen where he could escape the stares. Jean and her mother followed a few steps behind, and Polly scanned the room for the broom closet. As many times as she had visited in their home, she should know where to find it. At last she spied it and grabbed the broom and dustpan.

"Don't you worry with that." Mrs. Carpenter took them out of her hands. "You take care of your father. Are you all right, Mr. Jessup?" She spoke as she might to someone who was hard of hearing—slowly and loudly.

"I'll be fine if people stop screaming." His gaze took in the room and settled on Mrs. Carpenter. "Who are you? You're not my Mary."

A puzzled look crossed her face, and she took a step back. "No, I'm your neighbor. Rose Carpenter."

Pa blinked. "You're not Mrs. Carpenter. She is." He pointed at Jean.

Please, heavenly Father, not now. Polly had never seen Pa this confused. He clutched his coat close about him and crossed his arms, staring at the floor. "I'm so sorry." At least the kitchen afforded them some privacy, preventing the other guests from seeing him disintegrate before their eyes. She'd known the Carpenters all her life; they were good, decent people.

"How can we help?" Mrs. Carpenter asked, but her gaze shifted to the door.

"I think he just needs peace and quiet. I'll take him home." Polly swallowed her disappointment.

Jean hugged her. "We'll talk later. I'll tell you all about it."

"No need for the rest of your family to leave." Mrs. Carpenter went to the door. "We'll make sure they get home safely."

Polly nodded. "Come on, Pa. Let's go home."

He accepted her arm. "Whatever you say, Mary."

Mary might be her real name, but Polly knew that's not what Pa meant. He thought he was talking to her mother.

What next?

—∞—

Joseph stared at his mother and sister as they scurried through the door after Polly and her father. He took a half step in their direction before realizing someone had to attend to the rest of the guests. If he could divert people's attention from whatever happened, he would be doing everyone a favor—perhaps Polly most of all. The fathers of the newly affianced couple talked together, and Abe looked lost without Jean by his side. Joseph decided to take charge.

"Please, everyone, help yourselves to a glass of lemonade while we prepare to serve the cake."

Mrs. Mott took her position behind the table with the bowl of lemonade while Joseph headed in the other direction. Chocolate icing stained the carpet like muddy boots after a rainstorm. He grabbed a napkin to pick up the cake crumbs.

"Do you have to do that?" Alice's soft voice tickled his ear. "You'll get the legs of your trousers dirty."

At the touch of her hand, his knee dropped to the floor. As

she predicted, chocolate frosting smashed into his dark twill trousers. He brushed at it with the napkin, dropping all the pieces he had managed to pick up in the process.

"Joseph," Alice squeaked and searched around the table for more napkins.

For a fleeting moment, he wondered why Alice wasn't helping clean the floor. Then he reminded himself that she was his guest, not a family member.

Frustrated by his lack of progress, Joseph headed for the kitchen and met Jean at the door, broom in hand. She saw the guests clustered around the punch table and sighed in relief. "Thanks, brother." Within a couple of minutes, she had swept the mess away and cut the remaining cake into pieces.

Joseph took two pieces and joined Alice by the window.

"Poor Polly. Mr. Jessup works at the bank, you know, but after today, I don't see how Father can trust him not to make mistakes." Alice nibbled at the cake like a rabbit, one tiny bite at a time.

Something about Alice's comment set Joseph's teeth on edge. She had no right to make fun of Polly or her family. "Mr. Jessup is one of the finest men I've ever met. He taught me most of what I know about the Bible."

Alice leveled an indulgent look at him that bade him stay quiet. "You haven't seen him for a long time. He changed after his wife died. Everyone says so."

Joseph was considering the implications of Alice's assertion when a stranger, an older man with salt-and-pepper hair, approached and extended a hand to Joseph. "I was hoping to make your acquaintance today, Mr. Carpenter."

"You have the advantage of me, sir." The men shook hands. "I don't believe we've met."

"Gabe Noell, at your service. The fine folks at Breading Community Church have invited me to carve a life-size nativity scene as part of this year's Christmas celebration. But I've been wanting to meet you to talk over some business. Can we get together on Monday morning?"

Did Mr. Noell represent Joseph's first client in Breading? "I'd love to, but where shall we meet? I confess I don't have an office yet."

The bearded man waved away Joseph's concern. "We can meet at the church if that's all right with you."

Something in the man's gray eyes captured Joseph's attention. "At eleven?"

"Eleven it is." The hand that grasped Joseph's was strong, calloused, the hands of a workman.

"He comes well recommended as a wood-carver," Alice told him. "I wonder why he wants to see you."

Joseph made a noncommittal sound. If the man wanted to discuss business with a lawyer, Joseph wouldn't reveal it to anyone.

"Joseph." Jean approached them next. "You must come. People are anxious to speak with you."

If not Gabe Noell, another person would be Joseph's first client—and that person probably stood in this very room. It was time to celebrate Jean's engagement and reacquaint himself with his friends and neighbors.

Polly packed hay around the gravy boat, turkey platter, and cake plate. She loved sharing Mama's Flow Blue china of royal blue patterns swirling against a white background, but at the same time feared something irreplaceable would break. Irreplaceable in terms of both monetary and sentimental value.

Today the Breading Community Church would celebrate the first Sunday of Advent, as well as the Sunday after Thanksgiving. People brought whatever leftovers remained from their individual family feasts and enjoyed fellowship together. Polly looked forward first to hearing the pastor's sermon. Every year he preached a special series related to the

Christmas season, something that always added to her anticipation of the holiday.

Better to wonder about the pastor's sermon than when she might see Joey again. After the embarrassment at last week's engagement party, she wouldn't blame him if he avoided her. Who would be interested in a young woman who came saddled with a ready-made family and a father given to unpredictable behavior?

Because they were bringing Mama's china, Polly sat in the back of the wagon. She kept the box containing leftover pie, turkey soup, and the Flow Blue as steady as possible. Dolores took Polly's usual place next to Pa on the front seat, while Hazel nestled next to her on the wagon bed. Her twin brothers rode with their legs dangling over the back.

Getting to church was much easier since Pa had sold the farm and moved into town to work at the bank. Polly hoped to arrive early and get Pa settled in, but the Carpenters' surrey already stood beside the building. Joey caught sight of Polly as he assisted Jean from the carriage and waved a greeting. The moment Jean had both feet safely on the ground, he headed in their direction.

"Good morning, Mr. Jessup, Dolores." Joey shook Pa's hand and glanced at the back of the wagon. "Polly."

Polly's heart melted. Joey greeted them as if nothing had gone wrong at his sister's party.

"Joey." Pa's face lit up with pleasure and recognition. "It's good to have you home again."

Joey helped Dolores from her seat, and she giggled. Polly waited for her brothers and Hazel to climb down before she scooted forward, her skirts scrunching beneath her, hampering her progress.

"May I help you with that?"

Amusement gleamed in Joey's blue eyes, and heat rushed to her cheeks. *I must look ridiculous.*

"It's my mother's china. I'm always careful whenever we bring it."

He bent over the side of the wagon and tugged at the box. "Is this it?"

"Yes."

"Let me take it out first so you can be sure it's safe. Then I'll help you down."

Before she could protest, he hefted the heavy box onto his shoulder and, whistling, carried it to the church hall where they would enjoy the fellowship meal. Mrs. Denton, the pastor's wife, met him at the door to let him in.

Why am I sitting here like a lady waiting on her escort? Now that her movements wouldn't jostle the china, she could move about more easily. About the time she reached the end of the wagon bed, Joey trotted back, a frown on his face.

"I asked you to wait for me." He put his hands around her waist and lifted her from the wagon as easily as if she were Hazel's size. His hands lingered on her waist for a moment after her feet touched the ground. "Don't you know I just want to help?" he asked in a low voice.

Unable to look in his face, Polly's eyes sought the ground. Heat poured through her from the inside out, causing her to shiver where the cool air struck her hot skin. Joey tucked her shawl about her shoulders.

"Joseph! There you are!"

At the sound of Alice's voice, Joseph stepped away from Polly. Enough heat to cook an egg rushed into her face.

—w—

"Please turn in your Bibles to the first chapter of Luke, verse forty-six," Pastor Denton addressed the congregation.

Beside Joseph, Alice took out her fine-tooled leather Bible and rustled through the pages. His eyes strayed across the row in front of them where Polly put her arm around her little sister's shoulders and helped her find the spot in her Bible.

"Please stand and listen as I read aloud."

By the time Joseph found the passage, the pastor had started reading. He could see Polly mouthing the words as if recalling them from memory. " 'And Mary said, My soul doth magnify the Lord, and my spirit hath rejoiced in God my Saviour.' " Polly didn't miss a bit until Pastor Denton concluded his reading of Mary's song.

"This year for Advent we will be considering the character of Mary, the woman God chose to give birth to His Son. We can learn a lot about the person God wants us to be by studying her life. First, we are going to look at her capacity to glorify the Lord. Look at the words she uses in the burst of praise she gave voice to when Elisabeth greeted her. She glorified the Lord, she rejoiced in God, she said He had done great things."

For the remainder of the sermon, Pastor Denton outlined many ways Mary lifted up the Lord. "Was Mary having a mountaintop experience when she arrived at Elisabeth's house? No. She had gone to her cousin's home because of the rumors flying around Nazareth about her pregnancy. But she still rejoiced in what God was doing in her and through her and for her, regardless of the difficulties it presented. Can we say the same?"

His words sobered Joseph, and he remained thoughtful after the service. God had led him to return to Breading, although he could have joined a profitable practice near his school. Whatever challenges he faced paled when compared to what Mary endured. He prayed he would praise God whatever the future brought, starting with his meeting with Gabe Noell in the morning.

On Monday morning, Joseph arrived at the church a few minutes before eleven and heard someone whistling. He followed the sound and found Gabe Noell working in a lean-to behind the building. Bundled in a jacket and overalls, the woodcarver was studying a chunk of pinewood in front of him.

"Mr. Noell?"

"Ah! Joseph! You found me. I was about to head inside."

"I followed the music." Joseph smiled. "But we'd probably be warmer inside."

"If it's all right with you, I'd like to stay out here. At least until I show you what I'm working on."

That surprised Joseph. Most artisans he knew preferred to work in private. But the carver laid out several good-sized pieces of pine. The trees grew in abundance near Breading and seemed the logical choice for the manger scene. Perhaps Gabe felt more comfortable telling Joseph his problems if he kept his hands busy.

"Let me tell you about my plans," Gabe said.

His plans? Did he need Joseph to draw up a will?

"The church wants a manger scene that can be displayed outside, to remind all the people of Breading of the reason for Christmas."

Joseph wondered when Gabe would get to the point, but he played along. "How many figures have they asked you to make? Joseph, Mary, and the baby Jesus? Or more as well?"

"Well, that depends partly on you."

What? Did he need Joseph to negotiate a contract for him? "I'm sorry, I don't understand."

"The church wants the figures painted as well as carved. But if I do that, it'll slow me down. Besides, I'm a wood-carver, not a painter. So you see, I thought another artist could help me design their faces." He handed Joseph a piece of paper with rough sketches of the three main figures. "Work together, you see. So. Are you interested?"

Joseph blinked. Had he missed something? "I'm sorry?"

"Are you willing to help me with the manger scene? I would pay you, of course. I understand you're quite an artist."

Joseph almost dropped the paper with the sketches and backed away from Noell. "I thought you wanted to consult me on a legal matter."

A smile creased Noell's face. "Ah. I'm sorry I didn't make

myself clear. Just like me—I let my carvings do my speaking for me. No, I'm seeking your help about a different matter. Please say yes."

Joseph studied the sketches Gabe had made. The faces were blank, ready for an artist's brush. He could picture them in his mind. The strong, faithful man. The sweetly slumbering infant. But Mary. . . His mind flew back to the pastor's sermon yesterday. Mary praised God. What else did he know about her? He couldn't picture her in his mind. "I usually paint from real-life models. I don't know. . ." *Am I actually considering the project?*

"You don't know who is worthy of representing the Lord's human family? I understand your dilemma." Gabe chuckled. "Ask God. He'll show you."

Joseph took Gabe to mean he should search for someone who looked like Mary inside and out. *I'm foolish to even consider it. I need to start my business.* But he heard himself say, "I'll give it a try."

Noell shook Joseph's hand. "So it's agreed. I'll meet with you again on Thursday."

—∾—

On Tuesday morning, Polly headed for church after the children went to school. Was it only last year that Miss Berry, the teacher, had encouraged her to attend normal school? Polly liked the thought of teaching, but Pa and the family needed her too much at home. Leaving to go elsewhere would only indulge her selfish desire to remain in the comfortable confines of the classroom. A part of her had held on to the hope that her Prince Charming, Joey, would sweep in and rescue her, but she knew that was no more than a childish dream.

At least I do get to teach, at Sunday school. At the age of fourteen, she had taken over the little ones at church at the same time Miss Berry had asked her to lead the youngest reading group at school. So when the pastor asked her to help plan the Christmas program, she accepted. This year she had written the script for the play. She clasped the pages of the manuscript in front of her, hoping the committee would be pleased with the result.

Sunday's meeting had been brief. In addition to Pastor and Mrs. Denton, Mr. Post attended to discuss the music they would use. The pastor mentioned that he was looking for another person to help with the rehearsals. He liked for most of the work to be done by church members, to "spread the blessing." Had he found a volunteer?

When she arrived at the church, she heard whistling and followed the sound around the corner to where Gabe Noell worked in his lean-to. Hoping not to disturb him, she watched him studying a block of wood almost as tall as he was, making marks here and there along the length of it. How could someone create things that looked alive out of tree limbs? She had seen samples of his work, forest creatures that looked as though they would jump off the tree branch where they sat. She couldn't wait to see the finished manger scene.

"How's he doing?"

At the sound of the familiar, deep voice, Polly stumbled back a step—and into Joey's broad chest. "I didn't know you were there." Breathy, her voice sounded accusatory.

He put out an arm to steady her. "I'm sorry. I didn't mean to startle you. Are you here for the meeting about the Christmas program?"

Her eyes opened wide. "I am. Are you the new committee member?" *Joey?*

"Don't act so surprised. I guess Pastor Denton figures putting on a play can't be much different than defending people in court." The corners of his eyes crinkled in amusement. "Come to think of it, he might be right."

Polly relaxed. This was the Joey she remembered, even if he was hidden underneath a breasted suit and vest. "Putting on a play is one thing, but what about the twenty children we have to corral to get it together? We need to start rehearsals right away. I'm worried we don't have enough time to get ready before the program."

"I wouldn't worry. People enjoy watching their children—even the mistakes. Maybe especially the mistakes."

Maybe parents did, but what about the children? "That's no excuse for poor preparation." How well she remembered the humiliation of stumbling through her one line in her first Christmas play five times before she gave up and ran, crying, to where her mother sat in the audience. She never forgot her lines again and, in fact, went on to excel in memorizing scripture. She hoped this year's program would spark the same passion in the youngsters who participated.

"Oh, Polly." He tucked her arm beneath his and headed for the door. "I can tell we're going to have fun."

Pastor Denton was arranging a small circle of chairs when they entered the sanctuary. His wife murmured a greeting.

"Here they are." The pastor smiled. "Joseph, I believe you know Mr. Post."

"Very pleased, I'm sure." Mr. Post extended his hand.

"How is your mother faring these days?" Joey asked.

That was Joey all over again, a born politician. Polly would remind herself as often as necessary that he made everyone feel special. Anyone who kept company with Alice Johnson couldn't possibly be interested in someone like her.

Polly became aware that the group had turned quiet.

Pastor Denton cleared his throat. "Miss Jessup, we're all interested in hearing your ideas for the program."

She shuffled the pages in her lap and took a deep breath. "My idea is to let Mary tell the story." She handed out different copies to everyone. "I've used Mary's actual words where they're recorded in the Bible."

"That will tie in nicely with my sermons." The pastor thumbed through his script quickly. "I see that you're covering everything I intend to preach about this month. I like it. A lot."

Joey's face wrinkled as he read and reread the first page. "This is a lot for one person to memorize. Do you have someone in mind?" He smiled, as if to take the sting out of his words. "We're not all as gifted as you are."

Pleased at his compliment, Polly glanced away, hoping to hide her blush. "I was thinking of Jemima Fuller." She caught her breath, waiting for reactions from the others.

"Jemima." Mrs. Denton's voice was thoughtful. "I confess I wouldn't have thought of her, but now that you mention it, I think she'd be perfect. She always studies ahead for Sunday school."

"I hope doing this play will encourage her to keep learning. I'd like to see her in the scripture contest this year. It would mean so much to her if she could win something like that."

"Doesn't Jemima have a pack of brothers?" Joey asked.

"Six of them." Polly nodded. "I hope they'll take part as well. We can never seem to get enough boys interested."

"Are they as rambunctious as I remember?"

"They can be. . .high-spirited," Mrs. Denton said.

"Sounds like fun." Joey chuckled. "I'm glad you asked me to help." He winked at Polly.

Polly drew in her breath. With Joey involved, did the stakes for the Christmas program now include her heart?

CHAPTER 3

Alice Johnson has offered to help with the Christmas play," Mrs. Denton told Polly before rehearsal the following Monday.

Her nerves, already stretched, threatened to snap. *Alice?* Alice had never taken part before. Polly could think of only one reason why she had changed her mind this year: Joey. "That's nice," she stammered, her heart protesting against the intrusion. *Be kind,* she reminded herself.

How far she fell short of the biblical Mary. Yesterday Pastor Denton had preached about her obedience and humility. When God called her the most highly favored among women, Mary replied that she was only His servant. *Some servant I am, if I can't accept Alice's help without questioning her motives.*

In spite of her resolution to accept Alice's help, Polly felt relieved when she didn't arrive before they started rehearsal. As Polly hoped, Jemima needed little direction as she rehearsed Mary's response to Gabriel's visit. The pastor's son Peter, as the angel, stumbled over several words.

"Let's try that again," Polly said. "Peter, it's acceptable to read the script for now. Stop and let me know if there are any words you don't understand."

Midway through, Alice swept in with a young woman Polly didn't recognize and marched up to her.

"I understand you've written a little play about Mary for this year's Christmas program."

"That's right." Polly's throat almost closed from the effort to keep her tone pleasant.

"Martha has been the star in several programs at her church in Dallas. I'm sure she would be perfect for the role."

From the look on Martha's face, Polly guessed she hadn't suggested this invasion. The expression on Jemima's face told Polly all the confidence she had displayed could drain out of her more quickly than runoff after a hard storm. She had to speak, now. "But as you see, we already have someone to play the role of Mary. Would Martha be interested in portraying Elisabeth?"

Martha spoke before Alice could protest. "I'd love to be Elisabeth, or even one of the angels." She smiled. "I just love Christmas. As long as I can be in the play, I'll be happy."

Polly's heart warmed toward the girl. "We'll be practicing the part with Elisabeth in a few minutes. Why don't you read the script while we finish running through this scene."

Alice harrumphed and took a seat in the front pew. Polly shifted her attention back to the scene in front of her. "That was good, Jemima. Peter, that was better. It's okay to speak slowly. Just speak up a little louder. Let's start again from the beginning of the scene, and then we'll move on."

Whatever the reason, Jemima didn't do as well the second time through. Alice whispered in Polly's ear, loud enough for the children to hear, "I thought you said she could act."

Polly chose to ignore both Alice's comment and Jemima's second-rate performance. "That's an excellent start. Martha, are you ready to practice your scene?"

Martha nodded, and Polly held her breath, hoping the girl would do well. To her relief, Martha's reading of the "Who am I, that the mother of my Lord should visit me?" speech sounded genuinely heartfelt. She hugged Jemima, an extra touch not written in the script. Jemima relaxed and hugged her back, and Polly's fears fled. These two girls could work together and be friends, in spite of their elders. *Thank You, Lord.*

"Excellent, girls. Let's take a break while I call in Mr. Carpenter and the boys for the scene with the shepherds."

Going above and beyond his responsibilities on the committee, Joey had taken the boys outside to run off energy. Like Mary, he gave of himself with a servant's heart.

Polly turned toward the door and was surprised to see Joey in the back row with half a dozen boys gathered around him, sitting quietly. He smiled and touched his fingers to his eyebrow in greeting, and her heart flipped.

The Fuller boys had worn out Joseph sooner than he thought possible. Too many years had passed since he played rough-and-tumble with a gang of kids instead of hunkering down with a pile of law books. They had accepted with good grace his suggestion that they end the game and followed him inside.

They slipped through the door as Alice was introducing Martha to Polly. When he mentioned the play to Alice, he hadn't expected her offer of help. Polly handled the situation with her usual charm and common sense. She would make an excellent lawyer herself, if women did such things. The rehearsal had made good progress under her direction.

"That'un's a keeper." Gabe's soft voice carried only as far as Joseph's ears. A few minutes earlier, he had noticed the woodcarver slip into the sanctuary.

"Polly's got a good head and a good heart," Joseph agreed.

At that moment, Polly turned around and saw him. Her step hitched, and a faint pink blush stained her cheeks. Alice turned her head around then, her wide, fruit-crowned hat looking out of place for a midweek meeting. Polly's plain dress suited the occasion better, but her beauty still shone through.

Beauty. He shook his head. Never before had he thought about Polly in those terms. But already since his return he had seen she was a woman with wisdom and tact who loved God's Word. A woman who found joy in serving others.

He rose to his feet before his thoughts ran too far ahead of him, fighting the nerves that tingled along his arms and hands, the same way he felt when he stood before judge and jury for the first time. "Are you ready for the boys now?" He rubbed his hands together, as if he could rub out his uneasiness with the action.

"Yes, we're about ready to practice the scene with the innkeeper and the shepherds, and then we're done for the day." Polly smiled at the boys and beckoned them forward.

Entranced, Joseph watched as she worked with the children for another half hour. She encouraged, prompted, assisted, but never scolded. Even shy little Reuben Fuller managed to kneel when the angel appeared. Because of Polly's efforts, these children would understand Christmas on a whole different level.

While they rehearsed, Alice promenaded down the aisle with Martha trailing behind. The girl looked over her shoulder, watching the action at the front. They paused by the pew where Joseph sat, and Alice bent slightly toward him. "I'll see you at dinner tomorrow night, won't I?"

Joseph had forgotten the invitation until that moment. Acceptance meant implying his intention to court Alice Johnson; refusal could create repercussions for his fledgling practice. The banker could direct a lot of business his way. He managed a weak smile. "I wouldn't miss it."

"Wonderful!" She started to clap her hands together and then, with a glance at the children practicing, thought better of it. With a quick look over her shoulder and her hips gently swaying, she left the building with Martha in tow.

"I'm sure you'll do the right thing." Gabe put a hand on Joseph's shoulder and slipped out.

Joseph thought about his commitment to paint the figures the wood-carver was working on. How would he paint Mary's face? He had no more idea now than he had when he started.

The sky had deepened to twilight by the time they finished their afternoon practice and Polly headed home. She considered stopping by the emporium to look for ideas for Christmas presents. Perhaps she would see something she could make at home. The few coins in her reticule might purchase some penny candy, but not much more. She bypassed the shop and headed home.

A faint odor of something burning disturbed the crisp cool air, mixing with the scent of pine that was as much a part of Breading as the church steeple. She thought back to the breakfast Dolores had scorched last Saturday and shook her head. Her sister still didn't cook well, but only practice would improve her skills. The scent grew stronger as she approached their house, and her steps sped up. Smoke fogged the kitchen window. She dashed into the room and removed the guilty pan from the stove. Couldn't Dolores fry up a bit of ham without burning it to a crisp? Where *was* her sister, anyhow?

First things first. She removed the pot from stove. Most of the beans seemed unaffected except for a layer stuck to the bottom. Setting them aside, she pulled corn bread from the oven. God had spared them in His goodness. If she hadn't come home when she did, why, the house could have burned down around their ears.

In the silence that descended after her mad dash around the kitchen, she heard Hazel's voice crooning to her baby doll. Out the window, she caught sight of the twins chopping firewood. But she didn't see any sign of Dolores—or Pa. He should have returned from work by now.

Where could she be? Polly pondered what to do next.

The door rattled and Dolores ran in, eyes open wide in panic. Seeing Polly, she sagged against the table in relief. "Oh, Polly, thank goodness you're here. After I left, I realized I had forgotten to take the corn bread out and I was afraid. . ."

Before Polly could utter a word of remonstrance, she heard two other, deeper voices on the front porch.

"Here you are, Mr. Jessup."

Polly recognized that voice. *Joseph.* What was he doing here?

Moments later his broad shoulders filled the doorway as he led Pa inside.

"This isn't my home!" Pa looked bewildered. He saw Polly standing by the stove. "What are you doing here?"

"I, uh, saw Mr. Jessup headed down toward your old farm." Joseph shuffled his feet. "When I was escorting the Fuller children home. He seemed to have forgotten that you have a house in town now. . . ."

"That's where I was headed," Dolores said. "Miss Berry said she saw him going in that direction." She sniffed and seemed to notice the odor permeating the kitchen for the first time. "Did anything burn? I'm so sorry."

Polly wiped the back of her hand across her forehead. How much more would she have to deal with tonight? First the house could have burned down, and then Pa went wandering.

Pa sat down at the table, looking lost and forlorn, and Polly's heart went out to him. She dished out beans and corn bread on a piece of Ma's china and set it in front of him. "This is home, Pa. See? Here's Ma's china. No one else would have it in their house." She held back the tears that flooded her heart.

Pa pushed the beans around the plate, as if the pattern on the china would change if he moved them enough. "This does look like my Mary's china. But I don't recall this house, no, I don't."

"Go ahead and eat. You'll feel better then."

Pa brought a spoonful of beans to his mouth and sighed with

pleasure. After refilling his plate, she set out dishes for the rest of the family. She paused with an extra plate. "Do you want to join us for dinner? It's the least we can offer after all your help."

"Another time." Joey beckoned Polly to follow him onto the porch.

What else had Pa done?

"When did your father start to lose his memory?" he asked.

CHAPTER 4

Joseph walked home, grateful he hadn't chosen to ride on this particular day. Walking and thinking went together like blue skies and sunshine, and he needed to process what he had learned.

According to Polly, her father had been in decline for some time. Her mother's death might have triggered it, although that impression came more from instinct than anything Polly had said. At home they adapted to the imperceptible changes in his behavior, but lately she had worried something was wrong. The first, and so far the only, time he had revealed his weakness in public happened at the engagement party.

Joseph could sense Polly's embarrassment. "People have big hearts. They'll realize he's ill, given time." But she wasn't ready to tell anyone else yet, not until she had no choice.

"I don't know if I should continue working on the Christmas program," she had confided. Joseph insisted she must. She was the heart and soul of the play. Without her, the children would shrivel up on stage. What could he do to make things easier for Polly?

He hadn't found a solution when he arrived at the church for the afternoon's rehearsal the following day. A subdued Polly was already there, as well as Alice, dressed in her almost-Sunday best.

I'm supposed to have supper with her family tonight. The

events of the previous twenty-four hours, including an interview with a potential client, had all but driven the appointment from his mind. If it wasn't so late, he would decline to attend. He doubted he would so easily forget an invitation from the woman he loved.

Alice wasted no time in staking her claim on him. She shifted a particularly peculiar hat—complete with velvet ribbons and poinsettia flowers—to a coquettish angle as she looked up at him. "There you are, Joseph! I'm hoping we can leave rehearsal a little early to stop by the emporium. I would appreciate your advice on some Christmas presents I'm buying."

"But I'm needed at the rehearsal."

Their conversation had reached the front. Polly looked composed if somewhat pale. "Go ahead and enjoy yourselves. We'll be fine. Won't we, boys?" She winked with her usual good humor.

They all chorused their agreement. Joseph noticed a platter of cookies waiting for them and sensed a reward for good behavior had been promised. Why he would rather stay and eat cookies with the children before walking Polly home rather than enjoying fine dining with the Johnsons, he couldn't say.

But a commitment was a commitment. He tipped his hat to Polly and offered Alice his arm. "See you tomorrow night, then." They skipped rehearsal on Wednesday afternoons, due to the midweek prayer service.

Joseph turned his mind away from Polly and focused on Alice. "I see Martha didn't come today."

Alice shook her head. "No. Elisabeth is only in one scene, and they're not practicing it today. She wanted to come ahead, but I told her to stay home."

If Martha didn't come to rehearsal, how long would Alice continue? Joseph wasn't a conceited man; otherwise, he might think she wanted him to herself without her niece's interference.

Joseph decided to make the best of it. Being seen on the arm of the daughter of the richest and most powerful man in town wouldn't do his reputation any harm. He could think of worse ways to spend an evening than in the presence of a lovely, witty woman, even if she was shallow at times.

"Do you mind stopping at the emporium?" Alice asked. "I'm not certain what my brother will like, and I hope you can help." She explained what she had observed of his tastes since his return to Breading as they approached the store.

"I'll help if I can." He stepped forward to open the door.

Before he put his hand on the knob, a man exited. He was piled so high with packages that Joseph couldn't see his face until he passed. Mr. Jessup, looking lively and as pleased as Santa Claus's elves on Christmas morning.

"Why, Joseph, I thought you'd be at the church." He juggled his arms so the packages settled more securely and lifted a finger to his lips. "Don't tell Polly my secret. It seems God has answered my prayers and provided a bountiful Christmas for us!" He looked as though he wanted to clap his heels and leap for joy.

A glance at the pile of parcels suggested a stellar Christmas morning for the Jessup household. "God be praised, sir. I am mightily happy for you." If Alice hadn't tugged his arm to enter the store, he would have offered to help carry the packages. He settled for asking, "Are you headed straight home, sir? To Dover Street?" He wanted to be sure the man remembered the location of his house.

"Of course I am! Where else would I go?" Jessup looked surprised at the question. Had the previous evening's events passed out of his mind? "I'll see you later." He traipsed down the sidewalk, singing "O Little Town of Bethlehem" off-key.

Alice glanced over her shoulder at his departing figure, her nose wrinkled, before shrugging her shoulders and entering the mercantile. Joseph paused inside the door to breathe in the familiar scents of tobacco and licorice overlaid with the smells that always reminded him of Christmas: pine needles and cinnamon and peppermint. Something more warmed the air, and he turned his head, seeking the source. There it was. In the corner, the merchant's wife was pouring out hot chocolate with peppermint sticks for stirrers.

At the counter, Alice was leafing through the latest catalog from Montgomery Ward. She motioned for him to join her. "I value your opinion. After your years at college, I'm sure you have a better sense of current fashions for men than. . .anyone here in Breading."

The hat she had chosen for her brother had in fact been common back at college, but Joseph feared it might make him look like a dandy here in Breading. "That was a popular style at school. I'm sure whatever you think would be fine."

"Maybe I should ask the milliner to make one." Alice took out a piece of paper and traced the pattern.

Joseph excused himself and headed for the corner where he had seen the children with the hot chocolate. "Is that only for the little ones, or may I have some, too?" He smiled at the young woman, the store owner's daughter.

"Whoever wants it. Christmas, chocolate, and chilly days just naturally go together. But you're only the second adult to indulge." She poured him a cup.

He thanked her but refused the peppermint stick. Cradling the cup in his hands, he blew on the hot liquid. "Oh? Who else imbibed?"

"Mr. Jessup. He was so happy, saying how God had given him a surprise gift so his family could have a good Christmas. He drank the chocolate while Father rang up his purchases."

"I ran into him on the way in. He seemed to be in fine spirits." Joseph sipped the warm drink.

"Are you ready?" Alice returned from the catalog counter.

Joseph gulped down the rest of the chocolate and placed the cup on the table. "I am now."

—∞—

"Merry Christmas!" Pa called merrily as he entered the kitchen.

Polly turned around from where she was hanging up her coat after returning from church. To her surprise, a half dozen packages weighted down his arms. She took the top bundles and placed them on the table. He looked happier than she had seen him in a long time, almost like back when Ma was alive.

"Where did all this come from?" The family's finances didn't allow for this kind of extravagance, whatever the parcels held.

"God dropped a gift in my lap!" Pa took some coins from his pocket. "I even have some left over. I was on my way to the emporium to buy some nails to fix the front steps and there was a twenty-dollar bill. I don't remember putting it there, but I must have. After I paid up our account at the mercantile, I still had enough money to buy presents for Christmas."

How *did* the money get there? Maybe Mr. Johnson had given his employees a bonus. He had done that a few times. That must be it. Polly couldn't help thinking the money could have gone for more urgent matters than Christmas presents, but she wouldn't dampen Pa's happiness for anything. "Where do you want to put these?" Polly reached for the top package.

"Oh no, my dear. I must have my little secrets." Pa chuckled and handed her a different bundle. "Carry that one. I'll keep them in my room until Christmas."

Polly followed Pa to his room. She made a note of the nooks and crannies where he stashed the items away, in case he forgot between now and Christmas. Now and again that happened. Pa would wander around the house, looking for his glasses or a missing sock. Polly had become the guardian of Pa's memory.

She looked at the package Pa had grabbed out of her hands. He had included something for her, too. A little piece of her gladdened at the thought. When was the last time she had looked forward to opening presents on Christmas morning?

She told herself she didn't need them. Gifts were for the

little ones, and she had everything that mattered in Jesus.

But now she had something to look forward to, like everybody else.

—∞—

"What can we give to the children in the play?" Polly asked her fellow committee members when they gathered for rehearsal the following afternoon. Pa's shopping trip triggered her thinking. With the gifts Pa had bought, she could contribute the money she had saved for her family.

"Why, I have that all taken care of." Gabe Noell walked in on their discussion. "Don't you worry about it."

"You know the church can't afford to pay you any more," Pastor Denton said.

"No need." The older man waved away the objections. "Consider it my gift to all of you." Whistling, he headed for the front door.

As he went out, Pa came in. What was he doing here in the middle of a workday? Her mind raced with possibilities, none of them good. Had he forgotten to return to the bank after lunch?

Pa paused beside a stained glass window, light illuminating his features and easing away the years. He looked as uncertain and lost as a child. When he saw Polly, his face crumpled like a baby's.

"Polly." He sank onto one of the pews.

"I'll take over here," Joseph said. "You go take care of your father."

She hurried to Pa's side. "What's happened, Pa?" She lowered her voice. "Did you forget where you are?"

He shook his head. "I came to the church. I didn't know what else to do. I knew I would find you here."

Each statement left Polly more confused than the last, but she kept her composure. "What is it? Is someone hurt?"

Pa sat on the bench, rocking back and forth. Polly heard the door open but didn't look up.

"Shall I go for the doctor?" Pastor Denton had joined them.

"That won't be necessary." Jack Hurd, the town sheriff, had entered the sanctuary, followed by the banker and Alice. "We're here to arrest Mr. Jessup for bank robbery."

CHAPTER 5

Joseph couldn't have avoided hearing the sheriff's unexpected and unwelcome announcement even if he had wanted to. His voice rang louder than even the pastor's during a heated Sunday sermon.

At the interruption, Jemima and her brothers stopped in the middle of the scene with the shepherds. No one spoke for the span of a few seconds.

"That's enough for now." Joseph broke the silence. "Mrs. Denton has cookies waiting for you at the parsonage." He reached Jessup in three long strides. "The church is usually a sanctuary against arrest."

"He can't use this building to hide out from his crimes," Mr. Johnson scoffed.

Abashed, Sheriff Hurd put away the handcuffs he had ready to clap on Mr. Jessup's wrists. "If you'll just come with me, sir."

Mr. Jessup looked at Polly in bewilderment and sank lower on the pew, looking ready to put his arms over his head and curl up in a ball. She placed herself between her father and his accusers.

"What is all this about?" Joseph refused to let them waltz out with Polly's father without some kind of explanation.

"That's none of your business."

"He stole the bank's money, that's what he did." Mr. Johnson had no qualms about spilling the beans. "Walked out of the bank with twenty dollars of the day's receipts in his pocket."

"That was a gift from God." Mr. Jessup's words were as good as a confession.

Polly's face turned as pale as translucent oilpaper, and Joseph noticed that the arm she had draped around her father's shoulder trembled.

"So you admit you had money in your pocket when you left the bank last night?"

"It was a gift from God," Mr. Jessup repeated. "I didn't steal it."

"I'm afraid you'll have to come with me," the sheriff said. Jessup didn't struggle but shuffled down the center aisle of the church after the law officer and the banker. He glanced around him, almost as if he expected worshippers to arrive and music to begin.

Casting a despairing, pleading glance in Joseph's direction, Polly followed her father. Before he could respond, someone tugged at his elbow. Her face puckered and she turned away.

"Let them go," Alice spoke fiercely. "I knew something was wrong when we saw him with all those packages last night. The Jessups have never had that kind of money. The nerve of that old man."

Joseph straightened his shoulders. "That *old man*, as you call him, is a friend of mine. And he needs my help." He hastened down the aisle.

"But what about my father?" Alice's voice trailed after him.

Joseph didn't tarry long enough to hear her complaint.

Polly stumbled out the door only moments after her father. She hesitated in the middle of the street, uncertain which direction to head. Spitting snow, unexpected this early in the season, punched the air. Even as she sped down the street, the snowfall increased in intensity, more like sleet, biting into her hair and skin. She pulled her shawl closer around her and wished she had worn an overcoat. This kind of storm was fine, as long as she was inside beside the fireplace to watch it fall.

Pa won't have a fire. She hated to think of him, confused, cold, and alone, but the family would expect both of them home soon. Since they were old enough to take care of themselves for a little while longer, she decided to go with Pa. How long he could manage on his own in the town jail was uncertain.

Last night Pa had been so pleased with his unexpected windfall, one he thought God had provided. He didn't want it for himself; no, he delighted in providing an extravagant Christmas for the family. What she perceived as Mr. Johnson's generous bonus for his employees had generated genuine goodwill toward the banker in her spirit. She blinked back the tears that threatened to blind her. How had last night's happiness transformed so quickly into today's disaster? Had Pa somehow pocketed money that belonged to the bank?

With all the thoughts circling around Polly's head, she almost passed the jail. She turned on her heels and her foot slipped on the icy ground. Stumbling forward, she grabbed a lamppost, and her fingers stuck to the cold metal. A few tears spilled, melting the snowflakes that landed on her cheeks. Wiping away the dampness with her hands, she straightened and crossed the boardwalk into the sheriff's office.

Mr. Johnson sat at the sheriff's desk, alternating between dipping his pen into an inkwell and scribbling on a sheet of paper. At the sound of the door opening, he glanced up and his eyes narrowed into a glare. "Miss Jessup." He said her name as if she were guilty by association.

"Mr. Johnson." With quaking heart, she knew she must speak up for her father. "I'm sure this must all be some unfortunate misunderstanding." She glanced over his shoulder, hoping to spot her father or the sheriff, but the door to the cells was closed.

"There's no mistake." The banker infused sympathy into the

words, but one look at his face told Polly the truth. He had Pa in a vise, and he intended to take advantage of it. "I've already told the sheriff, and I've written it out here." With his forefinger, he tapped the papers he had been writing on.

Anxious to know the nature of the accusations, Polly reached for the papers, but Mr. Johnson pulled them back. "Now, Miss Jessup. These don't belong to you any more than that twenty-dollar bill belonged to your father, and I can't let you look at them without the sheriff's say-so."

Polly wanted to scream. After a scant five minutes at the jail, she had already antagonized Pa's accuser further. She took a deep breath and walked past the banker to the door. "Sheriff Hurd? It's Polly Jessup."

An anguished cry and clanging bars reached her ears through the thick door, followed by scuffling feet. The sheriff opened the door, his heavy key ring jangling from his belt.

"Miss Jessup. You shouldn't have come down here. There's nothing you can do."

Polly tried to peer around the sheriff without success. The slim line visible through the crack in the door didn't reveal Pa's whereabouts. "Can't I at least see Pa?" Her voice cracked. "Make sure he's warm enough? What are you going to do about his supper? Does he have a blanket?" The questions tumbled out of her as if she were a parent leaving her children with friends overnight.

"No one's going to starve in here. Mrs. Hurd will bring him a sandwich later tonight." He closed the door behind him.

A cold supper wouldn't warm him like the spicy stew simmering on the stove at home. Polly told herself to stay calm. "Thank you kindly. But what about a blanket? He wasn't dressed for the cold."

"Miss Jessup." The sheriff had reached the end of his patience. "No one has ever died of cold in this here jail. We don't coddle the prisoners. Now you go on home. We'll see about getting your father legal representation. You can come back in the morning with some fresh clothes, seeing as how we'll have a hearing tomorrow, since the judge will be in town."

A hearing. "So soon?" How could she prepare in so little time, when she still didn't know the exact nature of the allegations? "Can't I at least know what the charges are?"

"Your father is the one on trial here, not you. We've advised him of the trouble he's in. Now you get on home and take care of your family."

I should never have come alone, Polly thought bitterly. *The sheriff wouldn't talk to the pastor that way.*

A blast of icy air tore at her throat and announced the arrival of someone in the office.

"Sheriff, I'm here to see my client."

Joey Carpenter stood in front of the door.

Joseph could tell he'd arrived in the nick of time. Polly looked as wilted as a starched apron on a hot summer day. He wanted to pull her close and comfort her, if she would let him. Where did that thought come from? He was here as a longtime friend of the Jessups, nothing more, and he had urgent matters to address.

"You're going to represent Jessup?" Skepticism laced Mr. Johnson's voice.

Joseph straightened his spine, willing away all doubt. "If he'll have me."

"Isn't that—what do they call it?—a conflict of interest with your business with the bank?" Mr. Johnson raised an eyebrow, urging Joseph to abandon this crazy crusade.

"I can't say until I know the nature of the charges." Joseph felt the weight of Mr. Johnson's standing as the town's foremost citizen pressing on him, but he'd learned to face down intimidation in the courtroom. He looked at the man, who had until now been his prospective father-in-law, without blinking.

Mr. Johnson's mouth closed. "It's all here." He thrust the papers at Joseph.

"Thank you." Joseph took them. "May I see my client now?"

Polly took a half step forward. "May I. . . ?"

Joseph almost agreed, to set her heart at rest, but he needed to speak with Jessup in private. "Not now. I'll come by your house after I've spoken with your father." Noticing she wore only a shawl for protection against the elements, he said, "Take my coat with you. I'll pick it up when I see you later."

Polly opened her mouth to protest before demurring and accepting the coat. At the door, she glanced at him over her shoulder, anguish written in her eyes.

"Go ahead," he said, wishing he could do more to make this easier for her. "I'll be there as soon as I can."

Nodding, she opened the door, and a world of white swallowed her. When Joseph returned his attention to the office, Mr. Johnson was speaking.

"When do you think the hearing will be?"

The sheriff shrugged. "It depends on when Judge Heffner gets here. Before noon tomorrow, if we're lucky."

"The judge is coming here? Tomorrow?" So soon? How could he possibly prepare?

"Unless the snow keeps him home."

In either case, Joseph faced a long night of preparation. He doubted he would get much sleep.

Mr. Johnson took his leave. He paused as he brushed past Joseph. "I won't expect you for dinner." Whether he meant it as a statement of Joseph's plans for the evening or a permanent dismissal of his daughter's suitor, Joseph couldn't tell. At the moment, he didn't care. The front door slammed.

"I suppose you want to see Jessup?" the sheriff asked.

"Yes."

Sheriff Hurd unlocked the doors and escorted Joseph into the first of the jail's two cells. Jessup sat on a cot, staring through the bars as if they weren't there. The look on his face reminded Joseph of the day he'd found him heading toward the farm that used to belong to him. When he saw them approach, he stood to his feet, his eyes begging for enlightenment.

"Sheriff. What am I doing here?"

Sheriff Hurd worked his mouth, as if searching for words to explain. Joseph suspected that no answer would penetrate the haze that surrounded the man in the cell, at least not in his present state. "Why don't I let your lawyer here explain it to you? Mrs. Hurd will be here shortly with some grub." He said the latter as much to Joseph as to his client.

Joseph didn't know how much he could explain, even if Jessup could understand. Until he reviewed the documents, he didn't know the details of the charges beyond "bank robbery." He thought back to the previous evening, to the shopping spree Jessup had enjoyed at the mercantile. Could there be any truth to the accusation? He mentally shook himself. Everyone was innocent until proven guilty in a court of law.

Even if his lawyer harbored severe doubts.

CHAPTER 6

He doesn't remember taking the money," Joey told Polly. "But there's no doubt it's gone."

Polly sipped her coffee, hoping the fiery liquid would help her take it all in. An air of unreality pervaded the night. Once she'd arrived home, she had fed stew to the rest of the family and only explained that Pa had been detained. When she sent the others to bed, Dolores stayed behind.

"What's happening?" she asked.

Polly struggled with a desire to spill the story to her sister but refrained. She saw no need to burden the young girl with suppositions and possibilities. Tomorrow morning, once she heard what Joey had to say, would come soon enough.

"I don't know," she had said. "Not everything. I promise, I'll tell you when I do. But right now, the little ones need your help. Especially Hazel. Can you do that for me?"

Dolores had agreed and gone to bed with the others. Polly waited for Joseph to come. One hour went by. Then two. The clock had chimed nine times before she heard a knock at the door.

She'd hoped for good news, feared bad. "You think he did it."

"I'm saying money is missing from the bank." Joey paced the kitchen floor, as if in rehearsal for the coming hearing. "And there's more." He bit his lip, the most candid response she had seen from him so far.

"He spent a lot of money at the emporium last night." She said it for him. She didn't know how he knew, but apparently he did. Probably a lot of people did.

A look of resignation replaced a fleeting look of relief on his face. "So you know. I met him leaving the store last night."

"I helped him put away the packages." She thought about the wrapped parcels waiting in her parents' bedroom, thought of the money they cost. That brought another concern to mind. "You know we don't have money to pay you at this time. But we'll take care of it, somehow."

He waved that aside. "I'm not worried about that." He came to a standstill and slid into a chair across from her. "I need to ask you some questions. You might not like what I have to say, but I need to know."

The determined set of his mouth told Polly he believed Pa was guilty. But he still wanted to help. The truth was, Polly didn't know what to believe. "All right."

"Do you know how much money your father makes a week?"

Polly thought back to the chaotic condition their finances had reached before she had convinced Pa to let her manage money matters. From then on, she gave him money to settle their debts—and then checked to make sure the money had reached the intended hands. Sometimes Pa had forgotten, and she had learned to factor that into their expenses. But nothing like this had ever happened.

"I can do better than that. I can show you." She brought out the ledger where she kept track of their income and expenses, as well as her pitiful attempts to save against the day she feared her father would no longer be able to work. "You can see there's not much there." Except a possible motive to take easy money? She shook away the doubts. "Pa might get. . .confused. . .sometimes but he's as honest as the day is long. I'd stake my life on it."

"Polly." Joey looked at her, a heart-turning half grin on his face. "Or should I say Mary? Anyone grown-up enough to take care of all this"—his gesture took in the books, the house, her life—"deserves to be called by her real name, not a child's nick-name."

Heat burned through her, and she felt a moment of giddy relief from the worry weighing down her shoulders.

"I wish I had better news for you."

The heat that stained her cheeks might have come from happiness at the compliment or despair. "What is it?"

Joey tapped his pencil on the pad of paper in front of him. "The bank puts a special mark on each teller's bills. So if there's a discrepancy, they can tell who made the error."

Polly knew what was coming before he said it.

"Everyone else's money tally was complete."

She waited for the final blow.

"And the money he spent at the store—well, it was marked with his initials." He sucked in a deep breath before daring to look at her. "The money he spent at the mercantile was from his till. There's no doubt about it."

Joseph hadn't known how he would break the news to Polly, but he knew he had to. He wished he could take the words back, take back the past twenty-four hours, undo all the burdens placed on her young shoulders.

The least he could do was share the burden with her. He waited through her long silence.

"What will happen at the hearing?" Polly spoke in a low voice. "Will he—go to jail?" Her voice trembled but didn't break.

Joseph frowned. Polly might not approve of his trial strategy. "I think we can avoid that, if you're willing to testify."

"You just said they've proved he's guilty. And I can't prove any different. In fact—" Now a sob shuddered through her. "Oh, Joey, what am I going to do?"

He wanted to get out of his chair and take her in his arms and comfort her, but he settled for taking her hands in his. "I'm going to see you through this. I know it's what God wants me to do." Did that sound cold and uncaring? "It's what I want to do."

"Thank you." Bright wetness shone in her eyes but no tears fell, and she stood. Moving to the sink, she stared out the window at the falling snow. "I don't see how the judge can get here in this weather. Can we discuss this in the morning?" She coughed. "You need to get on home before it gets any worse. You can't spend the night here."

"I already thought of that. The sheriff said I could bring some personal items for your father tonight. After that, I'm going to the boardinghouse where Gabe is staying. He already offered to share his room." Ice crystals had formed on the window, and he, too, wondered how anyone would travel. He sighed. "Let me at least tell you my basic defense strategy, in case the hearing is held tomorrow. Then I'll come back over for breakfast and tell you the rest."

Polly stood as still as an ice statue for a brief moment, eyes closed in prayer. When she finished, she nodded and rejoined him at the table, much calmer.

"Tell me what you need me to do."

—∞—

Joey had plenty of time to prepare after all. The storm had kept the judge from reaching Breading that day or the next. Of course, that also meant Pa spent the weekend in jail.

By Sunday, the sun was shining and the snow, now a distant memory, had melted into the muddy earth. Polly searched for the Christmas spirit that had danced through her heart over the previous few weeks, but couldn't find it. She didn't know how she would continue, even if Joseph's plan worked and Pa got to come home.

"Polly." Shaking her hand, Pastor Denton greeted her as warmly as ever. His kindness brought tears to her eyes. He was letting the whole congregation know that he stood behind them in their current situation.

"Polly, there you are." Jean came up behind the pastor, Abe at her side and followed by her parents and Joseph. "We are counting on you taking dinner with us." Another public proclamation of friendship.

Polly didn't want to socialize, but knew she must accept the invitation, if only for the sake of the children. "We'll accept, gladly."

Gabe walked in next, leading the children's Sunday school class like the Pied Pier of Hamelin.

"He's been working with them on the Christmas program this week," Pastor Denton said. "He's amazing."

He'd what? Before she could think about it further, he'd settled the children with their parents and hurried to her side. "How are you, Miss Jessup?"

"Mr. Noell, I'm so glad you're here." Mrs. Carpenter spoke before Polly could answer. "We wanted to invite you for dinner today, to repay you for your kindness in taking in Joseph the other night."

At that moment, the church doors opened again, and sunlight outlined the members of the Johnson family. Martha waved at Gabe, but the others all turned a stony profile and walked down the aisle to their usual seats at the front on the organ side. They had donated the instrument to the church, after all.

Polly glanced at Joseph, wondering how he took the snub. He rolled his shoulders and smiled in her direction, and relief ran through her.

"I'm afraid I must get to the front," the pastor said. The organist was playing the introduction to "What Child Is This?".

After the singing of the carols, Pastor Denton invited them to turn to the passage in Luke that dealt with Jesus' presentation at the temple. The knowledge God had given to Simeon and Anna about the identity of the baby Jesus amazed Polly yet again.

"Today we'll be looking at the most difficult event Mary

had to face, one that would break the heart of every mother. Her perfect, divine son was born to die. When Simeon held the squirming newborn baby, he saw into His future. He told Mary, 'This child is set for the fall and rising again of many in Israel; and for a sign which shall be spoken against: (Yea, a sword shall pierce through thy own soul also.)'".

Mary couldn't have known what that meant, not then, at the dedication of her miracle baby. But only the blink of an eye later, she stood by His side at the cross, her son condemned to die a criminal's death. How could that be God's will? How could any good come of it?

Polly's personal problems dimmed in comparison. The pastor walked through Mary's life, showing how she always placed her troubles in the Lord's hands, even for something as mundane as running out of wine at a wedding. Polly vowed to do the same.

At the end of the service, the owner of the mercantile, Grant Richards, approached Polly. "Miss Jessup, may I speak with you privately for a few moments? Pastor Denton suggested we use the Sunday school room in the back."

The mercantile. Polly's throat went dry. Did Mr. Richards plan to prosecute Pa as well? His face reflected nothing but kindness and concern. *Remember Mary,* she reminded herself.

"Go ahead and go with the Carpenters," Polly told Dolores. "I'll be along in a few minutes." Out the study window, she looked to the lean-to where the manger scene that Gabe Noell was crafting stood. What would his Mary look like? The roof showed the effects of the snow, and she wondered how the adverse weather had affected his progress. She prayed while she waited for the storekeeper to join her.

A few minutes later, Mr. Richards came in with Pastor Denton. "I don't ordinarily encourage this kind of business on the Sabbath." Denton held out his hands to Polly. "But these are special circumstances."

Someone knocked at the door, and to Polly's surprise, Joey entered.

"Carpenter. Good, glad you could make it." Mr. Richards rose to his feet and shook Joey's hand. Everyone turned their attention to Polly.

"I feel terrible about what's happened with Mr. Jessup." The merchant took off his hat and turned it around in his hands. "I feel like it's my fault for turning that money over to Mr. Johnson like I did."

Polly couldn't speak past the lump in her throat.

"The truth is, you and your pa have always done right by us. Always made sure you paid your account. I'd be happy to let you keep the things your pa bought. But Joseph here"—Mr. Richards nodded at Joey—"thinks it best if you return the items Mr. Jessup bought. Do you know where they are?"

Polly thought about Pa's bedroom, the joy he had felt in hiding away presents for Christmas morning. "Yes." She couldn't manage any more. "I'll get them back to you first thing in the morning. I should have thought about it before now."

"You've had a lot on your mind," Pastor Denton said.

"And I'll testify to that judge about your pa's character. He's been a little—confused lately, but he's never taken so much as a peppermint. Anybody who knows your pa knows that."

"Thank you, Mr. Richards." Polly held back the sniffle that signaled a desire to give way to weeping—something she refused to do.

"We're behind you," the pastor said. "Everyone's prayers go with you into the courtroom tomorrow."

Everyone except the Johnsons'. Polly kept that thought to herself.

—∞—

Joseph accompanied Polly to his parents' house. As they trudged through the icy mud, he studied her appearance. Given the circumstances of helping defend her father and taking care of the family, he feared she would neglect her own needs. At least she had dressed warmly and put on sensible boots. Her brown hair shone against the dark red of her coat. In her mature dignity, she looked more beautiful than ever. Beauty from the inside outshone Alice's Paris fashions.

"I'm sorry about coming between you and the Johnsons. You didn't have to take Pa's case, but I'm glad you did."

"Think nothing of it." How like Polly. Instead of worrying about her own difficulties, she thought about his.

"But what about Alice?" Polly hesitated, her face turning the same shade as her coat. "You seemed to be courting her."

Why had Joseph ever thought stepping out with the banker's daughter was a good idea? Outward wealth couldn't mask her inward paucity of spirit. "I have no interest in a woman who doesn't understand that it's my duty to represent anyone who gets into trouble with the law."

Polly frowned.

What had he said wrong? He deeply regretted increasing Polly's pain.

He prayed he wouldn't have more to regret after tomorrow's hearing.

CHAPTER 7

"In view of the fact full restitution has been made to the bank, Jacob Jessup is hereby sentenced to jail time not to exceed thirty days provided he pays a fine of fifty dollars."

Polly slumped back against the hard seat. They hadn't received everything they had hoped for, but it could have been much worse. At least the judge hadn't bowed to the power of the Johnsons.

Whether or not the sentence was reasonable, nothing changed the fact that they had no income and no savings. A five-dollar fine would have been difficult; fifty dollars, impossible.

Pa looked at her, eyes clear and full of understanding, sadness etching more lines onto his forehead, adding years to his age.

I will not cry, not here, not now. Polly summoned the will to smile at him. Once she had regained her composure, she would go to visit him at the jail.

After the deputy escorted Pa back to jail, Joey sought her out. Grinning, he looked as excited as a preacher who had seen a dozen people come forward after a sermon.

"Polly, this calls for quiet conversation over good food. Mrs. Denton said to come over as soon as the hearing finished."

At least he hadn't called it a celebration. Polly didn't feel joyful. "I should tell the children. . . ."

"They'll be there. We can tell them together." He helped her over a mud puddle. The cold temperatures had created a few patches of ice.

Polly accepted his arm. What would they have done without him? Without his help, things could have gone so much worse. Her champion. Her heart flipped. In his presence she rested, quiet and easy. But she wasn't sure she wanted to rehash it all, even with the Dentons. Her steps faltered as they approached the parsonage.

Before they reached the house, Gabe Noell came out of the lean-to. "I heard what happened at court. I'll continue praying for you and your family, Miss Jessup."

"Thank you." Gabe's kind words helped Polly decide. She couldn't handle any more pity. "I'm sorry. I don't feel like talking with anyone just now. Please give the Dentons my regrets, and ask the children to come home."

She turned and marched in the opposite direction, toward Dover Street, before he could stop her.

—ɯ—

Joseph stared after Polly, sensing he shouldn't chase her.

Gabe stopped beside him. "Give her time. She's been hit hard."

Joseph frowned. True, the judge hadn't given them everything they had asked for, but no lawyer expected that—especially when your client insisted on pleading guilty. "I thought she'd be pleased."

Gabe only smiled and shook his head. "Spoken like a lawyer. You're right, you did a good job." He didn't elaborate. "I've nearly finished carving Mary and Joseph. You can paint them whenever you have time—as long as it's before Sunday."

Joseph wondered what he meant while he flexed his fingers. Maybe some time with a paintbrush in his hands would calm his roiling emotions after the turmoil of the past few days. "I've got some unexpected time on my hands this afternoon," he said. "I'll explain the situation to Mrs. Denton and join you a little later."

After the meal—Mrs. Denton said she would package up the leftovers and take them to Polly later in the day—Joseph joined Gabe in his lean-to. In spite of the cool temperatures, a small campfire kept the space cozy and warm.

When Joseph came in, Gabe was carving individual pieces of straw in the manger around the figure of the baby Jesus. As he had many times before, Joseph marveled at the intricacy and beauty of the craftsmanship. Works of art, the simple pine figures didn't need further adornment in his opinion. But the church had requested they be painted, and he had agreed.

He held a precise picture of Joseph in mind—someone a bit like Gabe, with salt-and-pepper hair, kind, peaceful eyes, and gnarled fingers used to working with wood. But he still didn't know how he wanted to paint Mary.

What had Gabe told him? To think about the character of Mary? At first, Joseph thought about using Alice as his model. She was beautiful, and he had fooled himself into thinking she possessed more godly characteristics than she did. The last of his illusions about her fled out the window when she condemned Mr. Jessup without a hearing.

He sighed and studied the figure Gabe had carved. All the things Pastor Denton had preached about were present. The hope and glory of God shone from her face, while the pain that would pierce her soul shadowed her eyes. He only needed to bring what was already there to life. He assembled his paints and brushes before him and set to work, praying all the while.

When the afternoon light faded to the point he could no longer do detailed work, he set aside his brushes. His shoulders ached from bending over the figure, but he felt happy with the results.

Gabe studied his work, a slow smile indicating his pleasure. "Mary, the mother of our Lord. God chose good parents for His Son."

"Yes, He did."

Gabe pulled a tarp over the work to protect it from the elements. As Joseph cleaned his hands at the pump, he realized all his concerns and worries had fled while he worked. Polly had no such release. Guilt assailed him. But what could he do?

"Give her time, Joseph." Gabe seemed to read his mind. "Wait until tomorrow."

Joseph nodded. When he went, he wouldn't go empty-handed. What would Polly take from him that wouldn't offend her pride?

By the next morning, he still hadn't reached a decision. Painting the nativity scene on the previous day proved to be fortunate. Representing Jessup hadn't done his reputation any harm. Three different people stopped by his office, seeking an appointment with Breading's newest lawyer.

Grant Richards expressed the common sentiment. "I want someone who's brave enough to stand up to Albert Johnson representing me." The shop owner asked him to review some shipping contracts.

The morning sped by before Joseph had the opportunity to get to the mercantile. Without a clear idea of how to help the Jessups, he asked God to guide him. He had considered asking Richards's opinion when he came in but refrained. His office was not the place to ask about personal matters.

As Joseph approached the store, he paused, remembering the joy on Jessup's face when he exited with arms laden with presents. Joseph wished he could duplicate his purchases, to give the family the Christmas their father had dreamed of, but Polly would never agree. Besides, neither one of them knew what was in the packages. They had returned them to the store unopened.

Joseph considered other options—perhaps a gift for the family. Strolling through the store, he resisted his usual pull to the books. Only the Bible would benefit the entire family, and they already had one of those. Something for the kitchen? Not food. Mrs. Denton had already spoken with him about a food basket for Christmas.

In the corner he spied a table decorated for Christmas, a cheery red tablecloth adorning the pine wood surface, set with a single setting of blue and white china. A sign announced Service for Twelve Available. It looked vaguely familiar. Not the china the Johnsons used. Probably he had seen it at one of the fancy dinners he attended while in law school. He wondered why the store was carrying it. Few people could afford it.

Shaking off the sense of familiarity of the china pattern, Joseph perused the store. Nothing struck the right chord as a gift to give to the Jessups for this season. He'd think about it and come back.

CHAPTER 8

"You shouldn't have done all this." Tears splashed down Polly's face as she unearthed jars of strawberry preserves and green beans and bags of potatoes and dried apples. Not to mention two hams, pumpkin and mincemeat pies, flour, sugar, lard. . .the list was endless. They had enough for Christmas dinner with much more besides.

"Lots of people contributed," Mrs. Carpenter said.

Mrs. Denton nodded. "We were so relieved when we learned that your house was paid for. We hope this tides you over until you figure out what to do."

What to do. Polly didn't know. The fine had been paid, at considerable sacrifice, and Pa would be released from jail in a few weeks. Of course, he had lost his job at the bank and might not get another anytime soon. Mr. Richards had offered to hire Polly at the mercantile but a clerk's salary wouldn't support a family of six, even with the discount they offered on foodstuffs.

"God will provide, dear. Don't be afraid to ask if you need help." Mrs. Denton said a prayer and they left.

One look around the well-stocked kitchen confirmed the truth of Mrs. Denton's words. They had everything they needed and more than she hoped for Christmas. God had provided today's daily bread and tomorrow's as well. Thanks to Mr. Richards's generosity, the Lord had even given her a way to pay

Pa's fine. How could she doubt God's provision for her future? Humming, she prepared to leave for the final rehearsal for the Christmas program.

"Joy to the world!" Dolores sang. "I'll have the beans ready when you come home. With some corn cakes?"

Her sweet sister had shouldered more responsibility around the house without grumbling, and the children hadn't complained about the unvarying diet of beans, beans, and more beans. Chili and beans. Beans with salt pork. Sweetened beans. Pinto beans, black-eyed beans, kidney beans. . . Beans with every conceivable spice. "That sounds good. And maybe some of the pumpkin pie? I'm afraid it might spoil before Christmas."

"Oh, can we?" Dolores smiled. "What a treat. I'll see you later, then."

Polly went outside, her shawl the perfect protection against the cool December air, crisp and clear and full of promise. Her heart skipped, and she was glad Joseph and the pastor had insisted she come to the final rehearsal. Spending time in the Lord's house would take her mind off her worries.

Although she expected to arrive early, she opened the door to find everyone already assembled, even Martha Johnson.

"Miss Polly!" Jemima saw her first and ran to her. "You're back!" She was dressed in costume, a delicate blue cloth wrapped around her head and down her gown, a perfect match for her deep blue eyes. "Come on. We can't wait for you to see the play." Her wide smile was infectious, and more of the Christmas spirit seeped into Polly. She let herself be propelled to the front pew.

Jemima came to the middle of the makeshift stage together with Peter. As Polly listened to their well-delivered lines, she wondered who had taken over the rehearsals. Pastor Denton had only told her not to worry; everything was taken care of.

Joey came out from behind the organ and motioned for them to leave the stage. *Joey* had taken over the play? On top of going to trial with Pa and spending so much time with her?

She thought back to her childhood dream that he would come home and claim her as his bride. Such a sweet, considerate, *wonderful* man. Any girl would be blessed to marry him. Since he had stopped keeping company with Alice Johnson, why not her? But he would never look twice at someone like her. What lawyer would marry a woman with a convicted felon for a father and a ready-made family to care for? Friendship, yes. He had proven that. But marriage? Never.

In fact, who would marry her? Maybe no one. One look at Jemima and Martha rehearsing the scene between Mary and Elisabeth, and Polly put that thought aside. If God provided a husband for Mary, unmarried and pregnant, He could do the same for her. Someday. Although it was hard to imagine anyone more wonderful than Joey.

Jemima did a terrific job, as did Martha. When they finished, Martha took a seat next to Polly. "Miss Polly," she whispered as the shepherds prepared for their scene.

Polly faced the young girl, who had all the beauty of her aunt Alice, plus a sweet spirit. She was brave, too, to defy her family. They couldn't approve of her continued participation. "I'm so glad you're taking part in the play."

"You are? You don't mind?" The girl fluttered her hands in a helpless gesture.

"Mind?" Polly smiled. "Of course not. You're *perfect* as Elisabeth. There's no one I would rather have in the play." She hugged the girl, and some of her resentment against the Johnsons and their clan dissipated.

The cast sped through the remainder of the play with scarcely a hitch. Although the church would hold a party after Sunday's service, complete with luncheon and gift bags for all the children, today the cast of the play threw their own celebration. They traipsed to the parsonage for hot cocoa and sugar cookies.

"I'm sorry I didn't bring any cookies. I had forgotten about the party," Polly apologized to Mrs. Denton.

"Your presence is our gift, dear." The pastor's wife patted her hand. "The children couldn't be happier."

The children held back from starting the party until Jemima and Martha arrived. When they came in, they each carried a package. They stopped in front of Polly.

"We wanted to do something special for you," Martha said.

"You worked so hard to write the play and helped us and all," Jemima said. "Some of the ladies from the church helped so we could get it done in time. Otherwise we couldn't have done it."

Polly teared up as she studied the elaborate packaging. Big white bows sat atop boxes wrapped in shiny red paper. Both boxes looked big enough to hold more food baskets, only they were too light for jars and cans and cuts of meat. She could feel her mouth widening in a smile, using muscles that almost hurt after the heaviness of the past few days. With the children, she didn't mind. She untied the ribbon and worked her finger underneath the wrapping paper of the first parcel, sensing the softness of whatever it covered.

Underneath lay a crazy quilt made of patches of outgrown dresses, torn dungarees, and towels originally destined for shepherd's headgear. She also spotted some material she had lingered over at the mercantile. Altogether it was a beautiful piece of work.

"When. . .how. . ." Polly didn't know what to say.

"Well, it's been cold. And we figured you needed to keep warm. You and Mr. Jessup," Martha said.

"So we all brought things we didn't need anymore." Jemima's words tumbled over each other in her rush to get them out. She probably loved having a chance to give to someone else. Polly had never realized how hard it could be to be on the receiving end until she experienced it herself these past few days.

"I showed them how to cut the squares," Mrs. Denton said. "And we had a quilting bee last weekend."

Last weekend. Before they even knew the outcome of the trial, the children had planned this surprise.

The second parcel—the one Martha carried—held hand-knit scarves in every color imaginable. "Even the boys helped make these." She smiled.

"I cut the fringe." The youngest Fuller boy pointed to bright blue yarn dangling from the end of a lopsided scarf.

"They're beautiful. Thank you so much." Polly hugged each of the children. Masking the tears that threatened her voice, she said, "Now you'd better drink your cocoa before it gets cold."

Joey smiled at her over the pile of presents in front of her, and she knew who had dreamed up this special surprise.

Friendship, she reminded herself. *Nothing more*. For now, that would be enough.

—∾—

Joseph studied the manger figures one last time, eyeing them from several angles.

"Never quite satisfied with our work, are we?" Gabe had exchanged his overalls for Sunday clothes. The church had invited him to distribute gift bags to the children—complete with the little toys he had carved for each of them in his spare time. In a plaid shirt red enough for Santa Claus, he looked the part.

Joseph couldn't imagine uncertainty clouding Gabe's mind. His work was so sure, detailed—masterful. "You, too?"

"All artists feel that way." Gabe looked at the figures. "Mary is your best work, in my opinion."

Joseph sucked breath between his teeth. "I tried." Capturing the spirit of the woman God had chosen as the mother of His Son had hovered beyond his reach.

"You had excellent inspiration."

"I wasn't thinking of anyone in particular," Joseph said. He looked at the manger scene without prejudice. "Whatever beauty is there is from your original work."

Gabe shook his head. "There's more to it than that, but you have to figure that out for yourself." He tapped Joseph's shoulder. "Ready or not, today our work is unveiled. It's time to go in to the service."

Joseph spared one last look at the crèche, a sheet shrouding it for now from the congregation's sight. After this morning, the manger scene would be set up in front of the church. The congregation hoped the people of Breading would take a minute to remember that first Christmas morning when they stopped to enjoy the display.

The set for the children's play took up the remainder of the platform. The pulpit had been moved to the front between the aisles. After Mr. Post led rousing renditions of "Joy to the World!" and "O Come All Ye Faithful," the play began.

After the days of practice, Joey could recite each line as well as the children. Polly's play put the familiar story into a new and thought-provoking format. After a few moments' discomfort in front of an audience, Jemima settled in and spoke clearly so that all could hear. Martha, her hair powdered gray, welcomed her into her home. Joseph shook his head. Who would have expected those two girls to become friends?

The other children did well, and Joseph listened as if hearing it for the first time, right to the last lines. Jemima looked straight at the congregation. "What a night it has been. Angels announced the birth of my little baby boy! Shepherds came to visit! The Savior has been born!" She touched the wiggling baby she held in her arms. "What stories I will have to tell You about the night You were born. I will treasure these things always and will think about them often."

A hush spread over the sanctuary as the children sang "Silent Night." Joseph rose to his feet and clapped, and soon the building rang with applause.

Pastor Denton came to the front, and the congregation quieted. "Mr. Noell will have gift bags for all of our children at the end of the service," he told the littlest ones who lingered near the front, looking for the promised treats. Laughter broke out. He looked behind him at the now-empty stage. "I don't know that I need say anything more, do I? They've said it all."

Scattered "amens" and "praise the Lords" arose from the congregation.

"I did want to talk about one other characteristic of Mary. Jemima has already touched on it during the play. Thoughtful by nature, Mary kept accounts of everything that had happened that first Christmas in her heart for long, long years until Luke interviewed her late in life. Out came the 'treasures,' as she called them. And thank God she shared them." He went on to talk about Mary's ability to hold on to the miracles of God in the midst of the trouble that later came.

Joseph's attention wandered. Soon they would unveil the manger scene. He prayed that his painting complemented Gabe's art and that the visual reminder of the reason for Christmas would lead the congregation in worship. Did the Mary he painted have a thoughtful face? He didn't know; he was too close to the project to tell.

By the time the sermon wound down, the hour had passed noon. Joseph's stomach rumbled from hunger as well as from nervousness.

"And now. . ." Pastor Denton smiled. "The moment has come to unveil our master craftsmen's creation."

Joseph's throat closed; he felt as nervous as he had before the trial.

Grant Richards joined the pastor at the front, and together they pulled back the sheet that hid the manger scene from view.

Spontaneous applause drowned out the initial "oohs" and "aahs." Joseph sagged against the back of his pew.

After the service dismissed, people surged forward to see Gabe's work up close. The wood-carver insisted Joseph stand next to him. Together they greeted each child by name and handed them bags of fruit, candy, and wooden toys.

Her face wreathed in smiles, Polly came forward with her family. He wanted to do everything in his power to keep that joy on her face.

"Why, look!" Little Hazel tugged at her sister's dress and pointed at the figure of Mary. "That's you, Polly!"

Was it true? Joseph looked from the figure to the woman standing before him. *Yes.*

Now what should he do about it?

CHAPTER 9

The following Thursday, Christmas morning dawned with fresh snow on the ground. As soon as Polly went downstairs to start breakfast, Hazel joined her. Soon all five of them were gathered in the kitchen. This afternoon she would go see Pa in the jail—Joseph had arranged for the special holiday visit. But this morning belonged to the children. Thanks to the generous spirit of the children in the play, they would have a Christmas. Scarves and mittens to warm their bodies and fresh fruit and delicacies of every imaginable kind to delight their palates. If only she could have served the Christmas feast on Ma's china, sold to pay Pa's fine. Polly repressed the thought. Life was about more than fine china. Above all days, today was about faith, love, and the gift of God's Son.

Both the Dentons and the Carpenters had invited them to join their families for Christmas dinner, but Polly had declined. The children needed things as normal as possible, and that meant Christmas at home. Thanks to the Christmas baskets, they would have a feast. She was kneading dough for dinner rolls when Hazel danced into the kitchen. "Someone's at the door."

Who would come calling on Christmas morning? "Dolores, would you find out who it is?" Her sister slipped out of the kitchen while Polly put the dough back into a bowl to rise again.

Dolores returned in a few moments, eyes wide. "You'd better come see."

"Is it Santa Claus?" Polly asked good-humoredly. She rinsed her hands and wiped them dry on her apron before heading to the front room.

Joey waited in the middle of the room, a gigantic box filling his arms.

"He's brought you a present." Hazel giggled.

Santa Claus, indeed. What was in the box? "You shouldn't have done any more. You've already done so much for our family."

"Not enough." His smile suggested a special meaning as he swept past her, into the kitchen, and set the box on the kitchen table.

Polly stared. Surely the carton didn't contain more food; but why else had he brought it into the kitchen? She bit her lower lip.

"Go ahead. Open it." He smiled.

"Let me guess." She lifted a corner to see if it rattled, but she could barely move it. Grabbing scissors, she cut through the string that held the package together and the brown paper covering it. Inside was a plain box.

"It won't bite, I promise." Joey's smile grew wider until it threatened to escape the confines of his face.

Mary opened the top. A delicate blue pattern peeked out between pieces of straw. Could it be. . . ? She dug her hand through the packing material and draped her fingers around the familiar shape of a teacup. Gingerly she lifted it from the box. It was! After that, she scattered straw on the floor, lifting out cups and saucers and plates. Every last piece of Ma's china. She turned her tear-filled gaze on Joey. "How did you know?"

Joey took a step toward her and stopped. "I recognized it in the emporium. Richards confirmed the source. I couldn't let you sell your mother's legacy."

Polly knew how much money Mr. Richards wanted for the china—too much. "But. . .you shouldn't have."

Joey surveyed the kitchen, looking at each child in turn, as if asking their permission for something. Hazel giggled. He closed the distance between them in a single easy step. "Polly, I once told you I would marry you when I came home from college—if you would have me."

Embarrassment toasted her cheeks. "I thought you had forgotten that childish nonsense."

"I had." His voice mellowed, turning warm. "I lost my way. But when I was working on painting Mary's face, Gabe Noell reminded me about what's important."

"Mary looks like our Polly," Hazel piped up. Polly squirmed, but Joey grabbed her hands and held her fast.

"She does indeed." Joey winked at Hazel.

Polly wanted to swallow her nervousness, but her throat was too dry. "What else did Gabe say?"

"He said I should model Mary's face after someone who reminds me of her, the woman highly favored by God. I didn't realize what I had done until Sunday, and I have Hazel to thank for it."

"I knew it." She reached for one of Joey's hands.

"*You* are like Mary, my dearest Polly. Like her, you obey God even in the hard times. Like her, you praise God always in your works and words and deeds. Even through the sadness of your father's situation. *You* are that highly favored woman, Polly. You are virtuous and beautiful and everything a man could want in a wife. You deserve whatever you want—this china is a very small thing. Believe me." He got down on one knee.

Polly put her hand to her mouth. *Can this be happening?*

"Polly Jessup, you will always be the face of Mary to me. Will you allow me to be your Joseph? Will you do me the honor of becoming my wife?"

Polly looked deep into the eyes of the man she had loved

since childhood and gave the only possible answer. “Yes, Joey, with all my heart, yes!”

She reached out her hands, and he stood. Taking her in his arms, he twirled her around and kissed her until she lost sight of the children around them.

In her mind, somewhere, she heard Gabe laughing.

Award-winning author and speaker, **Darlene Franklin** recently returned to cowboy country—Oklahoma. The move was prompted by her desire to be close to her son's family; her daughter, Jolene, has preceded her into glory. Darlene loves music, needlework, reading, and reality TV. Talia, a Lynx point Siamese cat, proudly claims Darlene as her person. Darlene has published several titles with Barbour Publishing.

Charlsey's Accountant

by Lena Nelson Dooley

DEDICATION

Thank you, Rebecca Germany, for allowing me the opportunity to bring Horsefly, Texas, to life.

And this past year, God has brought several new people into the critique group that meets in my home. Each of you joins the other members in improving my writing. Betty Wood, Kellie Gilbert, Julie Marx, Mary Williams, Marilyn Eudaly, Michelle Stimpson, and Carol Wilks. Happy to have you aboard.

No book is written without the love and support of my husband, James. We've walked a long road together, and it gets better every year. I thank God for bringing you into my life just at the right time.

CHAPTER 1

Horsefly, Texas, Spring 1890

Harold Miller III twisted on the train's bench, trying to find a more comfortable position. Every time he moved, all the thin padding under the leather upholstery shifted away from him. After spending the night in the Pullman, he wished for his plush feather bed back home. If his father hadn't insisted he come out West, he'd be rested, not aching and weary. Just the thought brought a strong twinge in his stiff neck. He'd also be working with the numbers he loved, instead of heading toward some godforsaken place in Texas. Why would anyone name a town Horsefly? He hoped it wasn't an indication of what he'd find when he arrived.

The monotony of rail travel compelled him to purchase a dime novel before he boarded. In any other circumstance, he never would have considered reading one. He preferred the classics to this drivel. After pulling the paperback book from his pocket, he studied the cover. A pen and ink sketch of a cowboy in full regalia—hat, boots with spurs, long-sleeved shirt, bandanna around his neck, and chaps over his trousers—was crowned with the title *Black Bart's Nemesis*. He opened it to the middle where he'd left off reading the exciting but preposterous tale.

James Johnson vaulted into the saddle from across his horse's rump and took off flying over the vast prairie after Black Bart. This time the dastardly outlaw would not get away.

Leaning close to Champion's neck, he urged the strong stallion faster and faster, hoping Bart wouldn't start shooting at him. He didn't want to have to kill the man. He just wanted him brought to justice. Thudding hooves stirred up smothering clouds of dust, and the outlaw and his horse left a wake of waves in the tall, dry prairie grass, much like the waves on the ocean.

Harold doubted the writer of this book had ever seen an ocean, especially if he compared it to dry prairie grass. And dust couldn't be compared to the salty tang in the cooling air currents blowing across open water. He remembered sitting on the dock at his family's cottage on Cape Cod, tasting the familiar fragrance, with the waves lapping under his feet.

James pulled his bright red bandanna over his nose to keep from breathing too much dirt into his lungs. Hot wind fanned by the mad dash across unfamiliar terrain jerked his hat from his head. If he hadn't had the cord knotted under his chin, he'd have lost his prized Stetson. Instead it bounced against his back, keeping time with the hoofbeats.

He was fast approaching his prey when suddenly Champion pitched forward and fell to the right. James had to leap sideways from his saddle to keep the gigantic horse from crushing him. Momentary fear robbed him of breath. Quickly he jumped to his feet, sucking deeply of the hot, dry air that brought a slow-burning sensation to his lungs. He pulled off his hat and surveyed the damage while he beat his headgear against his leather chaps, trying to get some of the accumulated tan dust off.

He walked wide around the troubled horse, trying to find what had tripped his usually sure-footed mount. Of course, the prairie dog town had been hidden by tall grass, and Champion stepped into one of the holes. "Oh, d—."

Harold refused to voice the curse word even in his thoughts.

"I hope you didn't break your leg."
The horse rolled back and forth, his hooves flailing, before finally making it up on all four hooves.James stared ahead, watching the figure of Black Bart and his mount recede until he was just a bouncing dot on the horizon. "Foiled again! But tomorrow is another day."

"Don't believe everything ya read in them dime novels."

Harold stared up into the face of the friendly conductor. "I'm sure that's true. I only brought it to help pass the time."

"Ya did say you're gettin' off in Horsefly, didn't ya?"

Feeling uncomfortable holding a conversation with the man who towered over him, Harold rose to his feet. "Yes."

"We'll be pullin' inta the station in about five minutes."

"Thank you." Harold tipped his hat before turning and shoving the book into his black leather Gladstone traveling bag.

The conductor ambled farther down the car.

"Sir," Harold called after him.

Without breaking stride, the man wheeled around and returned in a trice.

"Will I be able to hire a buggy in Horsefly, or will I need to ride a horse?" He hoped the conductor couldn't tell how much he dreaded the last alternative.

—∾—

"Hey, Charlie!" one of the cowhands shouted, catching Charlsey's attention. "Bring on the next 'un."

Charlsey Ames settled her sombrero more firmly on her head

and opened the chute. A half-grown calf stumbled toward her. She bulldogged the Hereford and slid it closer to the huge fire, trying to keep the smoke out of her eyes. Today was unusually hot for spring. It felt more like summer. Too bad they needed such a strong fire for the branding irons.

When the reddened metal touched the calf, the acrid stench of burning hide filled her nostrils, a truly unpleasant odor, mixed with excrement and other things that accompanied it. Branding wasn't one of her favorite chores, but she could rope the calf and tie its legs together faster than any of the other hands. That way the calves didn't suffer as much trauma because their branding was over quickly.

While she was bulldogging the next calf, her father rode up and dismounted. Funny how she could be intent on what she was doing, but also aware of all her surroundings. Pa said that made her the best hand on the ranch, though her sisters might disagree. And the cowboys respected her.

She released the calf and stood, winding her lariat into a manageable circle then swiping her sleeve across her sweaty brow.

"Charlie!" Once again the cowboy shouted for a calf.

Pa held up his hand. "Not right now. I need to talk to Charlie a minute. Why don't the rest of you take a short break?"

The cowboys rushed toward the chuck wagon for coffee, and Charlsey approached her father. "What's going on?"

"I forgot to tell you I received a telegram yesterday from Harold Miller in Boston." He took off his hat, wiped his forehead with his bandanna, then stuffed the soiled cloth into his back pocket. "He bought a packing plant in Chicago, and he's sending his son to buy some of our beef."

Charlsey broke up a dirt clod with the toe of her boot. "Have you met his son?"

"Nope, and I haven't seen Harold in over thirty years. Not since we worked the King ranch together. He lives somewhere back East." He put his dusty Stetson back on his head. "I was actually surprised he wants to buy cattle from us. I didn't know he'd kept up with me all these years."

Charlsey stared across the fence line toward the undisturbed pasture, brilliant with bluebonnets, Indian paintbrush, and buttercups. She loved the colors of spring and the fresh fragrance of wildflowers. "When do you expect the younger Mr. Miller?"

"Today or tomorrow. If I knew for sure which day, I'd send a wagon for him, but I can't have one of my hands sitting at the station most of two days." Pa reached for his horse's reins. "I've alerted your sisters. We might have company for a few days. You'll want to dress for dinner. . .and all that stuff."

His offhand wave told her what she needed to know about his expectations. She didn't mind entertaining guests, but it would be a bother in the middle of branding.

Harold exited the rail car onto the wooden platform. He surveyed the thriving western town surrounding the depot. Trees shaded many of the streets. Not the majestic white pines, hickory, hemlock, ash, and maple trees he was familiar with near his home in Massachusetts. The buildings were not the same either. Although a few were built of wood, most had rock walls. Others were part rock, part wood. *Interesting*. Not at all like in the dime novel he'd been reading.

He welcomed the coolness when he entered the depot. Stone walls evidently helped combat the higher temperatures. But even inside, he was glad he'd chosen to wear his lighter-weight suit, a blend of wool and silk. After glancing at the people around him, he knew the four-button cutaway and his flat-crowned derby would stand out in this town. Not one man wore a suit. Their headgear didn't resemble his either.

He hoped to conclude business in a timely manner and be on his way back to civilization. He'd have to purchase something to wear if he stayed more than a day or two. They all looked cooler in their colored cotton shirts and denim trousers.

When the stationmaster finished talking to the family clustered near the counter, Harold approached him. "Where can I hire a buggy?"

The man glanced up from the paper he was writing on and peered at him over the top of his spectacles. "Depends on where you're going."

Harold cleared his parched throat. "I need to get to the Ames ranch."

"Too bad you didn't get here half an hour ago." The man spoke with a lazy drawl. "One of their hands picked up a shipment. Could've hitched a ride with him."

"That would have been nice." Did everything in this town move as slowly as this conversation? Harold just wanted the information so he could find somewhere to get a drink.

"You'll have to cross the tracks." The man laid down the pencil and pointed. "Go about four blocks south. Livery's on the other side of the street. Can't miss it." He picked up the pencil again then looked back at Harold. "Before you go, you're welcome to head out back and get a drink from our well. I know how hot and thirsty you get traveling on the train."

The man must have been a mind reader. After thanking him, Harold hefted his bag and headed to the water. He cranked the wooden bucket down. It took awhile before he heard a splash. *A deep well.* When he finished cranking the filled container up out of the opening, he set it on the waist-high rock wall surrounding the well, spilling some of the water on the leg of his trousers in the process. With this heat, it should dry quickly, and the cold water felt good against his leg. He just hoped the fabric wouldn't wrinkle much more than it already had.

A long-handled metal dipper hung on a nearby nail. Rather primitive, but Harold was thirsty enough to drink out of almost anything. He dipped it in the liquid and welcomed the soothing coolness as it slid down his parched throat.

Three full dippers later, he trudged down the dusty street. Thankfully, several patches of shade kept the sun off most of the time. He passed cross streets with houses nestled among trees. Flowers grew in many of the yards.

With a name like Horsefly, he hadn't known what to expect. The town was much more pleasant than he'd thought it would be.

Soon Harold was ensconced in a black surrey with bright red fringe skirting the top. Reviewing the liveryman's detailed instructions, he settled back and enjoyed the ride. The horses handled easily, affording him the chance to study the landscape. He headed back north, and after passing the depot, he encountered a hotel. He considered checking in now but decided against it. He'd wait until he got back from the ranch.

Down the road a bit, a saloon stood on the other side of the street. Just before he reached the building, the swinging doors flew open, banging against the wall, and two men tumbled through. They rolled off the boardwalk, landing in the dust punching and kicking each other. Gawkers filled the open doorway, and their raucous taunts held many words Harold preferred not to hear. Maybe Horsefly was more like the dime novel than he had first thought.

Leaving the town behind, he turned onto the road the livery owner indicated he should take. It led over a couple of hills. Scattered trees and bushes rested beside large rock outcroppings, and grass seemed abundant. This area wasn't dry and dusty like in *Black Bart's Nemesis.* He shouldn't have even started reading that junk.

After the first couple of miles, he topped a higher hill, and a large valley spread before him. Glints of sunlight caught his eye from a river that meandered through the scene below. Trees grew along the banks of the river, and a meadow in the distance had a distinct blue cast to it. He knew they had bluegrass in Kentucky, but he'd never heard of any in Texas.

Finally, he topped another smaller hill and gazed across a field of blue flowers unlike any he'd ever seen. Other colors—red, pink, and yellow—dotted the azure blanket covering the ground. He just might like being in Texas—so different from what he'd heard and read in that stupid novel.

He knew the moment he reached the Ames ranch. Above the gate, ironwork proclaimed Rocking A, and at each end of the sign were capital *A*s on rockers. Probably the brand. Strong fences stretched as far as he could see. He followed the drive around another hill. It led to the two-story ranch house built out of the same sandy-colored stone he'd seen on some of the buildings in Horsefly.

Harold tied the reins of the buggy to the hitching rail by the fence around the yard and walked up on the porch. Before his fist had time to tap the door, it opened.

"You must be Mr. Miller." A tiny young woman with flashing brown eyes and dark hair smiled up at him.

He quickly removed his hat and held it in front of him. "At your service, ma'am."

"Pa said to send you out to the pasture." She continued to give him instructions, her hands doing as much talking as her mouth.

Harold followed the twin dirt tracks past various outbuildings before he topped another hill. On the other side, he found the Texas from his dime novel. Tall prairie grass covered the ground and rippling waves rolled in the occasional breeze, but it wasn't the dry brown as described by the author of *Black Bart's Nemesis*. Instead, the tall, skinny stalks were light green, not the rich green of grass back home.

A short distance away in a clearing without any vegetation, a raging bonfire stoked the heat in the already hot air. He thought about removing his suit coat, but he wanted to make a good impression. His linen shirt had to be a mass of wrinkles after the day he'd had, and they could already see all the wrinkles on the dried leg of his trousers.

As he approached the group of busy cowboys, a horrendous odor overcame him, making him want to retch. Whatever could that smell be? Surrounded by smoke, dust, and bawling cattle, he needed a breath of fresh air. Grabbing his handkerchief from his pocket, he covered his nose and mouth.

"Charlie." A raucous call rang out. "Bring on the next 'un."

A slim cowboy, in a hat larger than anyone else was wearing, pulled a lever to open a gate. A young cow stumbled out of the chute. That same cowboy jumped from his horse, roped it, tied all four legs together, then dragged the animal closer to the fire. Another man lifted what had to be a branding iron. Harold had never seen a real one before. When the hot iron touched the calf, he understood where the putrid burning odor came from as he heard the sizzling sound and watched steam escape from under the metal utensil. The ground was littered with filth.

Fascinated, he held the handkerchief closer to his nose as he watched the cowboy quickly untie the calf and release it. Then the one called Charlie turned toward Harold. Eyes the clear blue of the Texas sky above them stared hard, and a look of disgust covered Charlie's lightly tanned face. Or was it disdain? *What was that all about?*

CHAPTER 2

Under any other circumstances, Harold would have accepted the invitation to stay at the ranch until he and Mr. Ames concluded their business. But not today.

On the way back to town, he mulled over his options. He didn't fit here in Texas, and he hated the feeling. He'd always been secure and strong. He felt neither right now.

Since he had stepped from the train onto the platform in Horsefly, no one looked at him with respect as they did in Boston. That had to change. What was the phrase that caught his eye while he was reading *Voyages of Radisson*? "When in Rome, do as the Romans do."

He glanced around, glad no one shared the road with him. They'd surely think him daft to be talking to himself.

While he drove through town, he glanced at Kofka's Mercantile across from the saloon. Merchandise spilled onto the boardwalk out front, and enough dust and grime covered the windows that he couldn't see inside. He assumed many of the coarse men who frequented the bar across the street shopped in the mercantile. He could get outfitted there, but he wondered if there was a more appropriate place. He had noticed a store more to his liking on the way out of town, but his mind had been on other things. Just past the hotel, Eberhardt Emporium came into view, looking very much like a store back home. This one probably served more discerning customers. He wanted to blend in, but not at the expense of his superior standards.

After returning the vehicle to the livery, Harold headed up Main Street through the residential section and past the railroad station to the emporium. A bell above the door signaled his entrance. Although a couple of the customers glanced his way, they quickly returned to their own business. He headed toward the men's section, keeping his eyes out for any other men. He wanted to get a feel for what they wore.

He picked up a white shirt with a tiny black woven stripe. The cotton fabric had a good feel to it. He didn't want anything that would be too stiff.

The bell rang again.

"How are things at the bank today?" The friendly store-keeper greeted the newcomer.

Harold glanced over his shoulder and quickly perused the banker. The man wore a long-sleeved white shirt with a vest buttoned over it. His neckwear differed greatly from the cravat Harold had on. However, the man still looked businesslike, and he had to be cooler than Harold had been since he rode into the Texas heat.

As he moved through the men's section, he found black trousers made from a heavy cotton twill; but they weren't as stiff as the denim trousers he'd started to buy. Soon his arms held several items to purchase.

—∾—

Charlsey let her chestnut mare, Dancer, jog toward the house while she enjoyed every nuance of nature's display. Nothing was quite as breathtaking as a Texas sunset.

The blazing sun turned into a glowing red ball bathing trees and fields in a golden haze. As the sphere started sliding below the horizon, wide fingers of bright orange, yellow, and pink shot in an arc across the sky then melted into the twilight colors of plum, pale lavender, and rose. Molten gold rimmed the few clouds scattered around. They soon absorbed the mingled hues around them until the sky dropped its indigo shade pierced by twinkling stars.

Charlsey handed Dancer off to Bart, the youngest stable hand, and headed up to the house. She usually unsaddled her own horse, curried her, and fed her before going in for supper. But Bart would have to take care of her this time. With Mr. Tenderfoot from Boston coming, she had to hurry to be ready for their fashionably late dinner.

As usual, Sarah was working with a horse in the corral. All that girl ever thought about was horses.

"Sarah"—Charlsey stopped for a moment—"you'd better hurry up or you'll be late for dinner."

Sarah gave a quick wave, and Charlsey continued toward the house.

She took two steps at a time to reach her upstairs bedroom and flung open the door. "Oh, good."

Someone had brought in the large copper bathtub, and a little steam rose from the water. After flinging her sweaty work clothes and unmentionables into a heap, she slid beneath the surface and let the warm water soothe her aching muscles.

How she wished she could just relax this evening, instead of treating Boston like a special guest. At least he had declined Pa's invitation to stay at the ranch. He said he was staying at the hotel in town. She guessed spending an evening with the man wouldn't be too bad, since he wouldn't be underfoot all the time. She couldn't get his grimace when he arrived at the branding out of her mind. Imagine covering his nose with his handkerchief. *What a prissy tenderfoot!* Where did he think all those roasts and steaks he ate came from? They didn't magically appear on his table. A lot of messy things happened along the way. Maybe he needed an education in the facts of real life. Too bad tonight wasn't the time to do it. Maybe he'd be gone by morning, and she could get him out of her hair and out of her mind.

—w—

The hour had come to face his fear. Harold straightened his new white Stetson, curling the brim to match those worn by the other men. He squared his shoulders inside the western dress shirt and vest, straightened the lengths of his string tie, and pointed his booted feet toward the livery. So what if he hadn't ridden a horse since he was ten—when the wretched mare bucked him off and ran away, dragging him behind. He was now a man, and he would ride a steed to the Ames ranch this evening.

"When in Rome, do as the Romans do." The whispered words once again bolstered his courage.

The walk to the livery invigorated him. "Hey, Sam, where are you?"

The livery owner stepped from the tack room. He chewed on a piece of straw while he gave Harold an up-and-down stare. "So, Mr. Miller, back already?" He scratched his neck where the top of his red union suit peeked out. "Want me ta hitch up the surrey again?"

Harold wondered how the man could stand the added warmth from his winter underwear in this Texas heat. "Do you have a strong horse with a good disposition?"

Sam pulled the piece of hay from the side of his mouth. "You gonna ride somewhere tonight?" Skepticism tainted his tone.

In for a dime, in for a dollar. Harold wished these pithy sayings would stop popping into his mind. "I'll be dining at the Ames ranch. I thought I'd ride a horse this time."

The tall, thin man studied him for a moment before he turned toward the stalls. "Gotta gentle palomino mare. Sunshine. She'd be easy ta handle. Been out that way several times."

Harold hurried to keep up with Sam's long strides, hoping the horse's disposition matched her name. "She sounds like exactly what I'm wanting."

After they finished their business and Sam saddled Sunshine, Harold swung up into the saddle. . .*on the first try*. Wearing the right clothing made him feel like he belonged in the western saddle, which was very different from the English saddle he'd used as a boy.

"How long will the livery be open, Sam?"

"I close up before I go home to supper, but there are a few stalls out behind the hotel. You can keep Sunshine there until tomorrow."

Harold turned the mare around, and she danced a few steps in the dirt. She had a little spirit, too. He'd have to show her he knew what he was doing.

He headed north through town. The noise level at the saloon had reached a high pitch. Music, laughter, and loud voices blended into an unpleasant cacophony, complete with expletives Harold had never uttered, even when he was a boy trying to sound tough.

As he turned onto the road leading to the ranch, he felt as though he were on a different planet thanks to the bright moon steeping the landscape in a silver glow. As Sam said she would, Sunshine followed his lead, and soon they settled into an easy gallop.

After she finished her bath, Charlsey took awhile getting ready. The only time she usually dressed up was for church on Sunday or for a social. She had piled her abundant, fine hair into a poufy, upswept style with a cluster of curls nestled on her crown, but some of the strands kept slipping out of the confining pins. Tired of fussing with the ornery tresses, she left a few wispy curls along her cheeks and around the back of her neck. She stared into the cheval glass, actually pleased with the effect.

Now what should she wear? She pulled a dark skirt and white dimity blouse from her wardrobe then dropped them on her bed. She didn't want to look too stodgy. She wanted something to add color. After picking out several other garments and rejecting them, she finally chose a rose-colored dress sprigged with tiny white flowers. The bodice fit nicely and dipped to a deep point at the front of her waist. The round neckline dipped, too, but not far enough to be immodest. White lace outlined the waist, neckline, and cuffs of the long puffed sleeves.

Charlsey twisted and turned trying to get all the buttons fastened up the back. Her sisters were all down in the kitchen. She'd just have to go down there and have one of them close the gap she couldn't reach. Leaning close to the looking glass, she pinched her cheeks. Then she pressed her lips together until they glowed a soft red. Good. Nothing about her looked like a cowhand tonight.

Just as she reached the bottom of the staircase, a strong knock rattled the door. She took a deep breath and opened it, careful to keep her back turned away.

Standing in the light spilling from the opening was a complete stranger who stole her ability to speak. Breathless, she continued to stare, forgetting everything else.

He had removed his hat and held it in his hand. His smile fashioned a deep crease in one cheek. The bold spark in his eyes deepened their color to match the Hershey bars Charlsey loved. One errant curl sprang from his restrained dark hair and hovered above one eyebrow. If a more handsome man existed in Horsefly, she'd never seen him.

A chuckle started deep in his chest and rumbled out in a melodious laugh. "May I come in?"

Charlsey nodded, pulled the door open wider, and stepped out of his way. What was she thinking, keeping him standing there so long? And what did he think about her staring at him? "May I take your hat?" Her words came out breathy. *What is wrong with me?*

He handed the headgear to her. For a moment, she held it while he glanced around the foyer, and she studied him. Dressed in some of the finest clothes available in town, he must have shopped at Eberhardt Emporium to get that quality. The neckline of his black leather vest dipped low, and the bow of the black string tie couldn't disguise the strength in his chest and shoulders. She had a hard time breathing because his presence overpowered the room. Where had this man come from?

Finally, Charlsey found her voice. "I'll tell Pa you're here. You can wait in the parlor."

She led him to the doorway, whirled around, then fled.

—∞—

After the awkward welcome by the woman he now knew as Charlsey, the youngest of the Ames daughters, Harold enjoyed the warm reception by the other three sisters. He wondered how a man could have such a successful ranch with four daughters and not even one son.

The meal the women served proved as delicious as any he'd ever eaten: tender steak that almost melted in his mouth, vegetables that wouldn't be available in Boston for weeks, featherlight rolls slathered with butter. All of this topped off with the best peach cobbler his tongue had ever tasted—the kind that had a way of melting in the mouth all the way to a man's heart. These women would make some men very happy husbands.

The members of the Ames family were congenial dinner companions. . .all except Charlsey. The beauty with unbelievable blond hair and eyes the color of the Texas sky hardly talked during the meal. Every time he looked at her, a blush stained her cheeks, and she lowered her gaze and concentrated on the food. Occasionally, he caught her father or one of her sisters staring at her with a questioning expression. Evidently, this wasn't her usual demeanor. Maybe she was embarrassed because she'd turned her back on him with some of her buttons undone. He swallowed a chuckle, not wanting to make her feel any worse.

After they finished, Mr. Ames stood. "Charlsey, bring the coffee into the parlor, and we'll all enjoy a visit with Mr. Miller."

For some reason, this brought a deeper flush to her face. Every time he glanced at her eyes, they reminded him of someone. Harold hoped she would relax in the parlor so he could get to know her better.

CHAPTER 3

Harold leaned into the comfortable wingback. The bloodred velvet chair hugged him, reminding him of home. Even though the walls of the ranch house were built of rock inside and out, the parlor welcomed him almost as much as the one back in Boston.

"So how many head of cattle are you looking to buy?" Mr. Ames sat across from him, one foot propped on the other knee.

Bess Ames cleared her throat. "Pa, you can talk business in the daytime. Tonight is a social occasion."

Chagrin dimmed the older man's eyes, and he gave a sheepish smile. "You're right." He nodded toward Harold. "Forgive me. Since my wife's been gone, Bess often has to keep me in line. I find it hard to take time away from the ranch work."

Sarah rushed through the doorway. "I'm so sorry I can't stay and visit with you, Harold, but Larry just came to the back door. My favorite mare is foaling. I've got to go help."

Before he could answer her, she disappeared. He raised an eyebrow at Mr. Ames. "Does she always move that fast?"

"Not always, but that girl can be a real whirlwind." He rose and shook his head, chuckling. "I'm afraid I'm going to bow out, too. It's the mare's first foal. There could be trouble."

Right after he exited, Charlsey entered carrying a tray with a silver coffeepot and china cups and saucers.

Harold shot to his feet and relieved her of her burden. "Where do you want me to set this?"

She stared at him as if he had grown a third eye. Maybe the men around Horsefly weren't chivalrous. Or maybe the answer to his question was obvious.

"Over there will be fine." She waved toward the low table in front of the tapestry-upholstered couch. "I'll serve you."

He set down the heavy tray, and Charlsey perched on the front of the couch cushion, her back as straight as if a rod ran down her spine. *Mother would applaud her carriage and comportment if she were here.*

"Do you take cream or sugar in your coffee, Mr. Miller?" Charlsey glanced up at him without raising her head. "Or both?"

His gaze fastened on the long lashes framing her wide blue eyes. Fascinated, he couldn't tear his attention away. She looked as if she were waiting for something.

Oh yes, she asked me a question. He cleared his throat. "No. Black is just fine."

When Harold reached for the coffee, his fingers brushed hers. A jolt ran up his arm, startling him. The cup rattled until he steadied the saucer with both hands.

Charlsey sipped her coffee, not taking her eyes from him. Hers didn't rattle. Maybe she didn't feel what he had.

"This is really good, Charlsey." Lucy's voice intruded upon his thoughts.

He'd almost forgotten she and Bess were in the room.

"Yes. . .good." He drank too fast. The hot liquid made his eyes water and burned all the way down his throat. He set the coffee on the side of the table nearest him.

Wondering why all three women stared at him, he shifted in the chair. "So, Charlsey, did you attend a finishing school back East?"

Her mouth opened, but she quickly pressed her lips back together.

"Our mother taught us all we know about being ladies." Bess answered for her sister. "She felt it was an important part of a young woman's education."

Once more, Harold had blundered, but he hadn't meant to insinuate that the West was backward. Maybe he should just go back to town.

Bess rose. "Charlsey, I'm going to check on those in the barn, see if they need coffee to carry them through the night." She turned toward Harold, and he rose, too. "Good night, Mr. Miller. We enjoyed having you here."

He reached to tip his hat, but his hand encountered only air. So he raked his fingers through his hair instead. "The pleasure is all mine."

—~—

When Lucy followed Bess, Charlsey couldn't believe they had all deserted her, leaving her alone with the stranger she wasn't even sure she liked. When his fingers had brushed across hers, a tingle started churning in her stomach, and her coffee hadn't settled it down yet.

"How long do you think you'll be with us, Mr. Miller?" She forced a bright smile.

He studied her for an uncomfortably long time before answering. "I asked all of you at dinner to please call me Harold."

Rich masculine tones swirled around her, wrapping her in a blanket of unease. "Harold." She gave him a small nod, feeling entirely out of her element. None of the men from around these parts had ever unsettled her.

"And may I call you Charlsey?" His easy smile filled her with warmth.

She set her coffee back on the tray. She didn't need the heat. Glancing around, she couldn't see anything to fan herself with. "Yes. . .Harold."

Charlsey squirmed. Why did this man make her feel so uncomfortable? She glanced across the room, her gaze lighting on a new book.

"Harold, do you like to read?" Literature should be a safe topic. Next to working cattle, reading was her favorite pastime.

"Oh yes. I've spent many hours in our library." His eyes twinkled. She'd struck gold with reading.

"We don't have a library, but as you can see"—she waved toward a long bookcase—"we have a large assortment of books. And each bedroom has a similar collection." Charlsey gasped. Why had she mentioned the bedrooms? She felt her cheeks flush. Would he think her too bold?

He leaned forward. "So, Charlsey, what's your favorite book?"

She had to think a minute to decide which of the many she should pick. "I like biographies. We have a collection of them about American statesmen. I've read most of them. I also like *Imitation of Christ* by Thomas à Kempis."

"I've read that one, too. It gave me many days of thought-provoking insight." He leaned back, a pleasant expression on his face. No denying how handsome the man was.

"I know what you mean." Charlsey was anxious to further explore their common interest. "What's your favorite book?"

She held her breath awaiting his answer. His choice of reading matter should tell her a lot about the man. None of the cowboys had even a passing interest in books, so she hadn't had many discussions like this. Her pulse quickened, and she leaned forward.

"I've enjoyed biographies of American pioneers and statesmen—Washington, Franklin, Daniel Boone, David Crockett, even Kit Carson."

Quite a wide variety.

"Recently I picked up a copy of *Buffalo Bill: From Prairie to Palace*. I had started reading it, but alas, I didn't include it when I packed for the trip." He gave a rueful smile. Her heart flip-flopped in her chest. "I'll have to wait until I get home to finish it."

Charlsey laughed. "I hate to start a book and not be able to finish it right away, don't you?" Releasing a deep breath, she relaxed, surprised she was enjoying this city slicker.

He gazed straight into her eyes. "Don't you read anything just for fun? Everything you talked about was deep reading."

"I have enjoyed reading novels by Mrs. Mary J. Holmes, especially *Homestead on the Hillside* and *Lena Rivers.*" She clasped her hands in her lap. "I'm sure you haven't read anything by her."

He threw back his head, and a hearty laugh rang out. "No, I haven't. But novels are fun to read. I think I've read all of Hawthorne's." He paused and studied her. "I have a confession to make."

Whatever could it be? His look of chagrin made her think it might be unsavory. Maybe she shouldn't feel so comfortable with him.

"I actually brought a dime novel on the train ride."

She giggled, the depth of him as surprising as the next chapter of a new book. "What is the title?"

"*Black Bart's Nemesis.*" He emphasized the words as if he were reading one of the dime novels right now.

"You do know that most of the dime novels are exaggerations of life in the West."

He grinned and nodded. "Of course I do, but the rootin', tootin', shoot-'em-up story helped pass the time on the trip." He paused for several seconds. "Why in the world would anyone name a town Horsefly?"

"There've been lots of stories, but no one knows for sure." Charlsey smoothed a large wrinkle in her skirt. She'd heard the question often enough from visitors to their town. "The one I like best is about a German immigrant who said he'd never seen such large horseflies, so they called the settlement Horsefly, which has now grown into our lovely town."

They explored music, politics, even Texas cattle ranches before he finally rose from his chair.

"I hate to bring an end to our evening, but I must get back to town." Harold clasped her fingers and raised her hand to his surprisingly soft lips.

Charlsey hadn't ever had a man kiss her hand. *Or anything else for that matter.* She felt a hot shiver creep up her back. A second glance made her decide she liked a man with good manners.

After he released her hand, she followed him to the door. He settled the Stetson on his curls, still in disarray from his swipe through them. She wondered what he would have thought if she had straightened them for him.

Whew. When he was gone, she'd have to loosen her stays.

He opened the door and his boot heels clicked along the wooden porch. He glanced back at her before starting down the steps.

"Mr. . .Harold. . ."

Turning on the third and last step, he removed his hat and smiled at her. "Yes, Charlsey?"

They stood eye-to-eye. "Will you. . .be joining us. . . for dinner tomorrow?" *I can't even speak normally.*

"I'd be delighted to." His eyes twinkled. "Thank you for the invitation. Good night, Charlsey." He thrust his hat back on his head and whistled as he walked away, going around the house toward the barn. The way Harold's voice caressed her name gave it a femininity she'd always felt it lacked.

When Charlsey went into the kitchen, Bess had completely cleaned it up. *Good.* She wouldn't have to do it. She hurried upstairs to get ready for bed. When a knock sounded on her door, she was almost finished braiding her hair. It had to be Bess. She was the only one who knocked so softly.

"Come in, Bess." Charlsey continued staring at her reflection in the cheval glass. *How does Harold see me?* Probably not the way she saw herself. Too short, hair too light, eyes too big for her face.

Dressed in her nightgown and robe, Bess dropped onto the

foot of the bed. "Do you want to tell me what the problem was tonight?"

Charlsey tied a rag around the end of her long braid. "You mean besides making a fool of myself when I answered the door?"

"How did you do that?" Wrinkles of puzzlement divided Bess's brows.

A flush once again crept up Charlsey's cheeks. She knew how red they must look. "I didn't recognize Harold, and he flustered me so much, I turned my back on him. He had to have seen the gap in the back of my dress."

"Oh dear, maybe he wasn't looking."

Charlsey wished she could believe that, but she could still feel his eyes staring at her back, branding her.

"He didn't say anything about it."

Charlsey gave a very unladylike snort. "He's too much of a gentleman to do that." She wrinkled her nose. "But he wasn't that nice when he came out to the branding. Tonight he was like a different person. Which one is the real man?"

Bess stood and put her arms around her. "Charlsey, I've never seen you like this. You've never let any man affect you this much."

Charlsey hugged her back. "I know. What do I do about it?"

Bess chuckled. "Just give the man a chance, and talk to the Lord about it."

Charlsey had already been talking to Him about that most of the day.

—m—

Even though she had worked hard, Charlsey didn't sleep very well. When she arose just before dawn, her legs and arms recoiled from having to move, but those calves wouldn't brand themselves. She stretched to get the kinks out of her neck and shoulders. Before donning her denim trousers and long-sleeved plaid shirt, she braided her hair in one long braid, pinning it into a coil on the top of her head so it would fit in the crown of the sombrero.

After a quick breakfast, she rode Dancer to the branding corral. Without saying a word, she headed for the chute. When she finished bulldogging the first calf, she moved to the next one, establishing a rhythm that worked for over an hour.

"Hey, Charlie. Bring on the next 'un."

She was already tired of hearing that shout, but she pulled the lever, holding her reins in one hand and her lariat at the ready.

When she released the calf after it was branded, Pa's voice rose above the clamor. "Charlie, come with us."

Sitting on the large palomino next to her father, Harold stared straight into her eyes, but not an ounce of recognition flickered in his. *What is the matter with him? Where is the man who kissed my hand?*

She gave her dad a wave and headed toward Dancer, mounting her in one smooth motion.

"You men carry on." Several of the cowboys gave an offhand wave in answer to Pa's command.

She rode Dancer up to the side of Pa opposite Harold. That way, she could see him when she glanced at Pa. Even though he was dressed in a long-sleeved plaid shirt and denim trousers, Harold had gone back to being Boston, instead of the friendly man from last night. She rode along silently, listening to the two men discuss business and wondering if she'd done something wrong—something that displeased him.

"So do you only run Hereford cattle?" Even his accent was more precise this morning. "I had heard there were longhorn cattle in Texas."

"Oh, we have longhorns, too." Her father's deep voice felt comforting in her confusion. "Several cattlemen brought in Herefords, because they produce a higher quality of beef. More tender. But it wouldn't be a Texas ranch without longhorns.

Let's show him, Charlie." He wheeled his horse and headed toward the far pasture. "I like to keep them separated. Keep both strains pure." He had to holler to be heard above the hoof-beats and the wind whistling in their ears.

They loped over one hill and down across a valley. Boston kept up pretty well, but he didn't ride as smoothly as she or Pa. Maybe he was too focused on keeping his seat to give her any attention.

Wait a minute. I don't want his attention. Or did she? Conflicted, she rode silently, enjoying the feel of her powerful mare as Dancer's gait ate up the ground, allowing Charlsey to wrestle with her thoughts.

As they topped the second hill, the herd came into view. Pa reined in his horse. She stopped beside him.

Boston followed suit. "Wow. Look at the length of those horns. I wonder how they keep from hurting each other."

What a strange thing to say. Charlie stared at him, and he turned to look at her. His gaze roamed over her face and settled once again on her eyes. He looked confused. What was the matter with him?

If she had her way, she'd just turn around and ride back to the branding. But her father led them away from the longhorns and toward where the rest of the Herefords were pastured.

They continued all the way around the large valley, waving at the hands who were riding herd.

"So, Harold, I'll ask you what Bess wouldn't let me ask last night." Pa took off his hat and wiped his brow with his bandanna. "How many head are you wanting to buy?"

Harold planned to stop at Eberhardt Emporium on his final trip into town from the Ames ranch. These last five days were some of the most interesting he'd had in a long time. Being on Sunshine and observing the cowboys cut his cattle from the herd made him feel as if he were part of the West. . .almost.

The evenings spent with the Ames family proved lively. Sarah insisted he go to the barn and inspect the new foal. Lucy demonstrated her sharpshooting abilities, and Bess stayed near the house and made sure delicious meals were on the table every evening. Supper, as these Texans called it.

Harold wondered what Charlsey did during the daytime. She never talked about it. He enjoyed discussing so many topics with her in the evenings. She awakened his mind in a way no other woman had. If he were truthful, she awakened more than his mind; but he was destined to go back to Boston eventually, and Charlsey was a true Texan. He wished his time in Horsefly wasn't coming to an end, but he needed to accompany the cattle to Chicago. He'd watch the men load them into cattle cars on the train later today, then head for his place in the passenger car. And he had to keep a good account of the money he'd used.

He rode Sunshine to the livery.

"Sam, thanks for letting me get to know Sunshine." Harold unfastened the cinch.

"This the last day you'll need her?" Sam went about the business of removing the bridle.

"Unfortunately. We've become good friends." Harold reached for a brush to curry the mare.

"I'll take care of that, Miller. You go on along."

"Thanks, Sam."

Harold strolled north on Main Street, soaking up the feel of this Hill Country town. The quieter pace was deceptive. The mostly rock structures, the scrubby mesquite trees, the smell of dust baking in the Texas sun. A lot of business took place here. He'd have a lot to tell his parents when he arrived home.

He stopped in the Emporium to purchase a hand-painted china plate for his mother. The scene reminded him of the first time he saw a field of bluebonnets. He also needed to buy a bag to carry all his western clothes. When he found the store was out of leather Gladstone bags, he bought an extra-heavy canvas one instead.

—ɯ—

Harold took one last long gaze up Main Street toward the bank and hotel before he stepped up into the passenger car. He settled in his seat, but before the train pulled out of the station, a man ran out of the bank waving a gun and holding a bulging canvas bag. Dressed all in black and riding a black horse, he thundered out of town. Lagging far behind, but gaining on him, a cowboy, dressed like the one on the cover of the dime novel Harold read on his way to Texas, leaned close to the neck of his powerful mount.

Mesmerized, Harold stared at the first man. He looked exactly the way Harold had imagined Black Bart.

Immediately after Harold realized that, the outlaw cut out across the open prairie, heading straight for a rocky outcropping with trees clustered about. The second man turned, too, hard on his heels.

Harold leaned close to the window and stared after them until they entered a clump of trees. Maybe dime novels weren't all exaggerations.

As the train gained speed, Harold relaxed against the hard seat and relived each moment of the time he'd spent with the Ames family, Charlsey foremost in his thoughts. *Will I ever see your beautiful blue eyes again?*

CHAPTER 4

After Harold left town, Charlsey tried to forget the man, but he had invaded her heart and mind and settled in to stay. His behavior during their evenings was so different from the way he acted during the day. Maybe he had a problem with a woman wearing trousers and doing what many people considered man's work.

Charlsey had ordered a recently released book, *Strange Case of Dr. Jekyll and Mr. Hyde*, written by the Scottish author Robert Louis Stevenson. She had only read part of the story, but it reminded her of Harold.

In the evening, he was the perfect gentleman. *A very handsome gentleman*. They shared many interests. When they discussed books, she should have asked him if he had read Mr. Stevenson's. What would Harold think about the story of the man with the personality split along the lines of good and evil?

Harold's two personalities weren't good and evil, but he definitely exhibited two different ones. In the daytime, he was all business, concentrating on her father and not even speaking to her, even though Pa had her ride with them every day. The evenings were an entirely different thing—talking and laughing, enjoying each other. She'd never had a special relationship with any man the way she did with Harold's evening personality. That was the one she missed, the one tangled in her thoughts all day and in her dreams at night.

She couldn't spend her time thinking about the wonderful part of Harold without also taking into account his business personality. Daytime Harold, or Boston as she often thought of him, had been colder, calculating, and still something of a dandy, even in the cowboy clothes. How could she miss the company of such a man?

A month. Harold had been gone from Boston a very long month. Now he was aboard a train nearing his hometown. When his father asked him, he hadn't wanted to go to the wilds of Texas. He hadn't even wanted to leave the accounting office. *But I'm glad I did.*

He still liked balancing numbers. That skill had come in handy as he did business with Mr. Ames, with the railroad to transport the cattle, with the packing plant at the stockyards in Chicago, even for obtaining his tickets on the passenger cars.

In addition, his horizons had broadened. Exploring the vast country opened vistas of knowledge he never would've obtained any other way. The variety of scenery he'd ridden through amazed and delighted him. The large fields of colorful wildflowers. Valleys dotted with longhorn or Hereford cattle. The meandering river lined with mesquite and weeping willow trees. Picturesque Horsefly. *Texas isn't the only place I went.* But it was the one that stuck in his heart.

Look at his personal accomplishments. He could ride a horse as well as the next person. Well, maybe not the cowhands. Enough to know he enjoyed partnering with the animal stretching and bunching powerful muscles beneath him. He'd ridden herd with the Rocking A cowboys, helping them control the cattle he purchased.

Then there was Charlsey, the most fascinating woman he'd ever met. At that thought, his heart hitched, and he breathed out a deep sigh. He had to reason a way to go back to Texas.

The train pulled into the station. His parents waited on the platform. They must have missed him. Suddenly he realized how anxious he was to see them. Before the passenger car came to a complete stop, he stood on the steps, ready to alight.

"Harold!" His mother's velvety voice rose above the cacophony, and she rushed into his arms. "I missed you."

He kissed her cheek. "I missed you, too." He savored the familiar lilac scent that always surrounded her.

Father gave him a long, piercing look. "Did everything go all right?" At Harold's nod, he picked up Harold's canvas Gladstone. "Let's go home. The carriage is waiting, and Cook fixed all your favorites."

Harold waved toward the baggage car. "I have a couple more things. I'll pick them up and meet you out front."

Charlsey knew what would take her mind off the brown eyes alive with interest that haunted her days. She threw herself into ranch work, starting before dawn and not returning to the house until well past twilight. No matter how tired she was, that one-dimpled smile intruded into her dreams.

She let Dancer have her head as they started toward the barn. The mare stretched her legs in ever-lengthening strides on her way to food and rest. Charlsey wished she had somewhere to go and be totally alone for the evening, but who could be by herself with a houseful of sisters?

Tonight she turned her mare over to Bart and headed to the house, fatigue dragging every step. She didn't see any of the other girls on the way to her room. A tub of hot water awaited her. She'd have to thank someone. *Probably Bess.* She'd slipped deep into the water when her door opened a crack.

"Charlsey"—Sarah's head peeked around the corner—"can I come in?"

"Sure." She hoped her tone didn't sound as hesitant as she felt.

Sarah stood tall and slim, with dark hair and eyes. *Just like Bess and Lucy.* All her sisters took after Pa, but not Charlsey. She had to be like their mother. Not that she could remember her. Her earliest memories were of riding the range nestled in front of Pa, his strong arm keeping her safe.

"I wanted to talk to you." Sarah gathered up the dirty clothes Charlsey had left scattered around the room as she removed them. After piling them beside the door, she plopped down on the rug and sat cross-legged beside the bathtub.

"Okay." Charlsey picked up the bar of Cashmere Bouquet soap and sniffed the soft floral fragrance before using it to lather her washcloth. "What do you want to talk about?"

"You." Sarah just sat there staring at her.

Charlsey dropped the soap in the soap dish sitting on the floor and scrubbed her arms. "What about me?"

"You"—Sarah cleared her throat—"haven't been yourself since Harold came."

Not Sarah, too. "In what way?" Charlsey lifted one leg out of the warm water and scrubbed it.

"That first night he was here, you were so quiet at supper. You always keep conversation lively at the table."

"I talked to him afterward, didn't I?"

Sarah pleated the hem of her skirt with her fingers. "I don't know. I went to the barn."

Charlsey continued bathing as they talked. "That's right. Everyone left me alone with him. I had to talk to him. No one else would."

Her sister wouldn't let the subject go. "You spent every evening with him. What did you talk about?"

Why do you want to know? "I enjoyed being around him while he ate supper with us. We talked about everything from books to politics."

"And that's all?" A frown marred Sarah's face. "Didn't you connect in any other way?"

Where is all this coming from? "Actually, when we were together out on the ranch in the daytime, I didn't like him very much."

"Why?"

"He was so different. Didn't even acknowledge me. Now can you hand me that towel?"

Sarah obediently unfolded the cream-colored Turkish towel and held it up so Charlsey could step out and wrap it around herself. "You've been different since he left. More distant. And you're working yourself to death."

Might as well tell her what she wants to hear. "I'm trying to get that man out of my mind."

Sarah walked to the door and turned back. "Must not be working." Then she slid into the hallway, closing the door behind her.

"No, it's not." Sarah's words mocked her.

—∞—

As Father said, Cook had outdone herself preparing all of Harold's favorites. After eating heartily, he pushed himself back from the table.

"Amanda"—Father clasped Mother's hand in his—"I want to ask our son about the business side of his trip if you don't mind. He's regaled us with plenty of other information during dinner."

Mother frowned for a moment then smiled. "All right, but I may claim him for myself tomorrow."

Harold rose from the table and followed his father to the study. *I have to keep my mind on business instead of Charlsey.*

While Father filled his pipe with his favorite tobacco, Harold arranged his thoughts in an orderly manner and waited for Father to join him. Soon aromatic smoke wreathed the room as Father sat across from him in his favorite leather chair.

Father plied him with questions that drew an enormous amount of information from him. Finally, Father leaned back and blew a smoke ring toward the ceiling. "How is my old friend Frank Ames?"

"He's done really well for himself. He's one of the leading ranchers in the area."

"I heard he married. Tell me about his wife." Father set the pipe in a glass ashtray on the table beside his chair and leaned his forearms on his thighs. "Is theirs a happy marriage like your mother's and mine is?"

I didn't expect that question. "The only thing I know about his marriage is that they had four daughters, and Mrs. Ames died soon after Charlsey was born."

"I'm sorry to hear that. Must've been hard for him, raising daughters alone on a ranch."

Harold nodded. "I'm sure it was. But they're fine young ladies."

Father quirked his brow. "Are they, now?"

Harold wanted to distract him from that train of thought. "How well did you know Frank Ames?"

"When I went out West as a young man, we both worked on the King ranch in South Texas. A finer man, I've never known. That's why I wanted to buy our cattle from him. Why do you ask?"

Harold scratched the day-old whiskers on his cheek. *How should I word this?* "Do you think he would ever have a liaison with another woman?"

"I don't think so. Frank's the man who introduced me to Christ. Surely he wouldn't leave his Christian convictions behind. What makes you think he did?"

Harold didn't want to malign the man, but that young cowboy looked enough like Charlsey to be her brother. "A young man works for him, who looks enough like one of his daughters to be his son. He didn't eat with the family, or even come to the ranch house while I was there. I only saw him out on the range."

"That sounds strange. Maybe he's a cousin or something."

Father picked up his pipe again, puffing thoughtfully.

"Looking like he did, he'd have to be a first cousin." Hopefully that was true. Harold didn't want to believe Frank Ames would flaunt a love child. But then, maybe that was why Charlie never came to the house.

CHAPTER 5

Harold stretched one hand across his forehead and rubbed his temples with his thumb and fingers while he tried to focus his eyes. The long lines of numbers all melted together, and his thoughts took him back to Texas. A little break might do him good. He leaned back, folded his arms over his chest, and let the memories flow.

Charlsey Ames floated down the staircase, a smile illuminating her features. Lively sparks in her beautiful eyes dared him to come closer. She extended a hand toward him, and he pressed his lips to her fingers. Her lyrical voice welcomed him into the parlor.

His chair almost tipped over, and he sat up straight. *Stop thinking about her.*

Once more, he tried to make sense of the numbers dancing across the page. Why wouldn't they line up?

Since he arrived home, he hadn't spent a single day outdoors. Instead, he'd been trying to catch up with how the business had progressed while he was gone. He hunched his shoulders and stared at the columns of numbers. A fly started buzzing around his head. So hard to keep the pesky things outside. At least it wasn't as big as the horseflies in Texas. *Horsefly.*

He imagined himself stepping from the bright Texas sunlight into the cool dimness of the livery stable. Sam had

Sunshine saddled for him. Like a regular cowboy, Harold swung up onto the horse's back, settling into the comfortable western saddle. After riding north on Main Street, he and his favorite mount took the road that led out of town, then over a hill toward the ranch. Sunshine soon achieved an easy lope. The wind against Harold's face cooled him and invigorated his mind. His excitement built as the ranch came into sight. He left the horse in the barn and trotted up to the ranch house, anticipating his imminent meeting with the woman of his dreams. His knock brought Charlsey to the door. Texas-sky-blue eyes stared at him, surrounded by a cloud of white-blond hair swept up from around her face, except for a few wispy curls that caressed her cheeks and neck. Her smile arrowed straight to his heart.

Daydreaming was getting him nowhere. Every thought brought him back to the same thing. . .the woman who'd stirred his heart like no other. Pining away over her wouldn't balance the accounts.

Concentrate!

—∞—

Harold wondered why his father sent word for him to come up to the top floor of their building. As the electric elevator made its slow ascent to the fourth floor, a feeling of accomplishment swept over him. At least he'd finally balanced the books. Even if it had taken him more than a week, something that had never happened before.

When the car stopped, he opened the gate and followed the hall to his father's office. At his knock, the door opened wide, and Franklin, his father's secretary, welcomed him in before leaving, shutting the door behind him.

"You wanted to see me, Father?" He dropped into the leather chair in front of the desk.

His father tented his fingers and studied him for several long moments.

Harold revisited the day's events. Surely he hadn't done anything wrong. Had he? Not that he could remember. At least, not since he arrived home from his business trip.

"Son, are you happy?" The question broadsided him.

Am I happy? He didn't know how to answer. He'd come back to the accounting he hadn't wanted to leave in the first place. After a long line of checks and balances, he enjoyed conquering the numbers; but that wasn't as satisfying as it had been before he'd gone to Texas.

Thoughts of Texas always led to Charlsey. *What is happiness anyway?* Talk of happiness drew him to the woman who filled his daydreams.

Father stood and came around the desk to sit on the corner nearest him. "From your hesitation, I take it that you're not sure."

Nothing like getting right to the point. "I'm not really unhappy." He shifted in the chair.

Father crossed his arms. "I know you didn't want to leave your office and go on the trip to Texas and Chicago, but I thought it would be good for you. Broaden your horizons."

"It did that, all right."

Harold wondered where his father was going with this conversation. He didn't waste business time on idle chatter.

"I get the feeling you wouldn't mind going back to Texas." Father stared at him under his beetle brows.

His heart lightened, and he smiled. "You're right." He didn't want to give away the real reason.

His father gazed across the room at the painting of cowboys and Indians by Frederic Remington that he'd recently acquired. Harold wondered if his father was remembering his own trip to Texas as a young man.

"Going to Texas and working on a ranch changed me. It gave me a whole new perspective on life." His father rubbed one hand across his chin and cheek. "What would you think about us buying a ranch in Texas?"

Harold's breath caught. *Where did that idea come from?*

"I heard about one for sale north of Fort Worth, and I'd like to invest in it."

That was quite a ways from Horsefly, but a lot closer than Boston. "Where do I come in?"

Father stood and stuffed his hands into the pockets of his suit trousers. "I thought I might send you back to the Ames ranch to learn all about ranching. If we purchase the new property, you could take over the management."

"Do you mean—?"

"I haven't thought it all out yet, but once you got the ranch organized, you wouldn't have to spend all your time in Texas. You'd want to keep a watchful eye on all our holdings. Everything will belong to you someday."

"That's a lot to think about." *What an understatement.*

"You don't have to decide right now. Think it over. But I'll want you sitting in on all the meetings about the possible purchase of the ranch."

"I'd like that." Maybe seeing Charlsey again wasn't just a dream.

—~~—

It's not working. No matter how hard Charlsey toiled or how exhausted she was when she went to bed, Harold Miller III would not leave her alone. . .day or night. While she was out on the range, he galloped through her thoughts. In the few days he'd been here, he'd developed into quite a horseman. Of course, he may have ridden before he came.

But if he could already ride, why did he come out in a surrey when he first arrived? Wouldn't it have been easier to ride a horse? When she and Pa took him around the ranch the next day, he'd seemed a little uneasy in the saddle. By the time they drove his cattle into town and loaded them on the train, he rode like a seasoned cowboy.

Nights were even worse. Harold waltzed through her

dreams. Sometimes she'd dream that he'd hold her close. While she stared up into his warm chocolate eyes, his face would slowly descend toward hers until it was a breath away. Then she would awaken with a start.

How would it feel for his lips to touch mine? No one had ever kissed her lips.

She would never know. She'd probably never see the man again, except in her dreams. How could she be so drawn to such a man? She'd just have to force him from her mind.

With the sun descending close to the horizon, Charlsey headed Dancer toward the house. She usually enjoyed the multi-color display, but today a gray mood doused the rainbow. Would this madness never end?

After taking care of Dancer, Charlsey went to her room to wash up. With all that riding today, she needed to change clothes, too. She cleansed her hands and face and loosened her braid from the pins, letting it fall over one shoulder.

She slipped into a housedress and stared at the mirror above the bowl and pitcher on her washstand. Although her skin held a healthy glow, dark smudges under her eyes revealed her lack of sound sleep. *Lord, I need Your help. I must get over this fascination with Harold.*

Everyone had arrived at the kitchen table before her, and they looked up expectantly when she walked through the doorway.

"Guess what, Charlsey." In place of Sarah's usually solemn demeanor, a huge grin split her face.

Charlsey slid into her chair and placed her napkin in her lap. "I'm sure I don't know."

"Mr. Miller wrote a letter. It's addressed to our family, so we wanted to wait till we were all together to read it."

Charlsey turned from Sarah toward her father, but he nodded to her oldest sister. "I asked Bess to read it to us."

Clenching her hands in her lap, Charlsey closed her eyes for a moment. She didn't care what the man had to say. If only she could get up and walk away from the table. If she tried, she'd have to answer too many questions.

Bess carefully opened the envelope. She pulled out two pages of expensive-looking paper and unfolded them.

Charlsey could tell from where she sat that the handwriting was precise. Not at all like Pa's chicken scratch. Sometimes his notes took her awhile to decipher.

"Dear Ames family, time has really flown by since I left you."

Maybe for you it has. Charlsey almost snorted at his words.

"Thank you for your warm hospitality while I was in Texas. All of you are often in my thoughts and prayers."

All of us? If he'd had traveling companions, maybe she could be thinking about more than just the one man. A warm flush crept up her neck and settled in her cheeks. She ducked her head, hoping no one would notice.

"It has taken several days to tell my parents about all of my adventures in Horsefly. We've laughed together about many of the things that happened."

Now we're funny. Nothing in her thoughts and dreams had been funny. Memories of the evenings blessed her heart, and the snubs on the range made her angry. She took a deep breath and slowly let it out.

"Father asked many questions about you, Mr. Ames. He counts your time together on the King ranch as some of his fondest memories. I was able to assure him that you've done quite well for yourself, and he was pleased."

The words about ranch work brought back the pain of the way the man shunned her during the day. Why had her resolve melted in the evenings when his smile stole her heart? *Stole my heart?* That couldn't be.

"Bess, I miss the wonderful meals you prepared for us, and the lively conversations around the dining room table." Bess smiled before continuing. "Sarah, I'm wondering how your new foal is doing. Have you thought of a name yet?"

Smiles must be contagious. Sarah caught one when Bess read her name. Charlsey didn't find anything to smile about.

"Lucy, I'm sure you're still practicing sharpshooting. I'd love to watch you again. Maybe we could have a shooting contest someday."

Charlsey watched a silly grin adorn Lucy's face, too. *Wonder if he'll say anything about me.*

"And I couldn't write a letter without mentioning just how much I enjoyed the evenings I spent with Charlsey. Of necessity, they came to an end far too early."

All eyes turned toward her, and the warmth spread over her from head to toe. *Must be the hotter weather this year.* Too bad she didn't have a fan with her, but she didn't want to call attention by using her hand or napkin to try to cool herself. She was glad when their eyes returned to the letter and Bess.

When Bess finished reading, she served supper. Charlsey had been hungry when she started to the house this evening, but each bite she took seemed to grow in her mouth instead of diminishing before she choked it down with a drink of water. She scattered her vegetables around her plate with her fork while her sisters chattered about their recent guest and ate every bite on their plates.

How could a man living over a thousand miles away keep turning her world upside down?

—w—

Charlsey let Dancer lope across the valley to the river. She didn't care what her mount did. All she could think about was that maddening man. She'd had a hard enough time trying to push him out of her thoughts. Then yesterday they'd received that letter, and now it was an impossibility.

His melodious baritone voice swept through her dreams the few times she'd slept last night. And his face. . .today she couldn't get his chiseled good looks out of her mind. Pa had given her a welcome day off from work, but she'd dressed in her men's clothes and gone riding, hoping to shake the visions of him from her head.

Dancer picked her way through the thicket and stopped on the riverbank. Charlsey slid from her back and dropped the reins, letting the ends touch the ground. She patted her horse's neck and walked out on a large rock jutting over the stream. As a young girl, she'd spent many a day lying in the sun in this very spot, hidden from prying eyes by the trees and underbrush. She studied the eddying currents for a few minutes before settling onto the rock to sit with her legs over the side, high above the rushing water below.

Summer heat made her want to shed her outer clothing and take a swim, but this time of year the river still flowed too fast for that. In August, the level would be low enough and a welcome respite from the oppressive heat.

She wished she had brought her fishing pole. Several good-sized catfish lived in this section of the river. A mess of fish would have made a delicious supper and maybe, just maybe, gotten her thoughts on other things.

Wonder if Harold likes catfish. What difference would that make? The sooner she forgot him, the better.

The sound of approaching hoofbeats snapped her out of her reverie. Whoever it was should pass right by without seeing her.

"Charlsey!" Lucy's voice sounded close. She burst through the trees on her horse. "I thought I'd find you here. Pa sent me to fetch you."

Charlsey stood and reached for Dancer's reins. "What does he want?"

"Come to the house." Lucy rested her hands on the saddle horn. "He just got back from town. Mr. Miller is in Horsefly, and he'll be here for supper."

He can't be. Charlsey's mouth opened and closed, reminding her of the big catfish in the river. "But we just received his letter yesterday. He didn't say anything about coming back."

"I know. Isn't it exciting?" Lucy, grinning as big as Texas, wheeled her horse and headed back toward the house.

That's not what I'd call it. What was the man doing coming back? Why did her heart jump into her throat? Her pulse pounded. Excitement rushed through her like the Guadalupe River below, churning and disrupting her almost settled thoughts about the man. Charlsey swung up into the saddle and turned Dancer toward home.

CHAPTER 6

Charlsey turned, looking in the mirror. This time when she saw Harold, there would be no repeat of their first meeting. Her cheeks turned pink thinking about it.

Taking another glance, she was glad she had purchased this gorgeous dress in the Eberhardt Emporium, even if it had been after Harold left for Boston. Now she'd have a chance to wear it and hopefully show herself to the best advantage. She loved the pastel flowers sprigged across the dusky blue background that emphasized the color of her eyes. She hoped he would notice.

The fitted bodice sported a line of white buttons up the front. She could reach every one of them. No gap, and she made sure each button was completely through the buttonhole with no chance of slipping out.

As she brushed out her hair and worked it into a passable upswept style, she wondered why Harold had returned so soon. Only one day after his letter, which contained not one word about him coming to Texas. She hoped seeing him again would help her push him out of her thoughts, especially when he returned to Boston, which he undoubtedly would do.

While she descended the stairs, a sharp rap sounded on the front door. She'd wanted one of her sisters to answer the door when he arrived, instead of her. *No such luck.*

Charlsey grasped the knob and pulled. As she glanced up, her gaze collided with Harold's and held far too long for her comfort. *Or maybe not.* Feasting on those chocolate eyes brought back all the good memories. Easy conversations that connected them intellectually. . .and on other levels. When his eyes danced with interest about a subject, they enticed her into the heart of the discussion. Such a kinship, a connection, she'd felt with him. But there was something else there, too. Something she couldn't quite name. Maybe that was the reason she couldn't rid her thoughts of him.

After the first shock of seeing him, she stepped back. "Harold, please come in." She bit the excitement out of her voice, she hoped.

Her words broke their gaze. He glanced beyond her shoulder. She turned, surprised to see Pa coming down the hallway. Why hadn't she heard his boots pounding a cadence on the wooden floor? Their guest captured her attention to the point that everything else around her disappeared.

Pa's face shone with genuine affection as he clapped Harold on the shoulder. "Glad you could join us for supper. I believe Bess has everything ready."

The two men headed into the dining room, leaving her holding the door. Almost the way Harold treated her out on the range, as if she were invisible. That put a damper on any warm feeling she had toward him, except her fingers itched to push back the errant curl that fell across his wide forehead.

She huffed out a breath, shut the door a little too loudly, and followed them to the table, quickly slipping into her usual place.

Harold eased himself into the chair across from Charlsey. He studied her face. With her downcast eyes, he felt sure she avoided looking at him. She hadn't done that when she opened the door. Their gazes locked and held in a strong, almost breathless way. Something he'd never experienced with any of the women Mother paraded through his life, hoping for a daughter-in-law. None of them ever touched that deep place inside him where he and Charlsey shared similar views on God, family, and the future. Not that they'd ever really discussed a future together, but the desire for one had tugged him back to Texas as much as his father's plan to purchase a ranch.

They bowed their heads before Mr. Ames pronounced the blessing on their food and their lives. But when Mr. Ames finished, Charlsey still didn't look at him. He hadn't meant to walk past her, but her father had interrupted them. Bemused, Harold followed along. Now he wished he'd said something to her before he left her holding the door. His mother had taught him better manners, even though Charlsey couldn't tell this evening.

Finally, her beautiful blue, piercing gaze speared him. "Mr. Miller, why have you returned to Texas?"

The icy tone of her voice didn't bode well for him. She'd called him Harold when she opened the door. *What happened to that?*

"Didn't your father tell you?" He glanced toward the head of the table.

"I wanted to wait until you were here, so you could tell the girls." Mr. Ames took a bite of his delicious-smelling steak.

Harold glanced around, and all four sisters trained their attention on him, stifling him. He looked straight at Charlsey. "My father plans to purchase a ranch north of Fort Worth. He wants your father to teach me how to run it."

After the initial surprise, her features hardened for an instant before she adopted a bland expression that completely hid her feelings. "How long do you plan on staying here?" The quiver on her last word cut straight through him.

"That will depend on your father. When he thinks I've

learned enough to be able to take over the ranch, I'll leave." Stated baldly like that, the plan sounded cold and unfeeling.

He was anything but unfeeling toward Charlsey. Maybe they'd be able to spend part of the evening in discussion as they did when he had been here before. That was what he missed most about Texas.

Unfortunately, when Harold finally took his leave, it was from the whole family, not just Charlsey. The evening had been enjoyable, but not one member of the Ames clan left the parlor until he departed. At least Bess hadn't stopped them from discussing business, and he and Mr. Ames had worked out all the details with the four sisters looking on and even making suggestions.

Tonight didn't go as I'd hoped. He slammed his hat on his head and started toward the barn.

Charlsey hung back while Lucy, Bess, and Sarah headed to the kitchen to clean. "Pa, can I talk to you a minute?"

He looked up from reading the *Horsefly Herald Gazette*, which he'd picked up as soon as Harold left. "This is the first chance I've had to look at the news. Is it important?"

She dropped onto the edge of the sofa. "It is to me."

Pa folded the paper and laid it on the table. "Okay, sugar, what do you want to talk about?"

She gripped her hands until they hurt. "I'd really like to head out to the north line shack tomorrow. Some of the fence needs mending. I could stay there a few days and take care of it."

Puzzlement quirked his brow. "Why'd you want to do that? I can send a couple of the hands out to take care of the fence. They would get it done quicker with two of them working together." He paused and studied her. "What brought this on anyway?"

Heat crept up her neck into her cheeks. She wanted to cover them with her hands.

Pa had already seen the blush, because his eyes narrowed. "Something about Harold bothering you, gal?"

This was worse than she had anticipated. "I'd just rather not work with him is all." She didn't want Pa to guess the depth of her feelings for one of the man's personalities.

"I can take care of that without you banishing yourself to the line shack." He picked up the paper. "You wouldn't even have a way to bathe out there. . .or anything else you need."

The snap he gave the paper before he opened it signaled an end to the conversation.

She flounced out into the hallway and up the stairs to her bedroom. How in the world would Pa help her stay away from Harold? . . . *And why would he want to?*

Harold rode his newly purchased horse, Sunshine, to the Ames ranch. In his saddlebags, he had enough western clothes for a week. He hadn't checked out of the hotel room because he planned to return to town to have his laundry done. He also needed a place to go if he wanted to have time to himself.

He hoped to catch sight of Charlsey as he rode toward the ranch office in the north end of the barn, but she was nowhere to be seen. After dismounting, he knocked on the frame of the open doorway.

Mr. Ames swiveled in his chair and rose. "You got here plenty early, Miller." He grasped Harold's outstretched hand. "Do you want to stay at the house or in the bunkhouse? Either's fine with me."

Harold shoved his hands into the front pockets of his denim trousers. "If I'm going to understand about a cowboy's life on a ranch, I'd better live in the bunkhouse."

The ranch owner shook his head. "Not much space for each man. Just a bunk and a place for a trunk if you have one. You're not used to living like that."

"If you and my father could do it when you were young men, then so can I." He rocked up on his toes and down again.

"Well, I respect you for it. You'll learn faster that way." Mr. Ames sat back down. "Do you want the boys to know why you're here?"

He thought about the idea for a minute. "Not right away. If we don't tell them, maybe they'll accept me sooner."

"Probably right about that." Mr. Ames got up and studied a chart on the wall.

Wanting to see what it was, Harold joined him.

With long, thin fingers, the rancher traced a line of boxes, most with names on them. "These represent the bunks. See, they're stacked two high." He looked back over his shoulder. "When your dad and I worked the King ranch, the bunks were stacked three high. I sure didn't want the top bunk."

When the man started toward the door, Harold followed him. They went to the bunkhouse that was nestled on a rocky knoll surrounded by live oak trees. Not far away, a small cottage sat facing the ranch house.

"Who lives there?" Harold waved toward the tiny house.

"The foreman and his wife. Actually, sometimes Martha helps the girls with the housework if they're too busy to do it."

Made sense to Harold. But if the girls needed help sometimes, what kept Charlsey busy during the day? Maybe she volunteered in town with the children or at the church. *A worthy endeavor, for sure.*

—∞—

For a week, Charlsey managed to stay away from Harold in the daytime. Sometimes she caught a glimpse of him across the way, but she'd been busy and so had he. Their evenings were a different story. Even though she'd hoped for a return of their happy times before he went back to Boston, they hadn't had a single evening alone. Pa and one or more of her sisters joined them in the parlor every evening.

Last night, Harold kept everyone laughing with his tales of reading *Black Bart's Nemesis* and expecting Texas to be like the dime novel. A smile tugged at her lips at the memory. He told about watching a similar event play out in Horsefly before the train left the station taking his cattle to Chicago.

She stuck in a final hairpin and tipped the cheval glass so she could check her hem. *Just right.* As much as she loved her family, maybe tonight she and Harold could spend a little time alone. She needed to catch a glimpse of the side of the man she'd come to, dare she say, love when he was here before.

After the lively dinner conversation, Sarah and Pa headed out to the barn to check on a sick horse. Lucy offered to help Bess clean up the dishes.

Finally, Harold held out his arm to escort Charlsey to the parlor. She slipped her hand through, noticing how muscular he was. Her fingers tingled from the rock-hard feel of his forearm under her hand.

She settled on one end of the sofa, hoping Harold would share it with her. Instead, he eased into a wingback chair and propped one booted foot on the opposite knee.

Wonder what direction our conversation will take tonight.

He cleared his throat. "Charlsey, I'm glad we're alone this evening. I've been wanting to ask you something."

Must be important since he seems so nervous, tapping his fingers on his leg. . .limb. . .or whatever is the proper thing to call it while he jiggles it up and down. "What do you want to know?"

He dropped his foot back on the floor and rose in one fluid motion like the caged tiger she'd seen when the circus came to town, pacing across the rug toward the fireplace. He rested his hands on the carved walnut mantel.

Will the man ever say what he wants?

After turning back toward her, he shoved his hands into the back pockets of his clean denim trousers and rocked up on his toes, then back down. She'd never noticed him doing that before. Maybe she should prod him to get to the question.

She started to open her mouth but shut it again when he finally spoke. "I'm wondering about the young cowhand who works for your father."

Young? All the cowboys were almost as old as Pa.

"I saw him more when I was here before, but he doesn't live in the bunkhouse." He raked his fingers through his hair, making more than one errant curl dangle above his eyes. "I see him occasionally, but not up close." Once again he cleared his throat. "Is he maybe a cousin or something? He favors you more than your sisters."

Charlsey froze. Her heart stopped, then beat a staccato in her throat. He could only be talking about her. *Does he really not know?*

Harold turned his back toward her. "I even asked my father if your pa could have been involved with another woman."

She shot to her feet. "How dare you think such a thing!" She didn't care that she was shrieking. "You are so dense."

He whipped around, pain streaming from his eyes. "I'm sorry." He took a step toward her.

She backed up a step.

"I heard the other cowhands call him Charlie at the branding that day I arrived."

Trembling from head to toe, she tried to control her anger. "That was me!" She thrust her thumb toward her chest. "I'm Charlie."

His mouth dropped open as if he couldn't comprehend what she was saying. "You? . . . But he wore trousers."

"Of course I wear trousers when I'm working the ranch. Did you think I did it in a skirt?"

"I didn't know what you did all day." Shoving his fingers back through his hair, he stared at her. "Decent women don't wear trousers."

"You don't think I'm decent?" She spat out the bitter words, her fists clenched against her hips. "I thought we were becoming good friends, maybe more, but I can see now that we have nothing in common." She stomped out of the parlor and up the stairs, never looking back.

The nerve of that man!

CHAPTER 7

Instead of heading to the bunkhouse, Harold veered to a rocky outcropping bathed in silvery moonlight. He wasn't ready to face any of the other cowboys. How had he not known? When "Charlie" rode with her father and him the first time he came to Texas, she didn't join their discussions, so he didn't hear her voice. But those eyes. . .he'd always felt drawn to those eyes. Now he knew why.

If he'd had a lick of sense, he'd have remembered that Charlsey looked like their mother and the other girls took after their father. If Mr. Ames had been with another woman, the child wouldn't have looked like Charlsey. How had he even considered the idea about such a godly man?

What was he going to do? He'd been entertaining the idea that Charlsey might be the woman God intended for him. But that would never happen. Her scandalous behavior was completely unacceptable. What would his mother think if she ever found out the whole truth about Charlsey? If only he could talk to his father.

As he started toward the bunkhouse, he noticed Sarah leaving the barn and heading to the house. He made his way to the barn through the shadows cast by the mesquite trees and live oaks, careful not to stumble over a rock or step into a hole. By the time he reached the moonlight again, Mr. Ames was shutting the door.

"I'd like a word with you, sir." Harold stopped a few feet from the older man.

Mr. Ames studied his face a moment. "Sure. Would you like to come back up to the house?"

Harold thrust his hands into his pockets. After making his decision, he wanted to get it over with as soon as possible. "No. I just wanted to say that I need to go home right now."

With narrowed eyes, Mr. Ames gave him a puzzled look. "Something happen I need to know about?"

"No, sir." Harold concentrated on the toe of his boot drawing circles in the dust.

"You comin' back?"

How should he answer? He glanced up. "I'm not sure."

—~—

Charlsey muffled her sobs with her pillow. She wasn't even sure whether she cried because she was hurt or angry. She just needed to release a passel of pent-up emotions.

"Charlsey?" A knock followed Bess's tentative call.

She didn't answer. She didn't want to see anyone right now, especially not Bess.

The doorknob turned, but she had locked the door when she came in. She knew one or more of her sisters would try to talk to her. *But not right now.*

"Charlsey, open the door."

The doorknob jiggled, reminding her of Harold's jiggling leg, and she didn't want to think about that man.

"I know you're in there." Bess's tone had turned plaintive. "Let me in."

"What's going on?" Lucy didn't try to keep her voice down the way Bess had.

"I don't know. You heard the yelling as much as I did. That's all I know." Bess's answer was as loud as Lucy's question.

"Charlsey!" When Lucy rattled the knob, the whole door shook.

"Go away." Charlsey tried to keep her voice from trembling. "I. Am. Not. Opening. The. Door."

For a while they tried to wheedle her into complying but finally gave up.

She didn't know if she could ever tell anyone why she felt so foolish—allowing herself to fall for a man who didn't respect her. In her mind, both of the personalities of Mr. Harold Miller III coalesced into one man, a man she couldn't abide. Not now. . .not ever.

—w—

During the long train ride to Boston, Harold replayed his time in Horsefly. Before tonight, he'd considered it some of the happiest times of his life. He had really taken to ranching. With his accounting background, he'd caught on quickly to the office work. He hadn't realized how much bookwork ranching entailed. Keeping track of all the cattle, the breeding, the branding, the sales. The Ames ranch was very successful.

The time he'd spent out on the range with the cowboys had been enlightening, too. He'd learned to work with the other cowboys like a team, rounding up cattle, moving them to other pastures. He'd even helped fix fences. The other cowboys rode into town in the evenings, so they didn't realize he was spending time at the main house with the family. They accepted him as one of them by the second day. He hated to see that come to an end.

What could he do now? Charlsey wouldn't ever want to see him again. Even if she did, could he really introduce her to his mother? She would not fit into his world, and she surely didn't want him in hers.

If Father still wanted to buy the ranch, he'd run it for him. Even though it had only been a week this time, he felt he had a grasp on ranching.

When the train pulled into the station, his father waited

for him, worry puckering his brow. "What brought you home so soon? The telegram didn't give any details, except when the train would arrive."

"Can we wait until we're back in the office to discuss it?" He didn't want to get into a serious discussion in such a public place.

"Your mother expects us home. She's had Cook preparing a veritable banquet." Father picked up his Gladstone bag while Harold went for the trunk. "That woman spoils you."

Harold smiled at his father's quip. "She just knows I like to eat."

All the time they traveled the busy streets of Boston and throughout the meal, Harold kept a facade of normalcy. He didn't want to upset Mother, and he didn't want to talk to his father until they were alone. He had really messed up this time. Why hadn't Father left him to his accounting? He'd never have been in a fix like this.

When he followed his father into the study, he finally relaxed. As usual, Father sank into his favorite leather chair and started filling his pipe. Not until the aromatic smoke wreathed the room did Father ask his first question.

"Are you ready to tell me what's bothering you?"

Was he ready? He wasn't sure, but no way around it now.

"Have you already purchased the ranch in Texas?" If Father hadn't, then there might not be a problem.... Except that Father would make him face what happened anyway.

With a nod, Father asked, "Why is that important?"

"It's probably not." He stared at the Remington painting, wishing he were still out on the range. "I may have made a terrible mistake."

Father laid his pipe in an ashtray and leaned forward, his expression intent. "What kind of mistake?"

"Remember when I mentioned that young cowboy at the Ames ranch? Well, I was wrong. Mr. Ames didn't do anything wrong. Charlie is Charlsey." He rubbed the stubble on his chin.

"And you thought she was a man?" A hint of glee colored Father's words.

"Well, she wore men's clothes. A big hat, a big shirt, and loose. . .trousers." With the last word heat suffused his cheeks.

A loud guffaw bounced around the room. "Oh. . .this is. . . priceless." His father interspersed the words with more laughter.

Harold didn't see anything funny about it. He frowned. That set Father off again. This conversation was going downhill fast.

"Is that why you hurried home?" Father's tone grew serious.

Harold inhaled a deep breath and let it out slowly. "I wanted to talk to you."

With a nod, Father smiled. "I'm glad you did. So tell me all about it." He picked up his pipe and took a long draw, leaning back in the chair.

Might as well get it over with. In a monotone, he recounted his final confrontation with Charlsey.

After pondering his words, Father finally spoke. "You really did say she isn't decent?"

"I didn't mean it that way, but she wouldn't be acceptable in Mother's circle of friends."

Laying the pipe back in the ashtray, Father leaned forward with his forearms on his thighs. "The Bible talks about people looking at outward appearances but God looking at the heart. When you were home last time, you shared things with me that led me to believe you had a heart connection with the girl."

"I thought we did." He envisioned the times they'd spent together. "I was beginning to believe she was the woman God intended for me, but that can't be."

With a chuckle, Father stared at him. "The Bible also says that His ways are higher than our ways, and His thoughts than our thoughts." He got up and strode to the massive fireplace, stopping to stare into the mirror above the mantel. "I never told you about almost missing out on the woman God planned for me. I had too much pride."

"Pride about what?" This sounded interesting and took the attention off his own mistakes.

"Actually, the sinful kind that causes a man to be puffed up and not listen to the Lord." He turned and stared at Harold. "I was a poor cowboy, recently returned from the Wild West. Your mother, the daughter of a banker here in Boston. I misjudged her. Thought she'd consider herself above me. So I kept myself from being hurt by holding myself aloof."

Aloof? From what he'd seen of his parents, that wasn't a part of their relationship.

"I guess I considered her better than me, and she was, but my pride kept me from relaxing around her. We went to the same church. I tried to ignore her even though I felt drawn to her. She befriended me and slowly won me over. I think she even had the pastor and his wife helping get the two of us together."

Harold didn't really see what this had to do with his relationship, or lack thereof, with Charlsey.

"When we married, she was glad to live in a tiny cottage with me. She did things servants had always done for her, working beside me as we built the first horse farm into a thriving enterprise. Her father became sick, so we moved back to Boston to be near him. He brought me into the bank, and I was able to take over when he died. Your mother took her place in Boston society, but I still remember her helping me deliver foals. She didn't wear dresses when she did it, either."

That was a new image for Harold. His mother wearing trousers to help her father on a horse farm? Maybe she *would* accept Charlsey.

"Son, don't miss a chance at what God might have planned for you." He stood. "I'm going up to join your mother. It's been a long day."

That it had, but Harold knew his day wasn't over. He had to spend time with the Lord.

CHAPTER 8

Over a week since Charlsey had seen Boston, and finally she was coming to grips with all that happened. The man didn't understand what it took to run a ranch. Her father had taught them to do whatever it took to finish the job. No one else who knew them would *ever* consider her indecent. Boston had the problem, and she wouldn't let it affect her anymore.

She spent the morning in town buying supplies and visiting with friends. After helping Bess store everything, she changed into work clothes so she could get out on the range. She was heading toward the back of the house when someone knocked on the front door. *Must be a stranger; friends would come to the back or even to the barn this time of day.*

She retraced her steps down the hallway and pulled the door open wide. Frozen in surprise, she stared into the dark brown eyes she'd thought she would never see again. After a moment, she started to slam the door.

A scuffed brown leather boot prevented it from closing. Boston pushed the heavy wooden door as if it were hollow. She stepped back and crossed her arms, then stood tapping her foot.

"What do you want?" Anger and bitterness dripped from each word.

Pain glistened in his eyes, almost like the sheen of tears. "I am so sorry, Charlsey." His deep voice carried conviction.

"Sorry won't cut it with me." She let her upper lip curl in scorn.

How dare he think he could just waltz in here and say he was sorry and everything would be all right? He'd delivered a heart-deep insult that still ached even though she tried to put it out of her mind. Him standing there in her face brought all the pain back in full force.

He studied her as if she were the most interesting thing in the world, making her uncomfortable. "How could I not have known you? You're the essence of femininity."

She glanced down at the loose trousers and shirt, belted tight at the waist. *I look like a sack of potatoes. That's not feminine.* She opened her mouth but didn't know what to say, so she snapped it closed.

"I know I don't deserve your forgiveness." He moved a hand toward her shoulder, but she pulled it back out of his reach. "I'm here to prove how sorry I am and to earn your forgiveness."

"When h—" She knew he'd really think she was indecent if she said that out loud. "When it snows in August, Boston." That was the first time she'd actually used her derogatory name for him to his face.

He smiled. "Then get ready for a blizzard." He turned on his heel and headed back out the door.

She slammed it behind him. *How dare you!*

Harold hurried toward the barn, a smile tickling his lips. A woman wouldn't have that much fire if she didn't feel something for him. He looked forward to spending time around her while he broke down her defenses. No matter how long it took, he'd stay till the end. The only end he would consider was Charlsey as his wife.

Since the door of the office was closed, he realized Mr. Ames must be out on the range. Unhitching Sunshine, he jumped into the saddle and headed across the open land toward a cloud of dust. The cowhands had to be moving cattle.

Before he topped the hill, a lone rider headed toward him. Mr. Ames must be on his way back to headquarters. Harold rode Sunshine right into his path.

He knew the moment the ranch owner recognized him. The man slowed his horse to a walk the last few feet before he stopped in front of Harold.

"So, Miller, you did come back. I thought you might." A twinkle lit his eyes. "And you didn't stay away very long."

"No, sir." Harold rested both hands on his saddle horn. "I couldn't."

Mr. Ames took off his Stetson and swiped his bandanna across his brow before resettling his hat. "It's already a scorcher today."

"Yes, sir."

"So are we going to dance around each other all day, or are you going to tell me what's going on?"

Nothing like getting right to the point. "I need to explain something to you, sir." Harold swallowed and tried to decide where to start.

"I know my Charlsey's unhappy. I figure you're a big part of it. You want to explain that? Go ahead." A stern mask settled over the man's face.

"I was an idiot, sir."

"Stop calling me sir and tell me what you did to my daughter. I don't like to see her hurting." The man's horse shifted and his saddle creaked.

"Yes, s—I don't know how it happened, but I never realized that Charlsey is also Charlie. I know I was stupid, and when I found out, I said some things I regret."

"Why did you leave?" The stern expression didn't change.

"I went to talk to my father. I value his opinion, and he helped me straighten out my thoughts."

"What are you going to do about it?" Once more his eyes twinkled, and he gave a slight smile.

"I've already apologized to Charlsey, but she won't accept it. I just want a chance to prove to her how much I mean it."

"Is that all?" The man could see right through him.

"Actually, I'd like your approval to court her when she realizes I don't intend to repeat my mistake."

Mr. Ames stared out across the land for long moments before turning back. "If you can get her to forgive you, you have my permission to court her." He lifted his reins, and his horse danced in place. "But if you hurt her again, I'll nail your hide to the barn door. Understood?"

"Yes, s—Mr. Ames. I won't hurt her again." *I just want to cherish her.*

For the next week, Harold hardly caught sight of Charlsey, except at dinner with the whole family. She was more elusive than gold in a worked-out mine. After the meal, she didn't come into the parlor to visit.

Before going to dinner tonight, Harold pulled out his Bible and thumbed through it. He read several short passages from Proverbs. They all pointed toward patience. *Are You trying to tell me something, Lord?*

Go slow, son. Don't spook her.

Harold chuckled. Out here in Texas, God sounded like a cowboy to him. He decided right then to be the most patient man in this large state.

Over the next few weeks, circumstances changed. Maybe because of the commitment he made to the Lord, Charlsey started staying after dinner and visiting with him along with her father and sisters. Soon hope filled Harold's heart, but when he studied Charlsey's face as she talked, a slight hesitancy toward him shadowed her eyes. That had to go away before he could proceed with wooing her.

—w—

For the first few weeks after Boston returned, Charlsey felt wary of him—waiting for him to make one wrong move. When he didn't, she relaxed more and more.

Besides being the handsomest man she'd ever seen, he'd also become immensely more interesting. As the whole family came to know him better, she liked who he really was—neither Dr. Jekyll nor Mr. Hyde. Just an interesting man who loved the Lord and wanted to be a good rancher. He was already a good accountant. That combination spelled success in all the ways that mattered.

This year, August was more of a scorcher than usual. After she finished helping Bess can a couple of bushels of tomatoes, sweat dripped off Charlsey's face and saturated her clothing. All she could think about was taking a dip in the river. Nothing was as refreshing as that, not even a tepid bath.

She tied a bundle of clean clothes to her saddle and headed Dancer to Charlsey's favorite spot. Knowing the hands were working in a different pasture made the slow-moving river a good choice. Since she'd grown up, Pa didn't want her swimming anywhere near the men.

Leaving Dancer grazing in the shade of a clump of weeping willow trees, Charlsey stripped down to her unmentionables and dove in. She stroked through the water, then turned on her back and floated. All her cares washed down the Guadalupe.

Finally, she dressed in her clean clothes before leaving the shelter of the bushes. Dancer raised her head and ambled over to nuzzle Charlsey's neck.

Soon she and Dancer were sailing like the wind across the prairie grass. Charlsey imagined it would feel like this to be a bird.

Abruptly, Dancer went down, and Charlsey sailed through the air, landing hard on her left ankle before her whole body slammed into the ground. Her breath whooshed out of her, and blackness descended.

When she once more became aware of her surroundings, everything hurt. Only a prairie dog hole could make Dancer go down like that, and she hadn't seen any in this area before. If she had, she would have been more careful.

Charlsey gingerly pulled herself into a sitting position with her knees close to her chest, and her surroundings began to swirl. She laid her head on her knees and took several deep breaths. Her ankle throbbed, and she wasn't sure she could put her weight on it.

Dancer stood a few feet away. She gave a whiffling sound with a whine attached. Charlsey studied her horse, noticing that Dancer kept lifting one foot.

"Come to me, girl." She gave a clicking sound that usually brought her horse to her side.

Instead, Dancer sidled over, keeping as much weight as she could off that one leg. No way could Charlsey ride her back to the barn, and Charlsey couldn't stand up. Here she sat in the hot sun, and no one knew where she was. *Lord, I need help right away.*

Dancer nudged her. Charlsey used the reins and saddle to pull herself up on her horse's good side. She untied the canteen then hugged Dancer's neck.

"Go home." She gave the horse a slap on the rump and watched her limp away.

The farther the horse moved, the lonelier Charlsey felt. She took a sip of the lukewarm liquid and recapped the canteen. She might need this water to last a long time.

Her thoughts kept returning to Harold. Why hadn't she let him know that she forgave him? More than forgave. All she wanted was to be with him the rest of her life. Hopefully, she wouldn't die out here before she could let him know. With the intense August heat and no shade nearby, death was a real possibility.

—∞—

Harold closed the ledger and stretched his back. He'd offered to make sure the books balanced for Mr. Ames. Since the older man didn't really like the bookwork, he was glad to get out with the cowboys.

Harold heard a horse with a strange gait approaching. He went to the open door and saw Dancer struggling toward the barn.

"Bart, get out here." His shout echoed in the large building. "Dancer's coming in without Charlsey."

The stable hand ran toward him. "That horse is hurt." He grabbed the reins and led the limping animal into the shade.

"Was Charlsey riding Dancer when she left?"

"Yeah. Wonder where she is."

"We've got to find her, but how?" Harold hurriedly saddled Sunshine.

"Larry is over at his house. I saw him come in a while ago." Bart started cooing at the tired mare. "He's good at tracking."

"Saddle up his horse. I'll go get him."

Tracking was a slow, tedious business. Harold wanted to ride fast and find the woman he loved, but the foreman studied the grass and dusty ground, taking it slow and easy.

They made their way across a vast sea of dry prairie grass like that stupid dime novel described. The grass was so tall that Charlsey could be lying on the ground hidden, so Harold held in his impatience and followed the foreman's lead.

An eternity later, Harold spied Charlsey's head above the waving grass. With her head resting on her knees, she looked wilted in the heat. His heart almost broke, seeing her that way.

He turned toward Larry. "You go on back and have them get a bed ready for her. I'll bring her."

He raced Sunshine across the intervening space. Charlsey raised her head when he leapt from the saddle to crouch beside her.

"Charlsey, are you all right?" He gathered her into his arms and held her tight, her head resting on his chest, a canteen clutched in her hands. *Please, God, let her be okay.*

"Harold." She looked up at him and ran the tip of her tongue along her dry lips. "You came for me."

"Of course I did." He let her feet slowly slide to the ground, but she groaned when one landed. "You're hurt."

She leaned into his embrace. "I think my ankle is broken or at least sprained."

"Do you need a drink?"

"Yes, I was saving the water in case it took a long time for someone to find me."

Still holding her with one arm, he opened the canteen with the other hand. She tipped it up and drank deeply.

"Not too fast." He pulled it away from her. "Don't want you getting sick."

She clung to the front of his shirt with both hands and gazed up at him. "My hero."

"Are you delirious?" He didn't want to believe it, but that could explain her smile.

His attention settled on her lips, no longer dry, but soft and inviting. He tentatively touched them with his own. She didn't pull back, so he settled his on them more firmly.

Her hands slid up his shoulders and clasped behind his neck.

He pulled her closer and lost himself in a world he never knew existed. A place where two hearts meet and intertwine and soar above the mundane to the sublime.

An eon later but much too soon, she pulled away and nestled her face against his neck. Her soft breath both tickled and soothed him.

"Charlsey, I love you, and I want you to be my wife."

She stiffened, then relaxed. "I'd like that."

"You would?" Surprise, then delight, shot through him. "You'll marry me?"

"Yes, Harold. I love you, too."

She sounded so meek, he laughed. "What happened to Boston?"

"That was my bad name for you." She chuckled.

"I like it. You can use it when we're alone. A secret between us."

He lifted her and set her on Sunshine. After mounting, he pulled her back against him.

"Do I see clouds laden with snow on the horizon?"

She twisted and looked up at him as if he were crazy. "This is the hottest day of the year, and I don't see any clouds."

"Ah yes, but a blizzard is coming, my dear, because you have forgiven me."

Their laughter intermingled in a cloud around them. He'd never felt this happy. *Thank You, Lord.*

EPILOGUE

Charlsey's eyes shot open. Today was her wedding day. Christmas Eve 1890. A day she'd never forget. While her sisters had been busy decorating the house for the holiday, Charlsey couldn't keep her mind on that. Too many other things had captured her attention—all of them connected to the man she loved and her upcoming wedding. While her sisters made bows and popcorn and paper garlands for the tree, she worked on her wedding dress of blue velvet with white lace.

So much had happened since that day in August. Harold's parents came to Texas at the end of October. Charlsey loved her future in-laws, and they welcomed her into the family. They accompanied Charlsey and Harold on a trip to the new ranch, which had a two-story house. Mrs. Miller took her shopping in Fort Worth and Dallas to replace the worn furniture while the men caught up on the financial security of the enterprise.

Their new home on the Miller ranch would keep her close enough to her own family to visit often. After all, in this modern day and time, the railroad could take her there so much faster than by wagon or on horseback. They could go to Boston or Chicago whenever Harold needed to for business. A very exciting arrangement. In addition, the railroad was going to take her and her accountant on a wedding trip to Galveston.

Life was wonderful. But it was going to get even better this evening when she and Boston exchanged their vows. Thinking about all that would usher into her life sent delicious shivers up her spine and stirred a longing deep within her.

By tonight, she would be Mrs. Harold Miller III. Mrs. Boston to her and her new husband.

Award-winning author **Lena Nelson Dooley** has had more than 800,000 copies of her books sold. She is a member of American Christian Fiction Writers and the local chapter, ACFW - DFW. She's a member of Christian Authors' Network and Gateway Church in Southlake, Texas.

She has been on both the CBA Bestseller list and several Amazon Bestseller lists. Her 2010 release Love Finds You in Golden, New Mexico, from Summerside Press, won the 2011 Will Rogers Medallion Award for excellence in publishing Western Fiction. Her next series, McKenna's Daughters: Maggie's Journey appeared on a reviewers Top Ten Books of 2011 list. It also won the 2012 Selah award for Historical Novel. The second, Mary's Blessing, was a Selah Award finalist for Romance novel. Catherine's Pursuit released in 2013. It was the winner of the NTRWA Carolyn Reader's Choice contest, took second place in the CAN Golden Scroll Novel of the Year award, and won the Will Rogers Medallion bronze medallion. Her blog, A Christian Writer's World, received the Readers Choice Blog of the Year Award from the Book Club Network.

In addition to her writing, Lena is a frequent speaker at women's groups, writers groups, and at both regional and national conferences. She has spoken in six states and internationally. She is also one of the co-hosts of the Along Came a Writer blog radio show.

Lena has an active web presence on Facebook, Twitter, Goodreads, Linkedin and with her internationally connected blog where she interviews other authors and promotes their books.

Plain Trouble

by Kathleen Y'Barbo

DEDICATION

To, Janice Thompson, who writes
the best dedications in Christendom.

O praise the LORD, all ye nations: praise him, all ye people.
For his merciful kindness is great toward us: and the truth
of the LORD endureth for ever. Praise ye the LORD.
PSALM 117

CHAPTER 1

November 12, 1893

He could still see the dead child, even in his sleep. Or what passed for sleep lately.

Ever since he'd stood on that side street in San Antonio and watched an innocent lad be used as a shield for the guilty, Texas Ranger Josef Mueller had found precious little reason to sleep.

A litany of if-onlys passed through his mind during the day, only to increase in volume when his head hit the pillow. The shooter was a known bank robber who went by the name of Pale Indian. Joe happened upon the scene by accident, practically tripping over the Indian's half-Mexican accomplice behind the livery.

Unfortunately, the Indian spied them first and hauled the livery owner's youngest boy against him as a shield. When Joe didn't shoot, some cowboy with more liquor than sense in his skull did, and in the ensuing chaos a child died and a killer got away. Though the money was returned and the Mexican was tried and convicted, Joe refused to let the death of that boy go unanswered. The cowboy did three days in jail for public drunkenness, a poor answer for his even poorer choice to play hero; but Pale Indian had yet to be prosecuted. Though he'd likely only be sent up on robbery charges, the

Indian killed that boy plain and simple.

With a calm he had to force back into place, Joe lifted his pistol and stared down the barrel at the three targets placed at random on the limestone boulder. His finger on the trigger, left eye closed—one shot and the tin can flew off the fence, proving his aim was true. Another shot and the second can flew, and then a third.

Joe lowered his arm. Three for three. Just like always.

And yet he hadn't the good sense to use his sharpshooter's aim when it counted—when he could have saved the life of a child by taking the life of that worthless murderer.

"I still don't understand why You let that happen, Lord," Joe said under his breath as he slid his weapon back into the holster then slipped his boot into the stirrup. "Or rather, why I wasn't up to killing a man who deserved it."

Following a tip on the Indian's whereabouts halfway across ten counties had seemed like a good idea until last night when the weather turned cold and the ground turned hard. Now he had aches in places he didn't remember existed.

Not that any of this mattered when his pride had taken the worst bruising of all. Pale Indian had been in his sights just as surely as those three tin cans, and he'd somehow let him slip away. Joe thought of the killer now, dressed as if he'd come off the reservation, his white-blond hair stuffed under a wide-brimmed hat that all but hid his face. They'd stood at no more than a hundred paces in that alley, and yet he couldn't say he saw him clear enough to know him in the light of day.

The moment replayed in Joe's mind. Eerie calm on the other man's demeanor, even as the child struggled and cried out. Then a volley of shots that went everywhere but their intended target. Chaos—and an escape. What the Indian would soon know is there was no escape, not when the Texas Rangers were in pursuit.

Joe rolled his shoulders to ease the kinks. To make things

worse, the telegram that found him by way of Sheriff Arrington's office in Hemphill County indicated Pale Indian had been spotted getting off a train at the Horsefly depot. Of all the backwater towns in Texas, why choose the one town Joe had worked so hard to escape?

No matter. Joe had a job to do, and he'd use the familiar territory to his advantage rather than concern himself with going back to a place with nothing but unhappy memories. Two hours later, he began to recognize the landmarks of his birthplace. Joe shook his head. He saw nothing to prove him wrong in thinking the best thing about Horsefly was the trail leading out of town.

He'd said that so many times that it figured he'd now be plagued with an assignment right here in the place he'd happily left some years ago. But a ranger went where he must, and today he found himself in Horsefly.

If Pale Indian was here, he'd soon be caught. In a town the size of this one, no one could remain hidden for long.

This he depended on as he skirted downtown and followed the curve of the Guadalupe River over rolling farmland. Here and there he remembered a spot, thought on the memory, then discarded it. It wouldn't do to get attached to any place, much less this one. His allegiance was to the rangers now, and a homesick ranger was a dead ranger.

Come morning he'd check in with the sheriff, but for now his belly complained. Likely, Mrs. Vonheim had a pot of something warm and delicious simmering and a spare bed made up in the guest room. She always did, though he rarely took her up on her open invitation to visit. Partly, he decided, because his work had hauled him too far from Horsefly to easily return, and partly because it was easier to chase memories away when they didn't live down the road.

The widow's charitable nature went way back, tying the Vonheim and Mueller family trees together with equal strands of good deeds and companionship. Mama cared for Ida Vonheim and Tommy Jr. when Tom Vonheim was shot in cold blood while riding fences back in '79. Not long after, Ida Vonheim tended both Ma and Pa until the influenza took them, then insisted he let her see to him, too. Too sick to climb out of bed for his parents' funeral, Joe fought the fever while the older woman kept cool compresses on his brow and clear broth in his belly.

By the time the fever was gone, so was any desire Joe felt to stay in Horsefly, though he remained long enough to finish his schooling. Thus far, his mind had not changed, though his conscience prickled a bit when he thought about how easy it would have been to post the occasional letter or detour to visit on those times the trail had led him near enough.

No, it was easy enough to remember school days spent with his best friend, Tommy, the widow's only son, rather than dwell on the unpleasantness that caused him to hightail it south and slap on a badge. At least Ida Vonheim had Tommy to keep her occupied, and unless he missed his guess, there'd be a whole slew of grandbabies to fuss over by now.

Tommy always was one to attract the ladies. One of Joe's regrets was that he couldn't manage to convince Tommy to ride out of town with him. "Someday," his friend would say. "Just not today." Then off he'd go extolling the virtues of the latest female who'd fallen prey to his charm.

Joe swiped at his brow and glanced up at a sky that promised rain before nightfall. Reining in his mount as he came across the rise, Joe spied the Ames spread off to the north. Pretty girls, those Ames ladies. *Bessie Mae, plain as day.* He cringed at the memory of the rhyme he'd pronounced at the church picnic after Tommy's ribbing got the best of him. The one that stuck far longer than it should have.

Likely Bess Ames—or whatever her married name was—had long forgotten the stupidity he'd invoked, but Joe knew it to bother him on occasion. If he saw her, maybe he'd let her know what a heel he felt for being the cause of it. Or maybe he'd just keep that to himself.

Women were funny about things like that. Saying anything might be akin to opening a can of worms.

Joe shrugged off the thought. Why was it that he could put himself into the mind of a cold-blooded killer quicker than into the mind of a woman?

—∞—

What was Pa thinking when he hired a man to patch the roof? She could have easily helped with the repairs before the rain set in. With her sisters married off and gone, it wouldn't have been the first time Bess Ames had been called on in a pinch.

His excuse? She huffed as she recalled Pa saying it was unladylike to be climbing on roofs. Since when was he worried about what was ladylike? Hadn't she been the one to fuss over her sisters in that department while he allowed them to work alongside him or flaunt tradition in so many ways?

Why question me now?

"That's the widow's influence," she muttered as she threw a cup of sugar into the pitcher then stirred with a bit more vigor than usual.

Lately Pa had been spending an inordinate amount of time over at the neighboring farm. Helping out, he claimed, though Ida Vonheim had an able-bodied son, Thomas Jr., who could have easily done the work her father now cheerily performed, had he not been overly occupied with his job at the railroad.

To top it off, Pa had taken to whistling. Bess heard it now even as she dropped the spoon into the sink and reached for two glasses, adding them to the pitcher of tea now on the tray. Surely the menfolk would be ready for something cool to drink, what with the temperature rising to almost warm after last night's surprise frost.

Not that a frost in November should be a surprise, but with the weather staying on the decent side so far, the chill slipped through open windows like a thief in the night. Now the sun's warmth did the same, but Pa swore rain would come before nightfall. At least that was what he claimed his bones told him.

"Maybe your bones ought to tell you to stay off the house and away from the widow next door," she muttered as she lifted the tray. Even as she said them, the words pierced her heart. That Pa was still able to work alongside the heartiest of the hired hands was God's great blessing given his age.

The fact that Frank Ames might find a moment's happiness with a woman after two decades spent mourning Mama was a blessing as well. This, Bess could admit in theory. Watching it unfold was altogether different, however, especially given the reminder that even Pa could find a spouse before her.

Bessie Mae, plain as day. The taunt gave ample reason why she'd been left to see to the care of an aging man. Bess sighed. "Unfortunately, I suspect he's an aging man in love."

Balancing the tray, she negotiated the porch steps to set the tray down on the old stump near the eastern side of the house. Shading her eyes against the sun, she peered up to see Pa's hired hand watching her.

"Thought you might be thirsty," she said to the fellow.

" 'Preciate that, miss," he said without breaking his gaze.

"Pa," she called. "I'm going to take the eggs to town." She waited a minute. No response. Only the steady stare of the stranger. "You hear me, Pa?"

Her father's gray head appeared at the roofline. "I hear you," he said. "Didn't think it required a response." He paused. "You plan to make lunch 'fore you go?"

Lunch? For some reason, the question tipped the scales on her brimming anger. "No, Pa," she said. "I figured your hired man could make lunch for you." A pause for good measure and she stepped back into the clearing. "Or better yet, have Mrs. Vonheim fix your lunch for you."

"Now that's a right good idea," Pa said, "except I figured to take supper with her. Meant to tell you not to worry over setting a place for me at the table tonight."

So she'd be eating alone? Again?

Consider it a blessing he's happy, Bess reminded herself. Yet all she could consider was what would happen should Pa do the unthinkable and put someone besides her in charge of caring for him. What would become of her then?

Frowning, she stormed to the barn and retrieved the basket of eggs she'd gathered on her rounds, then made for the road toward town. She'd almost reached the turn at Vonheims' farm when someone called her name.

The stranger, Bess realized when he loped up beside her. Until now she'd not been any closer than a few yards to the lanky man. Figuring him to be someone's relative from the old country, she first greeted him in German. At his confused look, she shook her head.

"What can I do for you?" she amended.

He stopped short then lifted his hat to offer a courtly bow. "Beggin' your pardon, miss, but Mr. Ames wanted to know if you're taking the buggy or walking to town."

Suppressing a groan, Bess squared her shoulders and picked up her pace. In her haste to show her father just how irritated she was, she'd forgotten all about the horse and buggy waiting for her. Now she'd be walking five miles each way, all for pride's sake.

"It's a nice day," she said as she stormed ahead, praying the Lord would see fit to send someone with a buggy to fetch her home before the rain soured her plan. "Is that all?"

"No, ma'am," the fellow said, his voice cracking slightly. "He sent me with a message."

Bess continued walking, though she reluctantly gestured for him to join her. So Pa was too busy to come speak to her himself. *Figures.*

"What might that be? Perhaps to fetch more sweet treats for our neighbor?" she asked when he'd caught up to her. "I understand Mrs. Vonheim was quite taken with the *kolaches* he delivered last time."

A stain of red spread over his freckled cheeks. "I don't know about all that," he said, "but he did mention that you might want to fetch back some of those. . ." He seemed to struggle with the word.

"Kolaches?" she offered as she shifted the egg basket to her other arm.

"Reckon so," he managed before shrugging. "Though he didn't say what he planned to do with 'em."

Of course. "Fine," Bess snapped. "Tell him I'd be glad to."

A look of relief all but erased the fellow's worried expression. "I'll let him know."

"You do that," she said, picking up her pace. "And let him know he can make his own lunch, too."

"Oh, I don't think that's a concern," the hired man called.

Bess sidestepped a puddle then glanced over her shoulder. "No?"

"No, ma'am. I'm on my way over to Mrs. Vonheim's place next to tell her we'll accept her offer of fetching us a noon meal after all."

Well, that does it. Bess might have responded, but in the words of the pastor, "the comment wouldn't have been edifying." So instead she marched toward town, being careful not to jostle the eggs, a difficult undretaking considering the length of the march and how very much she wanted to throw the basket and watch its contents break and splatter.

Only a fool would've given in to the urge, however, and Bess Ames was no fool. The paltry amount she made on these twice-weekly trips had grown into a tidy sum over the years. Enough, in fact, to buy her a train ticket to a place where she might be appreciated.

The only trouble was, Bess couldn't for the life of her figure out where that place was. Even as her sisters each married up and left home, she'd given no thought to leaving Horsefly. Why would she when Pa needed her so?

But now? As far as she could tell, she was about as needed as a screen door in the wintertime.

Bess let out a long breath then put on a smile as she stepped into Kofka's Mercantile to make the first of her deliveries, her feet aching. By the time she reached the sheriff's office on Post Oak Road, her basket was nearly empty.

"A half dozen's all I've got left," she told Miriam, the sheriff's stout Irish housekeeper who tended both the sheriff's quarters and the jailhouse. "But if you'd like to lay claim to a larger share than usual, I can fetch them to you day after tomorrow."

" 'Tis a pity," she said as she removed the eggs and set them gently into the pockets of her apron. "While the jail's blessedly empty this week, the sheriff's expecting someone important. A ranger out of San Antone," she said as if announcing some sort of royal visit.

"Is that right?" Bess counted the coins and dropped them into the drawstring bag she used as a money pouch. Her next trip would be to the bank.

"It's right indeed." She leaned close. "I know you can keep a secret, Bess Ames. You've always been the reliable Ames girl."

The reliable Ames girl. Sadly, that was her in a nutshell. Not talented or even interesting. Not a crack shot or handy with a horse. Not even pretty.

Reliable. *Bessie Mae, plain as day.*

Bess tucked the pouch back into her pocket then noticed that Miriam seemed to be waiting for some sort of answer. "Yes, of course."

Miriam cast a glance over her shoulder where the sheriff sat hunched over what appeared to be a pile of paperwork, his chin resting on his palms. Upon closer inspection, Bess could see that his eyes were closed.

The housekeeper grasped the handle of the empty basket.

"It's Josef Mueller who's coming to catch that Pale Indian fellow. Sheriff Arrington sent a telegram saying he was on the way." She glanced over her shoulder at the still-napping lawman, then back at Bess. "You remember Josef Mueller, don't you? Fine-looking fellow, that one, best I recall, and now he's one of those Texas Rangers. Likely he'll catch this Pale Indian fellow. Wonder who he is."

Miriam prattled on, but Bess's mind had stuck on two words: *Josef Mueller.* Indeed, she remembered him. Fine looking or not, he was the one responsible for the awful school-yard rhyme that upon occasion still intruded on her thoughts.

Bessie Mae, plain as day.

Of all the days to be reminded of that. And of him. Oh yes, she knew Josef Mueller. Pale Indian, however, she'd never heard of. Bess was about to ask when the sheriff roused to sit up straight.

"Miriam," he called. "Either we've got company needing to be invited in or a door that begs to be shut. Which is it?"

"It's just Bess," Miriam called. "Come to bring the eggs."

"Yes," Bess added with a sigh. "*Just* Bess."

"Well, inside or out with you," he called with a chuckle. "The breeze is going to blow away my paperwork."

"More likely you'll lose it to sleeping on it, Sheriff Kleberg," Miriam called as she gave Bess a wink then closed the door.

As she stepped away, Bess could hear the good-natured banter between the pair even as she cast about for the familiar face of someone who might offer her a ride back home to the ranch. Then the door flew open and the sheriff appeared.

"A word with you, Miss Ames," Kleberg said. "I'd appreciate it if you'd not say anything about what Miriam's gone and jabbered about."

"What might that be?" Bess shrugged. "Oh, about Josef. Of course."

His strained expression relaxed. "Wouldn't want to let this

Injun fellow know we're onto him."

She spied the pastor coming out of Eberhardt Emporium and waved in the hopes she'd caught him beginning his round of visits to parishioners instead of completing them. Perhaps she'd not have to walk home after all.

"Miss Ames?" the sheriff said.

"Oh yes. He'll never hear it from me," Bess said with the appropriate amount of sarcasm. It took a moment to realize the lawman was serious. "I was teasing, of course," she added. "I don't even know who this Pink Indian is."

"That's Pale Indian."

"Right." Bess shrugged as she watched the pastor turn toward the church. So much for begging a ride from him. With a sigh, she returned her attention to the lawman. "As I said, I've no idea who this fellow is."

" 'Course you don't." The sheriff's eyes narrowed as he studied her from below the brim of his hat. "See that you're careful till we catch him."

"Careful. Certainly." Bess turned away with a grin. The biggest trouble she'd likely find today was sore feet.

After all, nothing ever happened in Horsefly, Texas.

CHAPTER 2

Joe stepped out into the late-morning sunshine, his belly full of Ida Vonheim's pancakes, eggs, and bacon. Likely she'd clean up the breakfast dishes then start on lunch, after which would come supper. He'd noticed a lack of repairs on the old place but hadn't found a way to ask why Tommy hadn't been doing his duties to care for his mama. Maybe the railroad job that kept him too busy to find a wife also blinded him to the obvious. Familiarity tended to do that. Though figuring out the why of it didn't get anything done.

Thus, his trip to town had been delayed while he allowed Mrs. Vonheim to show him to the hammer and nails so he could take on the more pressing of the repairs. He'd finished the items on her list in short order and gone on to a few more he'd found before the clock over the now-mended mantel sent him scurrying for his gun belt.

Of course, before he could head to town, Joe was called back into the kitchen to taste fresh *springerle* just out of the oven. As the cookies were his favorite, the job wasn't an unpleasant one, but it did cost him another half hour of valuable daylight. When he finally got out the door, Joe was carrying two more springerle and a towel-wrapped mason jar of coffee in his hands.

"A week here and I'd be unfit to ride," he said as he settled onto the saddle. "If Tommy eats like this, he's likely round as a barrel." Hopefully, Tommy would pay his mama a visit before Joe caught up to Pale Indian and dispatched him back to San Antonio.

The mare picked its way across the rocky pasture then broke into a trot once she reached the road to town. Mrs. Vonheim's substantial fare kept him from having to stop for the biscuit and bacon she insisted he bring, though he did pause long enough to water the mare at the edge of the Guadalupe.

Soon enough, Joe caught his first glance at the growing town of Horsefly. Where once just a few sad buildings leaned against one another, now stood freshly whitewashed dwellings and the smart spire of the church. Up ahead where the surprisingly busy road ran into Main Street, Joe spied the saloon—his second planned stop of the day.

First, however, he had to check in with the sheriff. Giving a passing glance to Kofka's Mercantile, which had been considerably smaller last time he saw it, Joe turned the corner onto Post Oak Road. At least the sheriff's office still looked the same. There had obviously been no need to expand this place or the jail when it likely sat empty except for the occasional overcelebrated cowpoke.

Joe intended to keep it that way. If Pale Indian was hiding out in these parts, it wouldn't be for long.

Nudging past a pair of matrons comparing notes on the price of calico, Joe reached for the door of the sheriff's office only to find it fly open of its own accord. "Come on in here," a cheerful woman demanded. "The sheriff's been waiting for you, and I've got lunch on the stove. *Rinderrouladen* it is, and the best you'll find in Horsefly, that's for sure."

At the mention of the familiar German beef dish, Joe opened his mouth to protest, but the woman's hasty exit prevented it. Instead, he found himself shaking hands with a much-older-than-he-remembered Sheriff Kleberg.

"I'm not one for wasting time," Kleberg said. "That's why I had you hauled down here."

Joe shrugged. "But the sheriff over in—"

"It was me who told Arrington to get you heading this way," the sheriff said.

Joe's eyes narrowed. "I'm going to have to ask you to explain yourself, sir."

Kleberg chuckled. "Spoken like a true ranger. You don't sound anything like that kid who hung around the alley behind the jail and shot cans off the fence with his slingshot."

"I suppose not," he said. "But I'd still be obliged if you'd—"

"Explain myself. Right, well, what with the size of this town, do you think I'd be able to keep the fact that I know who this Injun feller is quiet if I marched down to the telegraph office and sent for you?"

"Why me?" he asked.

Kleberg shrugged. "'You were the only man for the job, what with you being his best friend and all."

"Best friend?" Joe shook his head even as the blood froze in his veins. "Not. . ."

"Tommy Vonheim?" The sheriff nodded. "It appears so, Josef."

"You're wrong," Joe blurted out. "If it were him, I'd have suspected. I saw Pale Indian not two weeks ago. It couldn't be. . ."

But as he said the words, he realized he *hadn't* seen Pale Indian clearly enough to identify his face. Not with his hat hiding what the crying child didn't. Joe stormed around the desk and yanked the topmost poster off the jumble of pages tacked to the wall. "You can see for yourself. That man isn't Tommy Vonheim any more than you and I are."

Yet as he tried not to stare, he had to admit there was something familiar around the eyes. And there was the scar just south of the man's left eye that looked a bit like the one Tommy got when Joe dared him to try to catch his mama's banty rooster bare-handed.

Still, it couldn't be Tommy. Joe let the poster drop onto the desk and turned his gaze to the sheriff. "How can a man whose father was shot in cold blood turn around and go the way of a killer?"

Sheriff Kleberg remained silent. As wearers of the badge, they both knew tragedy could just as likely turn a man to evil as to good, especially when the tragedy came as a result of a crime that had never been solved.

Finally, the older man shrugged. "Maybe it ain't. Maybe Tom's just working a lot of hours at the railroad and not able to care for his mama like he used to."

It didn't take a Texas Ranger to see the sheriff didn't mean a word of it. "Or maybe he's on the run and not keen on showing his face much."

Kleberg's expression softened. "Now you see why you're the only man for this job. Any other fella would kill 'im and think nothing of it; but seein' as we've both known that family just about long as we've been alive, I'd like to do the Widow Vonheim the favor of not having to see her son strung up from a tree or carried through town with a bullet in him."

"That is, if he's guilty."

A nod to acknowledge Joe's statement, and then the sheriff pressed on. "I'd like to ask you to haul him out of town quick-like before anyone here's the wiser. 'Cept me, of course."

"Yes, of course," Joe said. "But whoever's under that hat I saw in San Antonio, he'll get a fair trial."

" 'Course he will. You're a good man, Josef." Kleberg paused, watching Joe almost without blinking. "Always were. Like your daddy was. And his before him. You'll do right by Tom in finding out if he's not our man. And if he done it, you'll do right by that, too."

Thoughts jumbled then reformed. Tommy's long absences. The Vonheim home's slow slide into disrepair. Ida Vonheim's inability to look Joe in the eye when the discussion turned to her son. . . .

Two questions rose above the rest: Where was Tommy Vonheim? And was his mother hiding him, possibly right under Joe's nose?

—∞—

Bess took her time paying for the kolaches then slipped the paper-wrapped pastries into her coat pocket and headed for the door. Were she the defiant type, she might have conveniently ignored her father's request. Instead, she did as asked.

Good old reliable Bess.

Sighing, she stepped out into the heavy air and braved a glance at the clouds gathering overhead. Gauging the distance to the farm from here was tricky because she rarely walked the five miles.

"Pride goeth before a fall, you fool," she whispered as she adjusted the ribbons of her bonnet to hold it tight against the breeze. "In your case, it will goeth before a soaking."

Yet there was nothing to do but start walking. If Bess picked up her pace, she just might get home before the bottom fell out of those rain clouds.

Scanning the crowd, Bess saw plenty of familiar faces, but none she could admit her prideful mistake to. No, she'd stormed off without using good sense. It was only right that she'd likely end up walking home through that very thing: a storm.

Bess turned onto Post Oak then headed for the road leading to the ranch, only to remember that she hadn't put her egg money into her savings account at the bank. Tempting as it was to turn around and make the deposit, she kept walking even as the coins jingled in her pocket alongside the kolaches. Soon the town of Horsefly was behind her and nothing but rolling hills ahead.

In the spring and summer, the road passed through some of the prettiest land God ever created; and to take her mind off her already-aching feet, Bess forced attention on that fact. Still, where green pastures had stood just a few weeks ago, all was nearly barren now, what with the couple of chills they'd had. Oh, it would green up soon enough, but for now the mesquites sat short and squat on what looked to be miles of nothing much but brown.

Not that the horses seemed to mind. Or the cattle. From the top of the hill, she could see plenty of both. Ignoring the thunderheads didn't keep them from sliding over the sun and stealing what was left of the afternoon warmth.

Suppressing a shiver, Bess crossed her arms over her chest and tried to walk faster. Unfortunately, the steep uphill grade prevented much progress—but it did help ward off the chill.

When the wind kicked up, she tightened her bonnet strings and began to sing. Only out here, with no one to witness it, would Bess dare sing "Nearer, My God, to Thee" at such a volume. All three of her sisters had been gifted with voices worthy of the church choir, while Bess's was more suitable to the back row. But the cows didn't seem to mind and only a few horses skittered away, so she sang all the verses she could remember then went right into singing "Just as I Am, without One Plea."

Up ahead she could see the twisted oak that marked the edge of the Schmidts' ranch. Bess smiled. Somehow she'd managed to walk two miles in what seemed like no time. *Must be the singing.*

"Only three to go," she sang before launching into the first verse of "Rock of Ages." When the sound of thunder interrupted, Bess sang louder. She was halfway through the fourth stanza when she realized someone was singing harmony.

In a very beautiful, very male tenor.

CHAPTER 3

Joe grinned as the mare cleared the top of the hill. There he found the other half of his impromptu duet: a stunning brunette with a lanky frame and a dress of butter yellow to match her bonnet. She looked as skittish as a colt and just as long-legged, and she sang loudly enough to wake the dead. Dangling from the crook of her arm was a basket that appeared to be empty.

Just who was this pretty stranger? Must be new to Horsefly. She certainly didn't look like anyone he knew. Another glance confirmed it. If he'd met this filly, he'd have remembered.

Tipping his hat, Joe put on his friendliest smile as he reined in his mare and stopped short a few paces away. "Well, howdy, miss. I don't believe we've been introduced. I'm—"

"It wasn't funny then, and it's not funny now, so just keep on riding to wherever you're going and leave me be, Josef Mueller."

How did she know his name?

The woman continued to offer him her back as she marched down the dusty road. His mama had taught him not to stare, and yet stare Joe did as the basket at her elbow swung against her left hip bone.

He had to look at the basket. Anything else wouldn't be right, what with the fact he hadn't seen a woman this pretty since. . .well, ever, if he were to be honest. When she stopped, the swaying stopped, and so did Joe.

"Just pass me by, Joe," she said, her backbone stiff and her shoulders a notch past proud.

There was something in her voice that his ranger training caused him to notice. Not anger, but maybe something close to it.

The mare wanted to trot, but he held the horse to a slow walk so he could keep a proper distance behind the gal whose face he couldn't quite place. "Do I know you?" he finally called out once he'd gone through every school-yard sweetheart's name twice. "Because you'll have to forgive me for not remembering you."

That seemed to do something that his sweet-talking couldn't accomplish. She stopped short and turned to face him. "Look, Joe. I know you're here to catch that Pink Indian fellow, but—"

"Pale Indian," he corrected as his senses prickled. Kleberg had told him no one knew about the Indian. Could this be an accomplice? Tommy always did attract the pretty ones. "How do you know about Pale Indian?"

"I sold eggs to the sheriff's. . ." Brown eyes narrowed. "Why does it matter?"

Thunder rumbled in the distance, cutting short any idea of lengthy response. At this rate Joe would likely be drenched before he reached Mrs. Vonheim's place. Yet he could hardly leave her when he knew nothing but the fact that she knew too much.

Joe climbed down from the saddle and held tight to the reins. Maybe she'd open up to him if he met her at eye level. And given her height, he'd just about do that.

Yellow Bonnet commenced walking faster, and it didn't take a ranger to figure out why when the first fat drops of rain pelted him. The mare didn't like bad weather; this much he'd learned on the trail from San Antonio. And so getting her—and himself—and this woman out of the rain became a priority. Even if she were some kin to the Schmidt family, the ranch house was a good half mile back.

He slid back into the saddle and nudged the horse into a trot. As he came alongside the woman, he pulled back on the reins. "I reckon neither of us want the soaking we're about to get." Joe swiped at the rain on his saddle horn. "I'd be obliged if you'd let me take you where you're going."

She looked for a moment as if she might consider it then shook her head. "As I said," she tossed over her shoulder, "go ahead and pass me by. I can get home just fine."

Off in the distance lightning zagged across the sky, and Joe counted the seconds until thunder rolled toward him. "Best I can tell, the worst of this storm's a good three miles east," he called. "So unless you're just about home, I figure you're not going to get a better offer than mine." He wanted to add, "Whoever you are," but instead held his tongue.

Another crack of lightning, this one close enough to feel, lit the worsening gloom. Thunder followed almost immediately, and with it came a strong east wind. Quick as that, the shadows had faded to near-darkness until the afternoon looked the same as night.

Joe knew immediately this was no normal autumn storm. "Looks like neither of us is going to get home dry," he said as he made an executive decision and spurred the horse on, "but at least we're both going to get home safe. When I reach you, jump."

"And if I don't?" From what he could see of the woman, her face held a little bit of arrogance and a whole lot of anxiety.

The rain plopped down in drops the size of half-dollars on the road between them, and the wind began to gust. He shouldn't tarry, nor could he leave her here.

"You'll still end up on my horse, miss," he said as he jammed his hat low on his head, "but I guarantee it won't be near as soft a landing."

She looked doubtful until a bolt of lightning cracked behind her.

With that, the horse tossed her head back and tried to shake the bit. "Settle down there," Joe muttered as he held tight to the reins. "Another minute and you can run for the barn."

He guided the stomping mare as close as he could to Yellow Bonnet; then, holding tight to the saddle with his left hand, he reached down to wrap his right arm around her waist. In a move he'd as yet practiced only with ornery goats back in San Antonio, Joe hauled the woman up and over the saddle then situated her across his lap sidesaddle.

With the added weight, the mare pranced and threatened to bolt. Or maybe it was the lightning, which was now so close Joe could almost feel the electrical charge as it hit a mesquite in the pasture up ahead. The woman squealed but never loosened her grip, even when the wind whipped the ribbons of her bonnet across her face.

"Hold on tight," he said. "I've got a good horse, but she's not keen on this kind of weather."

"Nor am I."

She wrapped her arms around him and grabbed two handfuls of his shirt as the mare took off like a shot, nearly sending them both tumbling backward. Only Joe's instincts kept him in the saddle, though they were seriously tested by the presence of the now-damp female.

"Where's home?" Joe asked when he regained his balance.

"Since nobody's moved the Rocking A, it's just down the road, Joe."

"The Rocking A?" He took his eyes off the road just long enough to glance at his companion. "You one of those Ames girls?"

"Yes," she said against his ear, though her voice was nearly hidden by the sound of the storm.

A gust of wind brought a torrent of rain, preventing any

further conversation. So did the fact that Joe was acutely aware of the shoulder leaning against his and the scent of something flowery that seemed to come from beneath her bonnet. Then there were the arms wrapped around his back and belly.

A man who might consider any one of those things was a man who'd not get where he was supposed to be heading. Joe shook his head to clear the details and nearly lost his hat in the process. Thankfully the Ames girl caught it and placed it back where it belonged.

If only she'd taken a minute to set it on straight, he might have been able to see a little better. By the time the Ames ranch loomed ahead, however, the storm had grown to such proportions that Joe could barely guide the mare even if the brim of his Stetson hadn't shaded one eye.

Dense trees bordered both sides of the road, leading them over another hill and then down into a valley before the Ames home came into view. Set atop a hill with outbuildings behind it and the well off to the south, the ranch house was lit up downstairs and dark upstairs. Someone stood in the open door, likely Frank Ames.

Joe urged the mare up the hill while the Ames girl, whichever one she was, kept her grip on his shirt until her pa raced out to pluck her from his saddle. Oddly, Joe felt the absence of the thin beauty immediately, though he could still smell the flowers even as the rain pelted his face.

Looking past the elder Ames to the younger one, Joe couldn't help but notice that whichever girl he'd returned to her pa, she was definitely the pretty one. Even in her sodden frock and flattened bonnet. Even as liquid ice poured down his neck and soaked him to the skin.

The woman paused on the porch to right her bonnet then gave up and tossed it aside. Hairpins went flying, revealing a length of glossy wet hair the color of mahogany.

Concentrate, Mueller. He still had another mile to go before the Vonheim house would welcome him, but at least he'd done his duty and delivered the lady to her doorstep.

" 'Preciate you bringing my girl home," Frank called as he ducked back onto the porch. "Come on in out of the weather."

Movement behind Frank Ames drew Joe's attention. There in the hallway was a blond-haired man. A man who could have easily been the man on Pale Indian's wanted poster.

Even though she knew she must be leaving a trail of water puddles behind her, Bess held her head high until she reached the safety of her bedroom. Only then, with the door solidly closed, did she sling the wet bonnet on the floor and remove her shoes and stockings.

Next, Bess stepped out of her skirt and dropped it beside her bonnet then fumbled with her petticoat. She'd only just washed her favorite yellow dress, and now she'd have to do it again. "And look at the mud caked on the hem. I'll be scrubbing for days to get that out."

Then she spied her reflection in the mirror atop her dressing table. "Of all the people to see me drenched like a wet hen, it would be Josef Mueller," she muttered as she pushed away the reminder of how it felt to lean against his muscled shoulder, to feel his arm around her, even if it was merely to keep her from falling and tripping his horse.

Oh, but hadn't the years been kind to Joe? And a Texas Ranger? "Mercy," she whispered. Then came the reminder in the form of the rhyme; her handsome hero had once been a schoolyard bully with a wicked ability to rhyme and wound.

"Bessie Mae, plain as day. Well, isn't that the truth?"

Turning her back on the mirror, Bess made short work of changing into dry clothes then went back for her brush and wrangled her hair into submission. That feat accomplished, Bess walked to the window. Outside the fat pellets of rain peppered the pane and obscured the familiar landscape. She pressed her finger to the glass and traced the path of a raindrop, but her mind was back at the little schoolhouse on First Street. She was seven, not twenty-seven, and her papa told her almost every day that she was the prettiest girl in the second grade. Bess knew now that her father had learned to braid hair from the ranch foreman's wife, but back then she just thought he was good at braiding because he was good at everything.

Then came Josef Mueller, and she knew Pa hadn't been truthful with her. It was the second-worst day of her life.

"At least he's just visiting," Bess said as she rested her forehead on the cool glass pane. "Soon as Joe leaves, things'll get back to normal around here."

Then she thought of Ida Vonheim and the fact that her father would likely marry the woman sooner rather than later. Another drop traced a path down the glass, quickly followed by more, this time on the inside of the pane.

This time they were teardrops.

CHAPTER 4

Ten minutes after he'd deposited Bess Ames at the front door of her Pa's house, Joe had the mare in a spare stall in the barn and was sitting at the kitchen table waiting for Frank Ames to pour coffee. Despite the offer of a towel, his damp clothes were sticking to him in places that made lingering uncomfortable, and there was a chill in the room. Still, he had a job to do, and finding out about the blond stranger came before creature comforts.

"You worked here long?" he asked the man who stood nervously in the doorway.

"Today's my first day," he said without meeting Joe's gaze.

"Cal's quite the roofer." Frank set a steaming mug in front of Joe then took the seat across from him. "Thanks to him we got the hole patched before the bottom fell out of those clouds."

"Where'd you live before you came to Horsefly, Cal?" Joe asked as casually as possible.

His ears turned red, and then, by degrees, the color spread to his face. Still he would not look at Joe.

"He's cousin to the Schmidts," Frank offered.

"Is that right?" Joe toyed with the edge of the towel. "Where'd you live before?"

This time Cal braved a glance in his direction. "San Antone," he said.

Joe's eyes narrowed. Had he found the man who might be Pale Indian so easily? It seemed so. "Why'd you leave?" he asked evenly then punctuated the question with a lift of his brow.

When Cal didn't answer immediately, Frank pushed back his chair and shook his head as he rose. "Ida tells me you're a ranger now, Joe."

He tore his attention from Cal to find Frank studying him. "Ida?"

"Ida Vonheim."

Joe couldn't help but notice it was Frank's turn to look embarrassed. *Interesting.*

"I am," he said. "Ranger company out of San Antone." Joe stared past Frank at Cal. "Sounds like you and I come from the same place. Small world, isn't it, Cal?"

"Sure is."

"I'll say." Frank shrugged. "Look at how you just happened to be coming down the road at the right time to save my Bess."

Joe nearly fell out of his chair. That gorgeous woman was. . . "Bess?" Bessie Mae, plain as day, had certainly blossomed in his absence.

Frank chuckled. "She lit out of here this morning with more spunk than good sense. I reckon she took exception to the fact I had Cal up on the roof helping instead of her." Another chuckle. "Ain't that right, Cal?"

Silence.

Cal was gone.

Frank shook his head then took a healthy gulp of coffee. "Don't mind him," he said as he set the cup back on the table. "He's not much for conversation."

Most bank robbers-turned-murderers aren't. "What do you know about him, Frank?"

The older man shrugged. "Gus Schmidt come by with him last week. Said his nephew was new in town and needed work. Said he'd vouch for him. Why?" He paused to narrow his eyes.

"You're here on ranger business, aren't you?"

Joe only hesitated a moment before making the decision to draw Frank Ames into his circle of confidants. "I'm going to need your cooperation and your word that what I tell you won't leave this room before I answer that."

"You've got both," he said.

"No questions asked?"

"Don't need to," the rancher said. "Your daddy raised you to be a good God-fearin' man, and the state of Texas put a badge on your chest. That's good enough for me."

A sip of the strong brew, and Joe was ready to tell the tale. Choosing his words carefully, he caught Frank up on his reason for returning to Horsefly. "I'm not sure if Ben Kleberg wants me to take Tommy in or prove him innocent," he said. "I know what I'd prefer, but I've got to stay neutral."

Even as he said the words, Joe knew they weren't completely the truth. There was nothing he'd like better than to prove Pale Indian was someone—anyone—other than Tommy Vonheim.

Frank rose and walked to the stove then returned with the coffeepot to pour himself another cup. Joe waved away his offer of more then watched while the rancher studied him. Finally, he returned the pot to the stove.

"So either I've got a criminal for a neighbor or a criminal for an employee?"

Joe rose and carried his cup to set it in the sink. "Or neither."

The older man's expression was unreadable as he seemed to be considering both options. Finally, he straightened and stepped away from the stove. "All right, Ranger. How can I help you?"

"I'm already staying with Mrs. Vonheim, so I'll know if Tommy comes around." He paused to think a moment. "But I'll need access to your place, sir. If I'm going to keep an eye on Schmidt, it can't appear as though that's what I'm doing. I'll also need a cover story for anyone who wants to know why a ranger who's been long gone from Horsefly would return." A thought occurred. "And there's one more thing. Your daughter knows about Pale Indian."

He gave Joe a sideways look. "Oh?"

"Does Bess sell eggs in town? Maybe to the sheriff? She mentioned she did."

"She does. That's how she came to be walking back alone." He shook his head. "Actually, she generally takes the buggy, but she left here in a huff this morning. Guess I should've known she'd not take kindly to me dividing my time between her and, well, I just should've talked to her first. Then maybe she wouldn't have left like she did." Frank must have realized he was rambling, for he smiled. "Guess it's too late for the short answer, but that would be yes, Sheriff Kleberg's usually the second stop on her morning route. I believe the emporium's first. Or maybe the mercantile. I rarely go with her, so forgive an old man for not remembering."

Frank Ames was hardly old, so he let the comment slide by without response. "Then it would be reasonable to assume she likely overheard something about Pale Indian while delivering eggs to the sheriff's office." He chose his words carefully. "You understand I will have to be certain of that before I can completely clear her."

"Clear her?" Gray brows rose. "Of what?"

Joe gave the man an even stare. "Until I told you about him, had you heard of Pale Indian?" When Frank shook his head, Joe continued. "Seems like the only folks who have besides the lawmen who want to catch him are his victims and his friends." Another pause. "I'd like to be sure she's neither of those."

"As would I, young man, but before we go any further, there's something else you need to know. I've got a connection to the Vonheim family that ought to be out in the open if I'm going to be involved in catching Tommy or setting him free."

"All right," Joe said, already guessing what that connection might be.

"That Ida Vonheim, she's quite a woman, and her husband was a good man, rest his soul. And, well. . ." Frank cleared his throat and looked away. "I believe the Lord's trying to put us together, Ida and me, though I'm just as certain Bess isn't so keen on it."

Not a complete surprise, as his hostess had mentioned Frank Ames more than once during their brief time together. Joe settled on a nod as the appropriate response.

Frank's attention returned to Joe. "She's never said it, but I wonder if being the last Ames girl still under my roof hasn't caused her some measure of discontent."

"Could be." Hard to believe that one hadn't been the first to wed, at least if beauty were a measure of marriageability. "Which one are you going to listen to, Frank?"

A slow smile began. "Wise words, young fellow. And as for this situation with the Indian fellow, I believe I've got an idea that just might work."

Joe glanced out the window and noted that the rain had let up considerably. Maybe he'd take a look around the Ames place before heading back to Ida's dinner table. Likely he could find the elusive Cal Schmidt and extract an answer or two.

"Joe, you want to hear my plan?"

He turned his attention to the rancher. "Sorry, sir. Yes, please."

"All right, so you've got a man to catch and I've got a daughter to protect."

"Protect? I'm not looking to arrest her. Just need to be sure she's—"

"I know all that." Frank waved away his protest. "What I mean is, if either Cal or Tommy is the man you're looking for, then my daughter's living in close proximity to a criminal and she doesn't know it. Bess is a friendly gal, and she's known

Tommy since he was a kid in knee pants. Cal she's not so fond of yet, but he's right here sleeping in the bunkhouse. Then there's the issue of why you're in Horsefly. Can't exactly say you're hunting a local, now, can you?"

Joe waited while the man warmed to his topic.

"Yes, well, here's my idea, and understand I'm going to have to run it by the Lord before I decide it's something I'll be party to. But what say you tell folks you've come back to Horsefly on a mission of another sort?"

"A mission?" Joe shook his head. "What kind of mission would bring me back here? Most everyone knows I'm a ranger and have been for years. What could possibly bring me back to Horsefly? And what does that mission have to do with finding Pale Indian and keeping your daughter safe?"

Frank Ames chuckled. "Oh, that's the best part, young man." He reached over to clasp his hand onto Joe's shoulder. "You're a ranger, all right, but word is you've been promoted to a desk job up there in San Antone. Is that right?"

"Well, I do spend less time on the trail than I used to. Why?"

The hand on his shoulder gripped tighter. "How old are you, Joe?"

"I'll be thirty-two come spring. Why?"

"A ranger in possession of a good salary and a desk job is surely going to start thinking about a wife, don't you think? And what better place than Horsefly, Texas, to find one?"

Shock rendered him speechless. Then came the sound of footsteps. Had Cal Schmidt returned? Automatically, Joe's hand went to the revolver at his side.

"Pa?" came a familiar female voice from somewhere on the other side of the wall.

"Come on in here, Bessie Mae," Frank Ames said with a wicked grin. "Ranger Mueller and I were just talking about you."

CHAPTER 5

R*anger Mueller?*

Bess pasted on what she hoped would be a pleasant expression then allowed her father to give her a hug before facing Joe Mueller. "I didn't realize you were still here," she said to him. "If you'll excuse me, I'll leave you men to your conversation."

Before Pa or the ranger could respond, Bess scurried out the door and headed for the staircase. Her foot rested on the second riser from the top when Pa's voice stopped her cold.

"Elizabeth Ames, I've never tolerated rudeness in my home and I'm not about to start now."

Rude? Elizabeth?

She turned slowly while she adjusted her smile. There at the bottom of the stairs stood her father and Joe Mueller. While Pa wore a familiar irritated look, Joe just seemed to be staring, his soggy Stetson dangling from his left hand. Likely he rarely heard a grown woman being treated like a child.

Yet she knew she deserved the reproach. "I'm sorry, Pa. It was not my intention to offend."

Pa gestured to Joe. "Then you ought to come on down here and thank Ranger Mueller here for seeing you got home safe."

Back straight. Smile in place. Hand tight on the rail.

Bess made her way carefully down the stairs until she

reached the bottom riser. This put her just above eye level with her school-yard tormentor. Though she planned to make amends with Joe as her father asked, she ignored the ranger to address Pa first. "Forgive my impertinence, Pa." True conviction hit her swift and hard. "Starting with this morning. My behavior was inexcusable."

Pa seemed surprised. "It was, but I do." The look on her father's face told her there would be more discussion on the topic later. "Well, all right then. I'll leave you two to finish this conversation." He turned to Joe and offered his outstretched hand. "I'll look forward to seeing you around the ranch, Joe."

Seeing you around the ranch? While Pa disappeared back into the kitchen, Bess worked her surprised expression back into something more neutral before turning her attention to the rain-soaked ranger.

Their gazes collided, and Bess tightened her grip on the rail. In the parlor, the clock struck the half hour. "My father's right," she finally said. "I'm grateful to you for my safe return home." *Though I'll likely have bruises by nightfall.*

Joe ran his free hand through still-wet hair. "Though you'd likely have preferred not to have been tossed across my saddle like a sack of potatoes."

Actually. . . "You've got a point," she said. "A buggy might have been a bit more suited to the weather."

"A buggy." He paused. "I understand you went off without yours this morning."

Heat flooded her face. What else had Pa told the ranger? "It was a lovely morning for a walk."

Inwardly she groaned. *I sound like a silly schoolgirl.*

He didn't appear to know what to say next, so Bess decided to end the agony. "Well, I do thank you for all you did, Joe."

"What?" His shoulders straightened. "Oh yes, well, I should go. I'm sure Mrs. Vonheim will be wondering if I've drowned."

Mrs. Vonheim. She tried not to react to the mention of Pa's sweetheart.

"Something wrong?" Joe asked.

So it didn't work. "Wrong?" She shook her head. "No, nothing." *Nothing I'd be willing to tell you, anyway.*

Joe looked doubtful but, after a moment, set the hat on his head. "All right then. I suppose I ought to be going."

A scrape that could only be a kitchen chair against the wood floor echoed across the hall. "Joe, hold on there," Pa called.

So her father had been listening. Bess sighed and leaned heavily against the rail. She watched carefully. *What is Frank Ames up to?*

Joe turned and met Pa halfway. The pair shook hands and seemed to exchange glances before the ranger turned to leave. Or maybe she imagined it.

"Joe," Pa called as the ranger opened the door. "Bess makes a fine roast. What say you join us after church on Sunday? That would be nice, wouldn't it, Bess?"

"Nice," she echoed, unable to believe her ears.

Thankfully, Joe appeared ready to turn Pa down. At least that was what the undecided look seemed to say. "I'd have to be sure Mrs. Vonheim doesn't have plans to make her own Sunday dinner, though." He glanced over at Bess. "I'm staying at the Vonheim place while I'm here."

She gave a half nod, sufficient to let him know she heard.

"Then you'll definitely be here, because Ida told me just this afternoon that she'd be pleased to eat with us on Sunday."

Ida? Bess jerked her attention toward Pa as the words sunk in. "She did?"

"She did," her father said evenly.

"Well then, I'll see you both on Sunday." Joe tipped his hat to Bess then made good his escape.

When the door shut, Pa gestured for her to follow him into the kitchen. She did, reluctantly.

"I know what you're going to say, Pa," she said from the doorway. "And before you do, you should know that I'm very happy you've found some measure of happiness with Mrs. Vonheim."

"You are?" Pa settled in a chair and rested his elbows on the table. "You sure?"

Bess sighed. "I'm sure I will be."

He smiled. "That's my girl. Now what's for supper?"

"Supper?" Bess asked. "I thought you were taking supper with Mrs. Vonheim."

"I changed my mind." Her father shrugged. "Figured I'd rather spend time with my daughter tonight."

"That's not the truth at all, is it, Pa?"

"Bess," came his warning tone. "I changed my mind, and that's that. Now if you don't mind, I'm going to go check on things in the barn while the rain's let up a bit." He rose. "Go on and get started. I'd like to get to bed early tonight. It's been a long day."

"All right, Pa, but don't expect kolaches."

He stopped at the door and glanced over his shoulder. "Why?"

"Let's just say there's not much left of the ones I bought in town this morning."

Pa started to laugh. "Oh no."

"Oh yes," Bess said. "And it's going to take more than one washing to get the remains out of my pocket."

"Next time I'll fetch them myself," he said with a chuckle.

"Next time I'll take the buggy." Bess attempted to keep a straight face but soon joined her father in smiling even as she reached for the dish towel.

"Well, thank the Lord for Joe Mueller." When she didn't respond, Pa continued. "He's a good man, that Joe." A pause. "And he's spoken favorably of you."

Bess froze. "He's what?" She let the towel drop onto the

counter. "How can he speak of me at all? Joe Mueller doesn't even know me anymore." *And when he did, he treated me awful.*

"Now don't you take that tone with me, Bess Ames. I believe the Lord led Joe here, and I'll not hear anything about it from you."

"Why would the Lord lead him here? According to Marian up at the sheriff's office, the ranger's based out of San Antonio, so technically if he's here at all, it's not to stay."

Pa crossed his arms over his chest. "So you've been discussing him as well?"

"I've done no such thing. But try and stop Miriam when she's busy telling a story." Bess turned back to her dishwashing.

"Yes, well, just promise me you'll give the ranger a chance, Bess."

"A chance?" She glanced at Pa over her shoulder. "What an odd thing to ask of me. What sort of chance would Joe Mueller be asking for anyway?"

"I suppose we'll find out soon enough," he said, though Bess had the distinct impression her father already knew the answer to her question.

And that troubled her more than anything.

CHAPTER 6

The dining room smelled of roast beef and apple pie, and the table had been set in what was surely the Ames family's best china. Sunlight streamed through windows framed by curtains that matched the napkin stretched across his lap.

Joe looked across the table at Bess Ames, a vision in blue gingham, and wondered whether the pretty girl had forgotten how to smile. She'd certainly seemed unhappy when he slid into the Ames family pew at church this morning. When he sang, she frowned. On the ride back from town, she'd failed to appreciate the fact he'd arrived in a buggy rather than on horseback, something he'd done just to make her grin. And she'd only ridden beside him because her pa insisted.

Neither had his gift of her missing egg basket made her happy, though it had cost him several lost hours while he searched for it along the road from town. A muttered thank-you was all he'd received, and even that seemed reluctant.

It was enough to make a man think he'd lost his ability to woo a woman. Not that he was trying to do that, of course, though it did wound him a bit when she missed his attempt to help her from the carriage and stepped right past him.

"Didn't the reverend have a nice sermon, Joe?" Mrs. Vonheim asked as she dabbed at her chin with her napkin.

"Yes, ma'am," Joe said. "I've heard some preaching in my day, but today was exceptional." He slid Bess a glance and noticed she seemed to be studying him. When Joe met her gaze, the Ames girl looked away.

"Bess, wasn't Ida's pie delicious?"

This time Bess met her father's stare. "It was," she said. "Might I have the recipe, Mrs. Vonheim?"

"Of course, dear," Ida said, "but only under one condition."

The Ames woman set her fork down. "What's that?"

Frank relaxed visibly and then offered Bess a smile before reaching to place his hand atop Ida's. "Why don't I show you that new foal we've got out in the barn, Ida?"

"I would like that very much," Ida said. "But might I have a word with Bess first?" She hesitated. "Alone, if you gentlemen don't mind."

Joe rose first, unwilling to witness any family trouble. While he was willing to keep to his agreement with Frank to watch over Bess, he had his limits.

By the time he reached the porch, Frank was on his heels. "I think it's going pretty well, don't you?"

"Depends on what you're trying to accomplish, Frank." Joe stepped off the porch, avoiding the patch of mud still remaining from the deluge of the last two days. "I'd give that conversation that's about to happen even odds on whether it's going to be good or bad."

Frank clapped his hand on Joe's shoulder. "Have faith, boy," he said. "Ida and I have been praying about this."

"Well, good," he said. "Now about your employee Cal. I spoke to Sheriff Kleberg yesterday afternoon."

"And?"

"And it turns out Kleberg's known Cal since he was a kid. Something about Kleberg's wife and Cal's grandmother being kin." Joe shrugged. "It's enough to satisfy me for now, but I'm still not convinced. The sheriff's going to check out the suspect's whereabouts for the past month."

"The suspect?" Frank stopped short. "You sure you're still remaining neutral?"

"I'm trying," Joe said.

"Well, that's all we can ask, now, isn't it?" Frank pointed to the toolshed. "If you've got a few minutes, I'd like to show you the pistol I found behind the well yesterday."

"Pistol?" Joe shook his head. "Why didn't you mention this sooner?"

"Because it's an old flintlock, Joe, and not in any condition to be shot. Likely carried downhill with the flood. Have you ever seen one of them?"

"I have," Joe said, "but it's been awhile. Mind showing me?"

"Come with me. I've got it taken apart so I can clean it, but I think you'll still find it interesting." Frank turned toward the shed, and Joe followed. "About Bess, I couldn't help but notice things are a bit cool between the two of you."

Joe stepped over the rocky outcropping. "I don't know what I'm doing wrong, Frank. At this rate no one in Horsefly's going to believe I came here to make a wife out of Bess Ames. Why, she won't even give me the time of day." He paused. "I'd appreciate any advice you might give me. Otherwise, I'm going to forget about this plan and come up with another one."

"I wonder if maybe. . ." Frank paused to gesture toward the road. "There's somebody coming."

Joe followed his gaze to see the lone figure riding toward them. It only took him a minute to recognize the rider.

"Tommy."

"Bess, I'd like to speak to you woman to woman." Ida Vonheim settled back against her chair and rested her hands in her lap. "And not to talk pie recipes."

"All right." Bess fumbled with the napkin then set it aside to give her attention to the blue-eyed woman at the head of the table.

"I understand your father's spoken to you about me." Her gaze never wavered, even when Bess remained silent. "I love him, Bess, but I won't come between a father and daughter, and I'd never dream of taking the place of your mother in your heart."

Well, that wasn't what she'd expected.

The older woman sighed. "So I'm here to turn propriety on its ear and ask you for your blessing on our relationship."

"My blessing?" The words soured in her mouth. "But I don't have the right to—that is, my father's a grown man and he—"

"And he would never hurt you, Bess. Unless you approve of us, I'll leave him to you." She rose. "Much as it will pain me and, likely, Frank, I'll do it to keep from driving a wedge in this family."

Something softened inside Bess. "You do love him, don't you?"

"I do."

"As do I." Bess rose as tears threatened. Ida Vonheim held out her arms, and Bess fell into them.

"Well, aren't you two chummy?"

Bess stepped out of the older woman's arms to see Tommy Vonheim standing in the doorway. Behind him were Pa and Joe Mueller.

"Am I too late to get a plateful of whatever it is that smells so good in here?"

In between bites, Tommy entertained the group with tales of life on the railroad. By the time the last piece of pie had been consumed, Bess remembered why she'd always enjoyed her neighbor's company.

If only he hadn't been best friends with Joe Mueller.

"Much as I hate to eat and leave, I'd love to see my own bed tonight," Tommy finally said. "And my mother looks as if she might be tired as well."

Mrs. Vonheim didn't look that way at all to Bess, but she said nothing, and neither did Ida. While Pa walked mother and son out, Joe remained behind. "I'll help with the dishes, Bess," he said, rolling up his sleeves.

"No need." She turned her back and hauled an armload of dishes into the kitchen then reached for the pump to fill the sink.

A sound behind her told Bess that Joe had ignored her. One more trip to the kitchen and he'd cleared the table. *Maybe he'll leave now,* she thought.

But he didn't. Finally, Bess had enough of the lawman standing behind her. She whirled around to face him, prepared to do battle.

"Go home, Joe Mueller," she said. "There's nothing else for you here."

He appeared to consider her statement. A curt nod, and the ranger walked out, leaving her alone with her thoughts. She'd already returned to her work at the sink when she heard footsteps heading her way.

Good. It was time to talk to her father about making peace with Ida Vonheim. "Pa," she called as she reached for the dish towel to dry her hands. "I've got something to tell you."

"It's me, Bess," Joe said. "Not your father."

Bess threw the towel onto the counter but remained in place. Words escaped her. A good thing considering the fact she'd likely need to apologize should her thoughts be heard.

"Turn around, please," he said then waited until she did. "There's something I'm long overdue in saying."

She complied and found that Joe Mueller had moved closer than she expected. He reached out to touch her sleeve. "Bess, I did you wrong back in school, and I never have made it right." Joe shrugged. "If I could go back and change things, I would, but all I can do now is ask you if you'll forgive me for that awful rhyme I made up about you." He paused to grasp her wrist. "Will you? Forgive me, that is?"

All those things Bess had planned to say to Joe someday

dissolved under his even stare. "Forgive you?" she whispered. "I—that is, there's nothing to forgive."

His expression told her he didn't believe a word of it. Bess looked away to study the pattern on the kitchen rug. "All right, it did hurt." She lifted her gaze to meet his. "A lot."

"Bess," he said softly as he released her wrist. "I was such an idiot. I would have said anything for a laugh."

She hid her trembling hands in the pockets of her apron. "The fact it was true didn't mean you should say it."

"Oh, Bess." This time when he reached for her, it was to touch her shoulder. "When I look at you now, I can't believe I ever thought you were. . ."

Her eyes found his. "Bessie Mae, plain as day?"

"Not anymore." Joe leaned toward her and brushed his knuckles against her cheek as he moved a strand of hair from her face. "You've grown into such a—"

The front door slammed shut, and Joe took a step backward. "Joe, you still here?" Pa called.

"I am, sir," Joe responded as he scrubbed at his face with his palms. "In the kitchen with Bess."

"Good, because I decided to go fetch that flintlock. It's in pieces, but I think—" Pa rounded the corner with something in his hands then stopped short. "Oh, I'm interrupting."

"No," they said in unison.

"What is that, Pa?" Bess asked as she swiped at her eyes with the dish towel.

"You're crying, Bess Ames." He turned to Joe. "What did you say to upset her?"

"It's fine," she said, "and Joe didn't say anything to upset me." She glanced up at Joe. "Everything's fine, isn't it?"

"Yes," he said with the beginning of a smile. "It's fine."

"All right then," Pa said. "If you don't mind, Bess, I'm going to show the ranger this flintlock I found out by the well."

"No, go right ahead," she said. "We were done." Bess turned

back to tackle the dinner dishes, all the while listening to the conversation between the men.

"And you found it in the mud?"

"Saw the barrel sticking out of the mud after the big rain the other day," Pa said.

"It looks as if it was buried only a short time." Joe paused. "See, the only damage seems to be to the wooden stock and mother-of-pearl decoration. If it had been in the mud very long, you wouldn't have any of that."

"What do you make of it, Ranger?"

"It's a mystery," Joe said, "but lucky for you, Mr. Ames, I specialize in solving mysteries." The men shared a laugh; then Joe continued. "The gun seems familiar," he said. "So I'll ride into town tomorrow and send a telegram to headquarters to find out if someone's reported it missing or stolen." A pause. "After Tommy and I have a chat, that is."

"Yes," Pa said. "Been awhile since you two spoke, ain't it?"

"Too long. I'll have to find out why that railroad of his doesn't take him through San Antonio." A pause. "Or maybe it does. I bet there are records to answer that one. I'll make a note to check."

"Yes, Joe, you'd need to know that so next time he's in town, you two can get together and catch up."

Odd, but Pa's tone sounded anything but natural. In fact, their conversation had veered from casual to downright odd.

Bess turned to peek at the item they were inspecting and recognized it immediately. "That's Tommy's gun. Remember, Pa? He used to come over and shoot cans off the well with Lucy because his mother didn't like him shooting at their place."

Pa gave her a strange look. "Why didn't I know about this?"

She shrugged. "Probably because you wouldn't have liked it had you known Lucy was shooting that old thing. I told her it looked dangerous, but she'd laugh every time." Joe tapped his temple with his forefinger. "Maybe that's why it seems familiar to me," he said, though Bess could tell he wasn't completely convinced. "I'll let you know when I hear back from headquarters."

"Speaking of headquarters," Bess said, "shouldn't you be going back soon?"

Soon as the question was out, Bess knew it was the wrong thing to ask. Pa's frown told her as easily as Joe's surprised look.

"I'm not trying to hurry you," she quickly amended. "Just wondered."

The ranger seemed to study her a moment. In truth, she'd only blurted out the question because the thought of his leaving was suddenly something that didn't appeal.

Hadn't he almost told her she was anything but plain as day?

"I'm in contact with headquarters, but I don't have a timetable for heading back just yet." Joe gave her a sideways look. "Well, long as we're wondering about things, I've got something I'm wondering, too."

"What's that?" Pa asked.

The ranger turned to Bess. "I'm wondering if you'd take a buggy ride with me tomorrow, Bess."

" 'Course she will," Pa offered as he looked past Joe to dare Bess to argue.

CHAPTER 7

When Joe stepped out into the chill night air, Tommy and his mother were long gone. He took a deep breath and held it until his lungs burned then let it out slowly. The ritual helped him focus, a habit he'd learned on the trail.

The ranger in him had waited all evening for some sign that his friend had gone wrong. Anything—a word, a gesture, a mark on him—that might confirm what the sheriff claimed. Thus far, he'd only seen Tommy Vonheim, long-lost friend and railroad man.

Only once had he felt ire rise against the German, and that was when he'd paid a bit too close attention to Bess Ames. The joke they'd shared was something he now could not recall, but the way she looked at him, the smile she offered. . . . That had nearly sent him across the table—stupidity normally reserved for pimple-faced youths.

This fact alone made Joe want to avoid Bess Ames altogether. For somewhere between saving her from a rainstorm and promising her pa to keep a watch on her, he'd started thinking too much about her.

He barely knew the woman, and yet tonight in the kitchen he'd have kissed her if Frank hadn't walked in. *Kissed her.* Joe shook his head. A ranger never loses his focus. It could mean the difference between life and death. With Tommy back, so could it mean the difference in catching Pale Indian or letting more innocent lives be lost.

This thought carried him back to the Vonheim place, where he paused on the porch to listen to mother and son carrying on what sounded like a spirited conversation. "I am careful," Tommy said.

The cry of a barn owl broke through the night's silence, obscuring the sounds inside. When the bird's call ended, so had the discussion in the parlor. Joe reached for the doorknob only to find the door fly open.

"I wondered when you'd come inside," Tommy said. Eyes as blue as spring flowers stared at him. He'd caught many a woman's attention with those eyes. Somehow women seemed to be taken in by this fluke of nature, though Joe had never understood it. Now Joe stared back, wondering if he was looking into the face of a friend or a cold-blooded killer.

"It's cold out here."

"I like it," Joe said. "Long as I've got a bed to sleep in, I don't mind the weather."

"That's right—you're a ranger." Tommy stepped onto the porch and let the door close behind him. "Funny how that turned out. I always said I'd be the one who turned lawman."

"You wanted to track down your pa's killer." Soon as the words were out, Joe realized his mistake. The genial expression on Tommy's face had gone south, and in its place was a steely look that masked any emotion.

"How long's it been since you were in Horsefly?" Tommy finally asked. "I was just trying to figure that out."

"More'n ten years, I'd say." Joe leaned against the porch rail and stared past the small yard to the pasture and the sparse mesquites beyond. Here and there a patch of limestone rock seemed to glow brilliant white under the winter moon. "Nothing much has changed. I'll admit that. Town's a little bigger. That's about it."

Tommy chuckled, or at least it sounded that way. "Never will, far as I can tell." He came to stand beside Joe. "So why now?"

Joe shot him a look. "What do you mean?"

"I mean, why come back here now?" The owl hooted again, and Tommy turned in that direction, offering Joe a profile that had changed little since grade school. He was taller—fully over six feet—and broader across the shoulders, but other than that, Tommy Vonheim was the same kid who chased squirrels and knocked tin cans off walls with slingshots alongside Joe all those years.

The same kid who'd shared his mama when Joe no longer had one of his own. In the spirit of that friendship, Joe reached over to clasp Tommy on the shoulder. "A man needs a place to come back to now and then, don't you think?"

Tommy seemed to consider the statement a moment. "I suppose he does." He paused. "But doesn't he also need a reason to return?"

The casual tone was gone. Joe's ranger training kicked in as he straightened his backbone and turned to face his friend. "I'm afraid you've caught me."

His eyes went wide then narrowed. "Oh?"

Joe stuffed his fists into his pockets and shrugged. "I'm after someone."

Tommy froze. Then, by degrees, a smile began. "Anyone I know?" his friend finally asked.

"Could be." Joe let his arm fall to gently rest on his sidearm. "I'm still trying to figure it out."

It was Tommy's turn to face him. "Oh, that's priceless, Joe. Let me figure it out for you."

Fingers tightened on the gun, though Joe kept his face neutral. As far as he could tell, Tommy wasn't carrying a weapon; but he'd never been a man to depend on supposition.

"You always did have a crush on Bess Ames. Everyone but you could see it." Tommy snorted with glee. "Makes sense you'd finally come back for her," he said as he gave Joe a playful nudge. "Though I'll tell you you'd best marry up with her before I decide to. She's a real stunner, and smart to boot. Wait. That intelligence of hers might work against you."

Joe released his grip on the gun and let relief wash over him as he joined in the laughter. Shooting a friend on his mother's porch wasn't in the plans for tonight, especially when he hadn't proven his guilt or innocence yet.

Abruptly Tommy stepped toward the door. "It's cold out here. Come on in and have a beer with me like old times."

Joe shook his head. "Don't touch the stuff anymore."

Tommy gave him a look of disbelief before reaching for the doorknob. "You are getting old," he said as he disappeared inside.

"With age comes wisdom," he replied, praying it was the truth.

"Bundle up, Bess," Pa called from the dining room. "There's a chill in the air. And be sure to take him past that little plot where you're going to be putting in a garden. There's a pretty view from the bluff up there."

"Say, Pa, I've got a great idea. Why don't you go on this silly buggy ride with him?" Bess said as she gathered her wrap around her shoulders. "Since you're taking such an interest in all this."

"Don't be impudent."

"Then don't play matchmaker." Bess stuck her head in the kitchen doorway and spied her father immersed in today's edition of the *Horsefly Herald Gazette*. "You're not very good at it."

Pa snorted and went back to reading his paper. A knock at the door sent Bess back into the hallway. There she found Cal. "There's a horse and buggy coming up the road, ma'am," he said as he studied the ceiling.

"Thank you, Cal." She moved toward the door, leaving her father's ranch hand in the hall. When he followed her outside, Bess found herself in the uncomfortable position of having to make conversation with a man who seemed unable to speak.

"So you're cousin to the Schmidts," she finally said.

Cal nodded but offered nothing further. Bess glanced down the hill and willed Joe to hurry.

When Cal moved to stand beside her, Bess searched her mind to find another topic to discuss. "So," she finally said, "how did you come to be in Horsefly?"

The Schmidt cousin's face flushed bright red. "You ask a lot of questions."

"I do?" Joe's carriage came over the rise. Now he was close enough for her to hear the horse's hoofbeats. "I'm sorry."

Cal looked away. "Family," he said softly. "A man reaches a point and he needs family. Especially at Christmastime."

"Yes," she said slowly. *Family at Christmastime.*

Much as she rarely admitted it, Bess missed her sisters. With Charlsey, Lucy, and Sarah all happily married and spread to the four corners of creation, it was hard to remember a time when they'd all been under the same roof.

A plan hatched, and Bess tucked it away for consideration after she returned from her excursion with Joe. "I think you're right. Family's important."

She waved to Joe then excused herself to Cal, who glanced at his watch then back at her. "Would you tell the ranger I'll be right back?"

"Yes'm," he said softly. "I'll tell him."

Bess slipped inside and tiptoed toward the kitchen, pausing in the doorway to watch her father for a moment. With his spectacles affixed to the end of his nose and the graying temples he'd sported recently, it was obvious Frank Ames was no spring chicken. Yet he certainly wasn't too old for the plan she hoped she could carry out.

"Pa," she called. "Got a minute?"

"'Course I do, Bessie." He set the newspaper back down and slid the glasses off his nose to place them atop the *Herald*

Gazette. "But didn't I hear the ranger coming up the road?"

"You did, but I've got Cal entertaining him." She settled on the chair beside her father. "Pa, I never got to tell you what happened when Mrs. Vonheim and I had our chat."

He shook his head. "Didn't figure I needed to know. A man's shy of asking about what goes on among womenfolk."

She smiled and reached to touch his hand. "I like her."

Her father lifted his gaze to meet hers. "I like her, too, Bessie Mae."

"I know you do." Bess contemplated her words before continuing. "Maybe it's time, Pa."

"Time?" He shook his head. "Want to explain that?"

"Not really," she said as she rose. "Besides, I don't think I need to."

"Bess," her father called when she'd reached the hallway.

She backtracked to peer around the door frame. "What is it?"

"Stick close to the ranger, honey," he said as he reached for his spectacles and set them in place on his nose. "You never know what's out there, and he's a man trained to protect a lady."

Bess shook her head. "What sort of silliness is that? This is Horsefly, Texas. Nothing ever happens here."

CHAPTER 8

Joe slapped the reins and set the horses to a fine trot once they left the winding ranch road for the wider avenue to town. "A fine day for a drive," he said to the beautiful brunette at his side.

Only then did he notice that Bess had worn the same yellow dress as the day he met her at this very spot on the road. In the rain. With her shoulder pressed against his and the smell of flowers in her hair.

He swallowed hard and turned his attention to the road ahead. To the right was the Schmidt place. Joe made a note to call on Mr. Schmidt. Though everything about Cal Schmidt had checked out, he still found it hard to let the ranch hand leave his suspect list so easily.

What he couldn't decide was whether it was because he didn't believe the fellow was truly innocent or because to admit Cal wasn't Pale Indian was to start believing Tommy was.

Sliding Bess a sideways look, he found her staring at him. "Where are we going?"

"I thought we'd take a drive through town first."

What Joe didn't say was he'd been asked one too many times at church last Sunday why he was still in Horsefly. A ranger didn't stay in one place longer than it took to capture the bad guy unless he was either retired or. . .well, there wasn't any other reason.

So he'd decided it was time to take Frank Ames's plan to heart. Though Bess didn't know it, today was the day she'd be introduced to the people of Horsefly as Joe Mueller's potential sweetheart.

He sighed. Something about the ruse didn't sit right with him, but he was unwilling to try to figure out which part.

If Bess wondered why a glorious day that could be spent in the country would involve the busy streets of Horsefly, she didn't let on. Rather, she smiled, toyed with her bonnet strings, and then leaned back to lift her face to the sun.

Maybe Tommy was right. Maybe he had been carrying a torch for Bess Ames since grade school. His heart sure did a flip-flop when he looked at her. She was a fine woman from a fine family.

What was it her pa had said? A ranger in possession of a good salary and a desk job was surely going to start thinking about a wife. Was he?

No. Not when Pale Indian had yet to be caught.

Joe was awfully quiet. He'd hardly spoken on the drive to town. Now with the buildings of Horsefly in view, he seemed no more talkative. She was about to say something when he pulled up on the reins and guided the horses to a stop in a sunny outcropping well off the road. From there she could see the town in the valley below and the shimmering water of the Guadalupe River.

"I owe you an apology, Bess."

"Another one?" she asked lightly. "This has become quite the habit of yours."

It was flirting, plain and simple, and Bess felt the fool as soon as the ridiculous statement was out. What business did a twenty-seven-year-old spinster have playing the coquette to a broad-shouldered Texas Ranger?

He gestured toward town, seemingly oblivious to her silliness. "I have a selfish reason for taking this route."

"Oh?"

A nod. "I'd like it very much if everyone in Horsefly could see you riding by my side." With that, he slapped the reins and set the horses back on the road toward town. As the buggy picked up speed going downhill, Bess felt her bonnet ribbons give way.

"Stop, Joe. I did it again," she called as the bonnet flew from her head and landed somewhere behind them.

He hauled back on the reins and brought the horses to a stop. "What's wrong?"

Bess pointed to her head then shrugged, again feeling like the fool. "I've lost my bonnet. You see, I have this habit of worrying with the ribbons, and what with the wind and all, it just. . . oh, I'm rambling." She leaned forward to escape the buggy, only to feel Joe's hand on her arm.

"Wait here and I'll go after it."

When Joe didn't immediately return, Bess rose to turn around and see if she could spy him. Failing that, she slid over and took the reins to turn the buggy around. That was when she saw him facedown on a limestone ledge, his arms outstretched.

Pa's warning came back to her now. *Stick close to the ranger. You never know what's out there.*

"Joe," she called. No response, so she tried again.

Now she had to choose: Leave Joe and go for help, or leave the buggy to help Joe. She chose the latter, bounding from the buggy with her skirts flying. Rather than announce her presence to whomever had sent the ranger down the canyon, Bess elected to move as silently as possible as she picked her way from rock to rock until she was almost close enough to touch the still-prone ranger.

From her vantage point, Bess could see that while his body remained still, his right arm seemed to be grasping at something. "Joe?" she whispered. "Are you hurt?"

This time he turned his head in her direction, his face

flushed. "No. Go back to the buggy."

Bess surveyed the situation then returned her attention to him. "But I—"

"The buggy, Bess. Go. Back."

Reluctantly she nodded. Rather than retrace her steps, Bess circled around the ranger. When she reached the other side of the outcropping, she realized the problem.

"You're stuck."

He lifted his head to stare in her direction. If this expression was what criminals saw, no wonder the ranger had such good luck catching them.

Swallowing hard, Bess moved forward a half step. There she could see his fist wedged between two limestone boulders, the strings of her bonnet dangling in his fingers.

"Your hand. You can't. . ." Giggles threatened, but she managed to tame them by looking away. "Let go of the bonnet," she said, "and then you can pull your hand out."

Joe shook his head.

"Stubborn man."

His glare wasn't as effective given his position, but he seemed not to notice.

"All right then," she said. "I'll have to come and fetch the bonnet."

Bess made her way with ease over the rocky terrain, her skill honed after a lifetime of skittering up and down the hills on the ranch. In no time, she reached the ranger and thrust her hand toward the bonnet.

"Here," she said as she snagged the yellow fabric. "I've got it. Now let go and—"

That was when the rocks slid from beneath her, carrying Bess and the bonnet down the canyon.

—∞—

The slide wounded Bess's pride more than anything else. This she realized when she came to a stop against a boulder firmly embedded in the side of the hill.

She set her bonnet atop her head but hadn't time to tie the ribbons before Joe Mueller came bounding down the rocky incline. He caught her in his arms and held her to his chest, nearly knocking the breath out of her.

"I thought I'd lost you," he said. "You were there and then you were just gone."

Bess could hear his heart racing even as hers began to match it. "I was careless," she said as she braved a look up into his eyes. "Took a step without looking."

"Yes." His face was close. Too close. "You did."

"I forgot," she said, her voice reduced to a whisper, "to look where I was going."

He blinked, and impossibly long lashes swept high, tanned cheekbones. "Yes," he said softly, "sometimes that's how it happens."

"Yes, sometimes. . ." Words blew away with any remaining lucid thoughts as she leaned against a broad and familiar shoulder.

"Sometimes," he echoed, "it's better to go ahead and let go."

Her last sane act was to look into his eyes. The hands that held tight to his arms should have pushed him away. Instead, she held on tight and closed her eyes.

Besides, she was a twenty-seven-year-old spinster, and nothing ever happened in Horsefly, Texas.

CHAPTER 9

It was only a kiss. That's what Joe told himself when he repeated it. Twice.

From her lack of understanding of the technique, he easily deduced it was her first. And second. And third.

"Bess," he said against silky hair that indeed smelled as flowery as he remembered. "You've dropped the bonnet again."

Dark eyes opened and then widened even as she tried to move backward. Pinned as she was between a rock and a ranger, there was no place to go.

Acting the gentleman was never so difficult, and yet Joe knew he must. He rose and dusted off his trousers then stepped past her to retrieve the troublesome bonnet. By the time he returned, he found Bess sitting on the rock fretting over a smudge of dirt on her dress.

Gently he set the bonnet atop her head then, with trembling fingers, tied the ribbons into some version of a bow. Doubling the strings over, the bow became a knot.

"There," he said. "Now it won't come off."

Bess peered up at him, seemingly unable to move. He was about to ask if she'd somehow been injured in the fall or, heaven forbid, during the kiss, when she blinked hard and cleared her throat.

"Joe," she said softly. "Why did you kiss me?"

Why indeed? Any number of reasons occurred to him, but Joe couldn't find his voice. Finally, he managed a smile. "Because," he said as he offered her his hand, "I fell."

Dark brows gathered. "What does that mean?"

"Bess," he said as easily as he could, "don't ask me to explain."

Her stare confounded him with its innocence. How long had it been since he'd met a woman like Bess Ames, let alone kissed one?

"Why not?" she asked as she let him help her to her feet.

Joe looked beyond Bess to the canyon and the Guadalupe below. From where they stood, a good part of Texas was visible. No, he amended, *the* good part of Texas.

"Turn around and look at that," he said to Bess as he steadied her with his arm around her waist. "What do you see?"

"Is that a trick question?"

She glanced over her shoulder at him, and he saw the bee-stung look of lips he'd only just kissed, causing him to almost forget his point. Clearing his throat, Joe forced his gaze back on the expansive landscape. "That's home, Bess." He pointed to the horizon. "*Your* home."

Bess stiffened in his arms. "Oh, I see what you're saying. Well, don't worry about me, Joe Mueller." She whirled around, her back straight, and began making her way toward the road. "Don't expect me to be one of those women who kisses a man then expects him to marry her. Because I'm not. I'm just not, and even a kiss like yours—"

"Three kisses," he corrected as he followed in her wake.

"Three kisses like yours," she amended as she crossed the rocky ground as nimbly as a deer despite her womanly attire. "Nevertheless, I'm a woman of the world, Joe, and I understand that while these things happen, there's no need to lay claim to someone just because he—"

That was where he stopped her—with a fourth kiss. This time right there in full view of the horses, the buggy, and Cal

Schmidt, who happened to be riding by with his uncle, his aunt, and their eight children.

While Joe went over to shake hands with the men, Bess did her best to endure the reproachful stare of Mrs. Schmidt. A curt nod was all she could manage before slinking back to the buggy, knowing every grass stain and smudge of dirt would be highly visible on the yellow frock. From what she knew of Mrs. Schmidt's ability to spy a misbehaving child from long distances during Sunday school, it was very likely the woman was taking inventory at this very moment.

Before she came to town for tomorrow's egg delivery, Bess would likely already be the topic of conversation, for the other thing she knew about Mrs. Schmidt was that she adored offering up juicy tidbits clothed as prayer requests.

She sank back against the cushions of the buggy seat and waited until she heard Joe's boots approach. "I'm horrified," she said as he slid onto the seat beside her. "I'm sorry, Joe. I don't know what came over me. I've caused you quite the problem and I know it. It's just that I—"

Kiss five silenced her.

"Bess," he said, work-roughened hands still caressing her cheeks, "if you don't stop talking, I'm not going to be able to stop shutting you up with kisses, and then we really will have a problem."

His expression told her he meant it.

Bess lifted her forefinger to her lips and pressed it there. A nod told him she agreed, and he responded with one of his own. Too soon, the buggy was in motion.

"What are you doing?" she asked when she felt the contraption turning back toward town. "You can't parade me through town with a stained dress and Mrs. Schmidt's tales leading the way."

The ranger leaned her way and brushed her cheek with his

lips. She decided that one was kiss five and a half.

"Only the guilty slink away, Bess Ames. Now sit up straight, and for goodness' sake, leave those bonnet strings alone."

Moments later the buggy rolled into Horsefly with Bess doing her best impression of an innocent woman. *It was just a kiss*, she told herself. *And likely the only ones you'll get.*

"Ranger, Ranger," someone called.

Joe pulled up on the reins and swiveled to greet the telegraph operator. "Got something here for you," he said before tipping his hat to Bess. "Ma'am," he said.

She returned the greeting while she watched Joe's eyes scan the page. A moment later, he folded the telegram and stuffed it into his pocket.

"Something wrong?" she asked.

His nod was curt, his manner giving away nothing of the man who'd just kissed her in the canyon. "If you don't mind, I need to make a stop at the sheriff's office."

"No, of course," she said. "I'll find something to do, so don't worry yourself."

In his haste to leave the buggy, Joe barely acknowledged she'd spoken. Before she could blink twice, the ranger had disappeared into the sheriff's office, leaving her sitting in the middle of Horsefly with stains on her dress.

All she could do was hide behind her bonnet and wave to anyone who might recognize her until Joe finally bounded back out onto the sidewalk with Sheriff Kleberg right behind him.

"Think about my offer," the old sheriff called.

Joe seemed to be waving him away. "Not until this is handled," he said.

"Understood." The sheriff looked past Joe to make eye contact with Bess. "Howdy, Miss Ames," he called. "Nice day for a drive."

"Yes, isn't it, Sheriff Kleberg?"

"Give my best to your pa," he said before giving Joe one last look and disappearing inside.

"Joe," Bess said carefully, "is everything all right? You look troubled."

The ranger shrugged off her question. "It's fine, Bess. Just fine."

With that they were off, heading back to the ranch the same way they came: in silence. It took all Bess could do not to fiddle with her bonnet strings as they neared the canyon. From the looks of Joe's expression, he could use another detour and several more kisses.

Bess sighed. And so could she.

No, she decided. Any further kissing she did with Ranger Josef Mueller would be done in such a manner that she was neither hiding nor ashamed. She'd learned her lesson during the seemingly endless time she'd sat waiting for Joe.

A woman worth kissing was a woman worth wedding. If Joe only wanted to toy with her affections, he'd have to find someone else to kiss.

As Joe pulled the buggy to a stop in front of her house, Bess opened her mouth to tell Joe exactly that. Editing the marriage part, of course, for a lady would never bring up the subject of marriage to a man, even if she were a twenty-seven-year-old spinster and he an eligible single ranger with an uncanny ability to silence her with a kiss.

Unfortunately, Pa and a half dozen ranch hands were gathered near the barn, and Joe headed their way as soon as he lifted Bess out of the buggy and set her feet on the ground.

Not even a good-bye did he spare her, the cad.

"Well," she said loudly enough for him to hear, "of all the nerve." With that, she stormed inside even as her curiosity begged her to stay and listen to the men as they threw about words like "pistol" and "arrest warrant."

"No," she said as she bounded up the stairs. She couldn't care less what anyone said about anything right now. Joe Mueller had just kissed and fled, and that was an unpardonable sin.

Throwing open her bedroom door, she aimed for her bed then found it occupied.

By Tommy Vonheim.

CHAPTER 10

"So the gun was Tommy's after all?" Frank asked as his ranch hands gathered around.

"It was, and that's what's going to get him caught." Joe offered the telegram to Frank. "Says here the fellow who was caught with him in San Antone identified a flintlock pistol as Pale Indian's weapon of choice."

"Guess the fact he was facing the gallows loosened his tongue." Joe heard a scream and ran. "Bess," he called as he threw open the front door. "Bess, where are you?"

All he heard was the ticking of the parlor clock. Then came the muffled noises at the top of the stairs. Joe glanced behind him and saw the ranch hands bounding up the porch steps. "Wait," he said then met them on the porch. "You three go that way and cover the back. You," he said as he gestured to a pair of tall fellows, "one on each side of the house. The rest will cover Frank and me." He paused. "You all armed?"

Satisfied they were, Joe gave them one more warning. "Keep your weapons at the ready, and if anyone except me, Bess, or Frank here comes your way and you don't like the looks of 'em, shoot to kill."

Frank nodded his approval and the men scattered. "You thinkin' there's trouble with Bess?"

Joe gave the rancher a sideways look. "I've got a feeling

there's always going to be some kind of trouble with Bess." He chuckled. "And likely I'm overreacting. But knowing what we know now, I'm going to have to be cautious until Vonheim's in custody."

"So he's Vonheim now?" Frank asked. "What happened to Tommy?"

"Tommy was my friend, Frank. Vonheim's a killer and he needs to be brought to justice." Another muffled sound stole his attention.

"Likely she's dropped her hairpins again," Frank said. "She's prone to doing that. Well, that and her bonnet. She worries with those ribbons until I'm surprised they don't fall off. Always did, even as a little girl. Why, her mama used to—"

A scream split the silence. Joe bounded up the stairs, grasping for his revolver. "Which room's hers?"

Frank showed him. It was locked.

"Bess," he called. "Open the door."

Silence.

"Bess?" Joe threw his shoulder into the door twice before it flew open. There he found Bess crumpled on the floor. Beside her knelt Pale Indian.

The hat. The clothing. The Indian moccasins. All of these things he remembered from the alley behind the livery in San Antonio.

The face he knew from childhood as his friend Tommy Vonheim.

Joe leveled the revolver at the Indian. "Back away from her."

"I didn't mean to hurt her," he said. "I was trying to get her to hear me out and she wouldn't do it. She just kept telling me I had to leave and she wouldn't listen." He was almost in tears now, this man Joe barely recognized. "Frank," he continued, "you're why I'm here."

Joe tore his eyes from Vonheim for just a moment as Bess roused. "Stay put," he ordered her, and she either listened and complied or was unable to defy him. Joe preferred to believe the first option.

"What've I got to do with anything, Tommy?" Frank asked.

"I want you to take care of Mama." He shook his head. "I don't know that I'm worth getting a blessing from, but I sure would like to see you marry up with my mother. She'll need you when I'm gone."

"You're not going anywhere," Joe said, "except to face a judge and jury."

Vonheim shook his head. "You know that would kill my mother. I can't let her know what I've done. You can't do that to her, Joe."

Anger throbbed at Joe's temples. "I didn't do this, Joe. Your bad choices landed you where you are."

The Indian rose and offered up empty palms. "I'm not armed, Joe." When there was no response, Vonheim continued. "There's no good end to this, and I know even though you're my friend, you won't let me go."

"I can't," Joe said through clenched jaw.

"I know." He shrugged. "You were always the good guy. Me, I liked playing bank robbers and horse thieves."

"This isn't play, Pale Indian," Joe said. "This is real life, and you've got to pay for what you've done. That boy in San Antonio didn't get a chance, and neither do you."

Vonhiem dropped his hands to his sides and turned his back to Joe. "What're you doin', Tommy?" Frank said gently. "Can't we just let a judge and jury settle this? Your mama'll love you no matter what happens."

He turned around and looked past Joe to Frank. "Yes, I know she will," he said. "And she'll miss me something terrible when I'm gone. Promise me you'll take care of her, Frank."

"Well, of course I will. I love your mama, son, which is why I can't let anything—"

Vonheim bolted toward the window and threw himself

against it. Glass shattered as the windowpanes splintered and the Indian fell through. A volley of shots rang out, and then only silence.

Joe scooped up Bess and held her against his chest until she opened her eyes. "Tommy," she whispered. "He frightened me and I fell. He was talking about his mother. Something about you taking care of her." She spied her father. "Pa? Where's Tommy?"

Frank walked past her to look out what remained of the window. "Appears he fell, Bessie Mae," he said.

"Fell?" She made a weak attempt to stand then gave up and sagged against Joe's shirt. "What happened?"

Frank knelt beside them. "His mama mentioned he wasn't well," Frank said gently. "It appears he might have lost his balance over there by the window." The rancher gave Joe a direct look. "Ain't that what happened, Joe?"

Slowly he nodded, knowing Tommy's mother would hear the same story.

A week after Tommy Vonheim's funeral, Joe packed his saddlebags and showed up on Bess's doorstep to say good-bye. Bess tried not to cry even as he pulled her into his arms for a kiss. She'd lost track of the number somewhere between Tuesday and Friday, but she did count two more farewells before he disappeared down the trail.

"I'll come home for Christmas," he called from somewhere beyond the mesquites.

"You'd better," she replied as she returned to her room to read the letters that would make good on her plans.

That evening at supper, Pa was grinning. "What's got into you?" she asked as she set out the plates.

"I asked her, Bessie Mae." His grin turned into a chuckle. "I asked Ida Vonheim to marry up with me soon as it was proper. Didn't want to intrude on her grief."

"And what did she say?"

"She said she'd marry me tomorrow, Bessie." Another laugh. "Looks like I'm going to be a married man. Not sure I remember how."

Bess went to hug her father. "Pa, what about a Christmas Eve wedding? The church'll already be decorated."

"A Christmas wedding! Why, that's a great idea." He rose and hurried from the room.

"Where are you going?" she called.

"To tell Ida the good news."

Christmas Eve dawned bright and beautiful with a chill in the air that competed with the anticipation Bess felt. She was keeping a secret that Ida, her soon-to-be new mama, was in on. While Pa went to cut the tree for the parlor, Bess made short work of completing the arrangements for the wedding. By the time the tree was up and adorned with the Ames family decorations, Bess's nerves were stretched thin.

The only piece of her plan that hadn't fallen into place involved Joe Mueller. Thus far she'd had neither letter nor telegram from the absent ranger. By the time she climbed into the buggy beside the groom-to-be, Bess had decided Joe wasn't coming.

A thousand reasons pelted her mind, but she refused to consider any of them. Rather, she reached across the bench and grasped Pa's free hand then slid him a smile.

"We're still gonna need you at home, Bessie Mae. Don't you ever think you're not welcome."

Bess sighed. "Thank you, Pa. We'll see how things turn out." The last thing she wanted to be was the third person in a newlywed's home.

The buggy arrived at the church, and Bess slid out to hurry to the church's side door. There she found Ida waiting for her. The older woman looked beautiful in the new dress Bess had helped her pick out. "Where are they?"

Ida opened the door to the pastor's study, revealing the best Christmas gift of all: her sisters and their families.

Time for hugs and greetings was short, as the groom now stood at the altar beside the pastor. As the music rose, Bess gestured to the door. "Shall we go out oldest to youngest?" Charlsey asked.

"No, dear," Ida interjected. "Let's do the opposite." She shrugged. "For fun."

"Of course." Bess hugged each sister as she left the study on the arm of her husband. Finally, it was Bess's turn. "I guess I've got to go it alone." *Bessie Mae, plain as day.* The statement haunted her for the first time since Joe left.

Ida reached for her overlarge bouquet then divided it in half. "Here, dear," she said. "It'll give you something to hold on to."

Bess took it reluctantly, feeling a bit silly as she stepped into the church. None of her sisters held flowers, so what would possess Ida to insist?

If only Joe were here.

Then she spied him. Standing at the altar. Beside Pa.

Her sisters were grinning. A glance behind her told Bess that Ida was, too.

"Go on, dear," Ida said. "You and Joe can have your turn at the preacher first. Frank and I have waited this long. We can surely spare a few more minutes."

"But I. . ." She shook her head as she turned her attention to Joe. "He hasn't even asked me to marry him yet."

"About that." Joe moved toward her. "You see, a fellow takes his time getting to know the young lady, but I'm due back in San Antonio by New Year's Day. I'd have to say this makes our situation a bit of an emergency."

Bess glanced around at the citizens of Horsefly gathered in the old familiar pews. Even Mrs. Schmidt smiled at her. "But you. . .we haven't courted properly."

His gaze scorched her. "Considering the timetable we're working with, I'd say our courting schedule might be hurried up a bit."

"I see." She smiled. "So how long have we been standing here?"

"Two minutes," Cal Schmidt called, pointing to his watch.

Joe moved closer. "Two minutes already?"

"At least," she whispered. "Almost three."

"Guess that makes it time." Their noses were nearly touching as he wrapped his arm around her shoulder. "Definitely time."

"Time for what?" she whispered against his cheek.

"Time for me to make up a new rhyme about you." Joe paused to lean back a notch and look into her coffee-colored eyes. "Bessie Mae," he said softly, "you're going to kiss me today."

And she did.

"Excuse me, you two," the pastor called. "There's a little formality called a wedding vow you'll need to speak before you can do that."

"Shall we, Bess?" Joe asked. Then he shook his head. "Wait—all teasing aside, let me do this properly."

Right there in the middle aisle of the church, Joe got down on one knee. "Bessie Mae, will you marry me today?"

And the bride-to-be said yes.

MRS. VONHEIM'S SPRINGERLE COOKIES

(makes approximately 5 dozen)

4 eggs
2 tablespoons butter
2 cups sugar
4 cups all-purpose flour
2 teaspoons baking powder
¼ teaspoon salt
¼ cup anise seed

Beat eggs; then add butter and sugar. Cream together. Sift flour, baking powder, and salt. Add dry ingredients to butter mixture and combine. Knead dough until smooth, adding more flour if necessary to form smooth dough. Cover and chill in refrigerator for at least 2 hours. Roll onto slightly floured board to ½ inch thick. Roll springerle roller over dough to make designs. Cut at border. Sprinkle anise seed on clean tea towel and place cookies on top. Allow to stand uncovered overnight to dry. Bake 12 to 15 minutes at 325 degrees; then remove from oven and cool completely. Store in airtight container.

MIRIAM'S RINDERROULADEN

(serves 4)

1½ cups beef broth
4 flank steaks, approximately 6 oz each
2 teaspoons Dijon mustard
½ teaspoon salt
¼ teaspoon pepper
2 slices bacon
2 pickles, sliced in strips
1 large onion, chopped
¼ cup vegetable oil
4 peppercorns
½ bay leaf
1 tablespoon cornstarch

Heat beef broth and set aside. Spread mustard equally on each steak; sprinkle with salt and pepper. Cover each with bacon, pickles, and chopped onion; roll like a burrito. Secure with toothpicks. Heat oil in heavy saucepan; add steak rolls and brown well on all sides. Pour in hot beef broth, peppercorns, and bay leaf. Cover and simmer 1 hour and 20 minutes. Remove steak rolls and set aside to drain. In bowl, blend cornstarch with small amount of cold water and mix well. Stir into saucepan and bring to a boil until sauce is thick and bubbling. Pour over steaks and serve immediately.

Bestselling author **Kathleen Y'Barbo** is a Romantic Times Book of the Year winner as well as a multiple Carol Award and RITA nominee of more than fifty novels with almost two million copies in print in the US and abroad. A tenth-generation Texan, she has been nominated for a Career Achievement Award as well a Reader's Choice Award and Book of the Year by Romantic Times magazine.

Kathleen is a paralegal, a proud military wife, and an expatriate Texan cheering on her beloved Texas Aggies from north of the Red River. Connect with her through social media at www.kathleenybarbo.com.

Also avaiable from Barbour Publishing.

A *Basket Brigade* CHRISTMAS

Three women spread Christmas joy to wounded Civil War soldiers.

#

Sugar Crystal

Bring to a full rolling boil Stirring Constantly with a long Wooden Spoon, once it Start to Boil, Set a timer for 5 min Turn the heat down To Med So you don't burn your finger off. when timer goes off remove from heat & add Choc Chip, Stir Until all Chip are Melted, add Marshmallow, beat with a Wooden Spoon, add Vanilla. Pour in Pan, let Cool ~~to~~ room Temp

Also avaiable from Barbour Publishing.

Christmas and romance follow nine pioneer couples into untamed lands.

2 and 1/2 Cup White Sugar
3/4 Cup Butter
2/3 Cups evaporated Milk
12 ounce Pack (2 Cup Semi-Sweet
choc Chip
7 ounce Jar Marshmallow Cream
1 teaspoon Vanilla

Line a 8 or 9 in Sq Pan with foil
Coat with Spray, set aside
in a 3 quart Heavy Sauce Pan
over high heat, Combine Sugar
Butter & Milk, Use a Wooden Spoon
To stir Slowly Until butter Melts
scraping side of Pan To get all

Grandma recipe
Azeez Hassmattel

5101-95 HT